Praise for *The New Husband*

"Mother doesn't always know best in this thrill ride of a novel . . . gripping and twisted."   —Karin Slaughter, bestselling author of *The Good Daughter*

"Plenty of twists . . . will keep you turning the pages as you guess . . . and guess again."   —Lisa Scottoline, *New York Times* bestselling author of *After Anna*

"An acute, sensitive portrayal of family love under extreme stress . . . [with] a touch of Hitchcock."
—William Landay, *New York Times* bestselling author of *Defending Jacob*

"A thoroughly engaging read full of breath-holding moments and pulse pounding tension, D. J. Palmer's *The New Husband* is an incredible tale of secrets and obsession."
—*The Nerd Daily*

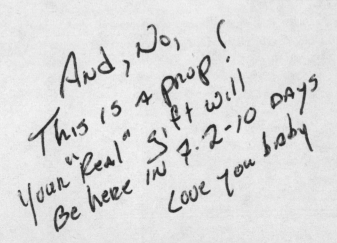

And, No,
This is a prop!
your "Real" gift will
Be here in 7.2-10 DAYS
Love you baby

ALSO BY D. J. PALMER

Saving Meghan

D. J. PALMER

THE NEW HUSBAND

St. Martin's Paperbacks

Published in the United States by St. Martin's Paperbacks, an imprint of St. Martin's Publishing Group.

THE NEW HUSBAND

Copyright © 2020 by D. J. Palmer.
Excerpt from *My Wife Is Missing* copyright © 2022 by D. J. Palmer.

For information, address St. Martin's Publishing Group, 120 Broadway, New York, NY 10271.

www.stmartins.com

Library of Congress Catalog Card Number: 2019048512

ISBN: 978-1-250-10750-3

Our books may be purchased in bulk for promotional, educational, or business use. Please contact your local bookseller or the Macmillan Corporate and Premium Sales Department at 1-800-221-7945, ext. 5442, or by email at MacmillanSpecialMarkets@macmillan.com.

Printed in the United States of America

St. Martin's Press hardcover edition published 2020
Griffin trade paperback edition published 2021
St. Martin's Paperbacks edition / April 2022

10 9 8 7 6 5 4 3 2 1

For Richard Glantz, who as my stepfather (and grandfather to my kids) has stepped up time and time again.

And to the memory of John Kristie, a mentor and friend who saw something in me I didn't see in myself.

CHAPTER 1

It was a chilly predawn morning when Anthony Strauss eased *Sweet Caroline,* his seventeen-foot Boston Whaler, from the trailer into water so dark it was indistinguishable from the sky. To the east, the rising sun raced along the riverbank, igniting the shoreline of Lake Winnipesaukee in a buttery glow. Anthony cast his lure about twenty feet out and was beginning to slowly reel in his line when he noticed a fellow boater some forty yards off his starboard.

In the early-morning darkness, the boat had been nothing but a black shape on dark water. The sunrise revealed a Starcraft Starfish, a great lake-fishing boat. The discovery was mildly disappointing. Anthony had thought he was alone out here and enjoyed feeling like he was the most dedicated fisherman. Still, it was polite to wave, and Anthony's hand went up almost reflexively. Nobody waved back. On second inspection, Anthony discovered that the figure he believed to be the boat's captain was, in fact, a dog.

Guiding his vessel closer to the Starcraft, Anthony watched while the dog—a golden retriever, he could now see—gazed forlornly toward land as though its owner might emerge at any moment from the dense forest abutting the rocky shoreline. The Starcraft, to Anthony's recollection, did not have a below-deck cabin, so he was surprised when he couldn't see anyone else in the boat with the dog.

The engine was off, but gusty winds pushed the unmanned vessel across the choppy gray water. The dog kept perfectly still while Anthony glided by, its black eyes locked on the same spot on the shoreline, golden fur rippling in the steady breeze. *Where is the captain? What if he's suffered a heart attack? What if he's fallen overboard and drowned?*

Anthony turned the wheel on his Whaler, steering the boat in a tight circle to make a second pass. As he neared, he called out: "Hello? Is anybody there?"

His barrel chest and solid build gave him a booming voice that should have attracted anyone's attention, but still only the dog looked his way. Slowly, the animal's gaze drifted back to the shoreline, as if it had assessed Anthony and determined he could be of no real help.

Steering the boat for a closer approach, Anthony hooked a set of bumpers onto his port side. As he neared, the dog moved, greeting Anthony with a wagging tail and lolling tongue. Gripping the gunwale with one hand, rope in the other, Anthony fastened the two boats together, using the bumpers to protect their respective hulls.

The dog barked three times in quick succession, as if trying to say something of great importance. Anthony appraised the animal thoughtfully before turning his attention to the Starcraft's interior. The deck was covered in deep red. *How odd,* Anthony thought, until his mind clicked over. A gasp rose in his throat as a sickening realization set in.

Anthony had gutted plenty of fish in his day, but none had ever bled like that.

CHAPTER 2

SEVENTEEN MONTHS LATER . . .

Nina told herself everything would work out fine. A cloudless August day gave the sun free rein to scorch the earth dry and bake her olive-toned skin a shade darker. She stood on the brown grass of her new lawn, facing the thirty-foot Ryder truck that held the majority of her life's possessions, all carefully packed inside corrugated boxes that were stacked neatly between the small pieces of furniture moved without the help of professionals. The bigger items were coming later.

"Anybody see the box cutter?"

Using her hand as a visor against the sun, Nina glanced at her feet and around her general vicinity, but did not see a box cutter. She did, however, catch the harsh look her thirteen-year-old daughter, Maggie, sent Simon, the new man in their lives, who was fumbling about the truck in search of the missing tool. That single glance reconfirmed Nina's greatest fear, that this move wasn't going to go as smoothly as she dared to dream. It was not a look of pure contempt, not the scathing, narrowed-eyed death stare any middle-school-aged girl could serve with the speed and accuracy of a pro tennis player, but still it smoldered with an unmistakable hostility.

Poor Maggie had so much on her plate, so many reasons to be angry, and for sure Nina was partly to blame, because she had opened her heart and soul to another man—a man who was *not* her daughter's father.

"Found it!" Simon yelled, holding up the box cutter like he was wielding a broadsword. As it turned out, the missing tool had been hidden in the tall grass of the sloping front yard, which needed mowing as much as it did water. Somewhere, buried deep inside that truck, was the mower.

Nina was familiar with her new neighborhood because it was still in Seabury, New Hampshire, a few miles from where she had lived only this morning. Even so, she had no friends nearby, and maybe for that reason it felt foreign here, as though she'd moved clear across the country. She was used to living near her very dear friends Susanna Garston and Ginny Cowling, but pop-in visits would be less frequent now that they lived fifteen minutes across town. For whatever reason, it felt much farther than that. Of course she'd adjust, and eventually she'd be as comfortable here as she'd been in the place where she'd spent the last fifteen years raising her children. She understood it would take time and effort for things to feel normal for everyone, and that applied to her new relationship as much as to her new home.

But today it all felt eerily unsettling.

At the far edge of her lawn, a splendid oak tree growing near her property line spread its thick branches from the neighbor's yard into hers, providing pockets of shade where a bold chipmunk escaped the August heat and observed the move with curious dark eyes.

Turning her head to the sound of scuffing footsteps, Nina watched nervously as her son, Connor, backed down the truck ramp clutching an oversize box in his outstretched arms.

"Careful, buddy. That looks pretty heavy," Simon said as Connor made a tricky pivot move at the bottom of the ramp that had heated to a steak-sizzling temperature under the un-relenting summer sun.

After deftly avoiding the family's five-year-old golden re-triever, Daisy, who had splayed herself out at the foot of the ramp, Connor sent Simon a confident look that carried no resentment, but then again, he didn't share Maggie's unreal-istic fantasies about their dad. He knew as well as Nina that Glen was gone, and gone for good.

Connor trotted the box up the wide front stairs with ease. Nina still could not get comfortable with how much he'd grown in the past few years. He towered over her and his younger sister. Not only was he tall for his age—sixteen go-ing on twenty-six, judging by his attitude these days—but he was also well-muscled, thanks to his dedication to the football team. He was as handsome as a Disney prince, too, with a wavy head of jet-black hair and an irresistible dim-pled smile. He'd gotten Nina's darker Italian coloring, and Glen, who was Irish through and through, had made plenty of milkman jokes over the years.

Inside, Nina caught Maggie, blue eyes brimming, survey-ing the empty rooms from the unfurnished foyer. The mod-est home was a good deal smaller than the one her daughter had lived in all her life, but square footage was not the rea-son for Maggie's distress. It was all about whom she'd be liv-ing with, not where.

It was all about Simon.

If somebody had told Nina a few years ago that she would end up living with the social studies teacher from her daugh-ter's middle school, in a new house they had bought together, she would have broken into a fit of laughter.

In another eight months or so, the court most likely would grant Nina her divorce from Glen, after which she might feel ready to say yes to Simon's marriage proposal so he could officially become her new husband. New Hampshire law was quite specific: spousal abandonment had to last two years or longer and required a demonstrated, willful desire to desert and terminate the marital relationship. Clearly, Glen's actions met those criteria. Or maybe he really was dead. Without a body, Nina had no way of knowing, while Maggie continued to hold out hope that her dad would soon return to them.

Nina directed Connor, still lugging the box, down the hallway to the kitchen. At some point, she'd hang her framed family photographs on the bare white walls, just as she had decorated her last home—only this time Glen would not grace any of the images.

With the windows closed, the empty house had turned into a sauna. Sweat beaded up on Nina's arms, and the cotton of her loose-fitting gray T-shirt stuck to the small of her back. But a tickle of excitement at the prospect of nesting helped her ignore the discomfort. Without the previous owners' furniture, the rooms appeared smaller than Nina remembered, though it was easy to visualize where she would put her things. The living room curtains would have to be shortened, but first she'd have to find her sewing machine, hidden inside one of those moving boxes.

Returning to the front hall, Nina found Maggie, looking serious, standing in the middle of what would eventually be a small first-floor office. Perhaps she, too, was imagining what the room would look like with furniture in it, though she would have to picture it with Simon's furnishings in the mix—if she could remember what he owned. Maggie had been to Simon's house only a few times, even though he lived just on the other side of town.

Before cohabitating, Nina had enjoyed plenty of afternoon delights at Simon's modest lake home, but she'd never spent the night. There was simply too much heartache, too much sadness, for her to leave the kids alone while pursuing personal pleasures. Still, she was no stranger to Simon's place, having gone there enough to commit his alarm code to memory.

When the movers came, Maggie would see that Simon had perfectly fine furniture, nothing too fancy, that would mix well with what they already owned. Then again, as Nina was learning, it was much easier to blend furnishings than the people using them.

"I hate it here," Maggie said, eyes watering, before Nina could utter a single word of comfort. She looked so much like Glen it was sometimes hard for Nina to hold her daughter's gaze. Maggie had fair skin like her father and the same straw-colored hair, hers descending to the middle of her back. She shared Glen's snub nose and big round eyes, and her sweet smile could melt the coldest of hearts. She was a slender girl with narrow shoulders and delicate arms. Her long legs were strong from skiing and lacrosse, but like a foal's, they did not yet fit her body.

Deep breaths, Nina, deep breaths.

"It's going to be all right, just give it some time."

"I wish we'd moved in with Nonni and Papa like we'd planned. I'd rather live in Nebraska."

Before Nina could respond, Simon sauntered into the room carrying a box labeled OFFICE, a smile on his face and sweat dripping into his eyes. Daisy followed him, panting from heat and thirst.

"We're making great progress—though gotta hand it to Connor," Simon said, breathing hard, "he's crazy strong. Football team's lucky to have him."

Nina forced out a smile while Maggie tried to discreetly wipe her eyes.

Practiced at checking in with his students, Simon took notice of Maggie's distress as he set down his box. He dropped to one knee, giving the youngest Garrity a temporary height advantage, and tried to make eye contact, though Maggie would not meet his gaze. Nina looked at him lovingly, appreciating his gentleness and compassion.

"I know you don't believe me," Simon said sweetly, "but it's going to work out fine. At school I might be Mr. Fitch, but here I'm just Simon. And I know we can all live together and be friends."

Channeling her social worker skills, Nina shared a few words of comfort and encouragement as well, though her daughter did not seem convinced. Worry turned her sweet face hard, older.

"I'm going to help Connor," Maggie said, sending a look back at Daisy to encourage her beloved dog to follow.

Simon stood and sighed as he pulled Nina into an embrace. Putting her ear to his chest, not minding the dampness of his shirt, she listened to the steady patter of his heart.

"It's too much," she said in a whispered voice, like an admission to herself. "It's too much, too fast."

Simon kissed the top of her head. "We knew what we were getting into, but what choice was there?" he said. "It was either this or you'd have had to move away, and neither of us wanted that."

It was true. Nina did not have the money to keep their family home and could not afford a new home without Simon. Before he had entered the picture her best, really her only option, was Maggie's current wish—to move to Nebraska. While Nina was close to her parents, her life was in Seabury, and there she wished to stay.

"People are talking about us, you know that?" Nina said. "We're the talk of the town."

Simon didn't look surprised, and for good reason. Both she and Simon had been touched by tragedy, and together they had raised eyebrows for the choices they had made in the aftermath. Nina had done what many had advised and moved on with her life, but apparently it was too quick for some.

"I don't care what people think," answered Simon. "I love you and that's all that matters. I know it's tough on Maggie right now, but she's going to get over it. I promise you it's going to work out. You'll see."

"I hope you're right," Nina said with audible desperation. *And I hope you know what you're doing,* she told herself.

In Simon, she had found a loving and genuinely caring companion who adored her and had guided her through the darkest days of her life. Still, she worried. How difficult would Maggie make this move for her, and even more so, for Simon?

CHAPTER 3

A week after move-in day, the house was still in complete disarray.

Moving boxes were strewn about in every room, and packing peanuts littered the floor like engorged confetti. Balls of crinkled packing paper roosted in corners of cluttered rooms with the grace of avant-garde sculptures. The television was still in the box, much to Connor and Maggie's chagrin, while the basement—which Nina hoped to convert into a kids' cave of sorts—needed a dehumidifier running twenty-four-seven before she could even consider laying down the carpet the movers had left rolled up down there. Simon, who was more obsessed than anyone in the Garrity clan with neatness and order, had assured Nina he was fine with the mess. But she knew that if she was feeling frazzled, he must have been in a total tizzy.

As the school's robotics instructor, Simon was good with technology, and had already gotten the wireless internet up and running. The Bluetooth Sonos speakers he had configured continuously pumped out high-energy classic rock music, but the boxes full of stuff were Nina's main job, and she desperately wanted to feel settled. Most nights she worked with Simon at her side, unpacking essentials, cleaning and scrubbing bathrooms, replacing the batteries in all the smoke detectors.

Despite these efforts, the place still felt like someone else's home, with Nina as a temporary guest. Maybe when she added plants, or had pictures hanging in the hallway, maybe when all her things were in place, it would feel like home. Or maybe she should buy new furniture, new everything, because the old stuff might serve only as a reminder of all she had lost.

With so much to do, Nina focused on tackling the laundry, because at least it was a task she could manage to completion. She was folding a basket of clothes while her endless to-do list tumbled disjointedly through her mind, just like the dryer itself.

Dog food . . . shopping . . . Maggie's dentist appointment . . . mend the hole in Connor's jersey . . . forms for fall lacrosse . . . order team sweatshirts . . . pick up prescriptions at CVS . . . enroll Maggie in CCD classes at St. Francis . . . the kids' physicals . . . nut-free ingredients for the football team bake sale (Maggie was deathly allergic) . . . and on . . . and on.

Moving didn't erase Nina's responsibilities, but rather added to them.

From down the hall, Nina heard an echoing "Hello?" and rose on achy knees to greet Ginny and Susanna, who had let themselves in. They were carrying two bottles of red wine, a foil-covered baking dish, and a cake box with WHOLE FOODS printed on the side.

"Happy birthday!" they shouted in unison, beaming at Nina as she approached.

"It's not my birthday," Nina said with a crooked smile.

"Well, the cake was on sale, so it's somebody's birthday—and it might as well be yours," said Ginny as she sauntered inside, delicately balancing the bottles as she stooped to give

Daisy a scratch hello. Ginny dressed like a J.Crew model, but despite the coastal palette of her cardigans and pleated pants, she still looked like a tired mom of three who lived in woodsy New Hampshire. She had a tousled nest of blond hair cut well above her shoulders, and a round, friendly face that was always quick with a smile.

"Where are the kids?" Susanna asked.

"Out," said Nina. "With friends. They can't take the chaos. Neither can I."

"And Simon?" Nina caught the slight hesitation in Ginny's voice, though she wasn't surprised. Not long ago both her friends had been trying to talk Nina out of making this move. They didn't have anything against Simon, per se, but each had reservations about the speed at which the relationship had evolved. They weren't the only ones.

Nina's parents hadn't embraced her choice to move in with Simon either. Her mother liked Simon well enough, but thought Nina was setting a bad example for the children to be living with him before they were married. It was an argument that didn't quite adhere to her mother's views on personal choice, but Nina saw it for what it was—a poorly disguised way of masking her hope that her only daughter would move back home to live with them. Her father, who had loved Glen like the son he'd never had, worried Simon was taking advantage of a vulnerable woman in a very tricky situation, concerns that Nina herself understood.

Before her life had taken a U-turn, Nina had scoffed at those dolled-up reality show contestants who professed their undying love for each other after a few staged dates. Now she knew there were more than a few kernels of truth to their mawkish sentiments—and that a TV show wasn't the only way to accelerate romance. Trauma, true bone-jarring trauma, did the job just as well, if not better.

"Love what you've done with the place . . ." Ginny said,

spinning around in a circle as she surveyed the disordered kitchen. Susanna sent Nina a sympathetic look. This was the third time since move-in day they'd showed up to help unpack, and the place still looked like it had been ransacked by raccoons. Nina had wondered if her lack of progress was a subconscious reaction from a part of her that wasn't wholly embracing the move. It wasn't only her daughter she worried about. As much as she loved Simon, Nina harbored a mostly unspoken fear of opening herself up to being hurt again.

After uncorking the wine, Nina cut three big pieces of vanilla buttercream cake. The lasagna could wait. Susanna went to the fridge after announcing her intention to whip up a quick salad, took one look inside, and had to think again.

"Someone's vying for the Mother Hubbard of the Year Award," she said.

Nina laughed. She might have lost her mind in the mess, but not her sense of humor.

"The children aren't starving, I swear. I just haven't made it to the supermarket."

"Like, since you moved in?" said Ginny, after checking the pantry.

"It's been hard," Nina said, slumping down on a metal stool at the kitchen island.

"A toast then," Susanna proposed, raising her glass. "To a happy, healthy home."

"Cheers to that," Nina said as all three clinked glasses.

Susanna took a sip of wine and then went to work emptying the box closest to her, aptly labeled KITCHEN. Nina felt supremely grateful to have such good friends in her life, and couldn't imagine where she'd be without them. Back when everything had first exploded, when her ordered world had become unmanageably disordered, Susanna had functioned as the family spokesperson. She was the perfect choice, already experienced with handling the media from her years as a reporter. An attractive woman with long chestnut hair and kind brown eyes, Susanna was a natural on TV. But now the cameras were long gone, and Nina's great ordeal was nothing but a tabloid footnote.

When Ginny went to help Susanna unpack the box, the first thing she pulled out was an old issue of *Real Simple* magazine. "Thank goodness you brought *this*," she said with a laugh.

But Nina wasn't laughing. She hadn't even realized she'd put that magazine in the box, but of course she had. She couldn't have thrown it away. It was a reminder, a memento from the day that everything had changed.

* * *

Nina had been in her living room—her old living room—ready to decompress during a rare moment of downtime. A cup of chamomile tea waited on the coffee table, and that *Real Simple* magazine sat on her lap. She was interested in the cover story about—of all things—making life simpler. The issue also featured an article on four summer recipes to make outdoor entertaining easier than ever, which she found annoying because it was only the first week of spring.

She got cozy beneath a soft fleece blanket, sinking deeply into the faded beige cushions of her couch. She flipped to the desired article and read a page until her eyes glazed over. She remembered thinking she should have been working on the PTA newsletter, or even getting an early jump on the live auction, but no—she had been cocooned, supposedly guilt-free, beneath a fuzzy blanket, preparing to relax.

Even when she worked at it, Nina could not quite get a handle on how to unwind. It simply wasn't in her DNA to turn off and do nothing. There was a time, years ago, when her entire life had been her career as a social worker. Then came

Glen, who was work-obsessed even during their honeymoon phase, and admittedly Nina was too, at least until the kids were born. Then they became her whole world, until they didn't need her as they once had. To fill the void, Nina found herself unable to say no to whatever favor, obligation, committee, or volunteer effort came her way. In this respect, she didn't stop working—she just stopped getting a paycheck.

Surrendering her downtime, Nina tossed the blanket aside. Today there would be no relaxing; she really had to work on that newsletter. Moments later, the issue of *Real Simple* lay atop a pile of other magazines on the floor by her cluttered desk.

It wasn't until Nina had returned to the living room to get her cup of tea that she saw a police car parked in her driveway. The car's roof-mounted light bar was off, and that gave her a moment's comfort: not an emergency. Still, her first thought had been of the children, always the children.

Maggie was with her best friend, Laura Abel, and Connor was at a weekend football practice, punishment for the team's lackluster performance during the previous night's game. She wondered if he had been hurt—but surely one of the team moms would have called if something awful had happened.

Nina watched through the window as two police officers, female and male, exited the car. They were dressed identically in khaki pants and blue polo shirts with official-looking embroidery stitched over the right breast pocket, guns strapped to their waists, their expressions grave.

Under normal circumstances, Nina would have felt a stab of embarrassment at the weeds growing between the paving stones. The yard didn't look all that great, either. Glen's busy work schedule left little time for the honey-do list. Nina could have used vinegar to get rid of those pesky weeds herself, but somehow—hello volunteering, organizing, chauffeuring, cooking, cleaning—she never seemed to have the time. Those quick thoughts fled as she opened the door to watch the two police officers make their way up the brick front steps.

"Can I help you?" Nina asked, a slight quaver in her voice.

"Are you Nina Garrity?" asked the man. He removed his sunglasses the way cops sometimes did on TV shows, slowly and full of intent, revealing eyes that were a striking, steely light gray.

He tilted his head slightly, his edginess giving way to something more congenial. Or was it sympathy? Nina couldn't tell.

"Yes. Can I help you? Is everything all right?" Her voice was tinged with dread.

"Is your husband at home?" the female cop asked.

"I'm sorry," Nina said. "Who are you? What's this about?"

"I'm Detective Yvonne Murphy, and this is my partner, Detective Eric Wheeler," the woman said. "We're with the Seabury Police."

They showed her their badges.

"Are you home alone?" said Murphy.

"Yes," Nina said. "I'm alone. Is this about Glen?"

"Glen is your husband?" Wheeler asked.

"Yes," Nina said.

"Do you know where he is?"

Nina answered Wheeler with a single word: "Fishing."

"What time did he leave?" asked Murphy.

"Before sunrise. Maybe four A.M. Maybe earlier—I don't really know, I was asleep. Is everything okay?"

"Was he going with anyone else?" asked Wheeler.

Nina shook her head slightly, trying to clear her mind so she could answer correctly. Her heartbeat quickened.

"Saturday is his fishing day. With the kids so busy on the weekends he almost always goes alone," she said.

"And do you know where he usually goes?"

Nina's pulse ticked up another notch, her throat tightening.

"The launch near Governors Island. Tell me, what's going on?" Her voice rose sharply.

The two detectives exchanged glances before Murphy headed back to the police car, leaving Wheeler alone on the front steps to answer Nina's question.

"Somebody found a boat, a Starcraft, floating near that boat launch this morning," Wheeler said.

"There was a dog aboard," Wheeler continued, "but no operator."

"Where's Glen?"

"Marine Patrol and Fish and Game are searching the water right now."

Nina's hand went to her mouth, but not in time to stifle a gasp that became a sob. "He fell overboard?"

"We don't know," answered Wheeler. "We also found a Ford F-150 parked at the boat launch. We've towed the truck and boat to our impound lot. Registrations show this address. Checked the dog's microchip, and believe she belongs to you."

At that moment, Murphy opened the rear door of the patrol car and out came Daisy. She bounded up the walkway at full speed, squeezing past the detectives to get inside, eager to be home.

"I guess she's your dog," Wheeler said, almost with a smile.

"Yes, this is Daisy," answered Nina as she patted her dog reassuringly. Overjoyed, Daisy reared up on her hind legs and placed her front paws on Nina's stomach. It was a habit of hers long ago broken, but instead of saying "Down," Nina noticed dried blood matting the fur around Daisy's paws.

"What's going on here?" Nina said, pointing to Daisy's paws.

"There was some blood found."

"Blood? Where?"

"In the boat," said Wheeler. "Look, why don't you take a minute to get yourself together. Make arrangements for your children if you need."

"Why?"

"Because you should come with us to the police station," Wheeler said. "Better if we talk there."

*   *   *

As the memory of that terrible day faded, Nina's eyes filled with tears. A cry broke from her lips, sending her shoulders quaking. Susanna and Ginny were at her side in a flash.

"Oh sweetie, I know it's not the *best* magazine, but it's not *that* bad."

Nina managed a weak laugh before she relayed what that magazine actually signified—that day, when she first got the news.

"Have you talked to somebody?" Susanna asked with concern.

"I talk to you girls," Nina said defensively.

"No, I mean somebody professional," Susanna said.

"A therapist," Ginny added, not that the clarification was needed.

Maggie and Connor were both seeing a therapist, but for some reason, Nina hadn't found one for herself. Everything was still so raw that talking about it felt like poking an open wound. And then, when Simon came along, her life seemed to stabilize. The welcome distraction from her troubles had made it possible to suppress her feelings, but maybe no more. Maybe her friends were right. The move was a trigger, and perhaps the time had come to get real help. She should have done it ages ago. She was a social worker and honestly knew better. But then again, the cobbler's kid not having proper shoes was a trope for good reason.

"Anybody have a recommendation?" asked Nina.

"Mine's great," Susanna and Ginny said simultaneously.

The three laughed and hugged, and Nina's fresh tears felt like a cry of relief.

CHAPTER 4

Dr. Sydney Wilcox worked on the second floor of a redbrick office building, in a neighborhood dotted with small businesses. The office itself was cozy and intimate with muted walls and a beige rug. The bland aesthetic was clearly intended to encourage patients to contribute their own color and energy to the environment. The soothing gurgle of a miniature fountain blended with the nearly inaudible hum of a white noise machine put there to ensure privacy. It was all carefully orchestrated to convey one critical message: this was a safe place to share.

Nina sat in an oversize armchair facing a stout woman in her early sixties who had a pageboy haircut that was more salt than pepper. Plastic-frame glasses gave Dr. Wilcox a professorial air, but there was nothing intimidating about her. She had her notebook open, her expression relaxed and nonjudgmental.

"How do we start?" Nina asked.

Nina kept her hands clasped on her lap, allowing her interlaced fingers to nervously caress her knuckles. *Why so anxious?* she asked herself. She'd been in the business of untangling human messes, and it wasn't like this was her first time in therapy. There had been some bumpy days early in her marriage, typical intimacy problems and communication snares that snagged lots of young couples shocked by the cold-water plunge of child-rearing.

"Where do you want to start?" Dr. Wilcox asked.

Nina should have expected her response—therapy was the fine art of asking questions. "Where do you want to start?" might as well have been "What brings you here today?"

Nina spoke of Glen, Maggie, and Connor, providing Dr. Wilcox with the necessary background information. She recalled the day the police came to inform her that Glen was a missing person, then told her that he was still missing, and that many months later, with the help of a successful quiet-title lawsuit that transferred the property title to her name exclusively, she'd sold her home in Seabury, bought a new one in the same town, and moved in with a new man, all in the span of little more than a year and a half.

Nina waited for a flicker of recognition to come to Dr. Wilcox's eyes—*Oh, you're* that *woman!*—but saw nothing of the sort. Maybe she didn't watch the news, or maybe, like anyone outside her immediate friends and family, Dr. Wilcox had forgotten all about the Glen Garrity story. After all, tragedy was personal, and like a wound, it mattered most to those people left with the scars.

"How has the move gone?" asked Dr. Wilcox.

"Good, good," Nina said, worried she sounded like she was trying to reassure herself. "I mean, Maggie is taking it the hardest."

Nina explained how Maggie had grown hostile when Simon became more than a friend.

"What about Connor? Does he get along with Simon?"

"Well, yes. Maybe because he's older. But Connor had some difficulties with his father."

"Difficulties?"

"Glen was something of a workaholic. My nickname for him was Glengarrity Glen Ross."

"From the play," Dr. Wilcox correctly noted.

"And movie about those crazed salespeople trying to save their jobs."

"He was a salesman?"

"No, he worked at a bank. Not in a branch, in the main office. He was a senior financial advisor. Always busy with something. The first night after his dad went missing, Connor confided how he was sad they didn't spend much time together."

Dr. Wilcox took notes with her pencil.

"I tried to convince him that his father loved him very much and that they *did* do things together. Glen always went to Connor's games, and they watched sports together on TV. But that wasn't the same—it wasn't what Connor wanted or needed, and Maggie had her own frustrations with her dad, mostly to do with his availability or lack thereof.

"When I tried to talk to Glen about his work habits, his obsession with his phone or email, he'd remind me that *all* the financial pressure was on him, and guiltily I'd let the behavior slide. I don't think I realized the effect it had on Connor, but that night he told me he didn't feel like he really knew his dad, which turned out to be true for all of us."

Dr. Wilcox's eyebrows rose slightly. "How so?"

"Maybe next session," Nina said. She knew it would be too much information, and therapy was a process, after all.

"Fair enough."

"Anyway, Connor wanted more from his father—more of a connection."

"And you didn't?"

Nina gazed up at the ceiling, trying to piece together her feelings.

"It wasn't a perfect marriage by any stretch," she explained, "but I guess it was enough for me. I had the kids, my friends, my life; in some ways it was easier not having Glen involved in everything. I could make decisions and not be second-guessed all the time. I got what I needed, Glen got what he wanted, but poor Connor felt like his father was uninterested in him, and that was hard to hear."

"Connor never talked about it with you before?"

"No, he could be stoic and stubborn, like his dad, so I only learned all this after Glen was gone."

Dr. Wilcox nodded in understanding. "Does Connor feel comfortable with Simon? Do they do things together?"

"Yes," Nina said as a pang of bitterness toward Glen and his failings came over her. "It's been sweet, actually. Simon is good with tools, more so than Glen, so he shows Connor how to do minor home repairs, that sort of thing. He's also studied YouTube videos to learn how to throw a football, and now he helps Connor practice all the time. And, miracle of miracles, he's gotten Connor interested in history. Simon's a social studies teacher as well as the middle school's robotics coach. He and Connor are building something robotic in the basement together. I'm just hoping it doesn't have arms."

"I see," Dr. Wilcox said. "And how does Maggie feel about their closeness?"

"I don't really know. She doesn't talk about it with me. She's angry, and I understand why. She thinks her father is coming back."

"But you don't."

"No, I don't," Nina said. "I think he's dead. I think he's down in that lake somewhere."

"Did the police explain why they couldn't find his body?"

"They did," said Nina. "Sometimes, depending on how a body settles—on its side, in a particular kind of growth, covered in some debris, or even trapped under a ledge—the sonar doesn't work. I'm a bit of an expert on drowning now, as you can imagine."

Dr. Wilcox's mouth stretched into a slight grimace, indicating she could imagine quite well.

"Normally a body will sink to the bottom," Nina continued. "But eventually it will surface as gas from decay forms in the tissues. Then wind drag, water density, even the topography can create movement underwater, so there was never any guarantee that Glen's body would be found near his boat."

"That must be hard for you—the uncertainty, I mean."

"It's hard for us all."

"What does Simon say about it?"

"Simon's fond of saying that if you're depressed, you're living in the past; if you're anxious, you're living in the future. He's all about being in the moment."

"Nice sentiment, if you can abide by it, but not easy to do. Speaking of pasts, how did you and Simon meet?"

Nina recalled that time last May when her life had pivoted away from Glen and toward Simon.

*   *   *

She and the children were still in the family home, the home they had shared with Glen. As she walked through her front door that day Nina felt a cold emptiness sweep through her body. Daisy always came running with a toy from her toy box clenched in her jaw. Now she was nowhere to be seen.

Nina rushed to the kitchen, the living room, all through the house, calling Daisy's name. Her stomach roiled with anxiety. The front door sometimes appeared to be closed, but needed an extra tug or two to pull it completely shut. With so much on her mind, it was entirely possible she'd forgotten to double-check. Daisy may have nosed open the door and then pawed at the screen, causing the latch to release. She wasn't boundary trained, and there was no electric fence to keep her contained, meaning she could be anywhere.

Nina got in her car and drove around the block, shouting for Daisy through the open window. Nauseous, her stomach in knots, she phoned Granite State Dog Recovery as well as the Seabury Police. Notices were put out on Seabury's Facebook page alerting the broader community to be on the lookout for a lost dog. Ginny and Susanna joined the search, while tips came in about animals spotted on streets as far as ten miles away, but none were Daisy.

As dusk was settling, Nina grew increasingly despondent. Memories pierced her heart. She thought of running her fingers through Daisy's thick coat, or how she rested her head on Nina's lap when they watched TV. As she consoled her shattered children, Nina bristled at how unfair life could be—how cold, cruel, and brutally unfair.

Then she saw a truck coming down her driveway and for a second did a double take, because it was the same make and model as the one Glen drove. A moment later, she noticed Daisy's glorious head sticking out the passenger's side window, tongue flapping in the breeze. The car came to a stop and out stepped Simon Fitch.

It was not the first time Nina had met Simon. That encounter had taken place five school grades ago, when Simon was one of three teacher representatives assigned to help Nina get a local D.A.R.E. (Drug Abuse Resistance Education) program off the ground. They'd had a few pleasant conversations during that time, worked well together as she remembered, but she hadn't seen him in years. Connor didn't have Mr. Fitch for social studies when he attended Seabury Middle School, and Maggie, being in seventh grade, wouldn't have him for a teacher until next year.

Nina didn't even remember what he looked like until he

exited the car, letting Daisy out his door and into the arms of her deeply relieved family. Simon had brown hair cut short, kind eyes, and a little dimpled chin that made his boyish face ruggedly handsome.

"Found her wandering along the side of the road on Whipple Street," Simon said. "My guess is she'd been in the woods."

There were licks galore, kisses, and laughs, and Nina felt a nest of burrs and twigs tangled in Daisy's thick fur.

"Lucky she came out when she did or I might have missed her as I was driving by. Glad you had her tagged."

* * *

"And that was how our relationship started," Nina said after she finished recounting for Dr. Wilcox the day that Daisy had inadvertently brought them together.

"What was your first date like?"

Nina smiled at the memory. "Well, it wasn't a date, but our first chance to spend time together was at my place. Simon remembered me, not only from the school program we worked on together, but because of Glen, because we'd been in the news. Anyway, I offered to have him join us for dinner, trying to think of something I could do as a thank-you for finding Daisy. I knew he wouldn't accept money. He declined my invitation, but sweetly said given what I'd been through I could probably use someone to cook for me. He told me he'd bring something by the next day because he was making his best dish for some school potluck thing and he'd make extra for us.

"I didn't really think I'd see him, but the next night he showed up with a baking dish of eggplant rollatine, which just so happens to be *my* favorite meal. It's my comfort food. My nonni—that's my grandmother—used to make it for me whenever I went to visit, and now I make it for my kids. They love it as much as I do. He showed up at dinnertime so I asked if he wanted to eat with us, and invited him in. That time he said yes."

"Did you think Simon was interested in you romantically?" Dr. Wilcox asked.

"Maybe. I wasn't really paying attention. I remember it felt strangely intimate to have him there, a bit unsettling, but I didn't think of it as a date. Honestly, I didn't think I'd ever date again after what Glen did to me—to us."

Dr. Wilcox glanced at her watch as though she were instinctively aware of how much time had passed.

"I'm afraid that part of the story will have to wait until next time," she said. "Our hour's up."

CHAPTER 5

I hate him. I absolutely, positively hate him.

Maybe, if after a year or something, Mom had wanted to go out on a date, sure, fine, go do it. But this was a *real* relationship. So yeah, my dislike of Simon was pretty much instant, and also justified. I told this to Mom a bunch of times of course, but she'd say everything was going to work out fine, and that eventually we'd become one big happy family doing all these Instagram-worthy things, like hiking and biking and whatever.

Screw that. I don't drink or vape, I get good grades—I do everything I am supposed to do, but still my life stinks and there isn't a damn thing I can do about it.

And it's all *his* fault—Mr. Fitch, aka Simon, aka Mr. I-Just-Want-To-Be-Your-Friend. God! He makes me want to puke. In five years, I'll be gone. Outta here. Off to college and that will be that. I won't ever, ever, come back, and my mom can cry all she wants, say how much she misses me all she wants, but I won't care. And that will be my revenge. And when she gets old and needs someone to look after her, I'll say, "Did you look after me? Nope! You moved me in with *him,* and for that you'll have to die alone and lonely. Sorry, I'm not sorry!"

Okay, that's not true. That's my secret revenge wish, but I'd never, ever, ever do that to my mom. I love my mom. Love her with a cap "L" and all that mushy stuff. But that doesn't mean I can't be pissed at her for what she's done. I still have feelings, you know. I still hurt.

One week into eighth grade and things are just as bad at school as they were at the end of seventh grade. I still eat lunch alone, thanks to Laura Abel's campaign against me (not worth getting into now), and then last week I twisted my ankle playing lacrosse (thought for sure it was broken). So I've got a stupid boot around my foot and too much time on my hands, and worse, I'm home when *he's* home. Students in my school are divided into different teams, each with different teachers, so thank God Almighty I don't have Mr. Fitch for social studies. But now that I'm not playing lacrosse, we essentially have the same schedule, at least on days he doesn't coach robotics, and I can't stand to be alone with him.

Since Mom's unpacked the house (well, mostly unpacked it), she's been talking seriously about getting a job. Worst-case scenario alert! That would mean I could conceivably have hours alone with Simon after school. Can you say: *Nightmare!*

At least the new house is comfortable enough, but it's not like I have any friends in the neighborhood. I don't really have any friends at all anymore (again, not worth getting into). My room—aka my sanctuary—is like my room in the old house, but it doesn't *feel* the same. Simon's energy makes it different. Somehow it gets everywhere, floating like an airborne virus.

Anyway, I knew my mom was worried about money. The move was super expensive, and we've had nonstop contractors since we got here—electricians, plumbers, painters, landscapers. Awesome, right? But Simon didn't think my mom needed to work at all. No, no, no. Mr. Fitch was set and ready to take care of us on his big teacher's salary. I don't know how much he actually makes, but it can't be enough to support a family of four.

Even though they are not officially engaged yet, it is going to happen, so Simon is essentially my stepfather, which is nothing but a stupid label. I looked it up online, and, married or unmarried, he has no legal right to make decisions on my behalf unless he adopts me. News flash—that is not going to happen, not ever ever ever. If Mom gets hurt, or God forbid worse, it would be up to Nonni and Papa to look after me, not him.

It was a Tuesday afternoon when bad went to worse. Daisy and I were on the couch watching TV. Some dumb Netflix thing, doesn't matter, and I was doing what I do best these days—feeling sorry for myself and being mad at the world. Lame, I know. I wasn't an orphan in a war-torn country. I had a roof over my head. I had my dog (I love my dog so, so much—and she makes a great couch cushion). I had everything except friends, my dad, and a Simon-free home.

Simon was in the kitchen. I could hear him messing about, putting together some kind of dinner for the evening. He's a good cook (a really good cook actually, I'll give him that), but I'd eat rice and beans for every meal from now until forever if I could have my dad back. It wasn't like my dad and I were the closest. I hate to admit it, but it was true. Even at home he was always busy with work, or on his phone doing something. He never seemed to have time for me unless we were on vacation or something. I know Connor kind of felt the same way about him, but he was still my dad. He loved me, and I loved him.

Sometimes I'd forget he was even gone. I kept thinking he was going to come walking through the front door, his suit a bit wrinkled from his commute home, a big smile on his face. But that door never opened.

Instead, Mr. Fitch came into the living room with this pleased-with-himself look on his face. He was trying so hard to be "Simon" here, not his school persona, that it was kind of sickening.

"Maggie, it's almost six," he said. "Your mom asked me to make sure you shut the TV off and get your homework done."

Your mom, he said, like he was my babysitter or something, like he doesn't share a bathroom with her. (Gross! Gross! Gross!) I responded by stretching out my legs on the sofa (*my* sofa, from *my* home), and did what I did best: ignored him. Daisy squirmed out from underneath me to roost on the bogus leather love seat that had come from Simon's place. So far, I had successfully avoided sitting (or leaning, or touching really) any piece of furniture that Simon had brought here. I even went around the area rugs that came from his house, just so I wouldn't set foot on even a thread he might have touched. Nobody but me knew about this silent protest of mine, not even Connor, who seemed to really like Simon. He was always tossing the football in the backyard with him or building some dumb robot, as if he forgot that he ever had a real dad.

"Hey, Maggie, I'm talking to you, could you listen, please?"

There it was, the teacher tone, his weapon of choice.

"What?" I answered snippily, as if I hadn't heard him the first time.

He sighed because teachers hate to repeat themselves. "Your mom asked me to make sure the TV was turned off at six so you could get your homework done."

"I don't have any homework," I said, finding that the lie came easily.

"Well, she still wants it off, please. Dinner will be ready in about an hour. Your mom is picking up Connor from practice on her way back from the gym."

As if I care . . .

Instead of off, I turned the volume up a bit louder.

"Hey," Simon said, sounding genuinely miffed. "Off."

Simon stood in front of the TV, his apron making him look like a contestant on one of those baking shows I liked to watch with my father—one of the few things we did together.

"Now, please, Maggie."

Up went the television volume. He was not telling me what to do. He had no legal right over me. This wasn't school. We were on my turf here, not his.

"Come on, Maggie. Please don't make this difficult for me."

Volume went up louder, as I stretched my legs out longer, and it felt good, oh so incredibly good, to defy him.

"You're being really unfair," he groaned.

"I don't have any homework," I said, knowing that the homework wasn't really the issue, and I did have a crap-ton of it to do.

Simon's face got red. He was powerless, and I was enjoying every second of it. He was nothing—a nonentity, a ghost person. He could talk and I didn't have to listen, because he didn't make the rules here.

"Look, Maggie, I'm not trying to replace your dad, but I am trying to do what your mom asked. Please, now. Cooperate."

I pointed the remote at the TV like a gun and turned the volume up louder.

And that's when I saw it. It was brief, just the flicker of a super-disturbing, dark look on Simon's face that came and went. I'd gotten in trouble plenty of times for being mouthy, or disobedient, or whatever, but I'd never, ever, seen a look like that before. It was full of hate, but somehow also empty, as cold as an ice storm—the only word I could think of was "soulless." I could imagine him smashing my skull in with a hammer with that same look on his face.

For sure, if he'd looked at his students like that, they would have snapped to attention and thought twice about making him angry again. There would probably have been calls to the school from worried parents. It was that kind of look.

Then the strange darkness gave way to a more familiar anger. Simon took two giant steps forward and snatched the clicker from my hand, quick as a frog's tongue grabbing a fly. I let out a cry of surprise, causing Daisy to bark with alarm.

"Give it back!" I shouted, springing from the couch like I hadn't quit gymnastics years ago.

Simon jerked the remote up and out of my reach, and with a push of a button, off went the TV.

"Go away! Leave me alone!" I screamed at him, feeling my face grow hot. I went storming up the stairs, stomping on each step as I went, and Daisy, dear, faithful Daisy, followed me into my bedroom, where I slammed the door and waited for my mom to come home.

CHAPTER 6

All of the endorphins Nina had built up during her strenuous barre workout with Susanna and Ginny vanished in a jiffy as soon as she set foot inside her new home. Maggie, who must have heard Nina pull into the driveway, bellowed for her mother to come upstairs. Simon was blocking the stairs like police caution tape, a silent warning that she wouldn't like what she'd find up there.

"What is going on?" Nina asked, speaking loudly to be heard over Maggie's urgent pleas.

Connor groaned and executed a textbook eye roll. "That girl's got more drama than an acting school," he said, tossing his dirty duffel bag to the floor.

"That," Nina said, pointing at the foul-smelling object, "needs to be emptied out. Dirty things in the hamper; cleats on the back porch." Nina redirected her finger at Connor. "And you stay out of it. Get started on your homework before dinner."

Connor skulked away, muttering something obviously unpleasant about his little sister.

"What is going on?" Nina asked again. She unconsciously adopted a defensive posture, arms folded across her chest as if to shield herself from the coming unpleasantness. She was still in her Lululemon workout ensemble, a carryover from the years when she'd felt secure enough financially to afford the luxury. If it weren't for Ginny and her seemingly unending supply of guest passes, Nina would have had to give up her barre workouts long ago. She was well aware Simon had money, more than a teacher should have—family money, he had explained rather vaguely, giving her the impression his deceased wife (will? life insurance?) factored into that equation. His reluctance to share any details kept her from prying.

Nina maintained her own checking account with an ever-dwindling balance. She had valid concerns about tying her finances to another person after Glen had left her and the kids nearly destitute to fund a different life she knew nothing about. Even so, Simon had been generous with his money, even putting Nina on his checking account in case something ever happened to him, or so he had said. But Nina wasn't going to ask him to pay for her workouts, not if she could help it.

As Simon explained the tiff with Maggie, Nina took a sharp inhale and held her breath. She could see why her daughter had reacted so strongly.

"I just wanted you to remind her to shut it off, not demand it," Nina said.

But the hard look Simon returned suggested a different narrative.

"No, you were very clear with me that the TV *must* be shut off at six. Those were your instructions exactly."

But were they? Nina scratched at the recesses of her mind, trying to locate the precise words she'd spoken, but what had seemed so clear moments ago was now as murky as the lake that had seemingly swallowed Glen. Had she issued Simon a mandate? She understood the power dynamics at play, and it would have been unfair of her to put Simon in such a position.

Of course Maggie would have battled back, if for no other reason than to make the point that Simon had no authority over her.

"I don't believe that's what I told you," Nina said. "And if I did, you should know you have to be gentle with her. She's very fragile right now."

"Which is why I specifically asked if you were sure that's what you wanted me to do," Simon said. "I know how young people think, Nina," he reminded her.

Again, Nina thought back to the conversation she'd had with Simon while rushing out the door. Ginny, waiting in the driveway, had given a second warning honk that they'd soon be late for the afternoon exercise class. Meanwhile, the house was still a mess, and Nina couldn't find a tank top to wear. It was entirely conceivable that in the rush and chaos she'd issued Simon a mandate that had set him up to fail.

From the start of their relationship Simon had been nothing but generous, empathetic, and almost superhumanly in tune with her feelings and needs. Most important, she loved the way he loved her. It was like that first dinner he had cooked for her (eggplant rollatine), the first present he'd bought (an opal necklace, a perfect choice), the TV shows and movies he'd wanted to watch that she did, too, the music he listened to—all of it perfectly aligned with her tastes and desires, as if the universe itself were sending signals to let her know she'd made the right choice. So if there was fault to pass around here, Nina considered it quite possible that it rested squarely on her shoulders.

In fact, in their brief history together there had been no fights, no misunderstandings, not even any minor tiffs for her to reference. The toilet seat was never left up. His clothes were never scattered about—or worse, dropped on the floor four inches from the hamper. He kept his side of the bathroom cleaner than Nina's, as was his nature, and anytime he borrowed her car, it always came back with a full tank of gas.

Their first evening alone together, before they were a couple, had been at a restaurant Simon had picked out, the Blue Nile. It was new to Seabury but came highly praised by *The Hippo,* a weekly periodical covering arts and culture in New Hampshire. Nina hadn't wanted to think of it as a date, because the word carried connotations she wasn't ready to embrace. She had told Simon to meet her there, partly because it felt less datelike to arrive separately.

Strolling into the restaurant, Nina felt guilty for wearing an outfit she'd taken pains to select. To quiet her conscience, she'd reminded herself of Glen's many betrayals. It was hard enough that he'd gone missing, but when his secrets surfaced (the waitress . . . the missing money) and his body didn't, it made things so much worse. So for that reason, Nina's petty revenge felt strangely sweet. The fitted lace bodice with semi-sheer sleeves paired with a pencil skirt, was both feminine and figure-flattering. She wore lipstick and mascara, something she saved for special occasions, but she had wanted to make an impression. Judging by how Simon couldn't stop looking at her, Nina felt it was mission accomplished.

But it wasn't a date. Her husband had disappeared only three months ago—twelve short weeks, and here she was, out with a man.

Simon had greeted Nina in the restaurant's sleek foyer. She felt something stir inside when his lips brushed against her cheek. He looked dashing in his tweed blazer, white oxford, and dark slacks, and Nina began to rethink her stance. It wasn't as if she had a marriage to mourn. As it turned out, she'd had no marriage at all. If Nina denied herself, it was only to adhere to some unspoken social norm. And it wasn't as if she had gone looking for Simon. He just happened. It was organic. In a weird way, it felt almost predestined.

They exchanged pleasantries—"Hello," "You look nice"—as he helped Nina with her coat. He thanked the hostess and before he took his seat, Simon pulled out a chair for Nina. She was glad to see chivalry wasn't dead. In fact, Nina found herself fluttering a little at being treated like a lady, though she kept those feelings to herself.

The first order of business was the wine. Simon barely glanced at the menu before he suggested a bottle of Thierry Puzelat, a red she had never tasted before.

"It's organic, unfiltered, and bottled without any added sulfites," Simon said.

Nina was impressed. "Sounds perfect."

And it was. Nina always shopped organic when she could. She was as careful about what she put into her children's bodies as what went into her own.

Simon smiled appreciatively. "Had a good hunch about what you might like."

"I'd say your hunch is very well informed."

Simon chuckled in response.

The wine came while they were perusing the menu. Simon made sure Nina got the first sip, and it was in fact delicious. The waiter poured two glasses before taking their order. Nina asked for the Scottish organic salmon with savoy cabbage and truffle vinaigrette. Simon ordered steak frites with an arugula salad.

"Tell me how you're doing with everything." Simon leaned in. Nina answered as best she could, sharing her worries, fears, doubts, and concerns for a future clouded by the smoldering wreckage of her past.

Simon had impressed Nina. He was so thoughtful and engaged, asking all the right questions; interested in her, but in a relaxed way. It didn't feel like an inquisition or a romantic tryst, but more like two friends getting to know each other better, chatting with ease. It felt nice.

"Kids are hanging in there," Nina said, answering one of Simon's follow-up questions. "They're trying to resume their lives, and I'm looking for therapists to help guide them, but it's hard, as you can imagine."

The evening flowed as easily as the wine went down. It wasn't until Nina got home, with only a friendly embrace and no kiss goodnight from Simon, that she realized how much she had dominated the conversation. They'd barely spoken of Simon's life, his hardships. It wasn't a big secret that Simon's wife had committed suicide some five years before. Nina didn't know how to broach the subject, and thought it best if he were the one to bring it up. But he never did. Maybe he didn't want to talk about it. Maybe the wound was still too fresh. Or maybe Nina was too consumed with her own misfortunes to discuss those of another.

She thought about this for much of the next day, wondering how to apologize for not encouraging Simon to speak about himself, when he showed up unexpectedly at the house with a toolbox in his hand.

Nina's breath caught, surprised at how good it felt to see him again.

"I was in the neighborhood and remembered you had a loose and leaky faucet. I keep a toolbox in my car, and had the crazy idea to come by and fix it." He swung his toolbox in the direction of the kitchen. Nina eyed him dubiously. She recalled the day Simon had brought over her favorite meal and she'd invited him in for dinner. He had fiddled with the faucet that evening, so his story was believable. But she was also aware of the general vicinity in which Simon lived, meaning the only thing that might have led him to this part of town was looking squarely into his sweet baby-brown eyes.

Nina was anxious about inviting Simon inside, as the

children were at home and his presence again would obviously raise questions. But she found herself stepping aside, then following Simon to the kitchen. There he opened his toolbox and got right to work.

"Shouldn't take but a minute," he announced, using a flashlight to examine the faucet carefully. The kids did not come to inspect the visitor, but Daisy did, and her olfactory memory earned Simon a lick on the arm.

While Simon toiled, half hidden underneath the cabinet, Nina worked in an apology for the other evening.

"We didn't talk about you hardly at all," she said, making no allusions to them both sharing a tragic past. "I felt bad about it when I got home."

Simon eased himself out from under the sink and met Nina's worried gaze.

"I had a wonderful evening," he said. "You don't owe me an apology for anything." And with that, he turned his attention back to the faucet.

As if on cue, Maggie came into the kitchen, surprised to see Simon there.

"Hey there," Simon said, pulling himself out from under, his expression becoming animated. To Nina's delight, he anticipated Maggie's question. "I was in the neighborhood and thought I'd fix the faucet. I noticed it was loose last time I was here. How are you?"

"Good," Maggie answered.

"Everything going well at school? I know getting back must be hard."

"It's okay," Maggie said in a soft voice.

"Well, it's almost summer," Simon said brightly. "I don't know who's more excited for the break—the kids or the teachers."

Maggie returned a polite laugh. She had missed almost three weeks of school—first for the search, later for the grieving—while managing to keep up with her studies from home. At first, to help her kids stay on track, Nina had kept the most damaging information from them. All they knew was that their dad was missing. She said nothing of their father's many misdeeds, nor did they have an inkling that their mom was beginning to develop feelings for another man.

Maggie didn't stay long. Adults had nothing to offer her, and if she did have questions about Simon's motives for fixing the sink or her mother's feelings, she'd never shared.

But she was sharing now.

Long after Nina and Simon had become a couple—after more dinners out, then movie dates; after long talks on the phone (something Nina hadn't done since she and Glen had begun dating); after a moonlit beach walk and dance in the sand with only the wind and waves for music; after their first kiss on the lakeshore by Simon's house and the first time they made love; after Simon professed his love for Nina (words he admitted to being too scared to say to anybody since his wife's suicide); after the rocket-ship trajectory of new romance—Maggie had found her voice, and had no trouble speaking her mind.

Nina trudged upstairs, anticipating a rehashing of her daughter's well-worn complaints: *He's not my real father. How could you just replace Dad? Why don't I have any say? How come I can't move to Nebraska and live with Nonni and Papa?* The real issue, of course, was Glen.

It took time and a lot of soul-searching before Nina had decided to level with her kids about what their father had done. She didn't expect them to comprehend the situation the way an adult would, but she had hoped it would make it easier for them to accept what she wanted out of life now: Simon, love, a second chance at happiness.

While Nina wasn't completely forthcoming, she'd given them the essential shape of the truth. She avoided using the word "affair," and downplayed certain details of their financial woes for the benefit of young psyches in no need of further scarring. The most important message Nina tried to convey—and thought she'd done a good job of it, too—was that their father was gone, never to come back. In nearly the same breath, she had reassured them that she would always be there for them, but she wanted, needed, and deserved to move on with her life—a move that, to Maggie's chagrin, involved Simon. This recent flare-up would in no way deter Nina's resolve to make everyone happy, including herself.

When she got upstairs, Nina found Maggie spread out on her bed, lying on her stomach, feet where her head belonged, listening to music on her phone (she was still in her pop phase). Daisy was on the bed with her, curled in a tight, furry ball, content as could be. A book lay open on the plush comforter: *A Wrinkle in Time* by Madeleine L'Engle, the novel Maggie was reading with Glen when he disappeared.

Nina sat on the edge of the bed, stroking her daughter's silky hair. Maggie wasn't crying, but her eyes were red, suggesting she'd only recently stopped. The whole room buzzed with her daughter's energy, her vibrant life force. The walls were plastered with a kaleidoscope of bright colors and handmade crafts Mags never tired of making: felt flowers, stuffed sock toys, painted rock animals, little creatures made from clam shells she had collected on a family trip to Sanibel Island.

Almost every inch of wall space was taken up with something Maggie had made, along with pictures of horses (her new obsession, though riding lessons were out of the question) and a lacrosse poster that read: I PLAY LIKE A GIRL. TRY TO KEEP UP! The furniture included a comfortable chair for reading, and well-stocked bookshelves. Mini blinds covered the windows. All in all, Mag's room was neat and ordered—unlike their lives.

"Want to talk about it?" Nina asked.

Maggie flipped over onto her back before pulling herself upright. "What's there to talk about? You won't listen anyway."

"You've been calling for me since I got home."

"Well, I thought it over and I realized there's no point. I'm stuck here . . . with him." She pointed at her wall, in the direction of downstairs.

"Can't you give him a chance?"

Maggie shook her head in a defiant no. "When Dad comes back, I won't have to."

"He's not coming back," Nina said, sensing her composure begin to fracture.

"You didn't see Simon's eyes tonight, Mom. His anger. It was really, really scary."

Nina gave a roll of her eyes that would have made Connor proud, thinking he was right to call Maggie overly dramatic. This was and had been her unending pattern: make big bold claims about everything falling apart and how it was all her mom's fault. But this was the first time Maggie had talked about being afraid of Simon. Clearly she was trying a different tactic to get a rise out of her mother.

Nina was mulling over how to respond when Simon came marching into the room holding a gun.

CHAPTER 7

I admit I panicked when I saw the barrel of the rifle. My first thought was, *This is it—I'm dead.* I've seen horror movies and true crime shows. *I'm going to be tomorrow's news today; a dead body in a room stained with blood-splattered walls.* But then my eyes went to work, and I realized the gun in Simon's hands was not going to be used to shoot my mom, my dog, or me. It was an antique gun, a musket to be exact, and was part of Mr. Fitch's well-known hobby of reenacting the Revolutionary War.

Every year, Mr. Fitch gives a big presentation on it to the entire school. Seventh- and eighth-grade classrooms gather at different times in the auditorium to see his one-man play. He dresses up first as a Redcoat and then a Patriot to show both sides of the conflict—you know, give us kids a complete picture of what was happening back then.

Even though I didn't pay much attention to last year's performance, a lot of kids really liked it. And our principal said it helped bring history to life, which is what Mr. Fitch, our "beloved" social studies teacher, got paid to do. Onstage, he paraded that musket around (yeah, school shooting concerns and all) like a good soldier. He spoke in this lame English accent and complained about not having enough food and ammunition to do some big battle or something.

Each year, around this time, Mr. Fitch leads a field trip for his classes to Strawbery Banke, an outdoor history museum that features a bunch of restored buildings from colonial New England. He goes dressed in costume and carries that musket with him like he is guarding the place from invaders. Only the kids who go on the Strawbery Banke field trip get to handle Mr. Fitch's musket, which cost over two thousand dollars from an antique gun dealer. They're allowed to load it with powder, even try out the bayonet on a tree—all under his careful supervision, of course. So once I figured out what the gun in his hands was, I knew he hadn't brought it into my room to kill me.

He'd brought it as a peace offering.

"I've come to lay down my weapon," Simon said, amusing only himself. He made a big show of putting his ancient musket on my bed, which annoyed Daisy, who up and left. My mother was looking at him like, *What the heck are you doing?* She didn't know the history of that musket, the cool factor it held for some kids—but not me.

"Look, Maggie, I'm sorry about what happened. Your mother and I had a little misunderstanding. Can you forgive me? I was headed downstairs to oil the musket, get it ready for the field trip, and thought maybe you'd like to help. Connor is working on that robot with me; I was hoping this could be our thing."

Oh joy, oh joy, I was thinking. *Nothing in the world would make me happier than oiling a gun—not!* I kept my thoughts to myself because I knew it wouldn't do me any good. Simon was all smiles and apologies, and my mom couldn't have looked more pleased.

"No thanks," I said.

Rather than fight it, Simon extended his hand to me. "Could we be friends again?"

Again??? I thought. *Whatever.*

"Sure," I said, trying to forget the look I'd seen in his eyes, that flash of something scary dark.

"Maggie, we've all got to try harder, okay, sweetheart?" Mom said as she got up from my bed. "This is a big adjustment for everyone, Simon, too."

I didn't say anything because sometimes silence speaks louder than words. Mom let go a heavy sigh.

"I'll try," I mumbled.

"You can do better than that," Mom said.

My mom didn't get angry very often, especially these days, when we'd already suffered so much. But I heard the shake in her voice, a little rumble telling me that if I pushed any harder, her volcano might blow. I backed off, saying I had homework to do, forgetting my earlier lie, so they left.

Simon took his dumb gun with him.

At some point, Connor poked his head into my room. I wasn't in the mood to talk, but he was in the mood to lecture.

"Hey, you've got to help Mom out," he said. "She's been through a lot too, you know."

I thought about telling Connor what I'd seen, that look from Simon, but I knew he'd say I was being dramatic, because that's what he always says. I was so done with him, with everyone. He could have Simon all to himself, if that's what he wanted. Go practice football with him, go make that robot, go do whatever. I didn't care anymore, because I had nobody. I didn't think it was possible to miss my dad any more, but I was wrong.

About a half hour later, I heard loud talking from downstairs. I snuck down the steps the way I did on those Christmas Eves years ago, when I thought for sure I'd catch my parents putting presents under the tree. By this point, I could maneuver in my stupid boot like I wasn't wearing it at all. I worked my way down the hall, careful to make sure Daisy wasn't around because she'd gladly give me up. I got close enough to hear my mother and Simon talking, let's just call it animatedly, about her going back to work. I kept my back pressed up against the wall, listening to the conversation coming from the kitchen.

"I can't sit around and let you cover all of our expenses," Mom said. "It doesn't feel right to me, even if you can afford it."

"But I *can* afford it," Simon whined. "We're fine. I'm making way more money than I thought renting out my house."

How does he have money? I wondered. Simon always bragged how he could provide for us, college and all, but I never thought it was possible on what a teacher made. Then again, he did own a two-thousand-dollar costume prop. Maybe he came from a wealthy family. What did I know? I hardly knew him.

"I don't get why you're so against me working," Mom said. "It's not the fifties, Simon. You do know women work."

Simon made a noise to convey his awareness of that fact.

"I know what year it is," he said. "Most of my colleagues are women. My point is I think it's going to be bad for Maggie."

For me? I thought. *Leave me out of it.* Before, I was against my mom working because it would have meant more time for me at the house alone with Simon. But now that I knew he was against Mom going back to work, well, I was suddenly all for it.

"I'm her mother; I think I know what's best for Maggie."

"I get that you're her mother, but it doesn't help me that you won't give me a voice in the house," Simon said. "I'm always going to be an outsider."

Damn straight, I thought.

"Some decisions need to come from me," my mom said. "Including my decision to go back to work. I want my own money, and honestly, I think it's good for Maggie to see me being independent, getting back on my feet. I want her to understand that no matter what life throws at you, you can always bounce back. Rather than tell her to be resilient, I can show her."

Connor came down the hall and I put my finger to my lips so that he would stay quiet. He wasn't a dummy. He was just as interested in eavesdropping as I was.

"That's a fair point," Simon said. "I'm just saying I've been around her a lot is all. I've noticed things about Maggie's behavior, and not just today."

Connor made a face at me that I wanted to wipe off with my fist.

"What kind of things?" Mom said. I could tell by her tone that she was worried.

"I think she's on edge. If you get involved in a new job, it's going to take a lot of your focus. That's how it goes."

"Thank you for your concern," Mom said. "But I think I know myself well enough to know how to balance a job and my family. My social worker credentials are up to date, I've got my résumé put together, and I'm starting to send it out tomorrow. I'm not asking for your permission here, Simon. I'm asking for your support."

But Simon didn't say anything, and for the first time in ages I felt great, really fantastic. I've never had a boyfriend, but I've watched plenty of TV, read lots of juicy YA books, so I knew cracks in a relationship when I saw them.

CHAPTER 8

On Saturday morning, Nina woke with a start. It was her father's birthday on Wednesday, but she hadn't gotten around to sending him a card with the kids' school pictures in it, something she did every year. It was the job search, she realized, that had distracted her, and in some ways the oversight supported Simon's assertion that she wouldn't be able to focus on work and the rest of her life while everything was in upheaval.

From outside, Nina heard the faint hum of a lawn mower, and wondered how late she had slept. A warm late-summer breeze pushed against the fluttering curtains, allowing in sips of light that painted the bedroom in an amber glow.

Nina stretched her arms skyward, then puttered over to the closet, where she retrieved a terry-cloth robe. It caught her off guard, still, even after all this time, to see Simon's clothes in there, leading her to wonder when he would become her new normal instead of her new man. Cinching the robe tightly around her waist, Nina went off in search of her family, as well as some coffee, hopeful that Simon had been his usual thoughtful self and made her a cup.

She could see from down the hall that Connor's bedroom

door was closed; no surprise there. That child could sleep until noon. Maggie's was open, meaning she was lurking about somewhere, probably parked in front of the TV, along with Daisy and a towering bowl of Honey Nut Cheerios.

The aromatic smell of coffee drew Nina downstairs as though she were a cartoon character following a scent trail. She poured coffee from the pot into her favorite mug, wondering why Daisy hadn't come to greet her. Usually it was Nina who fed the dog in the mornings, and the dog's hearing was especially keen on an empty stomach. The TV wasn't on and Maggie and Daisy weren't in the living room when Nina checked, so with mug in hand, she stepped outside and found Simon on the front lawn, standing on a ladder perched against the oak tree she loved, tying yellow ribbons around several of the limbs. These were the same ribbons her well-meaning friends had once tied around another tree in honor of her missing husband. This time they no doubt carried a different meaning.

At the edge of the property, somebody, presumably Simon, had spray-painted a jagged orange line from the curb well past the oak tree. Upon second viewing, it became apparent to Nina that some of the limbs from the neighbor's tree had unwittingly grown across the orange boundary line.

"What is going on?" Nina asked Simon from the base of the ladder. On a nearby table, Simon had rolled out an architectural drawing of their property. Nina guessed the spray-painted orange line corresponded to the property's defined boundary.

"Is that permanent?" she asked, pointing at the line.

Simon beamed at Nina from his perch up high before directing his gaze to where she indicated. "Oh, hey, honey, good morning. No, not to worry. It's marking chalk, comes off easily."

"Good. What are you doing?"

At that moment, Maggie and Daisy appeared from the back of the house.

Climbing down from the ladder, Simon wiped his hands on his faded jeans after reaching the ground. He planted a gentle kiss on Nina's forehead. "Did you get enough beauty rest?"

"Plenty," Nina said. "What's going on here?"

"Oh, this tree." He patted the thick trunk lovingly. "Some of these limbs, they're crossing into our property. Gotta come down."

"Yeah?" Nina folded her arms across her chest. "And the neighbors think so, too?"

"It's not their property," Simon said. "People have to respect ownership. There are laws for that."

Maggie, with Daisy following off-leash, came to the tree. She looked up and then over at Simon. "What's going on?" she asked.

Nina didn't answer her daughter, instead speaking directly to Simon.

"You can't cut those down without asking permission," she said sternly.

"But I have asked."

From the table with those drawings on it, Simon produced copies of letters he had sent the neighbors. Nina had not seen the Greens since they'd brought over cookies after she and Simon moved in. The letters Simon had sent announced his intention to trim the tree to his property line on this given date unless the Greens took it upon themselves to do the job. Simon then produced a copy of the law that made it legal for him to trim branches that extended onto his property line as long as he did not destroy the tree. He even got into a bit of the history of property law, not that anyone was interested.

"I've got these documents with me in case the Greens raise objections. It's clear the law is on my side."

"I don't care," said Nina, taking more of a tone. "I'm not going to have the Greens over here screaming about their mutilated tree."

"Well, what do you want me to do about it? Just leave it be? This is our property."

Maggie tilted at the waist. *Is this normal?* her eyes were asking. *Would Dad have freaked out about some dumb branches?*

"Unless you think those branches are going to fall on somebody's head, keep them on that tree where they belong," Nina said sharply. "I happen to like how it looks."

Simon's posture straightened at the rebuke. His shoulders went back as his neck seemed to lengthen. His stance grew rigid and Nina could see the muscles of his jaw tightening, while the corners of his eyes twitched several times as if dust had gotten in them. And then she saw something catch in Simon's eyes, a spark igniting in a brief flash before it dimmed, a look she'd never seen before. Was that what Maggie had seen—a fleeting darkness that bordered on anger, or something worse? Whatever it was, Nina found it unsettling.

But what came on quickly soon was gone. Simon's expression cleared and he returned to his normal self. A smile brightened his countenance and warmed his whole appearance.

"Of course," he said. "We've got to live next door to them. And if you like the tree as is, then I like it too."

He leaned in to again kiss Nina on the forehead, while Maggie looked on with a hopeful expression. The moment, though brief, had been illuminating for Nina on many levels. There were aspects to Simon's personality that would only be revealed with time. This, she understood, should be expected and embraced. She did not know he had a hang-up about property lines, but it fit with his personality (fastidious, far more rigid than Glen, a lot neater, too), so it made sense to her that he'd be somewhat obsessed with rules and order.

The incident with Maggie and the television remote suddenly took on new vividness for her. It better explained why rule-following Simon had been so insistent on shutting the TV off at six, ignoring common sense, while claiming a mandate she may or may not have issued. As for Maggie, a young girl without much life experience who missed her dad tremendously, who desperately wanted to get her life back to the way it had been, it was certainly conceivable she had misinterpreted Simon's angry expression as something more sinister. In some ways, it was a relief for Nina to see Simon's frustration, because now she saw what her daughter had seen, and it no longer concerned her.

CHAPTER 9

Summer turned to fall as Nina began her job search in earnest. In that time, she did a dozen drafts of her résumé, with Susanna's help. She updated her LinkedIn profile, reconnected with former colleagues and friends, all while sending inquiry after inquiry into the black hole of the internet, receiving no return responses. Somehow this was not supposed to dampen her spirits; after all, she was just beginning the process. Hadn't she taught her children that patience was a virtue and not to expect instant gratification? But in this day and age of social media and continuous feedback, she expected a certain degree of immediacy and tried not to take radio silence as a portent of things to come.

Nina was back in Dr. Wilcox's office, seated on the now familiar comfy chair, soothed by the sounds of the fountain and the white noise machine. *How should we start today's session?* she asked herself. Should she talk about Maggie and Simon, their argument about the TV remote that was really about so much more? Or maybe she should talk about her career; share her worries and fears about being professionally put to pasture and Simon's concerns over her resuming a demanding job?

As it turned out, Dr. Wilcox had a different topic in mind. Glen.

She glanced up from the notes she'd jotted down. "In a previous session you said you didn't think you'd ever date again after what Glen did to you. Can we talk about Glen now?"

A flood of memories rushed over Nina as if she were drowning in them. She remembered driving down her dirt road, dazed, seated in the back of the police car, where the prisoners usually go, on her way to the station to discuss her missing husband.

"I spent a lot of time with Detectives Wheeler and Murphy, answering their questions," Nina told Dr. Wilcox, who studied her with a look of sympathy and concern. "I thought maybe Glen had cut himself badly with a fishing knife, fell, hit his head hard, and somehow ended up in the water. He was an excellent swimmer, so he could have made it to shore, got lost in the woods, maybe he had a concussion and was disoriented. It gave me hope."

"But that wasn't the story?"

"No, it wasn't. Because the police searched the woods, with dogs even, and there was no sign of Glen anywhere. Then they asked me all sorts of questions. Was Glen depressed? Could he have been suicidal? They even wanted to know about our marriage."

"What did you tell them?"

Nina opened up about several issues that hadn't seemed worth mentioning to the detectives. They were little things, really, like how Glen still resented her for moving them out of the city. Seabury was too isolated for him, and moving there had only confirmed his belief that "rural" equaled "remote."

Nina, on the other hand, had adjusted quickly to their

new town. It was safe, the kind of community she'd always wanted to live in, a place where other mothers kept an eye out for her children, where everyone had each other's backs. Nina appreciated Glen's willingness to move, and told him so almost daily for the first few years. It was an idyllic community in so many ways—it just wasn't Boston, as Glen took every opportunity to remind her.

The marriage gradually became overwhelmed, thanks in part to the move north coupled with the daily grind of life. Spontaneity had yielded to schedules. Glen did what he always did: put his focus and energy into his work, moving up the career ladder, while Nina directed hers into the kids and home. As time wore on, and his work responsibilities grew, Glen showed increasingly less interest in her world—the mundane tasks of gardening, shopping, cleaning, laundry, the dog, and the kids—because he'd become too consumed with his.

The day-to-day went along smoothly enough, but Nina was also aware of a growing gulf between them as exhaustion replaced intimacy. Then again, wasn't that most marriages? Didn't most couples start off feeling some sort of imperative, an insatiable need for the other person, until those feelings became so familiar they went as unnoticed as breathing?

"But you never talked about divorce or separation?" Dr. Wilcox asked.

"No, no," Nina said dismissively. "We were happy . . . I mean happyish, right? I mean, who doesn't have problems? But I wasn't going to get into all that with the police. I felt the focus needed to be on finding Glen. Nothing else mattered. So eventually, I went home because I had to break the news to the children."

"How did they take it?"

"It was hard, of course. I know the words 'Dad,' 'accident,' 'missing'—they all came out in the course of the conversation, but for the life of me I have no recollection of saying them. All I remember is Mag's sweet voice cracking when she asked for her daddy. We hugged and cried together. Even Connor cried so hard he couldn't speak."

"How painful for all of you."

"Oh, it was. But it was just the start."

Nina recounted the first night after Glen had gone missing, reliving those moments in vivid detail for Dr. Wilcox's benefit. That evening she felt like she was hosting a wake for a person who wasn't dead. At least forty people were in the house, probably more, with cars lining the side of the road almost to the end of the street.

Several news vans had parked out front, their bright portable lights turning twilight into daylight. They had wanted a statement from Nina and the children. They wanted tears on camera, raw emotion that would make for a juicy tease to get viewers to tune in and satisfy advertisers.

Nina wasn't going to play their game, but she did want Glen's picture on the broadcast in case he was an amnesiac, lost and wandering. Susanna went on TV, functioning as the Garrity family spokesperson. Nina watched the News 9 broadcast live from outside her home. The picture they used for the report was of Glen smiling after a family hike to the top of Mount Monadnock. Susanna found the photo on Facebook, and everyone agreed it was the best one to use.

"Where were Maggie and Connor while all this was going on?" Dr. Wilcox asked.

"Maggie was hiding out in her room. It was too overwhelming to be downstairs. Connor wanted to go to the lake and search for his father—in fact, a whole group of us suggested we do just that, but the police didn't want us there. That part of Lake Winnipesaukee by Governors Island has all sorts of terrain, and they had professionals on the scene, and we would have been in the way.

"Connor was really upset about not being able to help with the search, and I did what I could to reassure him the police would find his dad, that everything would be all right, but I could tell he didn't believe me. Hell, I didn't believe me either."

"You implied things got even worse. Do you want to talk about it?"

Nina took in a breath to inflate her resolve. Some memories were harder to relive than others.

"Well, it was a chaotic night," she said a bit apprehensively, "with people coming and going. By eleven o'clock the house had nearly emptied out. At Susanna's urging I went upstairs to get some rest. I was probably a vodka tonic away from slurring my words."

"Understandable," Dr. Wilcox said.

"I had just closed my eyes when my cell phone chirped—an incoming text. It was a New Hampshire area code, six-oh-three," Nina said, "but wasn't a number I recognized, and it wasn't anyone in my phone's contacts. In fact, the text message started off by saying they were using an anonymous texting app that kept their identity a secret. Whoever it was didn't want to be involved, but they had something to share."

Bitterness rode up the back of Nina's throat, the memory still so raw and cutting it was easy to conjure up her initial shock and anger.

"What was it?" Dr. Wilcox asked.

"The texter—to this day I don't know if it was a guy or a girl—believed Glen was seeing a woman named Teresa."

"Teresa?"

"That was the name in the text. I'd never heard of her."

"And?"

"And . . . and for a moment I thought it was a prank, some sick person who had seen Glen's story on the news, knew all about him, looked up my phone number somehow, and was playing with my emotions for kicks. I imagined a group huddled around a phone, laughing at this poor woman they were taunting."

"But it wasn't a prank?"

"No. The texter sent a picture. Two pictures, actually."

The first picture Nina described had been too small for her to see clearly, but with a touch of her finger she'd expanded it into a larger image, filling her phone's display.

She saw Glen out at night, lit by a camera's flash, standing in front of a bar or restaurant Nina did not recognize, dressed in clothes she did recognize. He had his arm draped around a young woman who was heavily made up, hoop earrings almost touching her shoulders, choker necklace in place, dressed for a night on the town in a short black skirt, calf-high leather boots, and a tight-fitting black top that showed off the swell of her breasts.

The woman's strawberry-blond hair fell well past her shoulders, framing a slightly freckled face with enviable cheekbones, vibrant eyes, and a generous smile that was the early stage of a laugh. She radiated sexuality, lust. Glen had his head turned, his face pressed up against her cheek, his lips puckered, attached to her like a remora on a shark. Even though it was a frozen moment, Nina could still tell it was an intimate kiss, not a quick peck. Glen's blue eyes shone with delight.

The second picture she received left no doubt about the sort of kisses they shared. Glen had his lips pressed firmly against Teresa's, their mouths locked open, his hands squeezing her backside hard enough for Nina to see the strain put on his knuckles.

Almost two years later, she could recall the follow-up text message verbatim.

> This girl is Teresa Mitchell. She's my friend. Saw Glen's picture on TV. Think he's your husband. Knew him as Teresa's boyfriend. They were in love. Didn't know he was married. Took these photos when we were out together. Sorry for everything. Thought you deserved the truth.

Nina's hands shook so fiercely, she could barely type a reply.

> Where? Where were these taken? When?

> The Muddy Moose Carson NH. Teresa works there. That's where they met. Sorry to be the one to tell you. You have my sympathy. Good-bye.

Dr. Wilcox took in a sharp breath. "What did you do?"

"Well, that same night I sent the pictures to the police, of course, and gave them the number of the texter, because after all my husband was missing, and this woman, Teresa, could have had something to do with it. But I was worried, you know, afraid how much worse it would get."

"Worse how?"

"We were about to become a living, breathing *Dateline* special. 'Cheating husband vanishes. Was the grieving wife all an act?' You get the idea."

"Indeed. I'm guessing there's more to this story."

"Much more," Nina said.

CHAPTER 10

Lunch.

Oh, the dreaded, dreaded half hour. Some people hate gym, or get stomach cramps before math, English, or Spanish, but no, not me. I love all those classes. I love school. Homework doesn't bother me in the slightest. I don't get knotted up over tests; I'm not a perfectionist like that. But I am abysmally miserable during lunch.

I should explain. Lunch is where the complicated social structure of middle school gets sorted out. Groups are defined mostly by where they eat: the football team has three tables; soccer has a few; drama and band each have their own section of our incredibly noisy cafeteria—and so on. According to our guidance counselor, all that BS we heard in grade school about being inclusive doesn't apply in the dog-eat-dog world of middle school. Here, our friend groups form because of how we spend our time outside of school, in various clubs, sports, and whatnot, which is why the jocks and nerds mix like oil and water.

Up until midway through last year, my friend group was made up mainly of the lacrosse team, a mix of boys and girls who played the game (club in the fall, school team in the spring) and hung out together all year round. We went to each other's houses for parties, swimming, goofing off on trampolines, that kind of stuff. Since this was my friend group, naturally we ate lunch together, or at least that's what we did until I got the boot, and no, I don't mean the kind you walk in.

I won't bother naming all the names, because they don't matter anymore. All except for two: Justin D'Abbraccio and Laura Abel. Justin is the cliché cute boy in school—star lacrosse player, drummer in the jazz band, alpine ski racer, floppy hair and dreamy green eyes. Laura Abel is the girl at the center of it all. She is an expert dresser, the gorgeous, all-American-blonde type, with a nose for sniffing out gossip the same way Daisy can locate a morsel of dropped food. She is the queen of conflict, starting fights or resolving them whenever she wants, and has a crucial opinion when it comes to picking sides. Basically, she is the person other kids turn to when they aren't sure how to think or feel.

It's Laura who gets invited to all the "cool" parties, Laura who wins the class elections, Laura who gets the most attention from the boys. Her social media posts are mandatory reads, always with an avalanche of comments decorated with colorful emojis. To get a comment back feels like being anointed with special powers, to be one of the chosen, even if your moment in the spotlight was as fleeting as a shooting star.

It's not as if people don't have a voice of their own, or they can't make something happen without Laura's involvement.

They just don't want to.

Everything between Laura and me turned sour in June of last year, near the end of seventh grade. By that point, the police had put out word they were looking for Teresa Mitchell in connection to my dad's disappearance, so everyone knew or at least suspected that he'd had an affair. They also knew (because Connor had said something to his

friends and word travels fast in Seabury) that my m[...]
Mr. Fitch were going out to dinner together, meaning I had
more than enough strikes to make me a social outcast. But
to my ex-friends' credit, they didn't seem to care about my
father's secrets or my mom and a teacher at school who
might or might not be becoming an item.

But Laura cared a whole heck of a lot that Justin
D'Abbraccio was being extra nice to me on account of
everything I'd gone through that year. You see, Laura and
Justin were dating. Dating in middle school meant eating
lunch together, texting each other constantly, and sending
pictures and messages over whatever social media thingy
was in fashion at the moment. It was basically a meaningless
label that had *tons* of meaning, if that makes any sense.

Now imagine this—Justin started texting me and liking my posts. He also started hanging out by my locker,
waiting for me to show up. It's not like *we* were dating or
anything. But his parents had split up the year before while
Laura's were still married, so maybe he felt compassion for
me. Maybe he understood I was suffering, and, God forbid,
wanted to ease my pain a little.

Laura didn't care one tiny bit about Justin's motives. She
cared about competition and nothing more. I wasn't as pretty
or as well dressed as Laura Abel, but I was a heck of a lot
better lacrosse player. Now, if I had Justin on my arm, it was
easy to see how damaging that could have been to her social status. Which was why Laura went on the offensive. She
started a campaign against me, backbiting, spreading rumors
("You won't believe what Maggie Garrity said about you!")
and making sure people knew that if they hung out with me,
they weren't welcome in Laura's circle anymore.

Well, it didn't take long for bad to go to worse. One day
I was poor Maggie Garrity, the girl whose world had been
turned upside down, and the next I was a rat-fink bitch of the

...acrosse friends turned into fren-
...tagged in pictures of parties I wasn't
...flagged me on Facebook for being inap-
...wasn't, and I don't use Facebook anymore).
...other bullying going on—like posts that went
...al media implying my father was a pedophile and
m... ...ve abused me; a website listing that basically adver-
tised a young girl looking for hot guys and included my mo-
bile phone number. (FYI, I got a new phone number.)

None of this, not one of the attacks against me, got pinned
on Laura, but trust me, she was behind it all. In the end, it
didn't really matter. Laura could be suspended or not; I could
do all of the self-esteem-building stuff the guidance counselor recommended, read all of her pamphlets on how to deal
with bullying—I'd still eat lunch alone.

It wasn't like I could go clique jumping (really, that's
not a thing), and the other activities I was involved in (student council and newspaper club) I had picked because that's
what the lacrosse kids were doing, so those were now off-
limits. I could have made waves with the principal, because
bullying is such a big deal these days, but instead I played it
down. The only thing I'd get by calling out my bullies would
have been more bullying.

Justin quickly realized that his allegiance was with Laura,
and just like that he acted like I didn't exist. Which brought
us to this point: me eating lunch alone with a stupid boot on
my foot, my dad gone, and terrible Simon in my house.

There were two chairs between me and Jackson and Addie, or Jaddy as they were better known, a new school couple who were so in love I could have sat on Jackson's lap and
he wouldn't have noticed me. I was stabbing a grape with my
fork, imagining it was Simon on the receiving end, when a
boy came over to my table.

I knew him, of course, because Seabury isn't a big school

and everyone knows everyone here. But if we'd exchanged a dozen words with each other over the years, I couldn't have said what they were. Benjamin Odell was not an athlete, but he was a mathlete—one of the best math students in the school, in fact, though I didn't know what class he was taking, because it was so much higher than everyone else's level.

Ben was rail thin. Whatever muscle he had went to moving his limbs, not much more than that. To me, it looked as though his mother cut his short brown hair, or maybe he did it himself, because it was a little lopsided in the front. Somehow it was sweetly endearing, a throwback to grade school, when most of us didn't realize what we actually looked like. He had a gap between his front teeth, and his wire-rimmed glasses seemed flimsy for such thick lenses.

"Can I sit here?" Ben said to me.

Ben was a rover during lunch period, a real rarity. He'd sometimes eat with the band kids (he played some instrument, I wasn't sure which), sometimes it would be with the other mathletes, or sometimes, sin of all sins, he'd sit with whatever teacher was assigned lunch duty. Today he wanted to sit with me, and I couldn't figure out why.

He brought his lunch from home, but I didn't think he had an allergy like I did, because he was never in my nut-free classes in grade school. All us "nut cases," as we affectionately called each other, were usually grouped together out of convenience.

I nodded my head toward the empty chair next to Jackson. *Sit,* I said without saying it, and down went Ben.

He organized his food: some kind of sandwich with mustard, a batch of baby carrots, a carton of milk, and a few cookies. I had a cheese sandwich, cut-up cucumbers, those grapes, and brownies Mom had baked. She did that from time to time.

"I've noticed you eat alone a lot," he said.

Oh great, I thought. *My social status has sunk so low that I'm getting sympathy from the class geek.*

"It's not a big school, Ben," I said. "I'm pretty sure you know why."

"Do you want to talk, or do you like to eat in silence?"

Ben was funny, not the haha kind, but the peculiar kind. He was nice enough, I guess, but all I really knew about him was that he was supposedly on the autism spectrum somewhere—like an Asperger's kid, I think. Wherever he was on that spectrum, if in fact he was on it at all, it would have to have been on the super-duper-smart end of it.

"I can talk and eat," I told him. "I'm multitalented that way."

"I heard you moved," he said. "How do you like your new house?" I was about to answer him, but Ben continued talking. "I moved last year. I hate my new house," he said. "It's smelly—like old cheese."

And then Ben smiled, and when he did, something inside me opened up—a little door that had closed to people like him, people different from me. Maybe it was because of my circumstances, or it could be I'd developed more empathy, or perhaps I was feeling especially glum that day, or maybe it was his gap-toothed smile. Whatever it was, I suddenly found myself feeling incredibly glad that Benjamin Odell had decided to sit down next to me at lunch.

A smile came to my face as I thought about Laura Abel, Justin D'Abbraccio, and all those fake people who'd pretended to be my friends. I looked at Ben like he was crazy or something, and then a laugh came out of me.

And with that laugh, for the first time in a long time, I felt less alone.

CHAPTER 11

Nina, Ginny, and Susanna emerged from the barre fitness studio into a dry, perfectly temperate late-September afternoon, sweat-drenched and ready for post-workout lattes at nearby Pressed Café. It was Ginny who had gotten the trio into doing the ballet-inspired workouts to build up core strength and boost their increasingly sluggish metabolisms. And it was Ginny who would bemoan the pitfalls of getting older—sagging parts that shouldn't sag, wrinkles that came and went like lines on an Etch A Sketch, battled away with creams and facials—while Susanna, far more pragmatic, would note that the grim by-product of never having another birthday meant saying sayonara to this life.

For what it was worth, Nina felt increasingly comfortable with the changes of aging. Her long dark hair, which could be wavy or straight depending on the humidity, still had plenty of body and only sporadic grays to pluck. Her lips were full, and the prominent nose she had wanted reduced in high school now seemed to fit her heart-shaped face perfectly fine. The creases around her brown eyes had grown deeper from stress, but Nina wasn't about to erase them with Botox injections.

She was perhaps eight pounds over her ideal weight, but

it was a soft eight. Her arms and legs were well-toned from the barre workouts, but more than those exercise classes, Nina gave Simon the credit for the recent boost in her self-esteem and comfort with her appearance, years be damned. His support and admiration, the love he gave so freely, made it possible for her to stop blaming herself for what Glen had done.

It was natural, her friends said (and Dr. Wilcox later confirmed), for Nina to experience feelings of self-doubt and inadequacy after Teresa appeared on the scene. As time went on and the wounds felt less fresh, Nina invented several intentionally cruel names for Glen's paramour—Tarty Teresa and Strawberry Shortcake being two of her favorites, though these sobriquets she shared only with Ginny and Susanna. Nina often asked herself why Glen strayed. Was she not enough of a wife, mother, or lover to make him happy?

"Screw him," had been Ginny's response. "What an ass. You don't deserve any of that."

Of course Nina agreed; strongly, in fact. But it was one thing to agree, and quite another to believe. When Nina and Simon fell in love, those doubts she'd harbored about herself retreated like the tide, and a renewal of mind, body, and spirit came about, one that had made it possible to believe what her friends had been saying all along.

"It wasn't you. It was him, wherever he may be. Dead or not. Lake or not."

Screw him was right.

Now the ladies were sipping lattes and reliving a class that had had more pliés than *The Nutcracker*.

"The Heritage Commission had a meeting last night," Susanna said, changing topics, and Nina caught a hint of trepidation in her voice. Susanna knew, as did Ginny, how Nina had once taken great pride in her numerous volunteer commitments, trying as they might have been. She

had been "that woman"—the one who morphed from devoted mom to dedicated volunteer without missing a step.
Nina pinned the Busy Badge to her chest like some medal
of honor, and wouldn't have traded it for anything in the
world. But Glen's disappearance had changed everything.
In the aftermath, it had become impossible to stay involved,
and so she had simply jettisoned her commitments, Heritage Commission included, but took with her feelings of
guilt for backing away.

"Stephanie Abel was there, talking as always."

Nina failed to stifle a groan. She knew all about Stephanie
Abel, long before Maggie had had her dealings with Stephanie's daughter, Laura.

"Let me guess," Nina said, stirring frothy milk with her
spoon. "She's finally realized what a terrible child she's
raised."

Nina wanted to escalate Maggie's bullying plight to the
superintendent if need be, but had bowed to her daughter's
wishes to stay out of it.

"No, and no," Susanna said, eyeing Ginny warily—*How
much to share?* said the look.

"Don't handle me with kid gloves," said Nina. "I'm a big
girl."

"She was talking about you and Simon," said Susanna.
"How it was inappropriate for you to be living together so
soon after Glen—you know."

"Cheated on me, then vanished or drowned? We can use
the words, it's okay."

"Yes, that," Susanna said.

"Don't give that bitch any brain cycles," Ginny chimed in.
"She's not worth it."

"No, she's not," Nina agreed. "But I don't need any of that
getting back to Maggie. She's had a hard enough time with
Laura Abel as it is."

"Actually, Stephanie mentioned something about Maggie eating alone during lunch period and how your choices were going to alienate her even more."

"My choices?" Nina said, aghast. "Does she have any clue it was her bratty kid who caused all the problems in the first place?"

"I'm sure she's in denial," said Ginny.

"Of course she is," Nina said with disgust.

She contemplated ways to engage Stephanie Abel, thinking the best way to put an end to her gossiping was to plant a boot on her throat, when her cell phone rang. It wasn't a number Nina recognized. She answered, half expecting a robocall, but in fact, the caller was a real live human being, one who worked in Human Resources at The Davis Family Center, a support services organization specializing in family matters.

Nina had interviewed there the previous week and did not think the conversation had gone particularly well. Then again, she had done several interviews, none of which had led to a second meeting. Still, the economy was doing well, and she had reason to remain optimistic. Now she was feeling downright jubilant, trying not to let her burgeoning excitement get the better of her. Nina's girlfriends sensed something big afoot, and instinctively leaned closer to catch whatever snippets of conversation they could.

"That's wonderful news," Nina said, eliciting more excited glances from Ginny and Susanna. "When would you need to know? I see. Yes, yes of course. I can do that. I just need to talk this over with my . . ." Nina hesitated ever so briefly. *My what?* She hadn't yet said yes to Simon's marriage proposal, though she was closer every day, and "future fiancé" made her sound downright unstable—a woman with a story at least, which she was. Partner? Future husband? New husband? She went for none of those options. "Talk it over with my family. And thank you, David. Thank you so much. This is wonderful news, very exciting. I'll be in touch soon."

She ended the call, and her friends' beaming expressions demanded a quick reveal.

"I got a job," Nina said. And what followed were cheers that drew glances, hugs, and a few tears in Nina's eyes.

"I'm so happy for you," Ginny said, with Susanna echoing that sentiment.

"I can't believe it," Nina said, and then she paused as Simon's words of concern came to her. Would it be detrimental for Maggie, as he had suggested, to have her mother preoccupied, especially when she was struggling emotionally and having difficulty at school? And what about Connor? He was going through a huge upheaval as well. How would it be for him if his mother were suddenly less available? Perhaps he might go off the rails, so to speak.

Nina had more questions than answers. It was a good thing she had a therapist appointment in the morning.

CHAPTER 12

At therapy, Nina decided not to discuss Maggie's struggles. The night before, she had spoken to her daughter about the bullying at school, revealing what Stephanie Abel had said at the Heritage Commission meeting. When Nina learned of Maggie's new lunch companion, Ben Odell, the welcome news of their unlikely friendship offered a ray of hope that she might come out of her funk, feel less angry toward Simon, and maybe ease the transition for everyone. Talk of her job offer Nina thought could wait, too. Instead, she picked up right where she left off—with two pictures a stranger had sent of her husband kissing another woman.

With those photos, Glen became a stranger to her, and Nina was like a stranger to herself. Her completely ordered world had been shredded and taped back together in a poor imitation of what had been. Her vision of her life was nothing but an illusion—a cruel trick played on an unwitting patsy. There was, however, one truth Nina took from the terrible ordeal, an abstract notion that with time and rumination calcified into a harsh new understanding: just because you love someone doesn't mean you know them.

Nina told Dr. Wilcox about the morning after she received the pictures of Teresa and Glen together. She woke up as though she'd not slept a wink, and fed the children their breakfast in a daze. Time passed in a blur, with the secret weighing heavily on her heart.

The next day, the police gave permission for community volunteers to help with the search effort. Nina headed to the boat launch, her mental state echoing the fog that hovered ghostlike above the choppy water of Lake Winnipesaukee. Professional search-and-rescue teams continued their hunt for a body that seemed determined to stay hidden, and the U.S. Coast Guard also joined the quest, just as Detective Wheeler said they might. They brought along two specially equipped Boston Whalers, giving the New Hampshire Marine Patrol and State Police some welcome assistance. Nina didn't know if the police were rushing to Carson to track down the waitress, but she assumed the focus was still on the search for Glen.

She recalled standing at the lake shoreline, watching the search teams motor about in an organized fashion, craning her neck to follow the helicopter's purposeful circles. Her black boots sank into the mud as a steady rain pelted rhythmically against her green umbrella.

"Maggie said she thought the rain was her dad crying. That he was letting us know he would miss us."

Dr. Wilcox smiled wanly at the bittersweet sentiment, her right hand jotting something down. "She thought he had drowned?"

"We all did," Nina said, pausing before adding, "Some of us still do."

"Connor?" Dr. Wilcox remembered.

"Yes, Connor for sure," said Nina. "He thinks his father is dead."

"And you?"

"Jury is out. Maybe he's dead. Maybe he just wanted to start over. Fake his death and begin anew without the burden of child support and alimony. People snap, you know."

Dr. Wilcox's eyes glimmered ever so briefly. "What happened during the search?"

"I tried to redirect my energy to my kids and the volunteers," Nina said. "But I kept seeing those pictures in my head, Glen kissing that woman, his eyes glowing with lust—with love, maybe?

"At first I was paralyzed. I had no idea what to do," Nina went on. "I didn't tell anybody but the police about the pictures."

"So the search went on and nobody, not even your close friends, knew about the affair?"

"That's right. I think there were at least a hundred people out looking for him. I manned the volunteer tent, feeling like I was deceiving every last one of them."

"Why's that?"

"They weren't looking for Glen, the loving husband and devoted family man. They were searching for an adulterer, a man with secrets as hidden as he was."

Nina recounted how groups of volunteers, arms linked, headed out into the woods by the boat launch and returned cold and soaking wet, without any leads. Coffee couldn't warm them, and she sensed the mood shift late that day. By then, the enthusiasm for the search, so infectious in the morning, had fatigued, along with the searchers themselves.

It had been painful to think of spending another day thanking people for their kindness and sacrifice, hugging them, presenting a face of grief while she ignored the other feelings invading her bones. But that's exactly what she did the next day, too: she lied to herself and to others.

"I didn't know what else to do. I knew eventually the truth

would come out one way or another. But that wasn't the only thing upsetting me."

Nina took a moment to collect her thoughts and let the painful memories resurface.

"During the search I noticed that nobody from Glen's work was there," she began.

"He worked for—?" Dr. Wilcox let the question hang, prompting Nina to fill in the blanks.

"Center Street Bank. He was a senior financial advisor in the consumer banking division."

"I see. Is that what brought him to Carson?"

"I thought maybe, yes," said Nina. "Maybe he went there to scout a location for a branch, and got it on with a wait-ress while blowing off steam. But Glen didn't work in the retail side, so he'd have no reason to help open new bank branches."

"Got it." Dr. Wilcox took another note.

"While I thought it was odd that Glen would have even gone to Carson, it was even odder that nobody from the bank bothered to contact me. I mean, he was all over the news, but I didn't receive one phone call, no emails even."

"Why do you think?"

"I didn't know," said Nina. "So when I got home from the search I called his office."

"And?"

And . . .

Nina relived those moments in detail, letting them unfold for Dr. Wilcox as they had unfolded for her.

* * *

She dialed the main number and asked for Human Resources. A pleasant-sounding man with a nasal voice answered the phone after a few rings.

"Dan Kastner. May I help you?"

Nina had to take a deep breath before she could speak. "Yes, hello. My name is Nina Garrity."

She expected to hear a gasp, a heavy sigh, some weighty noise that preceded expressions of sincere sympathy, but no. There was only silence.

"Yes? What can I do for you, Ms. Garrity?"

"Um—" Nina cleared her throat. "I'm Glen Garrity's wife, Nina."

"Glen . . . Garrity?"

"Yes," said Nina. "He's the boater from Seabury, New Hampshire, who's gone missing. Surely you've seen the news . . . ?"

"Oh yes, yes, of course. Of course, I have. I'm truly sorry, Ms. Garrity. What is it I can do for you?"

Do for me? Dan's response had baffled Nina. *He's your employee,* she thought. *Where have you been? Why hasn't anyone called?* It was more than a strange choice of words—Nina struggled to come up with something Dan could actually do for her. By this point, after days without recovering a body, she, along with the police, had all assumed that Glen was dead.

"Well—um, I'm curious about health insurance, first," Nina said, stammering a bit. "Our daughter Maggie has nut allergies and, well, if she needs to go to the hospital, you know, how long will we still have insurance?"

Nina figured she'd eventually work her way up to asking why nobody from Center Street Bank had been in touch, feeling idiotic for fumbling her way through the conversation.

"This is for Glen Garrity, right?"

"Yes," said Nina, now annoyed.

"Hmmm—Mrs. Garrity, could you give me a moment, please?"

Nina pinned the phone between her shoulder and ear, breathing deeply. The hold music sounded like a Bon Jovi tune re-created on the marimba. Why *did* he put her on hold? Was there a problem with the insurance? Eventually, she heard the line click over.

"Mrs. Garrity?"

To Nina's surprise, it was a woman's voice, not Dan's.

"Yes," said Nina.

"Hello, I'm Jill Fleishman, the vice president of Human Resources for Center Street Bank. Dan told me you called asking about benefits in connection with your husband, Glen."

"Yes, that's correct."

Nina felt short of breath. Her skin had gone tingly as a terrible feeling sank into her chest.

"Um—Mrs. Garrity, I'm not sure how to say this. I know you're dealing with a tremendous shock."

"Please, just talk to me," she said. "Is Glen in trouble at work? I'm trying to figure out why he's been spending time in Carson—that's where he's been going. I'm assuming he was doing a job for you there?"

"Mrs. Garrity, I don't know about Carson, but what I can tell you is that your husband hasn't worked here for the past two years."

Nina was sure she'd misheard. "Excuse me? Could you repeat that, please?"

"We terminated Glen's employment two years ago," Jill Fleishman said.

"Terminated?" Nina's head was buzzing.

"Yes."

"Why?" Nina hoped she hadn't shouted the question.

"I'm afraid that's privileged information."

"I'm his wife. He's missing."

"Yes, I know. I'm sorry, but our confidentiality policy extends to all current and former employees of the bank."

Nina knew this was an argument she wasn't going to win, so she changed subjects. "You said this happened two years ago?"

"Yes."

"But that's impossible. He—he went—"

Nina stopped herself. She was going to say he went to work every day. But actually, he just went out the door. He got into his car. He drove away. He could have been in Chelmsford, or Carson, or Cleveland for all she knew. He could have gone anywhere.

"I can send you some paperwork—but I would—I would need a death certificate to release it."

Nina's throat closed up, but somehow, she managed to get out the words: "Thank you for your time."

* * *

If Dr. Wilcox found Nina's story shocking, it did not register on her face.

"That's another profound betrayal," she said.

"I nearly fainted," Nina replied. "Anyway, the first thing I did was go to the file cabinet where we kept all our financial documents. I'd seen our tax returns, but I'd never studied them. I just signed the page Glen gave me to sign; I never asked to *see* the numbers or look at the deductions, because I simply didn't see the need. I trusted him."

"I'm guessing that was a mistake."

"Quite. You see, Glen and I established a division of labor. I took care of the house stuff—the kids, the meals, shopping, that sort of thing—and he did the bills and filed all our financial statements. I had a general idea of what we had, but I really only paid attention to what was in the checking account. Those numbers went down and then up every two weeks as he got paid.

"He made a good living, but it wasn't a windfall. He still worried about money all the time, which is why he pushed himself so hard at work to get a promotion, maybe stock options, you know the routine."

Nina hadn't bothered with all the details, but after the 401(k) contribution, money Glen put in the stock market, taxes, food, utilities, home repair, insurance, what little they gave to charity, the occasional vacation, the random charges that seemed impossible not to rack up on the credit card— new clothes for Connor, summer camp for Mags, sports camps for Connor, fitness clubs, doctor, dentist, car payments, auto repair, all the random stuff—maybe they had four thousand dollars or so available in disposable income at the end of the year.

Maybe.

"And I thought of what they told me—two years, he'd been fired two years ago. I was thinking, hoping really, that he had a secret job to go along with his secret girlfriend and secret life in Carson."

"Did he?"

"No. He didn't." Nina grimaced. "I went through all the bank statements, all of our investments. I thought we'd saved about two hundred thousand dollars, maybe more, but there was only forty grand in all the investment accounts, including the 401(k)."

"What happened to the money?" Dr. Wilcox asked.

"It seems Glen drained our investments like he was running a mini Ponzi scheme. He took from one account to give to another, college funds included, all to hide the fact that he'd lost his job. We had about enough money to last us a year, but not much more. He even bought us pricey health insurance after the COBRA ran out, to keep up appearances."

Nina paused here, processing a thought. "It made me won-der," she said, "for a man with so many secrets, if maybe he'd done something else, something at his job, the reason he got fired, that had made it necessary for him to disappear."

"Do you know the reason?"

"No," Nina said grimly. "I eventually got them to send me some paperwork, because death in absentia takes ages to process. What they sent was vague at best—they cited 'underperformance' as the reason for firing him. I know as much about Glen—his motives, his choices, his fate—now as I did back then."

Dr. Wilcox returned a grim expression of sympathy. "How are your finances now?"

"Now? Well, with Simon they've gotten a whole lot better. Without him in the picture, I would've had to move away, go live with my parents, no choice there. That would have been okay, but I love Seabury and didn't want to leave. Anyway, Simon has family money, he told me, and his teacher salary, plus rental income from his lakefront home. For the most part we've kept our finances separate, but now you could say my finances have gotten another boost."

"How so?"

"I got a job. I'm going to be working with The Davis Fam-ily Center doing social work. The offer came yesterday."

Dr. Wilcox brightened. "That's wonderful news," she said.

"Simon's concerned. He thinks it's going to be too much on me, and hard on Maggie not to have me as available."

"What do you think you should do?"

Nina thought about how to put her feelings into words.

"I won't be making a fortune, but it would be something. And it would be mine."

"That must feel good."

Dr. Wilcox was doing her job—leading Nina to her own conclusions, not clouding things with pre-judgment.

"Yes. It feels quite good. I trusted a man with my family's financial future once before; I'm reluctant to do it again."

"Then I guess you know what to do."

Nina gave a nod. For the first time in a long time, she felt certain of a decision.

CHAPTER 13

Mom glared at me from across the dinner table like I should snap out of it or something. Sure, I had a sourpuss face, but she should have been used to it by now. After all, it's been my default expression since everything fell apart. Connor was a lost cause—too angry with Dad and too enamored with Simon (and their dumb robot that still didn't work) to see things clearly. At least I had Ben on my side.

It was amazing, really. I never would have given a kid like Ben the time of day before I got tossed out of my tribe. Not because I was stuck up or anything, but we didn't exactly run in the same circles. Thanks to a little bit of bullying (okay, a lot) I could see now what I couldn't see then. We were just people, with different interests, different tastes, and if you closed yourself off to people different from yourself, you might be missing out on something great. Super mature of me, I know. My guidance counselor would be so proud.

I knew Mom thought Ben was going to be the answer to all her prayers, but having someone to eat lunch with didn't change my feelings about Simon, not one little bit. He could cook all the yummy dinners he wanted—like the chicken he made tonight, with fluffy biscuits to soak up the thick gravy—and I'd still want him gone. He could play catch with

Connor until he got all-state honors and I'd still want to go to boarding school, or move in with Nonni and Papa. And now I had a new reason, a better reason to want Simon out of here, and gone for good: I'd seen the look in his eyes.

I told Ben all about it at lunch that day, and he got it right away.

"You're like Cinderella, only with the wicked stepfather instead."

"They're not married. They're not even engaged," I groaned.

"Oooh, living in sin," said Ben with an evil look in his eye.

I laughed, until Ben showed me printouts from StepTalk, "a website where stepparents go to vent." Seriously, that's the tagline. He would have shown it to me on his smartphone, but Ben is maybe the only kid in middle school I know whose parents won't let him have one.

"Married or not, he's close enough to make this relevant," he said.

The website confirmed what I had long suspected: there were loads of stepparents who hated their stepkids. Not all, of course, but enough that they needed a place to "vent" online. It wasn't a stretch to stick Simon in this category. I had no doubt he was putting on a big show for my mom. He wanted her all to himself, and we were the luggage he had to cart around. Maybe he accepted us as part of the package, but he resented me most, because I wasn't buying into his good-guy routine like Connor.

If I had to guess, I'd say Simon secretly hated kids, including the ones he taught. Why else didn't he have them with his last wife? And why did she have to die? If she were still alive, he wouldn't be here. He'd be with her. I know she killed herself, but I wonder if maybe she got him mad. Maybe she saw that dark look in his eyes, too. Maybe it was the last thing she ever saw.

I watched Connor top his mini mountain of mashed potatoes with peas before inhaling half the structure in a single bite.

"Coach is thinking about letting me throw the ball on Friday," he announced proudly with a mouth full of food.

"In a game?"

"Yes, Mom, in a game," he said, finishing that bite.

My mom followed Connor's football career close enough to know he played receiver, not quarterback.

"That's good, right?"

"It's a trick play," Connor said. "But I took some direct snaps in practice. I think Coach saw that my arm's gotten a lot stronger."

"Well, I guess you have Simon to thank for that," I said, after catching the appreciative look Connor sent across the table.

Simon sensed trouble brewing. "Now, Maggie, I just toss the ball with your brother," he said. "Connor's done all the hard work on his own."

Daisy was under the table resting her head on my boot, which was hopefully coming off in a week or two—not that I would be heading back to the lacrosse field. That Maggie was done and gone.

"Sure," I said, in a way that definitely poked the bear. Connor got the subtext right away.

"I can spend time with Simon and Dad won't mind," he said snippily. "Trust me."

"You don't know that," I snapped.

"He's not coming back, Maggie. Get real with yourself," he said.

"Don't say that."

"Hey, hey, kids, let's not upset your mother, okay?" Simon said, using a variant of his teacher tone.

"I'm not doing anything," I said, overdoing the persecuted

act for dramatic effect. "All I said was 'Sure.'" Next up came the eye roll, followed by a well-placed headshake.

"Maggie," Mom said, using my name to express many thoughts at once, *Back off!* being the most obvious of the bunch.

"Whatever," I said, looking down at my plate so I didn't have to look at anybody.

"Everyone take a deep breath," Mom said, taking one herself. "I have some news to share."

That got my attention. I had no idea what was coming, but I could see Mom psyching herself up for some big reveal. Simon actually seemed a bit uncomfortable. Maybe he didn't know either.

"I've accepted a job," Mom said. "It's with The Davis Family Center."

Connor perked up and looked genuinely happy for her. "Hey, that's great news, Mom," he said. "What are you going to do?"

"It's a social worker position, focusing on family issues."

Connor smirked. "Hmm," he said as if some idea came to him. "I know a family that needs some help." He eyed me nastily.

Mom returned his look, putting a quick end to any more snippy comments from my brother.

I got up from the table and hugged Mom tight. I was thrilled. Delighted. Overjoyed, to be precise—because I knew Simon was against it. While I congratulated my mom, I kept my gaze laser locked on Simon, waiting to see his face get red, waiting for the dark, scary look to return. But instead he beamed with a real smile, as genuine as Connor's.

"That's fantastic!" he shouted, rising from his seat. I moved away quickly before the three of us got caught in some weird broken-family hug. "When do you start?"

"Wednesday, two weeks from tomorrow," Mom said, and

then Simon's expression changed dramatically. He looked troubled about something. He got his phone, which was plugged into the charging station at the little desk in the kitchen, because, you know, he lived here, too. I saw him frown as he checked his device. *What could it be?* I wondered.

"Two weeks, you said?"

"Yeah," Mom said. "Why? Is something wrong?"

"Well—" Simon lowered his gaze. "I was going to surprise you, but—hang on a second."

And with that he left the room, giving Connor and me a chance to hug Mom and congratulate her some more. Even Daisy got in a few licks. I was extra excited, overjoyed about the news. I knew what Dad had done with our money, and why I'd been getting my clothes from a consignment store instead of the mall. But I also knew that money could buy freedom, as well as stuff, and with Mom having a job, she might not feel so dependent on Simon to keep a roof over our heads.

Simon returned to the kitchen holding a glossy brochure in his hand.

"I booked us a trip to Niagara Falls for that week," he said glumly. "Thursday through Sunday at the Sheraton, with views of the waterfall. I got an incredible deal, so I jumped on it. I was going to surprise you all tomorrow night."

"You did what?" Mom looked completely surprised.

"Niagara Falls," Simon said, handing over the brochure. "I knew Connor couldn't come because of football, but I figured he could stay with Luke or Joe for a few days."

I didn't like that Simon knew the names of Connor's best friends. It was like he had taken another piece of our family for himself. My guess, if Connor had to pick between Joe and Luke, he'd pick Luke, because Luke's dad was into duck hunting and he sometimes took Connor with him, something

I thought was totally gross. I mean, what did a cute little duck ever do to them?

"Since Maggie's not playing lacrosse right now," Simon continued, "I thought she could miss a few days of school, and we could have a little adventure together." He made a sighing sound. "Try to smooth over some of our rough patches. I already arranged it with the principal, but anyway, it conflicts with your start date, so I'll undo it. No problem."

But I could tell Mom thought there was a problem.

"I'll call the center," she said quickly. "Tell them I need to start the week after. I'm sure it's no big deal."

"No, no," Simon said, brushing off that suggestion with a wave of his hands. "That's not a good way to begin. Don't worry about it. We'll find another time to take a trip. I'm just really happy for you, *and* proud. It takes a lot of courage to put yourself out there, especially after everything you've gone through. They're lucky to have you."

Simon leaned in to give Mom a kiss on the lips, which I saw only because I didn't look away in time. Knowing Mom the way I do, I could tell she was feeling exceptionally guilty over a trip she'd known nothing about, especially because it would've involved making things better between him and me. What should have been a big moment for her, a rare happy occasion for my mom to celebrate, was now about Simon and how she had let *him* down.

It was so unfair I wanted to scream, "Can you please just let this one thing be about Mom?" But something else was knocking at the back of my head. I have a good memory for dates. It's a by-product of being a student athlete: you always need to be aware of potential schedule conflicts, and I was pretty sure there was some other conflict that had nothing to do with the start date of Mom's new job.

I excused myself from the table and went upstairs to have a look at my school calendar. And there it was. In print.

Clear as day. The big field trip to Strawbery Banke, the one Simon led every year, the one he went to in costume, with that rusty musket of his, fell on the same day as the trip to Niagara Falls that was now not happening. The same day! *What are the odds?* I thought.

So now I should go and tell my mom, right? I should let her know that it made no sense to me that Simon would book a trip to Niagara Falls, during the school week of all times, on a date that conflicted with his big field trip to Strawbery Banke. This Niagara Falls trip of his had to be a lie, but for what? I stayed tight-lipped about it, because I knew what my mother would say.

I knew without a doubt that she'd take his word over mine.

CHAPTER 14

Nina knew sleep would not come easily. It wasn't because of Maggie's refusal to make any accommodations for Simon, to give him a single benefit of the doubt. No, her big worry was still a little over a week away, when, for the first time in over fifteen years, she would set foot in an office building as a paid employee. She was in the middle of a mini fashion show for Simon, who lounged on the bed, hands clasped behind his head, pajama bottoms on and shirt off, giving Nina a clear view of his toned chest and the outline of well-formed abdominal muscles.

She'd acclimated to the round shape of his face, which would look boyish without the stubble, the plastic glasses he used to read, the khakis he wore to work, even how he was so particular about the way he folded his shirts. Maybe it was still that honeymoon phase, but Simon seemed to have none of Glen's shortcomings. He made a big deal of birthdays and listened to her without distractedly looking at his phone. He touched her often, lovingly—a gentle squeeze of her hand as he'd pass her in the kitchen, a brush against her shoulder as he served her dinner, and later in bed would offer massages without expecting favors in return. Perhaps the most notable distinction was how Simon enjoyed his work without letting it consume him.

On several occasions Simon compared his and Nina's relationship to the founding of America—one of his favorite topics to teach—citing how they, too, had unified under stressful circumstances, building something better together.

Yes, she told herself. *We can forge a more perfect union.*

The clothes Nina tried on (and there were a half-dozen mix-and-match outfits in her wardrobe) were recent purchases, all gifts from Simon. The outfits were professional, but not too buttoned-up—earthy colors mostly, cotton fabrics, no patterns. She was going for comfort and the pulled-together, approachable look of someone a person could confide in, as her clients would be expected to do.

She was showing Simon the pleated cream-colored boat-neck top and ankle-length slim-leg black pants she was thinking of wearing to her first day on the job.

Simon appraised Nina with hungry eyes.

"You look amazing," he said, as she finished her spin.

He lunged at her from across the bed, grabbed her waist, and pulled her to the mattress, where he kissed the spots that got her blood pressure rising. Nina slid out from under him, worried about wrinkling the outfit, still not sold on it as the right choice for her grand appearance.

"I'm so nervous," she said.

"You'll be marvelous," Simon assured her. "Trust me."

Nina flopped back on the bed and kissed him hard on the mouth. "You weren't always so happy about it," she said.

"It's hard for me to share you," Simon said, his hand rubbing the small of her back, teasing out jolts of pleasure that raced down Nina's legs and up her arms. She nestled into his embrace.

"I'm sorry this hasn't gone smoother with Maggie," she

said, switching to that subject because it was never far from her thoughts.

"Don't you worry," said Simon. "It's a process. It's all going to be worth it in the end."

"I hope you're right."

Nina breathed out her worry while burying her mouth in Simon's neck, taking in his scent, an orangey, woodsy aroma that reminded her so much of Glen. She'd been meaning to buy Simon new cologne, but tomorrow she'd make good on that pledge. He did not use Glen's brand of aftershave, but their smells were too similar, the reminders too intense.

"Remember when we were dating—"

"You make it sound like it was *so* many years ago," Nina said playfully.

"It feels like a lifetime and also yesterday, if that makes any sense," said Simon.

"It makes perfect sense," Nina answered, because a whirlwind romance mixed with profound hurt and a great upheaval bent time like it did lives.

"Anyway, remember when we were out shopping and you had your eye on a Coach bag? You wouldn't let me buy it for you because you said you needed a power job for a power bag like that."

"You didn't," Nina said.

Simon flashed an impish grin before he slid off the bed and vanished into the closet. Nina heard some rummaging, and moments later he emerged, holding a bag she remembered as vividly as the first time she'd seen it. There was so much to love about it—the size, the expert stitching, the softness of the gorgeous pearled white leather. Simon gifted Nina the bag down on one knee, arms extended, as though he were reenacting the day in July when he had presented her with his mother's diamond ring, in the gazebo at the park overlooking the lake.

His proposal had come as a surprise, but given that they'd been about to move in together, Nina's first impulse had been to say yes. While her heart wanted to put the ring on her finger, her brain was telling her not yet. Simon had been disappointed, naturally, but not crushed, since they were still going to be living together. Selfishly, Nina wanted what Simon could offer—a chance to stay in Seabury, where her life was, where she'd put down roots. Moving in with her parents would have felt like giving up too much of her life, and it would have been especially hard on Connor, who was nearing graduation. But even so, she didn't feel obligated to rush into a decision.

She had explained her reluctance as too much change too fast, but in the back of her mind another thought lurked, one she didn't share.

Glen.

She still had unresolved feelings, and questions for which she didn't have answers. Whatever caused her hesitation, it wasn't Simon holding her back; it was herself. To his credit, Simon wasn't pressuring her, not one bit, which was one reason why every day Nina was closer to saying yes.

She took the bag, held it, felt it before opening it. A flash of something white caught her eye, and she reached inside to find a note from Simon, penned in his neat teacher's handwriting. She read it aloud:

Dearest Nina,
You've got this. I know you're nervous and scared about the new job, but I've never had more faith in anybody in all my life. You are magnificent in every way. You're kind, compassionate, brilliant, and bold,

and I love you more than words can say. I can't wait
for the day when I can call you my wife.
                    With all my love and admiration,
                                        Simon

Nina leaned forward to kiss Simon.

"You shouldn't have done this. That bag is very expensive."

"You bought me a leather work bag for my birthday," Simon reminded her. "Now we're even. And thanks to that bag, I never have to look for my wallet and keys."

"You are the best," she said, kissing him again. "What did I do to deserve you?"

"I keep asking myself the same thing," Simon said wryly.

He took the bag from her hands to show her the tag with her monogrammed initials—*N.G.,* for Nina Garrity. Before Simon, when the wounds were freshest, she wondered if she should take her kids away, start over like Glen might have done—find someplace new, somewhere not tainted with her husband's lies. She'd thought of changing her name back to Sansone, but her children were Garrity, and they'd want to remain Garrity, meaning a part of Glen would follow them anywhere they went. She'd kept the name, and now it was etched on her bag.

"It's easy enough to change the monogram," Simon said, a glint entering his eyes as though he were reading her thoughts. "If we get married, and you know I hope we do, if you want to become Nina Fitch, I'd be honored."

For Nina it would be her second marriage, but it would be Simon's third. His first wife, a woman named Allison, his college sweetheart, left him and moved away on their fourth anniversary. The breakup shattered Simon, but Nina understood young love. It could be impetuous and prone to sudden changes of heart, especially when there weren't children involved to complicate a divorce. Even so, betrayal at any stage can have lasting consequences. She knew all too well why Simon was afraid to open himself up to more hurt, why he had stayed single for years after.

His second wife, Emma, whom he'd met through mutual friends, eventually broke through his defenses. Her suicide years later had gutted him in a profoundly different way than the loss of Allison. In some respects, Simon's misfortune in love made it easier for Nina to trust him, and to believe he'd never betray her as Glen had done. His bruised heart wouldn't let him love her the way he did if his feelings weren't absolutely true.

With the new job looming, the idea of becoming someone else after being a Garrity for almost twenty years was too much to process. Nina pulled away, and Simon took notice.

"I'm sorry, honey," he said. "I shouldn't have gone there. This is a lot for you."

Nina looked at him appreciatively.

"If you don't want to do this, if you want to back out of the job, it's fine. We'll be fine. We have plenty of money. I can take care of us both. Promise."

Nina looked at him askance. "What happened to 'you've got this' . . . you've 'never had more faith in anybody'?"

"No, no, of course I have faith in you, absolutely. But it's going to be a lot of pressure, a difficult adjustment for everyone. It will be overwhelming, I'm sure. I'm just saying if you want to back out, it's fine. You can. I can take care of us, Nina. All of us."

Of course he was referring to the children. A part of her welcomed the news, felt relief even, and a thought, rapid and jarring as a flash mob, caused her to consider his offer. She could call The Davis Family Center in the morning, make a hundred apologies, and then walk away, be home for Maggie, for Connor. But a second later another voice rose up, this one reminding her what had happened last time she'd put her financial future in the hands of a man. This one told her she was taking the job for herself, *for* her family.

"Simon—I'm . . ."

The thoughts that had come to Nina, so crisp and clear, got stuck when she tried to voice them. Simon kissed her on the cheek.

"Forget I said anything," he said. "You'll be amazing. They're lucky to have you."

CHAPTER 15

Monday's hot lunch was a chicken patty sandwich, buttered carrots cut into coin-size shapes, and an apple. Ben Odell, my lunch buddy and technically my only friend, heaped on the mayo and ate his sandwich while flipping through the pages of the calculus textbook he was reading for fun.

The cafeteria was bustling with the usual chaos and noise, but it wasn't distracting enough to keep my attention from wandering over to Laura and Justin's table, where the happy couple sat laughing and talking with a group of my former friends. I tried to imagine the pain I felt in my heart was indigestion from the cheese quesadilla Mom had made for my lunch, but I knew better. I didn't miss them exactly, because I knew what they were all about, but rejection, even from people who totally stink, can still hurt.

There were plenty of other things for me to obsess over—my Spanish test for one, and there was an English paper I had to write on *The Pearl,* which had turned out to be a pretty good book. Instead, I focused on Simon, who made Justin and Laura seem like the nicest people on the planet.

"It just doesn't make sense," I said to Ben. "Why on earth would Simon skip his big annual field trip to Strawbery Banke to take us all to Niagara Falls? And why leave Connor out of it? We could travel later, after football's over. Those falls aren't going anywhere."

I had thought about it for days, and couldn't come up with a single reason, which led me to one conclusion: he had lied. There was no trip. Never had been one. I don't know why he would have made it all up, but I'm sure he had a reason. What I didn't have was proof, and I told this to Ben, who shared my belief and concern.

It was strange to admit, but I felt like I'd known Ben forever. A few weeks ago, we'd hardly said hello passing each other in the hall. Now we looked for each other between classes. He was different from the other kids. He loved school, and math especially, and he said odd things at odd times. The old me would have rolled my eyes at him, called him a geek or whatever, but the new me found freedom in being friends with him.

I didn't have to be a certain way with Ben, or say certain things, or dress like this person or that person. He didn't care how I looked or even if I cried in front of him, which I did when I saw all my FFs (former friends) at our Old Home Day carnival and they walked right past me—even worse, they looked right through me. It made me sad and I got all blubbery and yeah, that's a true story. But Ben didn't care, because he liked me for who I was, simple as that. You don't realize how much you need a friend like Ben Odell until you've got one in your life. I could say that now.

So, when I told him I thought Simon was being a sneak and a liar for reasons unknown, he took my side right away. He chewed hard on a bite of his sandwich, and it seemed he was chewing on some thought as well.

"Why don't you find out?" he said.

"Okay, genius, how do you want me to do that? Ask him?"

"No, because he would lie about it," Ben said, straight-faced.

"Yeah, I know. I was being sarcastic."

"Oh," said Ben. "You didn't *sound* sarcastic."

"You don't have to sound sarcastic to be sarcastic—" I was going to argue my point, but I stopped myself. With Ben, I had learned to tell when an argument was going to go in circles.

"Forget it," I said. "What are you thinking?"

"I'm thinking you should call," Ben said.

"Call who?"

"The hotel, silly." He shoveled a sporkful of carrots into his mouth.

"Like, I should just *call* them? What would I say?"

Ben's look told me it was a dumb question.

"Tell them you're Mrs. Fitch, or the future Mrs. Fitch— you know, you're your mom—and that you want to see about redoing the reservation. Then find out if he ever actually made one."

"Gross. So now they're married?"

"Well, duh," Ben said. He was one of those kids who sounded strange when he was acting his age. "Aren't they basically married already?"

"Yeah, I suppose," I said dejectedly.

"He told you where you were staying, right?"

He put "staying" in air quotes.

I thought back to that moment when Mom had announced her new job, and remembered Simon saying it was the Sheraton with views of the waterfall—which, by the way, I really wanted to see.

Now, I'd never forged my mom's signature on a permission slip, or a report card, or done anything even remotely questionable like that, so pretending to be her kind of freaked me out. But, I thought, who would know? It's just some random person who works at the front desk. They won't care. So I searched for the number on my phone, and it was easy to find. Sheraton, Niagara Falls.

Ben and I left the cafeteria, telling the teacher on lunch duty that we were headed to the library. If it had been Justin and Laura asking to leave before the period ended, we'd have been sent back to our seats, no question about it. But Ben could go anywhere and do anything because everybody, all the teachers, trusted him.

The library wasn't a good place to have a phone conversation, so instead we found a quiet nook near the gym that was far enough away from the cafeteria to talk without shouting.

I had to listen to a bunch of annoying promotions for the Sheraton until eventually a woman thanked me for calling and asked if she could help with a reservation. I told her my name, described the situation, and tried to make it seem like we were so super excited the trip was back on. I gave it my absolute best acting job, pretending to be my mom. (P.S. my last official part in a play was as the apple tree in the third-grade production of *Johnny Appleseed*.) I felt I'd really sold it, and even lowered my voice to make myself sound all grown-up.

"Do you have a reservation number?" the woman asked.

I wasn't prepared for that one and I stumbled to find my words.

"Um . . . uh, no," I said. "I have a name."

I wanted to slap my forehead—dummy!—but to my relief, that seemed to be a perfectly fine response.

"Sure," the lady said. I gave her my name, Nina Garrity, and the date of our trip. I heard typing and then she apologized because she couldn't find our reservation. I shook my head at Ben, who mouthed the word "Simon."

"Um, maybe it's under my . . . my—" I stumbled again because I didn't know what to call him. "My husband's name,"

I eventually blurted out, giving the name Simon Fitch, while keeping myself from gagging.

There was more clacking as the lady did more typing.

"No, I'm sorry," she said. "I don't have a reservation under that name, either."

There was another Sheraton on the Canadian side of the falls, she told me, but there was no reservation at that location. The lady told me that as long as the reservation was for a date in the future, she could look it up, even if it had been canceled. I ended the call with a big smile on my face.

"Now we have proof Simon was lying," I said.

Ben didn't look nearly as pleased. "That's great," he said. "So what are you going to do about it?"

I got quiet because, well, what was I going to do? It's not like I could say I happened to have stumbled on this information. Then I had another thought and decided to change topics.

"Why are you helping me so much, Ben?" I asked.

"Because you're my friend." He didn't hesitate to answer.

"Yeah, but you're like, *really* helping. All I ever do is talk about me—my stupid problems. Doesn't that annoy you?"

"I like a challenge. Your problems are like calculus in people form."

"Great," I groaned. "No wonder I can't understand myself."

"Don't take this the wrong way, but your issues are a lot more interesting than mine."

"Really? What are yours?"

Ben gave a shrug. "Grades. Test scores. That's how I'm measured at home. That's how people see me—the smart kid. If I ever got a C, I think my parents might disown me."

"Well, I don't see you like that."

"You don't see me as an Aspie either, you just see me as me. Maybe that's one reason I'm happy to help. Just accept it and let's move on, okay? Now, what are you going to do?"

"Aspie," I knew, was shorthand for "Asperger syndrome," and it was the first time Ben had mentioned his label. I didn't know how to respond, but Ben's expression told me I didn't have to.

"I'm going to tell my mom," I said, after giving it some thought. "And let her figure it out."

The rest of the day passed in a blur. I took the bus home, which felt weird, because I was so used to playing sports, or doing something, after school. Simon wasn't there when I arrived, but eventually he showed up. I hung out in my room with the door closed, Daisy with me. I tried to do my homework, but really all I did was read the same passage in my history book over and over again. I felt like a prisoner, especially with Mom at the grocery store and Connor at football practice, but Simon knew enough not to come check up on me. I even heard him walking around upstairs, but he got it—a closed door meant no company.

My mom finally showed up with Connor. He had his license and would have driven himself to and from football practice if we could have afforded a second car. I came running downstairs (a bit awkwardly, thanks to the boot I still wore) as soon as I heard the front door open. Daisy had gone ahead at a faster pace. Connor, smelling like he had just crawled out of a dirty laundry hamper, was carrying two grocery bags and told me to get the rest in the car. I ignored him (I'm good at that) and instead followed Mom into the kitchen, where I confronted her with the kind of excitement I typically reserved for a straight-A report card.

"Say that again." Mom looked utterly confused.

I repeated my breathless explanation about the nonexistent hotel reservation, including the motive behind it.

"You think he made up a trip to make me feel bad about my new job? Why on earth would he do that? And why were you even looking into this?" She said it as if I was wrong to go snooping into Simon's personal business, but I could almost see the gears in Mom's head churning to translate what I told her—Strawbery Banke, weird timing, no reservation. I thought: *We've got you now—liar, liar, pants on fire!*

But then Mom did something I didn't expect. She left and didn't come back for a good long while. I waited in the kitchen, because I didn't know what else I was supposed to do. When she returned, she was with Simon. Mom looked annoyed, but not angry.

"Will you please explain for the benefit of my exuberantly curious daughter why there might not have been a reservation at the Sheraton for the family trip that we're rescheduling for a later date?"

Simon did not look like a man about to get caught in a lie. Instead he looked like a teacher trying to stay patient with a disrespectful student.

"As I told your mother, I didn't book the trip through the hotel." Simon made it clear I was testing his patience. "I made it through a travel website, so they had the reservation, not the Sheraton. When I canceled, the reservation went away." Then he crouched down so I could see his face clearly. It wasn't looking happy. "Do you want to see the receipt, Maggie?"

Connor came into the kitchen, sensed the tension, and asked what was going on. We ignored him.

"Look, I was devastated to miss that field trip," Simon said. "But I felt it was more important to try to . . . you know, do something to bring us a little bit closer. And that deal was too good to pass up. Hang on, Maggie. There's something I want to show you."

With that, Simon left the room, leaving me to face Mom and her disapproving eyes.

"You've got to try to make it easier for us, Mags," Mom said. "We all need to get along, and Simon does a lot for us that you don't seem to appreciate."

I couldn't look my mom in the eyes, so instead I watched her fiddle with her opal necklace, twirling the dazzling pendant in her fingers. I recognized that necklace, of course: it was the one Simon had bought for Mom's last birthday. My mom loved opals, but the present had bothered me—the last gift my dad had bought Mom had also been an opal necklace.

"You really called the Sheraton?" Connor said, shaking his head in disbelief.

I felt burning shame rush into my cheeks, even though in my bones I knew Simon wasn't being truthful.

Eventually Simon returned to the kitchen, showing up in the middle of Mom's big speech about everyone trying harder, and presented me with a receipt he'd printed off a travel website.

"You can take it," he said. "It's authentic."

But Mom took it first.

"No, she can't have it, because I'm not encouraging any more of this behavior. It's utterly ridiculous."

"Honestly, Maggie," Simon said. "I don't know why you're so suspicious of me. But eventually, and this is a promise, I'm going to win you over, one way or another."

But the way he said it, darkly, with no hint of joy in his voice or eyes, made his big promise sound more like a threat. That's when an idea came to me, a burst of inspiration—a stroke of genius, I think is the expression. I needed Mom to see the real Simon, the angry Simon, the dark Simon who'd snatched the TV remote from my hand, the one who had lied about our trip and then lied again. To do that, I had to make him angry, *really* angry, and I knew just how to do it.

CHAPTER 16

It was Saturday night, four days to go before Nina started her new job. She was headed out to dinner with Ginny and Susanna to celebrate, wearing a cute black top she seldom wore and her favorite pair of jeans, which fit her curves much better since moving stress had jettisoned some unwanted pounds. Her makeup was applied in a way that smoothed out the years without seeming bent on recapturing her youth.

She was almost ready to leave when she heard an unmistakable sound emanating from behind the shuttered door to the master bathroom. Moments before, Simon had rushed upstairs and vanished within without uttering a word. Then came the retching, the splash, next a flush, followed by more retching.

Nina went to the door and gave a gentle knock, worry knitting creases in her brow.

"Babe?" she called out.

"Hang on." Simon's strangled voice had the raspy, breathless sound of extreme fatigue. Nina grimaced at a cringeworthy heave and splash. Eventually, Simon emerged, his complexion the color of glue, sweat beading on his forehead, standing shakily on his feet.

"Honey, what's the matter?"

"Dunno," he said wearily. "Came on like a freight train."

Staggering over to the bed, Simon fell with a thump onto the mattress.

"I hope this is gone by Monday," he groaned. "We're about to start the colonial settlements segment."

Kneeling beside Simon, Nina touched his forehead with the back of her hand. His skin was clammy.

"Oh honey," she said, scraping the side of her hand against the stubble of his cheek as she brushed back his hair. "Food poisoning?"

Nina noted how she was feeling. She had sampled a few spoonfuls of the mac and cheese Simon prepared for Maggie's dinner, but her stomach felt fine, thank goodness.

"I don't think so," said Simon, before letting out a little groan. "I really haven't eaten much. Feels more like a fast-moving bug."

A bug invited in a new alarm, and Nina bristled at the thought she could still catch something. Maggie, too, might have gotten it, though Nina had less concern for Connor, who'd been at his friend Luke's house most of the day.

Simon rolled over, exposing his back to Nina. She tried to caress him, but he shirked away. No surprise there. Glen never wanted to be touched whenever he took ill. Man-flu, she called it, a debilitating ailment that women somehow quickly overcame to resume their duties of wife, mother, cook, driver, coach, mediator, shopper, and so much more, despite suffering the exact same symptoms. But tonight, Nina made no jokes, and gave Simon her full attention.

"I'm so sorry. Do you need the bucket?"

"The bucket" was family shorthand for a wastebasket to puke in, and now Simon was part of that shorthand.

People get sick, Nina told herself, sensing her evening plans were now in jeopardy. *This is what sharing your life with someone is all about. You get the good times and the bad. You share the laughs, the hugs, and the bucket.*

"I think I'm all right for now," said Simon, rolling over onto his back. A great rush of sympathy welled inside Nina as she peered into those beautiful brown eyes of his. The way he looked up at her, helpless, with searing gratitude, thankful to the core for her care, opened Nina's heart another crack, making it possible to love Simon a bit more in this moment than she had the moment before.

"What can I do to help?"

Nina stole a glance at the time on her phone, realizing that if she did not leave soon, she would be late to meet her friends at Cucina Toscana, a new Italian place everyone in town had been raving about. Simon groaned in agony.

"Nothing, you should go—"

Nina sensed the "but" coming.

"But I'm worried, if I get sicker—you know, I don't want to be a burden to Maggie," he said.

Nina got it right away. She felt all sorts of guilt for leaving her daughter home alone with Simon, and now illness added more complications to the already tricky dynamics.

Simon's point was a good one. What if he needed Maggie's help with something? What if he got really sick? What if Maggie got what Simon had? How could she eat, drink, and laugh with her friends with all that worry knocking about? Would she have left Glen alone in a similar state? Maybe, yes—probably, in fact. But Glen was Maggie's father. It was different.

"I should stay," said Nina, thinking it through. "It feels strange for you to be sick, alone with Maggie, and—"

Nina did not finish her sentence because, with the speed of a sprinter responding to a starting gun, Simon bolted from the bed and dashed into the bathroom, where more retching and splashing took place. He emerged minutes later looking utterly bloodless, wobbly as a top about to tumble. Nina gently led him back to bed, guiding him with a hand on his wrist, helping him onto the mattress, where he collapsed with a groan.

"That's it. I'm canceling," she said.

"No, don't," Simon protested without much conviction. Nina guessed he probably did not want to be home alone with Maggie, just as Maggie didn't want to be alone with him.

There was some back-and-forth debating, but in the end Nina got her phone and made the call, disappointing her friends, who had not seen her since their last workout together.

"We'll reschedule," Nina said.

"I've heard that before," Ginny said.

Nina had forgotten that it was the second time she had canceled plans with them recently. The other occasion was last week, when Simon's car had broken down on the highway as he was coming home from grocery shopping. She and her girls were going to meet up for a movie night, maybe dinner after, but Simon needed rescuing twenty minutes in the opposite direction, with two hundred dollars' worth of groceries in a hot car.

"Lately, it seems like there's always something coming up with you," Ginny said, sounding a bit sour. "Are you sure you're all right?"

Nina held her tongue. She knew Ginny was dredging up old concerns that Simon had some weird character defect because of how quickly he had moved in on her after Glen was out of the picture. But it takes two to tango and Nina didn't appreciate the insinuation that she was somehow being duped.

"I'm fine. Stop worrying," she said. "I'll make it up to you. Dinner on me next time."

"We don't want your money, love. We just want your companionship. Tell Simon to feel better soon."

Ginny didn't sound overly sincere, but Nina thanked her friend for the good wishes nonetheless, and ended the call.

Yes, she had chosen Simon over her friends, Nina told herself, but these things happened. Cars broke down. Plans got canceled. Nina's parents, who had been married forty years, had taught her how it was the small sacrifices, made over time, repeated over and over again, that ultimately determined the health of a marriage. Knowing that Simon would have gladly made those simple sacrifices for her somehow gave Nina confidence that he wouldn't soon be taking up with his version of Teresa.

Going forward, trusting men would never be completely easy for Nina, but thank goodness Simon at least made it possible for her to try.

CHAPTER 17

Four hours later, Maggie was asleep. She and Nina had watched a movie together, some film with actors Maggie knew and adored but Nina had never heard of. They ate popcorn with too much butter, tried to keep Daisy from cleaning the floor of dropped kernels, and shared a couple laughs, but it was not light and breezy as usual. An invisible wall had come between them, and the reason for that wall was upstairs recuperating in bed.

"It'll be okay, sweetie," Nina had said after giving a goodnight kiss to her daughter, trying to coax out whatever it was that Maggie wasn't sharing—some new feeling, a new issue, something she was holding on to the way Daisy would a bone.

"Sure, Mom," Maggie said, sounding sure of nothing.

After lights out—and a text from Connor confirming that Luke's mom was fine with him spending the night—Nina went to check on Simon again.

He looked well, much better than at her last checkup. The color had returned to his cheeks; his eyes no longer had the glassy look of sickness. He sat upright in bed, wearing sweatpants and a T-shirt and reading, of all things, one of her glamour rags. It was not a magazine she remembered buying, but that wasn't so surprising. She had spent a good chunk of time this past year in a perpetual daze, and only now was she starting to feel like her former self. Thank you, therapy.

"Someone's looking better," Nina said, coming to the side of the bed. She touched his forehead, and it was the perfect temperature.

"I was hoping for a fast-moving bug," said Simon, offering a relieved smile. "Maybe I was sick at the thought of not being with you."

Nina returned a playful eye roll. "You do know how to flatter," she replied as she plopped down on the bed beside him.

"Thanks for sticking around tonight, and sorry again about ruining your dinner plans." Simon sounded genuinely remorseful. "I'm sure Maggie appreciated it as well."

"She did for sure," Nina said, deciding not to get into her concern that Maggie's anger and resentment were building.

"Emma never would have put my needs above hers."

Simon's comment caught Nina by surprise, especially because he delivered that remark quite nonchalantly. He seldom talked about his dead wife, Emma Dolan, and the reference to her, made as a passing thought, left her momentarily speechless. She opted to change topics rather than delve into his past.

"What are you reading that for?" Nina gave the *Vogue* magazine a gentle poke to indicate the object of her curiosity.

"TV was giving me a headache, and I couldn't concentrate on real reading," Simon said.

Nina's look of indignation was intended to amuse. "Hey, I know many ladies who would take offense at that remark."

Simon flipped the magazine around and pointed to an article featuring a photograph of a pristine aqua blue sea. "And I take it back. Here's a very well-written piece on great destination weddings."

Simon said it slyly, implying that the content of the article, not the writing, is what piqued his interest. Nina crossed her arms as if in thought. "Are you asking me again, Mr. Fitch?"

Simon's return volley was a cat-got-the-cream smile.

"I'm an extremely patient man," he said, flipping the pages before he became keenly interested in something else. He turned the magazine around to show Nina a picture of a model, tall and thin, with porcelain skin and striking dark hair (close in color to Nina's natural shade) cut in a medium-length bob, angled at the sides with mod-looking straight bangs. It was sleek and chic, textured in layers, a classic look that could have been in vogue in the 1960s or '70s.

"This would be a great look on you," he said, handing Nina the magazine. She studied the woman, thinking the model was twenty, if that, and a spaghetti strainer would look good on her head.

"I couldn't pull that off," Nina said definitively.

"Nonsense," said Simon. "I think you'd look amazing, absolutely amazing, with that cut. I swear."

He leaned forward, cupping handfuls of Nina's hair in his hands, and then lifted them up to chin level, emulating the hairdo to some degree.

"Gorgeous," he said, eyeing her with a hungry look, absorbing her, taking in each detail as though he were a painter analyzing his subject. "Absolutely gorgeous. Don't get me wrong. I think your hair looks great. I'm just not sure it's as flattering as this would be."

He studied her some more, adjusting the length ever so slightly, perfecting his masterpiece. The desire she saw in his eyes sent tingles through her body, making her feel that perhaps she could be that twenty-something model.

"I like my hair," Nina said, surprised at the slight catch in her voice. Did she like it as much as she thought?

"Maybe . . ." Simon paused, chewing on some thought.

The box spring creaked as he shifted his weight. She smelled toothpaste and mouthwash on his breath. "Maybe you should do it," he said.

"Do what?"

"Get your hair styled like this. Do it for your new job. A new look to celebrate a new beginning."

Nina appraised Simon as though the flu, or bug, or whatever it was that had felled him, had also left him mad.

"That's nuts," she said. "And even if I did want to do it, there's no way to get an appointment with my stylist. He's booked weeks in advance."

Simon grinned strangely. "Actually, it was supposed to be another surprise of mine, but—"

He got up from the bed, went to the dresser where Glen's clothes once had been, opened the top drawer (socks and underwear, just as before), and took out an envelope. Inside, Nina found a gift certificate to Aiden James salon, along with a card indicating an appointment for Tuesday morning—the day before her start date.

"I asked Susanna and Ginny what to get you that would make you feel, you know, ready to take on the working world again. They suggested a mani/pedi, so I booked you an appointment for that along with a cut and color just in case you wanted it. So . . . the appointment is all set. What do you say?"

Nina was rendered speechless. The idea was so out of the blue, so completely outrageous, she simply didn't have the words. Eventually, she managed a polite thank-you that did not convey much thanks.

"I think I'll keep my hair the way it is," she said.

Simon studied the magazine a few more beats before tossing it onto the floor as though he'd tossed the idea away with it.

"Yeah. It's kind of last-minute and pretty radical. It would take a lot of guts to really go for it," he said.

Nina rose from the bed quickly, because it was the only

way she could slug him on the arm as he made his way to the bedroom door.

"You take that back," she said.

"Take what back?" he said, turning.

"You make it sound like I'm weak or something."

Simon appeared to take offense at Nina's remark. "It is a big move. And I'm not surprised you don't want to go through with it, is all. I'm not blaming you. But I think a change like that would help separate you from Glen, from that time in your life. It would be like a metamorphosis of a sort, a butterfly emerging from the chrysalis. Anyway, no biggie. Your hair looks fine. I'm going to get some ginger ale from downstairs. You want anything?"

Nina eyed him indignantly. *Fine? Fine?!* How dare he put it back on her like that. Why was her hair suddenly just "fine"? It was more than *fine*.

But Simon did not stick around to discuss it. He headed downstairs, leaving Nina alone to look in the mirror at herself, to lift her hair slightly, up to the same level Simon had done.

"A metamorphosis," she said mockingly to her reflection as she adjusted the length of hair cupped in her right hand to make it more symmetrical with the length on the left.

Though she was still annoyed with Simon's remarks, he did make her wonder. Would a new hairstyle change how she felt? Would it help her forget what had been done to her? Would it be like making a statement: *I'm not the Nina from before. I'm not Glen's Nina. I've got a new look to go with this new person I've become.*

Nina didn't like being pushed into anything, but if she were being honest with herself, she'd have to admit that Simon had planted a seed of sorts. As she contemplated the idea, tried to picture it—could she? would she?—Nina had to admit (if only to herself) that she liked the thought of coupling a dramatic change with her new start in life.

Yes, she suddenly found herself liking the idea very much. (*I'll show you "fine"!*) But she wouldn't commit to it under duress, so she'd talk it over with her stylist first. And she certainly wouldn't give Simon the satisfaction of mirroring his suggestion exactly.

For whatever reason—pride maybe, or unwillingness to let a man subjugate her (even with good intentions)—Nina had to call her own shots.

CHAPTER 18

It was T-minus one and counting until J-Day, Job Day, the start of her new life, and Nina had come eager for a session with Dr. Wilcox. But first Dr. Wilcox had to process the new Nina, because the person who entered the therapist's office did not look like the same woman of two weeks ago. Nina's hair was cut short to her shoulders, a clear nod to a style popular when the Beatles had dominated the airwaves, but decidedly more modern. It was a shaggy, long bob with choppy bangs, blown straight, and it looked fabulous—at least, that's what Dr. Wilcox had exclaimed when she'd set eyes on Nina.

"You like it?" Nina sounded uncertain.

"Like it? I love it!"

"It was Simon's suggestion," Nina said, taking her usual seat. "He saw it in a magazine and thought it would look good on me."

"Well, it does. You look like a model!"

Nina stifled a little laugh. "I'm not sure I can trust your judgment anymore," she replied jokingly. "Anyway, I didn't get the exact style as that girl in the magazine. Her cut was a bit shorter, more layers, and swept forward on the sides with straight bangs. But I thought a new look would be good for my new job."

"I think it's fabulous," Dr. Wilcox said, still beaming as she picked up her notebook, a signal to Nina that the session had officially begun. "Speaking of jobs, how are you feeling about yours?"

Nina went into a lengthy oration about her apprehension, concerns about Maggie and Connor, fear of failure, a grab bag of insecurities and self-doubt, and eventually came to the conversation with Simon the night he gave her the Coach bag.

"Sounds like he was sending you mixed messages," Dr. Wilcox said. "Part of him is proud of you for getting the job, but another part is feeling insecure about it. Why do you think that is?"

Nina gave it some thought before shrugging her shoulders. "I really don't know," she said. "He's never been insecure before, at least not with me. He's actually quite self-assured. He has to be, to command a classroom."

"Maybe it stems from something in his history. Many of our insecurities have roots in the past. Have you ever talked about it with him?"

"No, certainly not in this context. We've discussed his difficult relationship with his parents," Nina offered. "His father was ex-military, very exacting and precise. Simon told me he was physically and verbally abusive to his mother.

"And his mom suffered from postpartum depression and had continued episodes of depression for years. To some degree I experienced depression as well after Maggie was born. So in that way I really can empathize with him and his mother. Simon's faced more personal challenges than most people I know."

"In what way?"

Nina hesitated, unsure how much to share.

"Well . . . his first wife left him," she eventually said. "They were very young, inexperienced, and, well, those things happen. Eventually he remarried, to a woman named Emma, who tragically committed suicide." Nina felt guilty for revealing Simon's personal history. At the same time, their lives were conjoined now, which helped to offset her misgivings. "Pills of some sort, it was an overdose. He found her dead in the bathtub. He was at school, teaching, when it happened."

Dr. Wilcox grimaced. "That's awful and deeply scarring for all," she said, sounding genuinely sorry. "Maybe your new job is bringing up repressed feelings for him. He's dealing with a lot of change, too."

Nina had not thought about Simon's issues in those terms, but it made sense. One evening the previous summer, when she'd been at Simon's place for dinner, he had shared with Nina the diary Emma kept, detailing her profound depression. The entries described a private pain that had haunted her for years: her exhaustion, her overwhelming sadness, her inability to connect or to care.

Nina had read only a couple pages before Simon grew anxious, but it was enough to get a clear picture. Simon had found the diary while packing up Emma's belongings, and he blamed himself for not knowing the dire extent of his wife's suffering. In error, he had believed that love and Prozac would be enough to pull her out of the darkness.

On top of the hurt and guilt Simon still felt, he was trying to rebuild his life, trying to reach Maggie, stay connected to Connor, do his job, adjust to a new house, a new neighborhood—poor guy had had nearly as many upheavals as Nina. And she'd just added one more to the mix with this job of hers.

"Maybe he needs therapy," Dr. Wilcox suggested. "I could certainly give you some referrals if that's of interest."

"That would be great," Nina said. "I'll talk it over with him."

But Nina had no intention of talking it over, because Simon had no idea she was seeing a therapist. She didn't want him to think she wasn't perfectly happy with him.

Telling Simon the truth about Dr. Wilcox might open up a number of issues, but lying to him took a different sort of toll. She'd already made up several reasons to keep him in the dark about her therapist. One time, Nina had almost arrived home from a session, but had to turn around and go to the market because that had been the reason she'd given for coming home late.

In truth, a part of Nina was still with Glen. She thought of him constantly. If he were alive, why had he abandoned his family? Nina was well aware men do have midlife affairs, but they generally don't run away, or strip the family of all security. Did she have a part to play in this? Or did it have something to do with why he got fired from the bank? She had no doubt that, alive or dead, Glen had taken these and other secrets with him, wherever he'd gone.

Simon made her happy, made it possible to love again, but below the surface Nina's heartache lingered. The slightest reminders of Glen—a movie on cable they had watched together, a photograph from a family trip, even something as mundane as seeing his brand of coffee on a supermarket shelf—could bring on the waterworks.

There was much to resolve, which reminded Nina to move on with the session so she could move past Glen and get on with her new life.

"I should talk about Teresa," she said.

CHAPTER 19

Dr. Wilcox turned a page in her notebook, flipping back to refresh her memory.

"Right," she said. "The other woman."

"I mean, I was dealing with a lot back then," Nina said. "Glen missing, losing his job, the lies, and the affair on top of it all. It was too much for me to process. But I was worried, you know?"

"About becoming a *Dateline* special."

"That's right," Nina said. "I knew the police were going to investigate the lead, but I didn't know when. And I was also thinking about the children—What would happen if word got back to them about their dad's affair before I knew the whole story?"

Dr. Wilcox nodded with understanding.

"So I thought I needed to get some answers for myself. I didn't want to wait around for someone else, and I was tired of feeling like a victim. I needed to *do* something, take some action of my own. In the back of my mind I was hoping that it was much ado about nothing."

"So what did you do?"

"I went looking for Teresa," Nina said, making it sound like the only logical choice. "I had to learn everything I could about the girl with strawberry hair, even if I got to her before the police did."

Nina did not know if Dr. Wilcox had ever been to Carson, if she was at all familiar with the town of eight thousand residents. It was typical of New Hampshire in that it was old (founded in the 1700s), steeped in history, and lacking in diversity. To the east lay Bear Brook State Park, and off to the west rambled the Connecticut River, the longest in New England. Main Street in Carson followed the rise of a gently sloping hill, and quaint brick buildings lined the street, with stores on the ground level and apartments above.

Nina still couldn't wrap her mind around the deceit. She and Glen had shared everything—a bed, a home, the children. How could she love someone heart and soul and not know him at the same time? He had a history of his own before they became a couple. Naturally, he shared stories from his past, but there were lots of years to cover and surely plenty of details omitted. And how would Nina know what was left out? They didn't grow up together, weren't high school sweethearts. In fact, they had met long after college. They were fully realized people when they started dating. People with pasts.

Before Glen, Nina had done what many twentysomethings did: worked her job, gone to the gym, and hung out with friends on weekends. The bar scene was fun until it wasn't, and that shift happened almost overnight.

What had become of Jerry Collins, the college boyfriend whose heart she'd broken, or Keith Middleton, the man who had broken hers? The only thing Nina knew for certain was that her jealousy had grown as her friends paired off, got engaged, married, and became young mothers while she stayed stuck on the scene. One by one her social circle had grown smaller, like a herd being culled by some super-predator.

Nina went out on dates, fix-ups with friends of friends, hoping to find that connection, believing in her heart she'd know when it was right. But it was never right.

She had worried about being too selective. Maybe something was wrong with her, not with all of her dates. When Nina suffered these thoughts, she reminded herself of the real issue: she gravitated toward a particular type. She dated broken guys, much like the people she saw each day in her social work practice. Men with issues she could unravel with the same delight she took in working with clients. They were mysteries, enigmas for her to figure out. Secrets to unlock.

The older Nina got, the more dismal her prospects seemed to become. She'd tried her best to break the wounded bird habit, but the younger men she dated were too immature, and the older ones too set in their ways. She had too many bad coffee dates that felt like job interviews. Some of the men were overly desperate; others too detached. Throughout it all, she avoided online dating. She wanted her romance to have a fairy-tale element—a story she could tell her kids, with glee in her voice and delight in her eyes.

I was at the grocery store, and I dropped a jar of pasta sauce on the floor. It shattered on the ground with a massive crash. I swear it looked like a murder scene, blood spilled everywhere. I was so embarrassed, but then your father— well, before he was your dad—stepped in front of me and acted like he was the one who dropped the pasta sauce. He even called for the manager and helped him clean up the mess, apologizing over and over for being such a klutz. Then we went out for coffee and—

But no, that wasn't Nina's story. It wasn't her story at all.

It was a friend from social work school in Boston, where Nina had moved after venturing away from Nebraska, who had made her see things differently.

"Face it, your grocery store scenario isn't going to happen," she had said one evening years back, when wine was all about the buzz and calorie counting didn't matter.

Not only did this friend know about Nina's fantasy, but more embarrassing, she knew about the time Nina had held a jar of pasta sauce in her hand and contemplated dropping it because a cute guy was standing in the same aisle. Nina's best chance of meeting somebody was through a setup, which was, her friend opined, the same thing as online dating.

"Just cast a wider net. What can it hurt?"

Nina created her online dating profile that very night. When she was done, she made a single click to see her first set of matches. There he was, the fourth profile on the page, handsome as a movie cowboy. She read his profile carefully. Thank goodness he didn't list "long walks on the beach" and "cuddling by the fire" as personal interests. He sounded confident and sincere and was genuinely funny. He wrote something about being an aspiring surfer and having a good relationship with his mother, which in hindsight turned out to be not entirely accurate. He loved life, he wrote. Enjoyed the outdoors. Travel! Restaurants! He kept it vague, saying he'd rather chat in person than write it all out. Nina noticed he had rendered some of the letters in his "Interests" section in bold type, and realized after careful study that it spelled out the words "NICE GUY."

Nina sent him a message through the website. She got the internet through AOL, and transmissions back then were slow and spotty, but he messaged her back quickly. That was all it took. Her first and only attempt at online dating had resulted in an eighteen-year marriage, two kids, a house in Seabury, and her in Carson, standing in front of the Muddy Moose searching for a woman who had apparently captured her husband's heart.

"The Muddy Moose was a rustic bar," Nina explained to Dr. Wilcox.

To set the scene, she described what she'd seen back then—the heads of various animals mounted on the wall, including that of a large moose (presumably their namesake) hanging over the bar. There was a group of people, all men, she recalled, chatting pleasantly at the long wooden bar, hunched over their beverages. The place still smelled of last night's fun mixed with powerful cleansers. The jukebox was on, playing something by the Rolling Stones.

"I didn't see Teresa there," Nina said. "But I was hoping maybe she was in the kitchen, or she might be coming in for a later shift."

"How did being there make you feel?"

"Empty," Nina said. "I felt absolutely nothing. But somehow I knew, even if I didn't get a chance to confront Teresa, that the thought of her was far, far worse in my mind than it would be in real life. In real life, she was just . . . just a waitress at the Muddy Moose. I'm not sure that makes sense, but I remember feeling utterly depleted, like all the anger left me in one great rush."

"Did you leave?"

"Not right away, no. I went up to the bartender with my phone in hand," Nina said. "He was thin as a marsh reed, I remember that clearly. I also remember trying to keep my emotions in check, but my heart was beating crazy fast."

Dr. Wilcox leaned forward in her chair.

"I showed him the picture—not the make-out session, the other one—and asked if he knew the woman, and if she worked there, and he said, yeah, that's Teresa Mitchell. I asked if I could talk to her, but he told me she was gone."

"Gone?"

"Like gone, gone. Like she'd up and left. Four weeks ago, he said."

"Four weeks before Glen disappeared?"

"That's right. He told me she'd done that sort of thing before, usually with some guy she'd met, but she always came back. But this time she didn't tell anybody where she was going, didn't say when or if she planned to return. She was just gone."

"Did the police look for her?"

"They looked, sure. I don't know how hard, but they couldn't find her. They eventually released her picture to the local press, which is how everyone found out about Glen's affair.

"I asked the bartender if he knew anything about Teresa and Glen, as a couple. He said they hung out together, were friendly for sure, but he didn't know anything more. Anyway, I wasn't about to go grilling the staff for information about my husband's extramarital exploits. What did it matter anyway? The details weren't going to do me any good."

"Probably not," Dr. Wilcox agreed.

"So I went outside. Really I wanted to bum a cigarette even though I hadn't had one in ages, but instead I just looked at the picture again. I took it all in—her clothes, how she carried herself in that photo, everything—she was just the opposite of me, so different from anybody I would have thought Glen would have been attracted to. It made the affair somehow seem worse, like Glen had sought her out because she was nothing like me. And the strange thing was, I wasn't sure I cared anymore."

"Why was that? I thought you were worried about the kids, how people would react?"

Nina had an answer at the ready, because she'd analyzed that one long ago.

"I guess when you shine light into the dark," she said, "you see it for what it really is, and it loses all power over you."

CHAPTER 20

The Davis Family Center was located in a neocolonial home with white clapboard siding, green shutters, and three dormer windows poking out of the roof. The middle window looked into Nina's cramped new office, where she had a desk, a phone, and a metal filing cabinet. There was no room for comfy chairs like those in Dr. Wilcox's office, but all personnel had access to the conference room on the first floor. Nina didn't have to handle billing, client intake, or a host of other duties, so she could focus on helping those in need to "achieve the maximum each day and successfully face life's challenges"—the center's motto.

She had a boss—sort of—a pleasant woman in her sixties named Rona Wosk, who had an affable smile, rosy cheeks, and a hands-off approach to management. Rona described her role as a facilitator. She would assign cases to Nina, help push through bureaucratic obstacles, and request updated status reports. For the most part though, Nina would be a solo operator.

Rona gave Nina a brief tour of the office, helped get her set up with opening-day paperwork, and introduced her to the other therapists, social workers, and mental health professionals who used the center as a home base for their private practices.

As a collective, The Davis Family Center offered a full spectrum of services, including family counseling, divorce and coparenting support, LGBT support, and substance abuse assessment.

Nina spent the morning meeting and greeting, signing documents, getting her email running on the company-provided laptop, and reading through various company policies from the human resources department (a department of one). Rona assured Nina she'd be given a decent-size caseload, one that wouldn't be overwhelming, and her ramp-up period would be a gentle one.

On her way out, Rona hesitated in the doorway of Nina's new office. "We're so happy to have you with us and we have all the confidence in the world in you." She paused, a thoughtful look coming to her face. "We know you've been through your own ordeal, but trust me when I say you'll do just fine here."

Nina thanked Rona for the encouraging words and hoped her faith wasn't misplaced. She had religiously completed her required forty hours of continuing education each year, doing some of her coursework at home and some in seminars and workshops. It wasn't like she hadn't thought about her profession since Maggie was born, but still, she did feel a bit like the Tin Man in need of oil.

She spent most of the morning refamiliarizing herself with New Hampshire family law. Rona had told Nina her first assignment would be a custody case, helping a judge make the determination for two children, ten-year-old Chloe Cooper and her eight-year-old brother, Chase. It would be her job to get to know the parents as well as the children. She had to understand the issues within the marriage, analyze the behaviors, and ultimately determine, in a neutral and objective way, what was in the best interests of the children—a finding that would profoundly influence the judge's decision.

"You'll do just fine," Nina told herself with a long exhale, echoing Rona's words, though wishing she shared her confidence.

Near midday, Nina found her way to the bathroom, where she caught a glimpse of herself in the mirror. She had tried not to feel self-conscious or fiddle with her hair during the day, not to tug, twist, and shape it into the original style Simon had suggested. If only Simon had gushed the way she had expected, she'd be quite happy with this new look. Even a tepid reaction would have been preferable to what had happened.

Nina returned to her desk, trying to put the haircut and last night's disaster out of her mind. She skipped lunch to continue her reading on New Hampshire custody law.

At a quarter to two, her cell phone rang. It was Simon. Her heart sank a bit. He was probably calling to talk about what happened—hopefully to apologize, at least for part of the catastrophe.

It had all started when she had walked in the front door. She had expected a lot of oohing, aahing, and fawning over her new "do," which she had gotten from Maggie and Connor, who both loved the fresh look. Maggie was especially complimentary and thought her mother looked younger and even more beautiful—her exact words. But Simon's reaction was completely unexpected. It seemed he could focus only on the sides, which weren't swept forward and angled, and the bangs, which weren't cut straight. It was different than the photograph he'd shown her, and he'd even fetched the magazine to drive home his point. He had said it was no big deal, that she looked great no matter what.

Nina had been crushed, and later, when they were in bed together and the children asleep, she told him that his reaction had been hurtful and maddening. Simon was all apologies after that. He explained that he had been fixated on the cut from the magazine, so sure it would be perfect on her, but he'd never imagined she'd actually do it. The surprise clouded his thinking, and he needed a moment to adjust his expectations. He assured her, over and over again, that he loved it, that her hair was gorgeous, and apologized profusely for suggesting otherwise.

Nina wasn't sure she believed him, but he kissed her neck in the right places to get her thinking she could accept his apology. His touch sent a shiver racing through her body. She tilted her head as his probing fingers found the perfect spot to massage. She breathed slowly, heavily, in response to an electrifying sensation as his fingers traced long lines up and down her arms.

As his touches intensified, his exploration became bolder, and Nina felt something unfurl inside. All thoughts of her new hairstyle evaporated with a shudder of desire. The moment their lips touched, Nina ignited inside. Her mouth opened hungrily.

Responding with equal eagerness, Simon pulled Nina into him. His hands were free to explore every inch of her body. He ran his fingers through her hair, undoing to some extent the hard work of her hairdresser, while each tug increased her passion.

Simon brushed his hands across the top of Nina's chest, then lowered them to her breasts while tracing his lips along the contours of Nina's neck. As he kissed her, Nina began a slow rotation of her hips, pressing herself into him with an increasingly desperate urgency. She needed this: lust, hunger, arousal. It was liberating. She felt unburdened. When their mouths met again, Nina's tongue worked more greedily than before. His kiss, touch, everything about his body felt so right and good, everything but that orangey, woodsy aroma that conjured vivid memories of Glen. How was it the new cologne still smelled like the old? Was Glen now haunting her sense of smell?

To purge herself of him, Nina closed her eyes, focused only on Simon, his body, his lips, his fingers in full command. She let Simon get on top, murmuring with pleasure as he rubbed against her, pushing his hands under her body before placing them on the front of her pajamas, pressing his fingers into her. Nina opened her legs wider, thrusting her hips into him.

Frantically, she pulled Simon's T-shirt over his head, tossing it to the floor. She kissed his chest, brushing her fingers over his stomach. She tugged at the drawstring of his sweatpants, undoing them with one try. Even though they had made love a few months after they'd begun dating, Simon was the first man other than Glen that she'd touched this way in more than twenty years. It still felt exciting and new, but also terrifyingly unfamiliar. He pulled back, cupping her head in his hands again as he looked deeply into her eyes, taking her in, all of her, loving her the way she needed to be loved. Her body trembled as she worked her fingers down inside his pants. The intensity of Simon's kisses, his labored breathing, the way he touched her, ached for her, made her feel more desired than she had in years.

Nina assumed Simon would be so excited he might explode at her touch. But to her surprise, when she placed her hand on him, he wasn't hard at all. It was like a crash landing. Nina pressed her palm against him again, expecting to coax the start of a rise, but got nothing in response. She was genuinely confused. Simon had initiated their lovemaking and she was certain that he wanted her.

"Tell me what to do," Nina said in a soft voice, trying to sound understanding as she pulled her hand away.

Simon climbed off of her.

"I'm sorry," he said. "I don't know what's wrong. I'm . . . I'm probably just tired." Simon sounded flustered as he tumbled off the bed. He felt around the floor for his shirt and sweatpants.

"We'll try again later," he said, with a notable lack of enthusiasm.

Confused questions ran through Nina's mind. Was it the change in her appearance? Was it that she didn't look just like the model in the magazine? Was it the tension at home? The job?

She had been up late with pointless worry, and come morning had needed extra foundation to cover the dark circles ringing her eyes. *Some re-entry into the working world.* Simon left the house before Nina, giving her a quick kiss good-bye and a few words of encouragement for the big day. Instead of talking about the night before, they'd talked briefly about him coming home early to let Daisy out and about maybe looking into doggie daycare now that she was working. That was it—until this phone call.

"Hey, babe," Simon said when Nina answered. "How's the first day going?"

"Good," she said rather hesitantly. As they talked, Nina became more animated, describing her office and giving vague details about her first case.

At some point, the conversation stalled.

"I'm sorry again about last night," Simon said. "I'm actually not feeling well. Almost had to call in a sub, but I think I'll make it through the day."

Simon's apology, while appreciated, did not make Nina feel better. She'd never failed to arouse him before.

"Is it my new hairstyle?" she asked apprehensively. "Are you upset about it?"

"God, no, you look beautiful. No, no, it's me, I wasn't feeling well, that's all."

But Nina wasn't going to test that theory out. She had already made an emergency appointment that afternoon with her hairdresser, and she'd even used her phone to take a picture of the model so there would be no question about how it should be styled.

And Simon would be delighted.

CHAPTER 21

Today was the day I would prove to Mom that Simon had another side to him—an evil side. There hadn't really been a good opportunity to execute my brilliant plan until now. Mom was at work (first day on the job, three cheers for Mom!); Connor was at practice; Simon, I think, was out in the yard; and I was in the basement, looking for something. There was a lot of junk in our basement: storage containers filled with snow pants and boots, holiday decorations, plates and dishes that had been banished here for whatever reason, lots of things we had moved that really should have gone to the dump.

There was also a wide workbench and cabinet with all of Simon's tech stuff for building robots. Nearby, on the floor, was Simon and Connor's creation, which they cleverly named Bob. It was shaped like a stop sign and had four wheels bolted to its metal sides. I thought Simon's love of tech and history was a bit odd, but he was fond of saying that the past informs the future.

I grabbed a fold-up chair and positioned it in front of a storage unit that was pushed against the back wall. If it were a dangerous weapon, something that could shoot more than one lead slug every three minutes, Simon might have kept it locked up in a safe. But we kids were older, and supposedly knew better than to play with guns or mess around with things that didn't belong to us. Besides, I didn't see any ammo around.

I got Simon's antique musket down with ease. It was wrapped in a soft fleece blanket, along with the bayonet, which wasn't attached. I didn't see any gunpowder or ancient bullets nearby, but I wasn't about to load the stupid thing and shoot Simon dead. I'm not a maniac.

The gun felt lighter than I expected, about the weight of a baseball bat, maybe a bit heavier. I stepped down from the chair and lifted the musket to eye level, picking up a faint scent of oil, like engine oil, or WD-40, some treatment to keep it in working condition. I examined the various components and saw there wasn't really much to it. The wood was dark and rough, like the hull of a ship that sailed in cold seas. The long gun barrel had some rusty spots, and plenty of dings, like it had seen some action, but it looked to be in pretty good condition.

I was mostly interested in the trigger mechanism. It was pretty cool to see it up close, I had to admit. Kids went bonkers to touch Mr. Fitch's rifle, and here I was holding it in my hands like I was playing soldier or something. The metal of the trigger was silver-colored and badly tarnished. There were some letters carved into a silver plate—HENSHAW, I think it read. I could barely make out a date, 1772, that had also been etched into the soft metal.

I called Ben at home, and he answered right away, expecting my call.

"I got the gun," I said.

"Well, yeah," he said, because that really wasn't the hard part.

"I'm just letting you know," I said, a bit annoyed.

"Okay, but where are you going to do it?"

"I'll do it right here, right now," I said.

"What about your phone, the proof?"

"I've got that taken care of."

"So do it," Ben said.

If he had a phone, I'd probably Snapchat him, or we might use Talkie, which was the new new thing, because there always had to be a new thing when it came to social media. Instead, I pressed the speakerphone icon and set my cell phone on the same chair I'd used to help me get the gun.

"Can you hear me?" I asked.

"Loud and clear," Ben answered, his voice calming me.

"Okay," I said, taking in a breath and holding it for a bit. "Here I go."

"You know he's going to have a right to be mad at you," Ben said.

I paused. "What do you mean by that?"

"I mean you might record him freaking out, but won't your mom say he had a good reason to be angry?"

"If I'm right," I said, "it's not going to look like normal anger to her."

"Yeah, okay," said Ben. "Go for it."

I began to pull hard on the gold-plated loop that arched over the trigger. At first, it wouldn't budge, but then I tugged it from side to side, harder and harder with each yank, until I eventually heard a crack of old wood splitting and the piece of metal snapped right off the gun with some splintered wood still attached.

Immediately after, I felt a lot of relief because I'd done it. Then, about two seconds after that, I felt sick to my stomach, because, you know, I'd done it.

"Wow. I heard that crack!" Ben cried out.

"Yeah," I said, sounding shaky, my words catching in my

throat. I could feel my heartbeat going way too fast. "Now for the fun part."

And upstairs, I went to look for Simon, to tell him what had happened.

* * *

I found Simon out in the yard, rake in hand, but he wasn't raking up anything. Instead, he was again eyeing the branches of the oak tree that extended from the neighbors' property onto ours. I didn't know what to make of that, but my bigger concern was the torn-up hunk of metal and wood I held in my left hand. Of course I was worried. Would Simon be pissed off to just the right degree of mad, enough so that I'd get grounded and that would be that? It was too late to try out a plan B, even if I had one. I couldn't exactly glue the broken part back on.

I had my phone in my hand because phones were always attached to teenagers' hands, like an extension of our palms. No suspicion there, no reason for Simon to think I might be recording his reaction to the bad news I was about to share. I still had Ben on the phone, just in case Simon started murdering me or something. At least Ben would be a witness to the crime and I'd have justice from the grave.

But the truth was I didn't think Simon was going to hurt me. My only goal was for Mom to see that angry look, get some video evidence, proof that her sweet Simon wasn't at all who he pretended to be. He was a showman, a liar, and someone we had to get out of our house right away.

I crossed the lawn, approaching Simon with the apprehension of a dog that had just gone potty in the house. I carefully held my phone so the display was facing me, the camera lens facing out toward Simon.

"Simon," I croaked out, realizing this was my second big

acting job in nearly as many days. "I have something to tell you." The nervous edge to my voice wasn't faked in the slightest.

"Well, I have something to tell you, too," Simon said, spinning around, bringing the rake along with him. "These branches are crossing over into our property. Now, I told your mother about it, but she won't let me cut them down, and the neighbor won't cut them down either. Property law, Maggie, is not something to trifle with. The framers of the Constitution treated private property as the cornerstone of a free society."

I was too worried about my covert recording and what I was about to tell him to try and make sense of his little speech.

"Speaking of property," I said, pushing the words past the lump that had sprung up in my throat. "I am really, really, really sorry."

I bit my bottom lip, remembering that flickering dark look I'd seen, praying I could capture it.

"Sorry about what?"

Simon grew edgy, and then noticed my closed fist, instinct telling him that's where he'd find the source of my sorrow. Adrenaline (I'd learned about it in bio) shot through my body and caused my sprained foot to throb. I shifted my focus to the ground, mindful to keep the camera lens pointed at him.

"I was downstairs, looking for something, and I sort of stumbled on where you kept your antique musket, and—"

I thought I saw the color drain from Simon's cheeks, but for certain I heard the sharp breath he took. He was bracing himself, like I did when Mom asked me to sit down at the kitchen table because she had something to tell me about Dad.

"What did you do, Maggie?" Simon asked warily.

"I was just checking it out and . . . and . . . and this happened."

I uncurled the fingers of my left hand to reveal the looping piece of metal and splintered hunk of wood with ancient screws still attached. Simon's eyes opened wide at seeing what was in my hand, and . . . and . . . there it was, the start of the flicker I'd been hoping for, that shift from Simon to Simon 2.0. At almost the exact same moment the transformation began, his eyes darted over to my other hand, to my phone, and I swear, *I swear,* he noticed the camera lens pointed right at his face.

I tried to keep my hand steady, but I'm sure my recording of Simon would look like it was taken during an earthquake. I felt light on my feet and started to get super dizzy, as if I was having an allergic reaction without having eaten a peanut. I tried to push past the discomfort to focus on Simon, but what I saw made me feel even sicker to my stomach. Instead of capturing the look I was going for, recording his other personality, or worse, documenting some kind of attack on me, what I caught was his expression shifting as fast as I could blink. The darkness slipped from his eyes, and to me, he looked like one of the poker players Connor sometimes watched on TV, men and women who tried like heck not to reveal their hand.

I was thinking to myself: *Did I get it? Was it enough?*

Simon shook his head from side to side to signal his supreme disappointment in me.

"Boy, oh boy, Maggie, this is really, really unfortunate," he said in an emotionless voice. "You knew you weren't supposed to play with that gun. Any gun. It's not safe. It's not primed to be fired, but you didn't know that. You could have been hurt." He reached out and took my wrists in his hands, like he needed to touch me to drive home his point. I felt him apply gentle downward pressure on my wrists, lowering the camera in the process, so the only thing I'd be recording would be his khaki pants.

"I thought you were more mature than this, Maggie. I'm really, really angry at you." But he didn't sound really angry; in fact, he didn't sound angry at all.

"I can't send you to your room. Honestly, I can't do anything," he said, coming across as more sad than mad. "So I guess I'll just have to wait for your mother to get home and she'll have to deal with this. Could I have the piece you broke off, please?"

I gave it to him, my hand shaking. As he took the broken piece into one hand, he continued to gently hold on to my wrist with the other, keeping pressure on it so I couldn't raise my phone and record his face. Then he did the strangest thing ever—worse than the dark look I was after, worse than anything I could have imagined. He cocked his head slightly to one side, keeping his expression a complete blank, the perfect poker player all the way. Then he looked me right in the eyes, cold as a snake's stare, and he gave me a wink.

CHAPTER 22

The second call Simon made to Nina on her first day at work was to apologize for his apology, which he sweetly worried hadn't sounded sincere enough. Simon's third call came while Nina was chatting with Dave in Human Resources, and that was to ask about dinner. The fourth call came twenty minutes after the dinner conversation to ask about weekend plans, something Nina patiently told him would have to be discussed at home. She couldn't remember what he wanted on his fifth and sixth calls, but by that point her annoyance was starting to grow and show.

While Nina appreciated that Simon cared enough to keep in touch, he was making it difficult for her to concentrate on her work. She remembered what Dr. Wilcox had said about the job bringing up buried feelings for Simon, unearthing dormant insecurities, and her anger faded.

"You need to stop being so anxious," she told him. "You're acting like a jealous boyfriend."

Simon laughed awkwardly, as though embarrassed at being caught. He promised he wouldn't bother her again.

"You're simply going to have to adjust," Nina said, taking a stricter tone. "I have a lot on my plate already, but I thank you for your love and support."

"Always," Simon responded. "And I'm sure by now they've figured out how lucky they are to have you."

At the completion of her workday, she was overwhelmed with a strange mix of elation, exhaustion, and dread.

Listen to Simon. To Rona. You've got this! You'll do just fine.

Nina walked to her car, the last one left in the parking lot. She felt buoyed from her private pep talk and ready to let her hairdresser, Derek, do his magic. This time she'd have it styled to Simon's exact specifications, because deep down she did not entirely believe that exhaustion was to blame for his never-happened-before impotence.

Hair emergencies and quick alterations were Derek's specialty, and he accommodated her as she'd hoped he would. At the salon, he studied the picture Nina had taken with her cell phone camera and went to work on those bangs first, taking them from chopped to straight in no time. Next, he attacked the sides to make the hair look swept forward, a feat he accomplished with the help of enough hair spray to hold the style in a hurricane, and he adjusted the length as well. It was far more hair maintenance than Nina desired, but she figured she'd try out the look for a little while.

Derek was finishing up, lathering on effusive praise as he lathered in some leave-in conditioner, when Simon called for the seventh time that day. Nina took the call, answering with a bit of an attitude. "Yes, Simon," she said, wondering what he could possibly want now.

"Sorry to bother you again," he said, "but there's a problem."

"Problem" was an understatement.

Nina drove home with a dark cloud above her head. *How dare Maggie! How could she?* Maggie was never this child. She was never in trouble at school. She was never disobedient, mouthy, or moody, or difficult in any way. But then Nina shifted her thinking as she remembered some basic truths: her daughter's age, her trauma, the new man in their lives, and how confusing this must be for her. Even so, Maggie was old enough to know better than to play with guns.

When Nina reached home she was a lot calmer, and with time in transit to process her feelings, she felt ready to confront Maggie without blowing a gasket. Connor, football in hand, stood in the driveway chatting with Simon, who looked calmer than expected. As she exited her car, Nina was taken aback by the strange looks she got from both of them. Then she remembered her hair.

"You like it?" she asked.

"Looks good. But why the change?" Connor asked, tossing the football a few feet in the air before catching it one-handed.

"Thought I could spruce it up a bit more," Nina said, knowing only Simon would fully understand.

She caught the bewildered look in Simon's eyes as he approached.

"Well," she said, noting the drip of apprehension seeping into her voice. *Does it look awful?* "Do you like it?"

She twirled, albeit a bit nervously, when Simon didn't answer right away.

"I . . . I . . ."

Simon gawked at her as though she were some exotic being, a nymph, something otherworldly.

"It seems I've rendered you speechless," Nina said. "Not exactly the reaction I was going for."

"You look . . . you look amazing," Simon finally managed.

Nina's whole face lit up at the compliment. "Really?" she said, twirling once more, lighter on her feet, all but forgetting what Maggie had done.

Simon came closer, pulled her into an embrace, a hug

that felt imperative, and whispered in her ear, "Absolutely amazing." He pressed against her and she felt him come to life. "Can I make it up to you tonight?" he said, and she got the subtext right away.

"Hmmm," Nina answered, stepping back, shooting Simon a coy look that all but said *Invitation accepted*. "Where is the accused?"

"I don't think there's much question of her guilt," Connor chimed in. "Has she been tested for a concussion?"

"You stay out of this," Nina said, giving Connor's muscled shoulder a squeeze as she marched past him, heading up the walkway—which, she absently noted, had no weeds growing between the paving stones. Simon, with his fastidious nature, wouldn't allow them to grow, leaving Nina grateful that he had inherited some good traits from his overbearing father.

She strode into the house and found Daisy there in the foyer, greeting her with a wagging tail and playful kisses as though Nina had been gone for years. In a way, it felt like she had been gone that long. Her body was completely fatigued, and she wondered how long it would take to adjust to the mental gymnastics of the workday. Nina paused to give Daisy some much-appreciated attention before trekking off upstairs in search of her daughter, believing Maggie's bedroom would be the most logical hideout.

"Hey there," Nina said at the sight of Maggie, who was seated at her small desk by the windows overlooking the backyard, a schoolbook splayed open in front of her.

"You cut your hair again," Maggie said, after turning in her chair to greet her mother.

"Thanks for noticing," Nina said.

"I liked it better before," said Maggie.

"Thanks for the honesty." Nina's tone implied thanks for nothing, but her annoyance went away when she sat on

Maggie's bed, taking in all the familiar sights and smells of youth, toys replaced with trinkets, all of it serving as reminders that this was a girl with more on her plate than most adults could handle. "So, what am I supposed to do with you?" Nina said as she shrugged her shoulders.

"You're the parent," Maggie answered with a shrug of her own.

"Oh, I forgot." Her rebuke was gentle. "So, since I'm the parent, why don't you tell me what you were thinking?"

"I was just messing around," Maggie said, but Nina caught a look in her daughter's eyes suggesting that there was more to the story.

"What's going on with you?"

"I said it was an accident."

"It was an antique and also a gun. You *know* better."

"I was curious," Maggie said. "I said I was sorry. I'll pay him back."

"When? Over the next fifteen years? It's worth thousands of dollars."

Maggie had no answer for that, not that Nina had expected she would.

"You're a smart girl, Maggie. You don't do things like this. Did you do it intentionally? Did you do it to upset Simon?"

There! Maggie's nostrils flared out and she blinked rapidly, two of her easy-to-spot tells, making her non-answer all but an admission of guilt.

"Why?" Nina said, letting her exasperation be heard. "Why are you making this so hard on us all? Do you want to see your therapist more? I don't know what to do to help you, but you have to come to terms with the fact that Simon is a part of our lives now."

As Nina thought for a moment, she went to pull her hair back out of habit, forgetting all the hair spray holding it in place.

"I can't let this go by without doing something," she said. "Hand it over."

Maggie knew what was being asked of her and tossed her phone onto the bed with attitude, where it made a small bounce and landed next to Nina.

"Take it," Maggie said dejectedly. "When can I have it back?"

"How about right now."

Simon's voice came from the open doorway, where he had hovered unnoticed.

"Sorry to be eavesdropping," he said. "But may I?" Maggie responded with another shrug of her shoulders—*Do what you want,* she told him silently, and so he entered her room.

"I don't think Maggie should be punished at all," Simon said, taking a moment to look around and appreciate all of Maggie's things. This was her space, and normally she would not have welcomed Simon inside.

"People make mistakes, and nobody got hurt," Simon continued. "She apologized and I accepted her apology. Worst case, I get a new musket; best case, I can get it repaired. I was going to drive over to Wicked Weaponry tonight—I sent their repair guru a picture of the damage, and he thinks he can fix it up and it'll be as good as old."

Simon waited for a laugh that didn't come.

"Yeah, that wasn't very funny," he admitted. "But no punishment at all. That's my plea here. It's fun to have, but I don't *need* it for the field trip. And I'll find another way to store it. That was my bad. Maybe I'll keep it at the gun store until I figure something out. Doesn't matter, none of this matters. I just want things to be better for us all, and this is one way I can think of doing that. Nina?"

Nina shifted her gaze to Maggie, who appeared placid but uncomfortable, like she was trying hard not to react to

Simon's overture in any way. She certainly appeared to be actively avoiding eye contact with him, though for a teen that was no surprise.

"Okay," Nina said, rising from the bed, putting herself between Maggie and Simon. "How about we shake hands and make a pledge to try and work harder to support each other."

"Deal," Simon said, jumping on the offer, extending his hand fast as a whip crack. Maggie held out a few beats before extending her arm to give Simon an extremely tepid handshake. Glen would have made some remark, as he believed strongly that a firm handshake and solid eye contact were signs of maturity, but Nina had had enough for one day to try any additional corrective measures on her kid. She was tired, oh so tired, and wondering how the heck she was going to get up in the morning and do it all over again.

You'll do it by putting one foot in front of the other, she told herself. *Millions of people do.* Nina kissed the top of Maggie's head, taking in the smell of marigold-scented shampoo, and then turned to Simon.

"Please tell me I don't have to make dinner," she said.

"You don't have to make dinner," he answered with a dimpled smile. "It's grilled chicken with lemon, capers, and rosemary. Already cooked."

"Oh, thank God," Nina breathed out.

"How about you take off your work clothes and I'll set the table—with Maggie's help."

The look he sent Maggie made it clear she owed him and not to complain. Maggie rose reluctantly from her chair.

"I'll have a glass of wine waiting for you downstairs, but I'm going to let you all eat without me," Simon said. "Want to get to the gun store before they close and see about fixing it up before the field trip. Might be able to avoid some disappointed kids."

Nina made a kissing sound that made Maggie sneer.

"Thank you . . . thank you," she said. "I'm a working woman now. I need to be pampered."

"You are a superstar," Simon said, "and soon you'll be a well-fed one. Maggie?"

Maggie slunk out of the room with footsteps that were close to being a stomp. Nina let out a big sigh once she was gone.

"You are a lot more understanding than I would have been. I was going to take her phone and ground her for a month."

"And give her more reason to hate me?" Simon said. "No, thank you. Let's let this go and hope for smoother seas ahead. It's all going to be fine."

Simon bent down and deposited a gentle kiss on Nina's forehead.

"Tonight," he said, this time planting a quick kiss on her lips as he took her into his arms. Nina sank into his embrace and felt the taxing day leave her body. "You look amazing," Simon said. "And you are amazing. I can't tell you how lucky I am to have you in my life."

"Are you about to say you complete me?" Nina asked, giving him a playful pinch so he knew she was referencing that famous movie quote in a loving way. She pulled back to appraise him thoughtfully. "Thank you for being you," she said.

Simon kissed Nina again before leaving Maggie's bedroom to deal with dinner prep and his broken musket. Nina showered and ate a quiet meal with Connor and Maggie, the way it had been before the short-term trio had become a quartet. There was no talk of the gun, or getting along, or any weighty subject. Conversation was limited to school and logistics, including a reminder that Maggie was scheduled to get another x-ray on her injured ankle.

After dinner, Connor helped with the dishes, while Maggie,

who had set the table, got a reprieve. Simon returned a few hours later with the good news that his musket could be repaired without the break being too noticeable, and might even be ready for Friday's field trip.

That was not the only thing he fixed.

Later that evening, when the kids had gone to bed, after giving Nina a foot massage, preparing her lunch, consulting with her on day two's outfit, and refilling her glass of wine, Simon took her in his arms and made love to her with exquisite tenderness.

"One phone call tomorrow, that's your limit," Nina told him as she nestled in his arms, basking in the afterglow. "One."

"I'll try," Simon said. "But I love to hear your voice."

CHAPTER 23

Ben and I, along with everyone else in the eighth grade, were in the middle of the hallway, shuffling past glass displays of student artwork, trophies, and other school paraphernalia, on our way to the school gym for an anti-bullying lecture that some expert had been hired to give.

As we neared the gym, Laura, Justin, and a bunch of my former friends pushed past me with enough attitude to knock me over. I caught a few nasty glares as they strode on by, an extra-harsh one coming from Laura, but no words were exchanged. It's not exactly a smart move to bully someone on the way to a lecture about bullying.

I noticed how Ben stood a bit taller, and you'd have to know him to see that he puffed out his chest, which was really sweet. He wanted to protect me, but Laura Abel and her crew of meanies weren't my biggest concern. No, that particular person stood guard at the entrance to the gymnasium looking all teacher-like, with his navy polo shirt tucked into his dumb khaki pants. He had that leather bag Mom bought for his birthday at his feet. So many times I thought of hiding it from him because I knew that's where he kept his wallet and keys.

My fellow students greeted him with pleasant smiles and

warm hellos all around—"Hi, Mr. Fitch. Hey, Mr. Fitch! 'Sup, Mr. Fitch."—and as I approached I had to think of what to say. Should I say anything at all? Should I call him Simon like I did at home? I decided it was best to try and slip past him unnoticed, using my fellow classmates as camouflage, but no such luck. Simon reached out a long arm and tapped my shoulder, a knock hello, like he thought maybe I had missed seeing him. He smiled as though nothing was wrong and said, "Good morning, Maggie."

I managed to grumble out a good morning in return. Ben and I found two seats together on the fifth row of the bleachers, next to Jaddy (Jackson and Addie), who were occupied not with each other, but with whatever was on their respective smartphones. In fact, most kids were looking at, or sharing something, on their phones.

"Do you think it's funny we're having a lecture on bullying and everyone is on the smartphone they use to bully?" Ben always made some keen observation.

"You're just jealous because your parents won't let you have one," I said, teasing him because we were friends now, and friends can tease.

"I think you just bullied me," Ben said with a smirk.

I said, "Guess you'd better report me," and we both enjoyed a little laugh.

A few minutes later, nobody was laughing, or talking, because Principal Fowler had come to the microphone and introduced the guest speaker, a guy named George something (admittedly, I wasn't paying close attention). When you live it, and know it the way I do, deep and personal, it's hard to get really excited about an hour-long chat on bullying. It's like going to a lecture about what it feels like to get mauled by a bear after a bear has mauled you. It was kind of a "been there, done that" moment for me.

Still, I joined everyone in applauding for George, who

was young, maybe a few years out of college, and hip in a *Diary of a Wimpy Kid* kind of way, with short dark hair and thick black glasses that made him look like Ben's cool older brother. He had on a polo shirt similar to Simon's solid navy one, but his had alternating dark and light blue horizontal stripes. At the cuffs of his dark jeans were Converse sneakers, what the emos and goths in my school wore, making him even more the alternative type.

His lecture, inspired by his personal experience as a victim of bullying, highlighted choices he made that didn't stop the harassment, but rather helped immunize him to it, like a vaccine, so he could better cope with the meanness. His story wasn't exactly groundbreaking—he wore glasses from a young age, some kid thought that was funny, then nobody wanted to be friends with him. The teasing escalated and everything spiraled from there, until by high school he was friendless, depressed, and contemplating suicide. Yeah, no joke.

He gave us a bunch of statistics (these I listened to: one out of seven K–12 students are bullied; 35 percent of students had been bullied online; etc.) and throughout it all I was feeling more and more uncomfortable. I was one of those stats, and everyone in the school knew it, so it felt like I had a spotlight shining on me the entire time George was talking.

At the end of his lecture, which included a few interactive skits about trusting your parents and teachers, George asked if anybody wanted to share a story about bullying with the assembly. He called it an empowerment moment, but nobody came forward. I wished I could have turtled inside my clothes to avoid any of the looks people sent my way, but instead, had to settle for the next best thing, which was looking at my feet.

I waited anxiously, my stomach in knots, for this assembly

to be over so we could all get on with our lives. One second of silence became two, and I was sure nobody was going to volunteer to speak. I started gathering my stuff, thinking we were at the point when George was going to call it a day, thank everyone for our time, remind us to be kind to each other, something blah-blah like that, when someone came to the microphone. It was the worst person imaginable. No, not Laura, or even Justin.

It was Simon.

He appeared calm and composed, like he was about to do one of his Revolutionary War performances. As he leaned down to speak into the microphone, he looked right at me.

"I'd like to say something," he began.

His booming voice, much deeper than George's, bounced off the concrete walls, which were decorated with felt banners of our division and state wins in different sports.

"That was an incredible lecture and I found it very moving. Thank you, George."

There was a round of applause led by Simon, who glanced at George with a smile of appreciation, before turning his head to look at me again. I sank lower in my seat, trying to make myself disappear. I tried to guess why Simon was up there, what he might say next, and the possibilities terrified me.

"I have been teaching for many years and I have seen how damaging bullying can be," he continued.

No . . . no . . . no . . . I was thinking. *Please stop! Please stop right now!*

"Each year students have come to me with their hurt and their pain. I have seen firsthand the heartache that comes from bullying."

A murmur rose up from the bleachers, because everyone knew that "firsthand" referred to me.

The noise didn't die down, and next I heard a little laugh

that was loud enough to get Principal Fowler to shush the of-
fender angrily.

"Please take to heart what George said today," Simon continued, "because your words and actions can cause people a
lot of real pain, and can lead to lots of tears and heartbreak.
It makes people contemplate things much worse than dropping out of school."

Oh. My. God. Did he just tell everyone that I've been
crying all the time? Did he imply to the entire class that
I'm suicidal? I wanted to scream. I wanted to run. I kept my
head down.

"Your words and actions matter," Simon went on. "Instead
of ridiculing others, try being kind. Instead of excluding
someone from your lunch table, invite him or her to eat with
you. You can make a big difference in a person's life, but it
all starts with a simple act of kindness."

He didn't have to say "Maggie Garrity," because everyone
knew I'd been booted (or self-selected out of) my usual lunch
table. When I looked up, Simon's eyes were still locked on
me. And that's when I knew—I knew for a fact this was pay-
back for his precious musket. This was why he had winked
at me. This was why he hadn't supported punishing me when
Mom wanted to take my phone. He knew we were having
this lecture, and knew he'd have the chance to humiliate me
in front of the entire class.

Now everyone was looking at me. Okay, maybe that was
an exaggeration, but for sure the whispered talk I heard
was about me, and without a doubt the hard poke someone
gave me from behind was no accident. I couldn't take it
anymore. I thought I was going to pass out if I stayed a
minute longer. My watery eyes made it look like everyone
was swimming, but I was the only one drowning.

I got up while Simon was in mid-sentence. I couldn't hear
what he was saying anymore. I couldn't hear anything over

the ocean-like roar in my head. Maneuvering as gracefully as one could in a stupid protective boot, I worked my way down rows of bleachers, not bothering with apologies to the people I pushed and shoved on my way to the gym floor. Everyone, Principal Fowler included, watched my escape.

I didn't ask permission to leave the assembly, I simply left, dashing through the metal exit doors as fast as my hobbled leg could carry me.

I took refuge in the girls' bathroom, locked inside a stall, blubbering like I was eight again. Eventually I ran out of tears, but I was still shaking. What were people saying about me? How would I face them again? *Okay, don't panic,* I told myself. But I was panicking, my mind going a million miles an hour. *Should I run away? Could I make it to Nebraska with what I have in my savings account?* I don't know how long I was in that stall, but it was long enough for the assembly to end. The quiet erupted into chaos as kids filled the halls and more than a few ended up in the bathroom with me.

"OMG, did you see Maggie? Could she have gotten out of there any faster?"

I knew the voice—Pam Epstein. Band kid. Not one of the meanies. But now even Sweet Pam was gossiping about me, thanks to Simon. I checked my phone to see what kids were saying on social media.

Sure enough, there were a few Snapchats about me, and even an Instagram post capturing my speedy departure (yes, they'd tagged me so I'd see it), but it was all pretty tame. I doubted *that* would last long. Kids would talk, and the story would grow from there. That's how legends were born.

I opened Talkie, the new social media thing. Talkie was a good place for me to go online, a safe space where I could track the happenings of celebrities and athletes who got tired of Twitter. Today I wanted to see what, if anything, was being said about me.

When I logged in, I saw that I had a new Talkie to Me, which is what Talkie called friend requests. It came from a person named Tracy Nuts. My heart stopped. I couldn't think straight. Everything was spinning super fast, and it felt like I was both falling and floating. I couldn't breathe. The bathroom began to spin. I was sure I was going to get sick. My whole body started to tingle.

I know only one person named Tracy Nuts, and she is me. It's my nickname, a little play on words about my deadly peanut allergy: Trace of Nuts. Get it? Tracy Nuts. The only person who ever called me that was the same person who'd given me the nickname in the first place.

My father.

It was kind of a jokey nickname for such a deadly serious condition, but my dad came up with it one day when I got sad because I couldn't eat any of my friend's birthday cake. He thought a little humor might make it sting a bit less, and well—he was right. There was a message accompanying the Talkie to Me request that I read a hundred times in the stall.

> Sweetie, it's me. It's Dad. Accept this request and I'll be in touch soon. But promise me, promise, promise you won't tell a soul I've contacted you. Not your brother, not even your mother. There are reasons, important reasons I can't get into right now. I'll try to explain later. But please, please, please, keep that promise for me, OK? If anybody finds out I've contacted you it will be very bad for me and I won't be able to reach out to you again. Try to understand. I love you to the moon and back and there and back again to infinity. xoxo—Dad

Maybe somebody, somehow, had learned about my Tracy Nuts nickname. Connor could have told somebody, so I considered it a possibility. It was also possible that somebody was being extra mean and cruel, piling on the pain after today's humiliation, trying to hurt me more by sending a Talkie friend request using that nickname, maybe knowing my father had given it to me.

But some things were never shared, like the private conversations between a father and a daughter, which is why nobody, and I do mean nobody, not even Connor, knew that every night before I went to bed, my dad would kiss me on my forehead and whisper how his love for me went to the moon and back, and there and back to infinity.

CHAPTER 24

Hours after the school assembly, Nina, Simon, Maggie, and Connor gathered in the living room for a family meeting. Family meetings were something Nina had tried out from time to time over the years. They seemed to always convene in moments of great crisis—problems with attitude, chores, bedtime, homework, those breaking points where the parent (typically Nina, occasionally Glen) felt like they were being held hostage by miniature creations of their own making.

When things improved afterward, which they invariably did, Nina would promise herself to have these meetings regularly, but life had a way of derailing the best of intentions. And so the cycle would begin anew—crisis, family meeting, resolution, crisis, family meeting, resolution, and so on, until one day Nina discovered her children had outgrown the small issues and graduated to bigger ones.

With or without today's incident, what Nina had seen six days into her new job convinced her these meetings were more important than ever, and she renewed her pledge to hold them weekly.

This was Simon's first family meeting, and he perched himself on the edge of the leather love seat that had come from his home. Nina and Maggie sat side by side on the couch, close in proximity but worlds apart from a solution. Connor was on the floor, playing tug-of-war with Daisy using her favorite rope toy.

"Please tell Maggie what you told me," Nina said to Simon as she rubbed her tired eyes. Once again she found herself dealing with lingering fatigue from another day spent reviewing case files on the Coopers and setting up home visits, all while planning the rest of her investigation.

She would have been home much sooner to deal with the crisis du jour, but Nina had several new cases on top of the Cooper case, two of them involving young people, each around Connor's age, who were addicted to pain medication.

Knocking around in the back of Nina's mind, erratic and cacophonous as a child banging a toy drum, were Simon's words of warning: how the job would eat away at her free time, to the detriment of her family. The seeds of doubt he'd planted had unfolded into a gnawing worry that she'd miss something important, some critical juncture, and this would send one or both of her kids careening off course, eventually landing them in the case file of a social worker like herself. Nina understood it was irrational, but at the same time her daughter was showing real signs of strain, and Simon was not helping the situation.

"I am so sorry, Maggie," Simon said with an anguished voice. "I had no idea how that was going to be perceived. Honestly, I was extremely upset with your situation, and felt compelled to speak up, to say something. I wanted the other kids to know there were real consequences for their actions."

If Maggie was moved in the slightest by his apology, she said nothing. She would not, or could not, make eye contact with him.

"Believe me, if I could take it back I would," Simon added.

"The last thing I want is to make you feel bad or put more distance between us. More than anything I want you to think we can be friends."

"I don't even see how it was so *embarrassing* for you," Connor chimed in mockingly. "Everyone knows you've been kicked out of your friend group, and news flash, they don't care."

"They were laughing at me," Maggie said defensively. "You weren't there. So shut up."

"Connor, stop it," Nina snapped. "You don't get to weigh in on how your sister feels. And Maggie, don't tell your brother to shut up."

"Look, I apologize, profusely," Simon said. "Did you get any mean text messages or see any posts about it?" He seemed worried that he had made a bad situation even worse.

"No."

To Nina's ears Maggie had responded too quickly, almost defensively, like she had seen or heard something upsetting but for whatever reason did not want to share it with the room.

"And Simon, I'm sure your intentions were noble, but nobody likes being singled out, and it's especially difficult for middle schoolers who are just coming into their own. You, of all people, should know better."

Maggie seemed to perk up a bit at Nina's rebuke. She had used the same stern tone she took whenever Glen wouldn't help with bedtime, or clean up after dinner, or any number of occasions when he'd failed to live up to his end of the marriage bargain.

"I honestly didn't think anyone would connect it to Maggie," Simon said. "But I can see now how they did and how counterproductive it was. Again, I'm really sorry."

"Well, thank you for the apology," Nina said. "But I'm not the one who counts. Maggie, do you accept?"

Maggie gave a shrug, which was good enough for Nina to continue.

"The reason I called a family meeting is because we're all going to have to do something to make things better around here. All of us."

Nina directed her attention to Connor, who was notorious for not pulling his weight around the house. The multiple chore charts that had come and gone over the years would have made a stack as thick as a novel.

"I can't do this alone," she continued, "so if you have any grievances, issues, or complaints, then let's get them out in the open right now. Because, like it or not, tomorrow I'm getting up in the morning and going back to my job, and after that I'm going to come home to you children, and to Daisy and Simon, and I could really use your support."

"I come after the dog?" Simon said, mock-offended.

Nina was in no mood to banter. "We need to be a team," she added. "So, starting tomorrow, what is everyone going to do to make things better around here? Hmmm? Who wants to go first?"

For a few tense moments, nobody spoke. Even Daisy clued in to the escalating tension and departed the living room for a less fraught location. It was Connor who broke the silence.

"I'll do the recycling," he offered. "And I'll walk Daisy, every day after practice."

Nina arched her eyebrows, impressed. "Okay," she said. "That's helpful. Simon?"

"No more speeches at school assemblies for me," he said.

Connor chuckled, while Nina did not look particularly amused, and Maggie sat stone-faced, her gaze elsewhere.

"Too soon?" Simon read the room correctly and quickly shifted gears to a more serious response. "It's one thing teaching kids, and it's another living with them. I have no experience in that regard. To make things easier I will from this moment and forever more keep home stuff and school stuff as separate as church and state. That's a promise."

"Sound good to you, Maggie?" Nina asked.

"Whatever," Maggie said, somehow upping her attitude a few degrees.

"Maggie, can you promise to try to get along with Simon?" Nina pleaded. "At least not be so hostile? We are all adjusting here, so I'm not coming down on you. I'm merely asking if you'd be willing to try harder."

"Whatever. Sure."

It was a better response than Nina expected.

"And you need to load the dishwasher every night after dinner," Nina added, pushing her luck. Maggie's next "Sure" and "Whatever" were barely audible.

"What about you, Mom?" Connor asked.

"Me?" Nina sounded taken aback. "I do enough for you all that I'm exempt here. I've earned the right to be a diva. Meeting adjourned. I'd say we should hug it out, but I don't think we're quite ready for that. However, I'd like Maggie and Simon to shake hands. We need to move on from this."

Nina was impressed with herself. Only a week on the job and already her conflict-resolution skills were sharp as ever. Even so, she worried; always worried. Damn Glen. Damn Teresa. Would she forever have to smooth over these conflicts at home? When could she stop worrying about blending her old life with her new one? Glen's behavior had made her suspicious, cost her that easy trust in people, had made her wonder if there was any truth to her daughter's accusations about Simon—the dark look, the trip, and now this assembly business. Could it be that she had brought trouble into her home?

Stop it! Nina scolded herself. *Just stop! Simon loves you, you love him, and this is Glen's fault, not Maggie's. This is Glen's betrayal lingering. Maggie will adjust or she won't,*

*but you won't let fear, uncertainty, and doubt get in the way
of your happiness.*

These thoughts came and went as Simon once again extended an olive branch of sorts, which Maggie took and shook
with perfunctory courtesy.

"Very well. We'll do this meeting thing again next week."

But if experience had taught Nina anything, it was that
this would be their last family meeting until the next crisis
erupted.

Later on, after the dog had been walked and the dinner
dishes were loaded in the dishwasher, after homework was
done and the goodnight routine had come and gone, Simon
crawled into bed more quiet than usual. He appeared to be
brooding, and Nina naturally worried that Maggie's behavior had been more upsetting to him than he had let on.

"It's Emma's birthday today," he said, as explanation for
his uncharacteristic moodiness. If they had been together longer, Nina would have known this about him, but a newish relationship came with constant discovery. Simon had always
been a bit guarded when it came to his past, something Nina
found entirely understandable given the pain many of those
memories evoked. "I get sad every year around this time, for
what we had, and . . . and how it was suddenly taken away,"
he continued.

Nina understood perfectly well how milestones like birthdays could awaken those feelings of sadness and loss.

"It was deeply traumatic for you," she said. "It's understandable."

"It seems women are always leaving me suddenly and
traumatically."

Nina thought: not only Emma, but Allison, Simon's first
wife, his first true love, who had walked away from the marriage without a word of good-bye.

"I'm sorry, babe," Nina said, kissing him tenderly, finding

his hand under the covers to give it a gentle squeeze. "I have no plans on deserting you, so you don't have to worry about that."

"Maybe I had Emma on my mind and that's why I wasn't thinking clearly today," Simon lamented. "God, could I make this adjustment any harder on myself?"

"You're doing great," Nina said reassuringly. "We knew this wasn't going to be easy."

"It's your fault," Simon said, a sardonic smile coming to his face. "If you weren't so damn wonderful I wouldn't have cared one bit that you were going to move to Nebraska."

"Thanks, I think."

"Kidding aside, thank you for your support with Maggie. I know I'm blowing it, but I loved you from the minute I saw you and I'm not going to let anything come between us. Certainly not my own stupidity."

Nina let Simon pull her into his arms even though she was still mad at him. She asked what she could do to help, and Simon said all he needed was Nina's love, that her love made him whole. It was like that "You complete me" line she had joked with him about, but this time she shivered because Glen had once said something quite similar to her years ago.

"I still think you need to quit your job," said Simon, after turning out the bedside light. "Today, what happened, the reaction, it's not all because of me. Maggie is struggling. I'm just not sure you can see it."

But Nina wouldn't quit, and she said as much. Working again, supporting herself, it felt too good, and she was too invested in her cases to back out now.

"I understand your reasons," Simon said, his voice taking on an edge that wasn't there a moment ago. "But I still think, for Maggie's sake especially, you should quit and let me take care of everyone."

"Please, Simon, please stop using my children as part of your argument."

Nina managed to tamp down her anger, feeling there'd been enough drama for one day, but she added that her employment status was not open for discussion. She had kept this conflict of theirs from Susanna and Ginny, not wanting to give them more reasons to question Simon and her choices, but doubted she could muster the restraint if he kept up the pressure.

"Well, if it goes the way I'm seeing it going, I promise I won't say I told you so."

He leaned over in the dark, fumbling a bit before he planted a gentle kiss on her lips.

"Goodnight, darling," he said. "Tomorrow will be a better day."

Soon enough Simon was breathing heavy, fast asleep, while Nina's thoughts darted about like a jackrabbit. Why was he so insistent on her not working?

She understood his stated reasons, even shared his concern, but part of her wondered if he didn't like the idea of his wife (or future wife) having her own career. Emma hadn't been working when she took her life; she knew that much about the woman who had made Simon a widower. His mother didn't work either, from what she'd been told. Perhaps he had some kind of set expectation for what a wife should be. But if anything, he was progressive, having a broad historical context to help shape his modern-day views on feminism. And surely he knew her well enough to understand her need for independence.

But how well did she understand Simon?

CHAPTER 25

Twenty-six hours and seventeen minutes after my father contacted me, I broke my promise to him. Well, in my reply back I didn't officially agree to keep the secret, but that was a technicality at best.

I decided to tell Ben, because I simply *had* to tell *someone*. If I didn't, I think I might have exploded, had some sort of freakish meltdown, gone all Exorcist (saw the movie on Netflix, super creepy!), and for sure my dad didn't want that to happen. I knew Ben could keep the secret the way I knew that one plus one equals two. Besides, I was basically doing what my dad asked by not telling Mom or Connor, who I think were his real concern. So Ben knew, my father didn't know I had told him, and I was fine with all my justifications.

I was with Ben in the library, working on a science lab that was worth 20 percent of our grade, which meant I was getting an A. Ben was as good at science as he was at math, not that I was any slouch. Together we formed an unstoppable team.

We used a basal thermometer and stopwatch to conduct our experiments on the effects stress had on body temperature. We had asked our test subjects (who included Mom,

Connor, and Ben's parents—but not Simon) to rate their stress levels on a scale of 1 to 15. We then recorded their body temperatures (yes, we had the thermometer properly sanitized each time). Next, we asked our subjects to put a stack of mixed-up numbered pages one through fifty, in sequential order, on a time limit. We told them to get as far as they could, as fast as they could, while a timer was counting down. Stressful, right? We then re-measured body temperature and recorded the results. Turned out that in most cases, stress did raise the body temp a few tenths of a degree.

We had charts and graphs and all that impressive-looking stuff. I was going to take it home, type up our conclusion, add some finishing touches, and 20 percent of our grade would be secure. But we were having a hard time focusing on the lab because my own stress was burning me up. I kept checking my phone every two seconds, hoping my dad (aka Tracy Nuts) had responded to the dozen or so messages I'd sent. All of my communications were variations on the same theme: *Dad is that you? Please message me back. Daddy I need to hear from you. I love you so much. Are you okay?*

"Don't you think you should tell someone, like your mom, for instance?" Ben asked.

He had a Web browser open on the library computer, researching terms like "serotonin" and "hyperthyroidism," looking to bolster our conclusion with the biological reason why our temps rise under stress.

"I can't," I said. "He was really, really specific about it. It's bad enough I told you."

I showed Ben the Talkie to Me request he'd sent as a reminder.

"And you're sure it's him?"

It was a bit embarrassing to share my dad's goodnight routine with Ben, but it was proof, or so I thought.

"My parents say stuff to me like that," he revealed, sensing my discomfort.

I hated that now I was suddenly filled with doubt. *What if it was a trick?*

"So, what are you going to do?" Ben asked.

"I'm going to wait for him to contact me. I can't risk it," I said, sick to my stomach at the thought of losing my father again.

"Why do you think he doesn't want you to tell your mom or Connor?"

"Connor is easy," I said. "He'd blab to Mom for sure. He couldn't keep a secret if his life depended on it. Dad knows that."

"So why not your mom?"

"That's the big question," I said, feeling frustrated. "I don't know. He must have done something bad, something that forced him to go into hiding."

Ben clicked through links about human anatomy, absorbing information at the speed of a computer. "Any ideas?"

"He was having an affair. Maybe something about her?"

I wished more than anything that I had the answer. I mean, what could make a devoted father, one who had kids who loved him, a wife who loved him, a great dog, and a great life, up and leave it? Not a word good-bye. Nothing. I said all this to Ben and we tried to piece it together.

"Let's make a list," he suggested.

And so we did.

1. The other woman.
2. Dad's bank job.

That was it, that was the extent of our list.

"Not very helpful," said Ben, looking it over.

"Not at all," I agreed. "Why not just run away? Why this whole elaborate setup with Daisy in the boat, cutting himself with a knife to make it look like some kind of fatal accident or something?"

"Maybe there was another person involved. Maybe he got cut in a fight, but maybe something worse happened to the other guy . . . or girl."

"Gross! So my dad's a murderer? You think he killed that waitress he was seeing?" I was horrified at the thought.

"We don't know, is all I'm saying," said Ben. "And anyway, let's say he committed some crime, something really terrible, maybe related to his bank job, maybe not—why reappear now?"

"Maybe he knows we're in danger," I said. "Maybe he's been secretly tracking us, and he knows Simon is some kind of freak."

As if summoned by magic, Simon came strolling into the library, hands clasped behind his back, looking real casual. He came over as if there was nothing wrong, like that dumb family meeting had fixed all our problems.

"Hey there, Maggie. Hi, Ben," he said, talking in that hushed library tone that wasn't nearly as quiet as people thought it was. "Happy accident running into you two. Say, do you have a few minutes to chat since we're both here?"

"Sure," Ben said, for some reason thinking he was a part of the discussion Simon wanted to have.

"Actually, Ben and I are doing our lab report for science," I said, spitting out the words, concocting some half-baked reason on the fly. "It's a huge project, worth twenty percent of our grade, so—"

So go away . . . so no, so I don't want to talk to you.

The teacher part of Simon understood the significance; the other part of him pretended to care.

"What's your report about?" he asked.

Of course, Ben told him. He even talked about hyperthyroidism.

"Very interesting," said Simon. "Listen, Ben, could I have a minute alone with Maggie? Would you mind?"

Ben grew noticeably uncomfortable, because he knew I would be uncomfortable, but he didn't know how to get either of us out of it.

"Um . . . um . . . um . . ." he stammered.

"It's okay," I said, coming to his rescue. "I'll take this home and finish it up. I know what to do. Just give me that paragraph on serotonin or whatever before the end of the day."

Ben got up from his seat, hurriedly collected his things, and left with a wave good-bye.

When he was gone, Simon said, "So, Maggie, I've been thinking a lot about what happened and I can't apologize enough for what I did. I was out of line and feel really stupid about it."

His words were kind, but his eyes were cold.

"That's okay," I told him, thinking maybe that would be enough and he'd go, but no, he stayed.

"I . . . I just . . ." Like Ben, he was struggling for the right words. "This hasn't been easy."

And I thought: *The understatement of the year award goes to . . .*

"I'm trying really hard here, but for whatever reason I keep messing up."

"It's fine," I said. "I broke your musket. We're even."

Not even close, but whatever. Winker.

"Forget about that, sweetheart," he said. "I just want this to work out for all of us."

And I wanted to scream: *Did you just call me sweetheart? What was next? Pumpkin? Oh. My. God. Please, please, please, just go away.* I was about to lie about needing to get to class when my phone buzzed. I glanced at it, naturally, even though Simon was still pouring his heart out to me, repeating his excuse about how teaching children and living with them wasn't the same thing. When my eyes went to the phone display, my heart leapt to my throat. I'd received a new Talkie to Me message from Tracy Nuts.

"So what can we do to make it easier on everyone, especially your mom?" Simon asked. "I've been thinking maybe we should start family counseling."

I only half heard him. All I wanted to do was open that message from my dad. I wanted to see it, read it, touch it. My head and heart hurt with a desperate need, but I didn't want to do anything to clue Simon in.

I knew my own weakness well, and if I broke down in tears in front of him, he'd ask questions, and that could lead to problems. It destroyed me to wait even a fraction of a second. Maybe my father wanted to chat—right now, online—and this was our only moment. Maybe the police were closing in on him (for reasons unknown) and this was it, our last chance to communicate before he vanished again for good.

I held my breath, tried to block out the images of my dad sitting in a car, or at a park, or somewhere, clutching his phone, eyes glued to the screen, sirens blaring in the background, and him going, "Come on, Maggie. Where are you? Where are you? I have to say good-bye. I have to tell you one last time how much I love you and how sorry I am for everything."

"It's fine," I blurted out, my legs bouncing like I had ants crawling on my skin. "Talk to Mom about it, okay? I don't know. I . . . I have to go." I gathered up my papers and books as fast as I could.

"I just want us to be friends," Simon said.

"Yeah, okay," I said, and off I ran, out of the library and into the hallway, bringing my phone to my face.

I opened the Talkie app and tapped on Dad's message, reading while walking.

Sweetheart it's me. Have your phone available Monday at noon. I'll have a few minutes to chat online with you. I'll tell you what I can, but I can't tell you everything.

CHAPTER 26

It's never going to end with Maggie and Simon, Nina thought glumly as she arrived at Dr. Wilcox's office for her afternoon therapy session. The big family meeting from the night before had produced a tense truce, but little more. Simon had told Nina in a brief phone conversation earlier in the day that he'd spoken with Maggie at school and tried apologizing again. He thought he'd made some progress, but said she was acting oddly, really distracted, visibly upset by something. He didn't get the sense it was related to him.

"I'm really worried about her," Simon said, and suggested to Nina that she and Maggie have a heart-to-heart conversation.

That was probably sage advice, thought Nina. Despite Rona's assurance about a gentle ramp-up period, the work had been piling up at a steady rate. Perhaps Simon was right to think Maggie didn't like the competition for her mother's attention.

As much as Nina wanted to get home to help sort it out, she had a more pressing need that required Dr. Wilcox's expertise.

Hours ago, Nina had wrapped up her first home visit since

resuming her career—a trip to Wendy Cooper's house to conduct a formal assessment for the custody hearing. While it was an extremely productive session, it had also dredged up feelings she desperately needed to discuss.

"So what was it about the home visit that has you so on edge?" Dr. Wilcox asked, parroting Nina's words back to her.

Nina mulled this over a moment. "Wendy was lovely and the kids were great," she said. "There were no red flags. I didn't sense anything amiss."

"But—" Dr. Wilcox correctly guessed there was more.

"But even though I was there as an impartial professional, I couldn't help but reflect on my marriage. I wondered if my story was somehow similar to Wendy's. I mean, her big complaint was that her soon-to-be-ex, Michael, was a workaholic, which was Glen's MO as well."

"It's natural for anyone to make comparisons and look for parallels to their life experience. Did you pick up on other similarities between you and Wendy?"

Nina nodded. "For sure. The kids came to Wendy for everything—a glass of water, help finding the TV clicker, help with homework. We were probably interrupted five or six times for this or for that. But I didn't think anything of it until after I left, because that was my life, too. I was the go-to person in the family for everything and Glen would breeze in and out when his work commitments allowed. I know it's a common story, but it definitely caused tension in my marriage, Wendy's, too, but what's strange for me, and I guess what I wanted to talk about today, is that it actually made me think of Simon. I kind of have the reverse problem with him. It's like I'm the workaholic, even though I'm not anything like Glen, or Michael Cooper, from what Wendy described."

"Can you say more on that?"

Nina gave it some thought.

She was reticent to admit it aloud, but if ever there was a safe place to share, it was here. "I guess . . ." She cleared her throat. "I guess, lately, this tension between us, over my job mainly, it's made me feel a little more uneasy about my decision to move in with Simon."

Dr. Wilcox's brow furrowed. "Why do you think that is?"

"I'm not sure," Nina said. "I knew getting married, even engaged, would be too much change too fast for Maggie and Connor, for me as well, but honestly I didn't think Simon living with us would create so many challenges. He keeps saying my working is bad for Maggie, but I get the feeling it bothers him for some other reasons."

"Maybe those insecurities of his."

"Maybe. And on top of all that, my good friends, Ginny and Susanna, are upset with me because I'm not seeing them nearly as much as I used to—dinner plans, movie plans, all canceled at the last minute. I know they blame Simon for it, but there's always a valid excuse."

Nina told Dr. Wilcox about the most recent incident, when Simon bought theater tickets as a surprise for the same night she had had dinner reservations with her friends.

Simon had been upset about the conflict, but told Nina to go to dinner if that was her preference. Of course she couldn't go; it didn't seem right, and those tickets were expensive. But finding a new date to get together with her friends was proving to be a bit of a chore.

"It seems I'm always canceling plans with them," Nina lamented. "And my new job isn't helping matters any."

"Have you talked to Simon about it—his issues with your work, your friends' concerns?" asked Dr. Wilcox.

"No, because I'm sure he'd deny it all. He'd say he was happy I was working again and that Ginny and Susanna were overreacting. I know he means well."

"Good intentions don't preclude your feelings. Perhaps

now would be a good time for Simon to come in and we could meet together, or separately if he'd prefer."

Dr. Wilcox's suggestion made Nina cringe. It seemed incredibly indelicate to bring this to Simon now that he, not Glen, was the focus of these sessions.

"You're hesitant for him to come here," Dr. Wilcox said after a brief silence.

Nina thought of several lies she could tell but opted instead for the truth. "I haven't told him I'm seeing you," she confessed.

"Really? Why not?"

Nina explained that she didn't want Simon to think she wasn't perfectly happy with him, or saddle him with doubts at the start of their new life together.

"It sounds to me, Nina, like what you're really confessing here are your own doubts."

"I can't afford to make another mistake with a man," Nina admitted.

"We've talked about this before, but let me ask again. Have you learned more about Simon's past, his family?"

Perhaps this was at the root of her mounting anxiety. Therapy was a magical thing, and Dr. Wilcox had helped reveal something Nina had tried to deny. The shock and wounds she'd suffered with Glen made it impossible to feel totally comfortable with Simon, and his newly revealed insecurities around her job were compounding the issues.

"There's not much on his family other than what I told you—father was strict, ex-military, rule oriented." Nina didn't go into Simon's fixation about the tree branches, and how his upbringing probably played a role in that obsession. "And from what Simon's told me, aside from her depression, his mother was a very kind, loving, stay-at-home mom. Both his parents sadly died when he was in his twenties."

A slim shadow crossed Dr. Wilcox's face. "Of what?"

"Ovarian cancer for his mom, and a heart attack for his dad a few years after. Simon says his dad died of a broken heart."

Dr. Wilcox's tight smile acknowledged the bittersweet sentiment.

"What about other family?"

"He was an only child," Nina said. "And I think there was animosity with extended family on both sides after his parents died. Bad blood from settling two estates. He hasn't been in contact with any of them for years, and he doesn't talk about it much."

"Not the first time that's happened. Death is easiest for the deceased. What about his past relationships? Do you know much about them?"

"No. Allison, his first wife, ran off, Emma killed herself, and that's all I know."

"Any photographs?"

"Of Allison, no," Nina said. "After she left him, Simon had a meltdown of sorts and burned all their photographs, thinking that would somehow ease his pain. All gone. Up in smoke." Nina raised her hands as though they were the smoke rising.

"And Emma?"

Simon might have had a photo album with Emma's picture in it, or a digital archive somewhere, but she imagined how that conversation would go:

"Hey sweetie, do you have photos of your dead wife I could look at? I'd like to have a peek at her. Get to know her because—well, well . . ."

She didn't find it unusual that Simon hadn't shared Emma's picture with her. It wasn't like Nina went around flaunting photographs of all her ex-boyfriends for Simon's benefit. Sometimes the past was the past, and opening doors served no purpose other than opening wounds. Emma's death had shattered Simon, and she could think of no good way to explain why she wanted him to relive that pain.

Nina explained all that for the benefit of her therapist.

"I see. No wonder you're feeling . . . unsettled. You have the stresses surrounding Glen and now a new man in your life who isn't a completely clear picture to you. It's difficult to know where his insecurities about your job, time with your friends, and all that come from, which naturally would bring up questions for you. I think you should come in together, or it would be fine if you want to find a couples counselor for a fresh start on your own. Either way, there are concerns here worth exploring in depth."

Nina folded her hands on her lap, no doubt a defensive posture, because Dr. Wilcox had just sunk an arrow into the heart of the matter. It was all about trust—trusting herself, trusting a new man who had been nothing but kind to her and the children. Wendy Cooper had been a mirror of sorts, and thanks to Dr. Wilcox, that reflection was now a bit clearer.

On her drive home, Nina ruminated on her session. Now that she was seeing things more clearly, a thought struck her hard. It was understandably hard to trust fully in the face of so many questions, so much missing information. Maybe, to Dr. Wilcox's point about unresolved feelings, it wasn't just Simon she had to better understand, but Glen as well. Maybe clearing that ghost would make it easier to clear the way for a new beginning with Simon.

Wendy had gone to great lengths to show Nina how capable she was at mothering compared to Michael, whom Nina would observe with Chloe and Chase at some point in the coming weeks. Had Nina gone to similar lengths to show herself as the more competent parent—the parent to seek out for approval, direction, and affection? Had Glen come to resent her for it? Who knows?

But the question did leave Nina wondering. What if Glen had confided in Teresa about his wife? Was it possible something he had shared might give Nina answers about his thinking back then, some concrete reasons for his erratic and completely uncharacteristic behavior? She had to know, desperately wanted to know, what role she had played, if any, in his destructive choices.

She thought of calling Ginny or Susanna to talk it through but didn't want to get an earful about the latest plans she'd canceled on them.

But there was another call she could make.

Pulling over on the side of the road, Nina used her phone to look up the number of the Muddy Moose. It was worth a shot, she told herself. Maybe she could track down the woman at the center of it all and get herself some real answers.

A female voice answered her call. Nina presented herself as a friend of Teresa's who had just moved back to town and wondered if she knew how she might get in touch with her.

"Well, you could show up here Monday afternoon," the woman said. "Teresa's scheduled to work. Can I tell her who's calling?"

Nina couldn't believe her ears. Teresa was "gone, gone," from what the bartender had told her way back when, as in never coming back to Carson.

She had called the Muddy Moose thinking she might get a lead on the waitress's whereabouts, not her damn work schedule. Could she be back with Glen? Had Glen emerged from the shadows to resume living his double life? Is that what had pulled Teresa out from wherever she'd been hiding? Nina's pulse spiked, pondering the possibilities. A plan formed in her head, one that cut through the initial confusion with razor sharpness.

"No need to say who's calling," Nina said. "Better if it's a surprise."

CHAPTER 27

Nina rose creakily on Saturday morning, hardly believing Monday would start her second full week on the job. Even though everything ached and had stiffened during the night, her mind revved up immediately. Jumbled thoughts of case files, forms, general worries for her clients—including the two young people who had required emergency admission into a treatment facility for their drug dependence—should have been overwhelming, but instead she was completely, almost euphorically, energized. She loved the job. The joy she got from serving others, making a real difference in people's lives, made her feel hopeful and renewed in ways she'd thought lost to her.

Before she reached the kitchen, Nina's phone buzzed with a message from Ginny. Of course she jumped at the chance to join her two girlfriends for a midmorning workout, some lunch, and maybe shopping after. It felt like ages since she'd seen them.

Nina put her phone away before getting sucked into social media or the news, thinking both would bring her down on what appeared to be a glorious weekend morning. She found Simon in the yard, raking leaves onto a blue tarp.

"I'm going to join Ginny and Susanna at the gym," Nina announced.

"On Saturday?" Simon sounded perplexed.

"I keep canceling plans on them, and it's going to be harder for us to work out together now that I have my job. I could use it."

"I was hoping we'd work on the yard," said Simon, making his disappointment known. "Fall is the best time to lay down new grass seed. I was going to rent an aerator from Home Depot."

"I'm not stopping you," Nina said. "But I'm going to the gym with my girlfriends. Maybe Maggie or Connor can help."

But Maggie, who had been in the yard tossing a ball to Daisy, bolted in the opposite direction at the mention of her name, running unencumbered now that her boot was off, leaving Nina and Simon to watch her go.

"She'll come around," Nina said encouragingly. "Give it time."

"Yeah, sure." Simon sounded only sure of the opposite. "Have a good workout," he said. "I'll see you when you get back."

Nina felt a stab of guilt. He was trying so hard to form a family with her and the kids, and she needed to give him every chance to succeed. She'd apologize for leaving him in a bit of a lurch, but later.

"I'll be awhile," Nina said. "We're going shopping after."

Something shifted in Simon's expression, and for a moment Nina thought he'd give her that look she'd seen on the day he almost cut down those tree branches, but no, it was only a squint against the bright sun.

"Have a blast," he said.

* * *

Nina did as Simon suggested—she had a blast. Las Tres Amigas, Nina, Ginny, and Susanna, together again, burned it up at the studio with leg raises, plié squats, and a host of other tortures. Afterward, the women enjoyed a light lunch, and Ginny ordered a glass of wine.

"Why do you think I work out?" Ginny said, raising her glass, and they all laughed.

A text from Maggie informed, did not ask, of her plans to go over to Ben's for the day, which for Nina was a major relief. No need for her and Simon to pal around, not when Connor (he had played a Friday-night football game) was home and could lend a hand. Ben had been a true blessing, and the Odells, who had picked up Maggie an hour ago, were an incredibly sweet family. The more she learned how they were raising Ben, with less tech and more culture, the more she respected and even wished to emulate them.

Nina had a passing thought: she didn't tell her daughter nearly enough how proud she was of her resilience. Maggie's fighting spirit often moved Nina to tears. Secretly, she wished a nasty case of shingles on Laura Abel and her mother, but thoughts of Maggie's unfair treatment at school yielded to the more pressing demand of planning the upcoming girls' weekend.

Their annual sojourn to Connecticut took place at the beach house Ginny's parents owned. Las Tres Amigas, along with three other women from town, would stay up too late, eat and drink too much, and justify it all with the long walks they would take, each Fitbit tracking calories burned and thus earned. Nina had her misgivings about leaving Maggie at home with Simon, but it was only a weekend away and Connor would be there to act as a buffer.

"We need a shopping list," Susanna said.

"Okay. Wine," said Ginny, as she sipped from her glass

out on the patio of Pressed Café, the lunch spot close to where they'd exercised. "Red and white. What else do we need?"

"Earplugs," Nina and Susanna said in unison, an obvious reference to Ginny's snoring. Everyone laughed, and in that moment Nina lost sight of all her troubles.

* * *

Simon was all smiles when she returned home some six hours after she had left, with a car full of groceries and bags from a shopping trip to the outlets. Thanks to her paycheck, she felt comfortable to splurge a bit on herself.

"What's gotten into you?" Nina asked, eyeing Simon suspiciously. It seemed she'd been forgiven for her choice to work out instead of pulling weeds. He was sweaty, but his pants weren't dirty from yard work, nor were his hands.

Simon's smile lengthened, making him look giddy as a teacher on the verge of summer break.

"I've got a surprise for you," he said, "but you've got to put this on first."

Reaching into the front pocket of his jeans, Simon removed a bandana that belonged to Connor.

"Um, babe. The children are home . . . or at least Connor is, and I'm not really into that."

Simon looked at her curiously until it dawned on him. "No, not that," he said. "Put it on. Trust me."

Nina took the bandana, unnerved but mildly intrigued. She tied the fabric around her head until the bright sunshine was no more.

"Can you see?" Simon asked.

"No."

"Promise?"

"Promise."

His voice sounded closer, and then from nowhere she felt a breeze near her face. She didn't flinch because she couldn't see anything, but guessed the breeze had been Simon waving his hand in front of her, testing the blindfold. He took hold of her hand.

Where is Connor? Nina wondered. *And what the heck is Simon up to?*

"Trust me," Simon said, his voice a bit flat and affectless, his earlier enthusiasm now undetectable.

Why? What is going on?

Nina battled back her nerves to allow him to lead her across the lawn, then up the front stairs, into the foyer, and then partway down the hall. She heard a door open, the door to the basement, and her heart revved slightly. *Why down there?*

"What are you doing?" she asked nervously, but he didn't answer. Instead, he led her down, step by step, into the musty basement.

"Simon, you're freaking me out a bit," Nina said. She listened for other sounds, wondering again where Connor might be. Hearing nothing helpful, Nina focused on Simon's even breathing, using it as a guide, but took no comfort from his proximity. Something felt off to her.

"Last step," Simon said, lifting her hand as he helped guide her to the ground floor. "Follow me."

Nina fought the urge to rip the blindfold off and advanced with trepidation, taking short steps, unsure what obstacles could be in her way or what awaited her. Maybe he and Connor had finally gotten their robot working.

As he pulled her to a gentle stop, Simon turned Nina around like she was about to play the piñata game. Then he came up from behind, leaning his body against hers as he fiddled with the loose knot he had tied. Putting his mouth to her ear, he whispered, "Are you ready?"

Ready for what?

Simon removed the blindfold with a flourish, allowing light to flood her eyes. As soon as her vision focused, Nina saw Connor standing there with a wrench in his hand. Next to him was a brand-new Bowflex home gym and elliptical trainer. A large area had been cleared of boxes to make room for the equipment.

"Now you don't have to worry about getting to the gym on workdays or not being here to help with the lawn," Simon said with a proud look on his face. "You can get all you need for your workouts right at home."

"It's awesome, Mom," Connor said, demonstrating the bench press for Nina's benefit.

"He was great at helping me put it together," said Simon. "I went to get the aerator at Home Depot, but Walmart was next door, and, well, I had a thought. They couldn't deliver until Monday, but luckily both boxes fit in my truck."

"What do you think, Mom?" Connor asked. He had a proud smile, wide as a canyon.

What did she think?

The equipment had to cost thousands of dollars. Glen never would have been so thoughtful, let alone as generous. She kissed Simon tenderly on the cheek.

"I love it," Nina said, knowing how hard Connor had worked setting it up, how much thought and money Simon had put into the gift. She hoped her voice didn't betray how she honestly felt—trapped.

CHAPTER 28

Monday couldn't come fast enough. All I could think about was my father and his promise to chat online at noon. Ben skipped lunch to be with me in the library, but it was his idea, not mine. We both shared the same concern: that it wouldn't be my dad on the other end of the app; that it was someone pretending to be him, someone who knew about Tracy Nuts and maybe got lucky guessing his goodnight ritual, because, to Ben's point, parents say stuff like that. Together, Ben and I came up with five questions only my father would know the answers to—five questions that would prove he was alive, he had reached out to me, and he trusted me, and me alone, with his secret.

"Are you ready?" Ben asked.

I checked the time: almost noon. I'd thought about this moment every second of the day. And it felt like every second mattered, too, because judging by the way Mom gushed at dinner about the new fitness equipment Simon bought her, it wouldn't be long before I completely lost her to *him*. Whatever. When she finds out Dad's alive, when he comes home, then Simon will have to be gone, and this will be something for me to talk to my therapist about.

"Ready," I said to Ben, as I looked over the questions I'd

written and rewritten at least a dozen times, searching for the right ones that would leave no doubt.

"What if it's him?" Ben asked. "Are you going to tell anybody?"

By "anybody" I knew he was talking about my mom.

"Not if he doesn't want me to," I said.

"Are you sure?"

"What if he vanishes again? There's got to be a reason he doesn't want my mom and Connor to know."

"Yeah, like the police," Ben said.

"I'm not going to break his trust again," I said. "I told you, I feel guilty enough about that."

Ben did not look convinced that keeping this secret was a good idea. Then again, it's easy to judge other people's choices. He didn't lose his dad for almost two years. He wasn't living with Simon. My throat dried up as hot tears flooded my eyes.

Ben touched my shoulder gently. "It's okay," he said. "Give it some time. He won't forget to call."

I don't know how Ben knew exactly what to say, but he did. I'd read somewhere that kids with Asperger's had a hard time reading people's emotions, but Ben could read mine just fine. Maybe the label was wrong, or maybe he and I had a special connection. Either way, now wasn't the time to figure that out, because my phone buzzed. It felt like lightning had hit my body. I tensed, then relaxed. I checked the display. It was a Talkie message from Tracy Nuts.

It read:

Hi sweetie.

My breath caught, and those tears returned, but this time they were tears of joy. I knew it in my heart, my soul, my gut—every bit of me knew with a hundred percent certainty (no, make it a thousand, a million percent) that I was chatting with my father.

Hi Daddy.

My hands shook so badly I could barely type the words.

I miss you, Bunny.

And there was one of my questions answered already, no prodding necessary on my part: What do you sometimes call me? What other nickname do you have for me besides Tracy Nuts? And the answer, since I was a little girl, was Bunny, even though I hated it and had wanted him to call me something cooler, like Bear, but he kept forgetting and called me Bunny instead. Those tears in my eyes rolled down my cheeks, and Ben, usually so in sync with me, suddenly looked really uncomfortable. I typed:

Where are you?

I'm not anywhere close. Can't tell you where I am.

Why not???

My three question marks could have been four hundred.

There are reasons. Reasons for everything.

Please tell me.

I can't. I'm sorry.

Why? I don't understand.

You will. In time. You're the only one I can trust,
Maggie.

Now I felt even worse about telling Ben, but I had some
trust issues of my own to get over. I was sure, so sure, this
was my dad, but my remaining four questions would be the
final proof.

I typed, imagining what a puddle I'd be if I heard his voice:

Can you call me?

Not today.

Dad, I have to make sure it's really you. You understand.

Yes. Understood. You're a smart girl. Always were.

I smiled because that was something my father would say.

Where were we when I slipped on some wet rocks and
scraped my knee on barnacles?

My dad would remember that fall. I had screamed like
I'd been stabbed, even though after we cleaned the wound it
wasn't much of anything at all.

Cranberry Island, Maine.

The response came back as fast as if he'd said it aloud. A
tingle shot through my body. I showed Ben the phone and
nodded.
Two right.
Three to go.

CHAPTER 29

Glen read the question and wanted to cry.

In the beginning, all he knew were tears. But at some point, he couldn't say when, the pain, his endless suffering, became less intense as it morphed into a persistent, almost dull ache. The relentless, piercing agony of those initial days, months even, after his disappearance couldn't have gone on forever. At some point the body and mind had to accept their fate. He had to do what humans had done for eons—adapt to survive. But what Glen was most thankful for was his capacity to endure. Otherwise, he'd have surely gone insane by now. And if he couldn't do what was asked of him—and much was asked—everyone would suffer.

Glen had to focus for Maggie's sake, at least until this conversation was over. There'd be plenty of time for tears later. All he had was time.

Who's my best friend?

Right away, Glen realized this was a trick question, and his pride for Maggie surged with her cleverness. She was thinking someone might have studied her, tried to learn her habits to pull off a ruse. She was right to be cautious. Glen knew better than most that people really *did* study others that way. So how to answer? He could have put down Laura Abel, or even Benjamin Odell, but he knew neither would have been correct.

He imagined his daughter at school somewhere, because for once he knew the time of day. If he closed his eyes, he could see her blond hair and picture her sweet twelve-year-old smile. Then he realized, no, he had missed her birthday, so she was thirteen now, and the hole in his heart somehow managed to burrow a few inches deeper.

He eventually provided the correct answer to her question: Daisy. Maggie always went around saying Daisy was her best friend in the world.

Glen pictured them in his mind, his family, together as they once had been, before everything changed. He put them in their old house, even though he knew they were living across town now. He might have been absent all these months, going on years, but Glen knew everything about them—every soul-crushing detail.

Maggie's next question arrived:

What was my favorite Christmas present before we got Daisy?

Before Daisy, who would be five now, Glen calculated. So it would have been a present from at least six Christmases ago. He thought a second, and soon it came to him. He lived his life over and over again in his mind. Memories were all Glen had now, so he collected, stored, and guarded them, like a starving man with dwindling rations. He'd go year by year, day by day if possible, trying to recall specific events, experiences that had once grounded him, but too often those moments were shrouded in the fog of time. Thankfully, this wasn't one of those moments.

He remembered that Christmas morning quite vividly. Maggie was six at the time, but the way she had cried with delight made it hard to believe something so loud could come from a body so small.

They were gathered in the living room, a fire roaring in the fireplace, with a bright and glittering tree nearby. The scents of pine and gingerbread came to Glen as though he'd been transported back there. Nina, beautiful Nina, hovered behind young Maggie, waiting with nervous anticipation. She had begged for a Barbie DreamHouse for so long, lobbied like she was running a political campaign, the wait had been almost as excruciating for them as it had been for their daughter.

The memory surfaced with an ache both raw and primal. Now having his daughter so close, being connected to her this way, made his pain unbearable. Tears sprang to his eyes as his throat closed up.

Glen gave his answer and once again he was right.

The next question he got right as well. The Family Kettle—that was the name of the restaurant they had vowed never to eat at again because of the terrible food and service.

Shifting position, Glen hoped to alleviate the persistent ache in his back, but there wasn't much space to maneuver. His secret room behind the basement stairs was made of concrete and smelled of dust and mold. The room was exactly eight-by-eight-by-eight. He had measured it with his hands and feet countless times, irrationally thinking it might somehow have become a little larger.

Technically the space *was* larger, but two layers of wall had been put in, with a double row of studs along each interior side. The layers had been filled with a noise-damping compound, applied with a caulking gun. Sound clips placed between the studs and drywall provided an additional barrier for sound. The walls and ceiling also had high-end sound-proofing acoustic panels. The carpeted floor was sound-proofed like the walls. Every crack had been filled in with that acoustical caulk. He had named the space behind the stairs "the box." With the door closed, nobody could hear Glen, even if he screamed.

Breathable air was a concern, and for that the room had been outfitted with an energy recovery ventilator, which brought in fresh air from outside while simultaneously pulling stale, contaminated air outdoors. In essence, the ERV system was the lungs of the space. Humidity and temperature were kept consistent and comfortable such that the space was warm during the cold months of winter and cool in the heat of summer. Glen didn't know everything about the engineering and installation. He knew only that it had been professionally done.

A single twin mattress rested on the floor, stained, no sheet, one blanket—his bed. A blue bucket, lined with lye to fend off foul odors—his bathroom. Dirty paper plates and fast-food wrappers littering the floor near his malnourished body—his food. A plastic pitcher and plastic cups—his water. A television was brought in only on special occasions, but it did provide one source of stimulation and entertainment. Food, shelter, water—Glen had the absolute bare minimum to sustain life, but alive he was.

Bolted to the floor in the center of his room was a heavy-duty cargo-securing base, a metal plate with a twenty-ton D-ring attached. Secured to the D-ring was a carefully measured length of grade 70 transport chain. Connected to the chain was a stainless-steel shackle, secured around Glen's ankle.

"You did good."

The voice, even after all this time, still set a chill against Glen's skin.

Simon Fitch knelt in front of the open door to the room behind the stairs with a cell phone in his hand. Markings on the floor, pieces of electrical tape, indicated the safe zone, a spot for Simon to stand where Glen, held back by his length of chain, would not be able to reach him. Simon had spent much time and money getting the box prepared just right, and he'd been happy to share his ingenuity with the room's lone occupant.

These days, Simon often ignored his safety zone markings. He knew Glen was in no condition to attack him, nor was he all that interested anymore. The fight had been sucked out of him. Simon had been Glen's only source of companionship for nearly two years, his sole human contact. These days Glen actually welcomed Simon's visits, hoped for them. Loneliness bred strange companions.

Glen always asked for news of his family, any chance to be connected to them, even by proxy. But this was the most contact yet. Maggie was on the other side of that phone, as if an invisible wire connected them. He'd never felt such joy and despair at the same time.

Simon might have taught history, but he knew technology, too. He figured out how to make those calls and texts to Maggie impossible to trace. Something about using internet proxy servers located overseas. As an extra precaution to make sure she never suspected him, Simon learned how to schedule messages so he could be with Maggie when she heard from Glen.

"I've got to get back to school," Simon said, sitting cross-legged on the cement floor of the basement just outside the box. Glen knew that his prison was in the basement of Simon's lake house. It was the same home supposedly rented to vacationers, and was a short drive from the middle school, making it a convenient distance for brief visits during lunchtime. The basement had no furniture on which Simon could sit. The only thing down here, aside from the HVAC system, was that TV.

Simon had constructed a secret door complete with a concrete façade, so when it was closed it looked exactly like a basement wall. There was a thin outline of a door, but it was hardly noticeable. He added a gate latch to one of the bricks in the façade. Push on a special brick just so—only from the outside—and it released the latch, allowing the door to open.

It was an ingenious hiding place, since anyone who happened to venture down into the cellar would see a wall and not the man held prisoner by a chain bolted to the floor behind it. The chain was an added precaution in case Glen somehow figured out a way to open the door. Most of the time Simon left Glen alone in his box.

In the early days of his captivity, Simon had been quite cruel. He took twisted pride in having total power over his captive. He reveled in taunting Glen with stories of Nina and the children, like an alpha dog marking his territory. Simon had wanted everything, every single moment Glen spent in the box, to hurt.

One time, before Simon and Nina moved in together, he brought her into the basement while giving her a tour of the house. He had placed a wireless speaker inside the box so Glen could hear her voice, but she couldn't hear him no matter how loud he called out to her.

Sitting cross-legged in his room behind the wall, tears streaming down his face, Glen had listened as Nina made comments about the basement being so clean and neat, how it didn't feel damp at all.

They didn't stay long, but Simon returned later to gloat.

"Your wife is so hot in bed," he had told Glen. "She loves doing things with me she never did with you. She told me I'm the best she's ever had. She's glowing right now, positively glowing, in my bed upstairs."

Glen had lunged at Simon, who stood in the safety zone, so the chain pulled tight, and his outstretched fingers brushed only air. He could move in any direction inside the box, but only within a six-foot radius. When Simon needed to get closer—to remove the ankle shackle so Glen could change his clothes, for instance—he always kept his Taser at the ready. But Glen had learned his lesson. There was no escape.

Simon, too, had become more subdued, even compassionate. Mutual dependency had forged a strange bond between captor and captive.

"We need to end this chat now," Simon said. "I'll do the typing, you answer any questions." A smile came to his face, eerily lit by the phone's bright display. "Let's see Nina keep working when her daughter's an emotional wreck," Simon remarked to himself.

Ever since Nina took that job, Simon had been pressing Glen for ways to force her to quit. Glen did not begin to understand this obsession, nor did he understand any of the forces behind Simon's behavior, including his all-consuming need for Nina. But Simon was right to believe that Nina would quit if she felt her job was negatively impacting Maggie. He understood this without any help from Glen.

"Remember what I told you," Simon warned. "Remember the consequences."

The consequences, as Simon had made abundantly clear from the start, were that if Glen failed to cooperate, tried in any way to warn Maggie, he would kill the entire family. He threatened to do it slowly and brutally and livestream it for

Glen to watch. He said he might even kill Glen and stage the crime to look like a murder-suicide.

Glen, broken in body and spirit, close to madness, had done Simon's bidding and deceived his daughter to protect his family. But how much longer could he do his part to keep them all safe?

CHAPTER 30

Ben handed me tissues he'd brought, knowing I'd need them even before I did. I started typing fast, my fingers flying over the digital letters, writing exactly what was in my head.

> Please come home.

> > I can't Maggie.

> Please. You've got to help. You've got to get him out of the house.

> > Get who out?

And that's when I stopped: Dad didn't know. He didn't know we'd moved. He didn't know that Mom was with Simon. He didn't know any of it, because he'd already been gone when it all happened.

> > What's going on? Is Mom seeing somebody? Are you living with this person now?

I hesitated before showing Ben the exchange, looking to him for guidance.

Tell him the truth, his shrug back to me said.

Part of me agreed. If Dad didn't know what was happening, he might not realize how important it was for him to come home—before Mom became Mrs. Simon Fitch. But another part of me worried about upsetting him, hurting him more than he was already hurting.

In the end, the truth won out. I texted him about Simon and told him everything, explaining it as best I could in textspeak, mostly letting him know we were in a new house with Simon and that I didn't trust him.

Why? he asked.

So many reasons. I'd have to tell you by phone.

I thought: *And I need to hear your voice.*

Is your mom happy? he wrote. Not the reaction I was expecting.

What does that matter?? He's not you!

I've done things. Things I'm ashamed of.

I know what you did. The waitress. Don't care.

No. You don't know everything. Nobody does. And I can't tell you. You just have to trust me.

Please tell Mom you're alive. I have to tell her. I can't keep this a secret.

MAGGIE, NO!!!!

All caps. Serious business.

IF SHE FINDS OUT IT WILL BE VERY BAD FOR ME.

All caps again.
Ok, I wrote, feeling really crappy about upsetting him and
guilty for having told Ben.

> I'm serious, Maggie. Mom will tell the police, and if you
> tell Connor, he'll tell Mom. I can't have that. OK? Wish
> I could explain but can't. Trust me. Tell me about this
> new guy.

I typed as fast as my thumbs could move.

> He's SUPER creepy. He was OK for a bit. Got worse
> when we moved in together and Mom started working.

I added a bunch of grimacing-face emojis—a yellow face
with clenched teeth—for emphasis.
I kept typing.

> He has this hidden rage. Saw it once. Like a serial killer!!
> Tried to record it with my phone. Broke his gun to get him
> mad but he winked at me like he knew what I was doing.
> And he freaked out about some tree branches. Lied
> about a trip. And made fun of me in front of the whole
> school! Too much to type. But trust me. He is CRAZY
> CRAZY!!

Nothing came through for a bit. I held my breath and
then . . .

> OK. I'll look into him. Promise.

I suddenly felt a whole heck of a lot better. Maybe my dad could dig up some dirt on Simon. Maybe with my father's help, even from afar, there was a way we could rid ourselves of him once and for all. I wanted to talk to my dad for hours, but he had other plans.

I have to go, he wrote.

When can we talk by phone?

Not sure. Stay strong, Bunny. I love you.

And that's when I burst into tears again.

The rest of the day passed in a blur. I read and reread our text exchange a hundred times, thinking about what he could have done that made it impossible for him to come home. I wondered what he might learn about Simon, almost hoping it was something bad, something serious, proof that we were in grave danger, and it would force Dad out of hiding. I didn't pay much attention in my classes until I got to science. Our lab was due—the one on stress and body temperature—but when I went to hand it in, I couldn't find it in my backpack.

I emptied my backpack, searched every folder and notebook, but it wasn't there. That was impossible—I remembered putting it in my backpack the night before. But my teacher didn't really care what I said I did. She only cared that it wasn't on her desk with all the other labs.

A thought came to me: Simon had been in the library with us that day. He knew about the lab and how important it was for our grade. When I called Mom, my voice shaking with anger, to tell her what had happened to my homework, why my science grade was going to be a D, why Ben was going to stop being my friend, and who was responsible for the missing lab, I got her voice mail. That damn job! So far, I think it was the only thing Simon had been right about.

On top of the massive guilt I had over the secret I was keeping, I knew I'd soon have a different challenge to face: convincing my mom that Simon had intentionally taken my lab report. How much, I wondered, could I take before I snapped in half like I was one of those tree branches Simon obsessed over and he was the saw, slowly, methodically, cutting me down.

CHAPTER 31

Nina got the phone message from Maggie, followed up by another call that she was able to answer. Her daughter was in hysterics, at points incoherent. The reason for her calls: her lab report was inexplicably missing and surprise, surprise, she was blaming Simon for the disappearance.

Maggie couldn't say why Simon might have taken it, only that she was sure he did. Eventually she calmed down because there wasn't anything Nina could do to fix the situation. She was headed to Carson after work, not home, though Nina had told Maggie that she needed to work late again.

"Glad your job is going so well," said Maggie after Nina made her evening plans known. It was a perfect blow to unleash a fresh torrent of guilt.

Nina had had that heart-to-heart with her daughter the previous night as Simon had suggested, but Maggie denied being upset about the job. It seemed her daughter was equally skilled as Simon at delivering mixed messages in that regard. Then again, it made sense to Nina that Maggie would try to hide her true feelings. Nina made it quite clear she loved working again.

Thinking of Maggie's sacrifice brought on a nearly irresistible pull to get home, but there was another pull with even more force taking her in the opposite direction. Nina had to know. She simply had to confront Teresa.

Nina called Simon after speaking with Maggie, to warn him of the coming storm.

"It's always something with her," Simon said, sounding more exasperated than normal. "Thanks for the heads-up. I'll prep myself. I'm not going to say I told you so, but—"

He didn't bother finishing his sentence, and Nina didn't need to hear it. The timing for her next bit of news couldn't have been worse.

"So hon, Rona's put a new case on my desk, and I have to jump on it right away, bit of a family emergency. I'll be home a little late. Do you mind eating without me?"

She pictured Simon alone with Maggie sulking at the kitchen table and guilt ate away at her anew. A protracted silence ensued.

"I'd say we've got a bit of an emergency on our hands, too," Simon said. "What time?"

His voice carried an edge, notable only because he so seldom spoke with one.

"Maybe after seven," Nina said.

A worry struck her: *What if he drives by The Davis Family Center and sees no lights on? But why would he?* she asked herself. *Because lying takes effort . . . because eventually everyone gets tripped up in their deceits . . . because secrets don't stay hidden forever.* Nina silenced the chorus in her head.

"Another late night," Simon said, still no joy in his voice. He wasn't asking for details about the new, albeit fictional case. No, he sounded downright angry. Nina contemplated abandoning her plan, but she was committed now.

"I know it's been hard," she said, putting extra sweetness in her voice. "I promise it'll get better once I get my rhythm going. It's an adjustment period, that's all."

"I understand, darling," Simon said, his tone brightening. "Not to worry."

"Thanks, babe." Nina breathed easier.

"You know," said Simon, "since you've been so focused on your job, and it's been a lot more all-consuming than either of us thought, and with all the issues at home, perhaps you shouldn't go on that girls' weekend with Ginny and Susanna?"

"What? No!" Nina sounded indignant. "We've had it planned for ages."

"Well, that's before you took a new job that's taking up all your time, and before I made things even worse with Maggie. And now this lab report disaster? I hate to say that I could use a buffer around here, Nina, but you're putting a lot on me."

"Connor can look after Maggie when I'm away; you don't have to do anything."

Nina's voice carried a gasp of desperation; she'd been looking forward to this weekend for ages, but her earlier misgivings, the same ones Simon expressed, had returned with a vengeance.

"That's really not my point, is it?" Simon rebutted. "Things are falling apart here. You're working all the time and then you're going off with your girlfriends. That leaves me to deal with everything and it doesn't exactly seem fair. That's what I'm talking about."

Nina swallowed hard, because a part of her understood his logic and agreed. She also wanted to avoid a fight at any cost, because right now her focus was on matters more pressing.

"I get it, I really do," she said. "I'll talk to Ginny and Susanna, maybe we can reschedule."

Maybe they can get even more upset with me, Nina lamented.

"Thanks for being so understanding, honey. I'll have dinner waiting for you when you get home."

"Sounds good," Nina said. "Thanks, babe. Love you. Bye."

On the drive to Carson, Nina vacillated between two thoughts: what she would say to Teresa, and how on earth to break the news to Ginny and Susanna that her participation in the long-planned girls' weekend was now in doubt.

Both those concerns vanished the moment she set foot inside the Muddy Moose. The smell alone, sawdust, cooking oil, and beer, took her back to the first time she had gone there searching for the waitress.

A cluster of men sat at the dark bar, just as before, hunched over their respective beers, backs aglow in neon, with the mounted heads of dead animals keeping close watch. Additional patrons sat at the scattered pedestal tables, and, given the hour, Nina assumed they were part of a regular after-work crowd.

From the jukebox, the Eagles serenaded the crowd with a story about a lonely desperado. At the back of the bar, two double doors swung open, presumably leading to the kitchen, and out came Teresa, wearing a black top over a short skirt, high boots, and enough jangling jewelry to turn her into a walking wind chime. Even from a distance Nina could see the hardscrabble living fused to Teresa's face. Still, she was extremely pretty with that strawberry-colored hair, sexy in the way she carried herself with confidence, and once again it was easy to see why Glen had sutured his lips to her cheek and then to her lips in those kisses.

For a moment, the anger remained visceral—to think her husband had junked her for this woman. Nina was the old model traded in for a flashy (or trashy) newer one. She'd been put to pasture. She'd been made a damn cliché. But then Nina remembered that she was here to get information, and simmering anger would turn Teresa off. With a few deep breaths and long exhales, Nina managed to let go of any lingering animosity.

Teresa weaved between the tables, expertly balancing a tray of steaming hot food, most of it fished from the depths of boiling oil moments ago. She delivered the goods to a table of salivating young people with a smile that made it clear she understood what it meant to work for tips.

Approaching from behind, Nina tapped Teresa on the shoulder after she had jettisoned the heavy food. The marginally perturbed look on Teresa's face when she spun around suggested she was anticipating some complaint: a missing beer, wings without sauce.

"Can I help you?" Teresa sounded genuinely relaxed, not a hint of recognition in her eyes. Nina waited for her to make a connection that didn't come. Certainly, she'd have known from the news that her missing paramour had a family.

"I'm Nina, Glen's wife," she finally said, wishing she could subdue the shake in her voice.

Teresa returned a blank stare as she switched her tray from one hand to the other. "Have we met?" she asked.

Nina had her phone and the pictures at the ready. Teresa studied the images for a quiet moment, before her expression changed to one of utter surprise.

"What the hell is this?" she said. "Where did you get these? Who are you?"

"I'm Glen's wife, Nina."

Teresa gave a deep-throated laugh. "Holy shit. Is this a revenge thing? Are you armed? Honey, I swear to you I barely remember that night."

"Night? You were in love."

"What?" Teresa's painted eyebrows went up. "No, no, darlin', you got that all wrong. We were in lust, one drunken night only. One." A single finger raised in the air emphasized her claim.

"But the message?"

"What message?"

Nina showed Teresa the text she'd received along with the pictures, and could see the shift happen like a tide of sympathy rolling in. Whatever hardness lingered in Teresa's gaze emptied on the spot.

"Okay, okay, I think I know what's going on here," Teresa said, talking sweetly. "Well, not about your husband, but at least about these pictures. Let's you and I sit and talk."

CHAPTER 32

Nina grabbed an empty booth under a stuffed bison head, while Teresa headed to the bar to get them two Diet Cokes.

"Can't drink on the job," Teresa said, handing Nina a tall, ice-filled glass.

"And I can't drink and drive," said Nina.

"Well, this is weird, huh?" Teresa's opener elicited nervous laughter from Nina, but nothing else in response.

"The police were looking for you," Nina said. "You were on the local news as a person of interest in my husband's disappearance."

"Me?" Teresa put her hand to her chest. "Why? Do they think I killed him?" Teresa took note of Nina's pained expression. "I'm sorry, that was rude of me. I just—Glen was a regular, we were friends, but I swear to you, I swear, I had absolutely nothing to do with his disappearance. I was long gone before he vanished. What's it been? Almost two years? Do you think he killed himself?"

"I don't know what to think anymore," Nina answered sorrowfully. "They can't find his body. Maybe he faked his death to run away, start all over without the messiness of a divorce. I really don't know. The pictures. Who would have sent them to me? Why would someone say you two were in love if it was just a one-night thing?"

The revelation that Glen might not have had an affair—Nina still wasn't sure what to believe there—was surprisingly liberating. Sex was one thing, but an emotional attachment was a betrayal of a very different sort.

"I bet you anything it was Chris."

"Chris?"

"Yeah, my crazy ex. A real stalker type. He couldn't accept it was over between us. That's the reason I left town. Had to get away from him. Didn't leave any forwarding information; not even my best friends knew how to find me. That guy was going to kill me, I swear. It had to be Chris who took the pictures and sent them to you."

"Why would he?"

"My guess—from what you told me—to get the police involved so they'd launch a search to try and find me."

"From what I understand, the police didn't really go all out to find you," said Nina. "So it wasn't much of a search."

"Shouldn't have been." Teresa sounded mildly offended. "Like I told you, I'd left a month before he went missing. Why would the cops waste their time tracking me down? I'm guessing Chris saw the news report about Glen, recognized him from that creepy stalkerish photo he took, and figured you'd tell the cops about me. That way he could get a little petty revenge on the guy I slept with and get the police to go searching for me at the same time. God, he's such an asshole."

"How long have you been back?"

"A few months," Teresa said. "My mom's got COPD, so I came back to care for her. Don't smoke. Don't start."

"Don't intend to," said Nina. "What about Chris? Aren't you still afraid of him?"

"Not anymore. He's in prison in Concord," Teresa said. "Beat up his last girlfriend, surprise, surprise, so I have at least five years, maybe more, without having to worry about him."

Teresa reached across the table and patted Nina's hand. "Okay, talk to me, sweetie. I can't sit on my ass for long. Much as I'd like to, the boss frowns on that sort of thing. What else do you want to know?"

Nina's question came free-falling from her lips like the Tom Petty song now playing on the juke.

"What about that night with Glen? Can you tell me anything about it?" Nina felt her cheeks go hot. "Not the details, I mean, just, you know, how it happened."

Teresa gave another throaty laugh as she tossed her head back.

"Like I remember!" She grimaced with embarrassment. "Sorry, that sounds really, really cold. But it was a long time ago and we were all pretty far gone."

"All?" Nina got the sense someone else was involved.

"Yeah, it was me, Glen, and this other dude at the bar tossing them back. I knew Glen because, well, he came here a lot. Had the ring, though." Teresa pointed to her finger. "So I kept my distance. I was good like that—well, normally, I mean.

"Anyway, we would talk about fishing, or sports, or the bar. He was great at helping me with this crazy place." Teresa gestured behind her, as if Glen might be there, dealing with some personnel problem. "You wouldn't think it gets political here, but believe me, there's all sorts of shit going on behind the scenes, and Glen was really good at understanding people, figuring out what to say, how to smooth things over."

"He was a financial advisor at a bank," Nina told her. "He

understood people as well as he did numbers. It was a skill he prided himself on."

Teresa had people skills of her own, and took hold of Nina's hand as if sensing her growing distress.

Nina had imagined this moment for so long, what she'd say, how she'd say it. She had rehearsed it like a play— coming in all hell on wheels. "You give me some answers!" she had shouted in her mind. But this moment was nothing like her fantasy. She had no anger at all. Teresa might drink too much, smoke too much, definitely partied too much, but all of that was a big "whatever," because something about her, the ease of her being, the relaxed way she spoke, how she called her sweetie, and touched her hand, made Nina like this woman immensely.

"I didn't know that about Glen, the pride and all. Didn't know much about him because it was just a one-night thing. I swear. I had the evening off, and was hanging out here 'cause what else was I going to do? We were having a great time at the bar, things got a little heated as we got drunk, and the other guy said we should take the party to my place, and I was like, why the hell not? I'm not proud of it, but I also wasn't thinking very clearly. Anyway, the other guy passed out on my couch, took off without a good-bye, but your husband—well, he stuck around."

Teresa cringed a little. "I'm really sorry it happened, but that's the whole story and the truth."

Nina's eyes were filled with doubt.

"I can tell you don't believe me," Teresa said. "And I don't blame you. But if you ever find Glen, ask him, and then you can be sure. It was one night only. I saw Glen maybe once or twice after that, and then I took off."

Nina gave a nod. She wanted to accept Teresa's story as the truth—part of her did—but she'd need to look Glen in the eyes to be certain.

"If Chris didn't send me that picture I never would have known any of this," Nina said, her voice getting softer.

"What are you doing here?" Teresa asked. "What is it you're chasing?"

"Answers," Nina said sorrowfully. "I hate not knowing."

"Why he cheated? I told you we were wasted."

"Not only that."

Nina quickly went through the narrative—the job Glen pretended to have and the money he stole from his own family to keep up the ruse.

"I don't know why the bank fired him, they wouldn't give me that answer, and now nobody can find Glen."

"Oh my, that's a lot of secrets for one man to keep."

"Tell me about it," Nina said, again exchanging a knowing look with Teresa. "When you hung out with him, did he say anything about me, his wife?" Nina's crooked smile acknowledged the silliness of talking about herself in the third person.

"Not much, no."

"He didn't . . . criticize her . . . me . . . any?"

Teresa got a faraway look in her eyes, maybe drifting back to memories of friendly chitchat at the bar before alcohol tore down all inhibitions.

"No, we didn't talk about you like that. You were the wife, that's all, and there were his kids, but he didn't talk about them much either. He told me he had business in Carson, but fished every chance he got. I got the sense there was more to the story there, but no idea what a screwed-up story it was. Like I said we were . . . you know . . ."

"Bar buddies," Nina said, allowing a little bit of bitterness back into her heart. The rest didn't need to be said. "And he didn't complain about me, his family, not ever?"

"No, but don't kill yourself trying to figure it out. Men can be crazy. The first time I broke up with Chris he faked having cancer so I'd feel sorry for him. Then, I found out it was all bullshit, and that's when I broke it off for good."

"That *is* crazy."

"It's no biggie," Teresa said with a wave of her hand. "He'll be away for a long time. But picking a man can be like reaching into a bag of jelly beans, you just never know what flavor you're going to get."

"I have a new man," Nina said, offering up the information like a reflex. Perhaps she was hoping Teresa, an impartial third party, could waylay her lingering concerns.

"Tell me about him," Teresa said, her eyes sparking a bit. "I've got about five minutes before I'm on the unemployment line, and much as I hate it, I need this job."

Nina talked about Simon, how they met thanks to Daisy, and about his job as a teacher, how she'd been judged for moving on so quickly with a new man, how his tragic past and hers might have helped speed up their union, and how wonderful he'd been to her since he'd come into her life. For whatever reason, Nina felt compelled to share, in brief, her struggles with Maggie. For sure it all took more than the allotted five minutes, but Teresa didn't complain.

"No surprise there," she said in reference to Maggie. "It's hard for a kid. It was hard for me."

"You had a stepfather?" Nina asked.

"I wish," Teresa said sharply. "I had four."

"Oh."

"Look, I know you didn't come here for my advice," Teresa said, "but I'm going to give it to you anyway, because you seem like a really sweet girl, and your husband was a real shit, so I'm going to give you my two cents and then I've gotta split. Time is money."

"I'm all ears," Nina said, leaning forward, catching that faint whiff of tobacco again.

"Make sure you really know this new guy of yours. Make

really damn sure. I made that mistake with Chris, and it's one mistake I'll *never* make again."

*   *   *

On the drive home Nina thought about Teresa's warning. There were still things about Glen she didn't know—why he'd lost his job, for one, if he had had other "flings," for another. She'd come to the Moose hoping that insights into his choices would help her feel more comfortable with her own. Instead she left feeling an urgent need to get windows into Simon's life. But how? His parents were gone. There was no extended family to contact. No place to turn for clues—or in Teresa's words, to really get to know him—unless of course she went to Simon himself for answers. But hadn't she done that? Hadn't they talked, and talked, but did she feel any closer to an understanding? No, not really.

Just before reaching home Nina had a thought and brought her car to a stop in a strip mall parking lot. She used her phone to access a usually reliable source of information.

Google.

She had long ago googled Simon's name, because of course she'd do that before bringing a new man into her life. What had come up was nothing remarkable: links to school-related matters, pictures of him in his Revolutionary War garb from the school website, articles about robotics competitions his team had won, and a few mentions of Emma Dolan's tragic suicide on news and tribute sites. She had researched Emma as well, but had never looked into Emma's family, because it didn't seem relevant. But now she was realizing there was a hidden history there she could mine for information.

Again, she heard Teresa's voice in her head, urging her along. Sitting in her car, she googled Emma Dolan's name, searching for other avenues to explore. She read the obituary.

There was a brother mentioned in addition to the parents, aunts, uncles, and husband she had left behind: Hugh Dolan. She googled Hugh's name and got a number of hits from—of all places—the Manchester, New Hampshire, police department website, detailing his numerous arrests for drug possession. It did not take a lot of research for Nina to conclude that Simon's former brother-in-law, Hugh, was a drug addict—heroin and oxy, according to the police logs she read.

He was also on Facebook. Nina matched a profile picture to one of his posted mug shots.

Before she knew what she was doing, Nina had sent him a friend request, with a short message introducing herself as Simon Fitch's fiancée, because "girlfriend" didn't sound serious enough. A moment later, Nina's friend request was accepted, and a return message hit her Messenger in-box.

So you're the one, Hugh wrote. *We should talk.*

CHAPTER 33

Glen felt sick to his stomach.

He had lied to his daughter. Deceived her. Tricked her. What kind of father would do that to his child? He imagined what people would say about him if they knew.

Should have given her obviously wrong answers, you idiot! Then she'd know something wasn't right. She'd have gone to her mom, broken that promise she never should have made. They would have gone to the police and figured it all out. The police would have protected your family from Simon, and eventually they would have found you and freed you. You fool! You dummy! You dolt!

They could think that, but they'd be wrong. They didn't live with Simon. They weren't *in* the box. The box changed a person. It broke them in every way.

He was afraid. It was as simple as that. One wrong answer would bring the worst consequences. He saw blood. Gashes to Nina's face, deep slashes across Maggie and Connor's throats. He saw himself watching their deaths via a live video feed.

The horrific visions consumed him. He believed Simon, took him at his word, and in his heart Glen knew he was right to believe.

So many moments over these months Glen had wished for death. He was already entombed; all he needed was for his heart to stop beating. He thought about using the chain to choke himself to death, or go on a hunger strike, even stop drinking water, but again fear held him back. He couldn't and wouldn't leave his family to Simon.

He knew eventually, soon perhaps, there'd come a tipping point. Nina would upset Simon more than she already had with that job of hers. Maggie would cross him one too many times . . . and then the blood . . . then the knife to their throats. So Glen existed—he breathed, ate, pissed, defecated, solely to keep Simon from acting impulsively—or worse, violently—taking from his situation the only parts he could control so that his family might live another day. He had no other purpose.

Horrible as it was to lie to her, it was also unbelievably uplifting to be connected with his daughter again. He felt human. The proximity was intoxicating. He felt like a castaway catching the glow of a distant rescue ship; his heart never felt so full. Alive again. Alive.

When he closed his eyes, Glen transported himself out into a field with Maggie, playing catch with lacrosse sticks and a ball. He felt the sun on his face, so bright and warm, the wind rustling through his hair; he inhaled fresh spring air deep into his lungs. Oh, how he longed to breathe fresh air again. Roll in the grass. Touch the earth. Gaze at the sky. Hug his daughter. Tell her how sorry he was for everything, for tricking her, for lying to his family.

Tricks.

That was how he got into the box in the first place—a dirty, nasty trick.

Suddenly, Glen wasn't in that field anymore. He was back at the Muddy Moose, reliving the day he first met Simon. He was at the bar, talking with Teresa, doing what he always did back then, nursing a beer because money was tight. Hiding out. He didn't want to be anywhere near Seabury, and Carson had good fishing, so it was as fine a place as any to try and get his life going in the right direction again. But that effort wasn't going anywhere; he wasn't lying to himself anymore. At least he liked the town. He liked the waitress, too. He even liked the man who called himself Bill, who was loose with his wallet and quick with the jokes. Bill had dark hair and a mustache, but those were disguises, worn in case Glen recognized Simon from home.

The whiskey went down easy and then easier. At some point the room was tilting and Glen's hand made its way to Teresa's leg. Or had Simon—as Glen now knew him—put it there? Glen didn't remember. He knew only that he was feeling very drunk. Confused. Then he was outside. A flash. Photographs. He didn't see anyone taking those pictures, but Simon had shown them to Glen enough times so he knew it had happened. He *had* kissed Teresa outside the Muddy Moose. But even more happened, and later on Simon would tell Glen about the roofie he had slipped into his drink.

Lowers inhibitions and awareness. It lowers everything.

"Got to be more careful, buddy," he had lectured, when Glen was in chains. "Never lose sight of your drink at the bar. That's drinking 101. But I guess that's what they teach the ladies."

Glen woke up with a hangover like no other and no memory of how he ended up naked in those rumpled sheets, the smell of sex in the room and Teresa lingering nearby.

"Well, that shouldn't have happened," Teresa had said as she poured him coffee.

And it never happened again. Simon got what he had wanted—those two pictures to complete his plan and set everything in motion.

The next time Glen saw Simon it was at the boat launch.

Simon had scouted that spot on Lake Winnipesaukee numerous times and correctly anticipated no one but Glen would be there at that hour. Glen was always the first on the lake. It was a thing with him, a source of pride.

Simon parked his truck near Glen's. It was the same make and model as the one Glen drove, a purchase Simon had made a year before, anticipating this day. He wanted everything for Nina to feel familiar. It was the same reason he wore Glen's brand of cologne.

Simon climbed out of the cab and, for good measure, erected a barricade across the access road on which he placed an official-looking ROAD CLOSED sign purchased from the internet.

He approached Glen and Daisy with a friendly smile on his face, but no fishing pole in hand. Daisy barked as Simon grew nearer, but he had a dog treat at the ready to win her over.

"Sweet pup," Simon said, as he crouched to give Daisy a pat. When he stood, Simon drew his Taser and blasted Glen with a jolt. Glen didn't have time to raise his hands in defense. He fell to the ground, grunting, convulsing wildly. Simon fed Daisy a second treat to quiet her down, and then silenced Glen with electrical tape over his mouth. After that, Simon secured zip ties around Glen's wrists and ankles to further immobilize him.

Glen had no memory of this, but Simon lifted him off the ground and effortlessly threw him into his boat. He slashed Glen's arm with a Bowie knife, releasing enough blood to make him even woozier. He quickly applied bandages to the wound, knowing he'd suture the gash closed when he brought Glen home, applying the skills he had perfected on pillows.

Simon used his Taser on Glen a second time for good measure. When he moved him from the boat into his truck bed, Glen was, in Simon's words, limp as a rag doll. With Glen subdued, Simon got his boat into the water and, using more treats, coaxed Daisy aboard before piloting the craft toward the middle of the lake. He was careful not to step in any of the blood covering the deck. He wanted the blood to throw everyone off balance. Keep them guessing. Make Nina uncertain and unsure, which he equated with more vulnerability. Accident? Did he drown? Did he fake his death?

At a spot that felt right to him, Simon dove overboard. He had left his shoes in the truck, and he swam to shore in his clothing. The entire sequence took fifteen minutes and forty-two seconds to complete, a bit shorter than planned.

He retrieved his barricade, checked for fresh tire tracks and, seeing none, drove home with his passenger in the back of the truck. Simon carried Glen downstairs, put him in the room he had spent months constructing, changed him into a gray sweatsuit, and put him in chains.

Simon took great pleasure in sharing every detail of his plan with Glen, boasting of his cleverness, beginning with that fateful setup at the Muddy Moose. He had been tracking Glen's movements for years, studying his patterns. He knew Glen was as predictable as the tide. Almost without fail, Saturday mornings were spent fishing on the lake with his loyal dog, Daisy, serving as first mate. Sundays he was with Nina and the kids. Sometimes he'd go with them to church. He spent Monday through Friday hiding out in Carson.

But now he was Simon's guest, every single day.

And every day was basically the same. Boredom. That was something Glen would never overcome. He had his exercises—yoga to keep his muscles from shortening too much, along with a bodyweight routine he'd developed to keep them from atrophying completely. Simon would make regular checkups, make sure Glen was staying healthy enough. Too much weight loss, any sort of hunger strike, was always countered with threats of violence.

Glen had the TV, but it was only an occasional treat. Every two weeks, Simon would provide Glen with five books, mostly nonfiction, often topics related to history. Simon said it was to keep Glen's mind sharp so his brain didn't go to mush. Five books in. Five books out. That was the routine. Glen had those two weeks in which to read them all. New book day had become as intoxicating as those whiskies had been.

But today was even better. Today, he'd spoken to his daughter—well, sort of spoke to her. Excited as he was, guilt and regret ate away Glen's appetite. He was always hungry, but the hamburger Simon left for him had gone untouched. Food, like the books and TV, was another reward.

Suggest the best present for Nina—get greasy fries.

Give Simon something to say, a perfect compliment, something Nina would like to hear—maybe earn a cup of hot coffee.

The first question Simon had ever asked Glen was food-related: *What's your wife's favorite meal?*

Glen had told him: eggplant rollatine.

He got treats like a dog for doing Simon's bidding, but now he couldn't eat. His stomach was the size of a walnut.

Once Simon moved in with Nina, Glen was certain that would be it for him. It was the milestone he felt he'd been marching toward, the plank on which he walked. But after move-in day came and went, Simon did what he always did—pumped Glen for information about Nina and the kids.

It was Nina's unwillingness to say yes to Simon's marriage proposal that Glen now believed had saved his life. Simon wanted a ring on Nina's finger. He taunted Glen with his plans for marriage, but didn't seem to trust himself to keep the relationship going without more and more insider information. That was Glen's job, and he knew that once Nina and Simon were officially engaged, or more likely married, he was as good as dead.

He started to cry. He seldom cried anymore, but Maggie had opened a door in his heart long shuttered. Alive. She had made him feel alive. Human again. And now the worst had happened—in through that open door, Glen allowed hope into his heart.

Hope was a dangerous thing down in the box. Hope didn't belong here. Hope was a trick of the mind. No matter how hard Glen tried to suppress the feeling, up it sprang, like a blade of grass sprouting from muddy earth. Hope lived inside him now. What to do with it?

Glen's thoughts were as dark as the room. Simon had taken away his only light—a small battery-powered LED fixture that stuck to the ceiling, bright enough to illuminate the closet-size space. It was punishment for Maggie's obstinacy. "How dare she call me a serial killer," he had howled. "She doesn't understand. But we'll get her in line, won't we, Glen?" He had said it in a threatening way. No hidden meaning there.

"It will be hardest on Nina," Simon had mused. "The grieving, but I'll be there for her."

Glen had been made to believe this was all about Nina, for reasons still unknown, so why did Simon care so much about what Maggie thought of him? While motives were scarce, Simon's reaction had been illuminating. Finally, after all this time, Glen felt he had a critical bit of information, a crack, a sliver, a fingertip-size handhold from which he could hoist himself up and actually do something. Something, yes, but what? Chain. Box. No way out. But now . . . hope. Think. Think. And then it came to him. One possibility. Like that blade of grass growing a tiny bit taller.

The conversation with his daughter had unwittingly

revealed something of Simon's fractured personality. No doubt the tactics had advanced Simon's agenda, but the way Maggie spoke of him, her utter contempt, had wounded him deeply. Even though he was intentionally manipulating Maggie, and Nina as well, Simon clearly wanted Maggie to like him. *Why?* Glen could only speculate, but clearly Simon understood the way to a mother's heart was through her children.

Naturally, Maggie hearing from her father after all this time would make her act increasingly anxious. A distraught daughter might serve Simon's purpose in one sense by forcing Nina to leave her job, but it might also create a new set of problems by making Nina rethink her future with Simon as tensions built at home. Knowing his wife the way he did, Glen could see her thinking that this new man, not the new job, was the source of Maggie's growing distress.

Hope.

Glen thought: What if he promised Simon he could turn Maggie from an adversary into an advocate?

If he could somehow convince Simon to change tactics, make him believe Nina would blame the relationship for Maggie's distress, that she'd leave him before she'd quit her job, he might find a way out of the box. What Glen really wanted was some reason to get back in touch with Maggie. He needed to send her a message.

NICE GUY.

That was how he and Nina had met—a hidden message Glen had created using bold type in his online dating profile. It had stood out to Nina; so much so that she felt compelled to make contact. If Glen could deliver one more secret message, this time to his daughter, something that would stand out to her as well, maybe, just maybe, he could warn everyone of the terrible danger they were in.

CHAPTER 34

Nina exchanged a flurry of short messages with Hugh, the last of which included her phone number. He had asked for it and she had given it in a moment of pure impulsiveness. Apparently, what he had to say, the reason he felt they had to talk, could not easily be explained over text. Nina checked the time, realizing if she didn't start the drive home now, she'd arrive later than promised.

She navigated heavy afternoon traffic in the dark of late October, already missing the daylight hours and the leaves on the trees. Her focus vacillated between the road and what on earth Hugh Dolan could possibly tell her. Why was it so important that they speak right away? Obviously, it was about Simon; something negative, she supposed. But what?

When her phone rang, Nina jumped in her seat, startled, even though she'd been expecting his call. There was no name on the display, only numbers, so it could have been a telemarketer—goodness knows she was getting more robo-calls by the minute—but somehow she knew it was Hugh making good on his promise.

"Hello?" Nina answered tentatively.

"Is this Nina?" The man's raspy voice, coarse as bark, suggested a pack-a-day habit.

"Yes. Is this Hugh?"

The air inside Nina's car grew supercharged. Her knuckles whitened on the wheel.

"Yeah . . . it's uh, Hugh." He sounded out of it, not entirely sure of his answer.

"Thanks for taking the time to call," she said, talking quickly, nervously. There was no easy entry into this conversation. "What is it you wanted to talk to me about?"

Hugh exhaled loudly, leading Nina to believe he had blown smoke out of his lungs. "Where do you live? Can we meet in person?"

Nina tensed. That was the last thing she wanted. She knew his history—or at least the part that had put him behind bars. Hugh could be completely unstable, desperate for money. He might think she was easy prey.

"No, I'm afraid I can't do that," Nina said, choosing not to elaborate.

"Suit yourself," said Hugh. He made it clear he thought she was making a big mistake. "Let me ask you this: How long have you and Simon been together?"

"Two years," Nina said, stretching the time a bit, but not by much.

"How did you two meet?" he asked.

Nina weaved through traffic as she maneuvered to her exit, calculating she had about five minutes to devote to Hugh before she had to give her full attention to Maggie, still reeling from her missing lab report.

"We, um . . . we met through a friend," Nina said, fumbling for the words, lying to protect her location.

Hugh scoffed. "Lucky you." He sounded a sarcastic note.

"Hugh, what did you have to tell me?"

Irritation rose up inside her. Nina's urge to have this call over and done came on strong. Her grand vision of gaining some useful insights into Simon's past now seemed not only foolish, but quite possibly dangerous as well.

"Yeah, about that," Hugh answered, sounding as though he were about to drift off to sleep. "Maybe we could . . . um-mmm . . . work something out."

"Work something out? I'm sorry, I'm not following—"

Alarms began going off in Nina's head.

Hang up. Forget this. It was a stupid idea.

"Look, I'm a little short," Hugh said, his way of an explanation.

It took Nina a moment to realize he wasn't talking about his stature.

"Are you asking me for money?"

"I'm asking you for a fair exchange," said Hugh. "Money for me; information on Simon for you."

Nina stammered, searching for footing here. She had professional training on implementing treatments for alcohol and other drug problems, the role of domestic violence in drug addiction, and a host of other competencies, but none of them covered how to handle a drug addict extorting her for cash.

"I'm not paying you, Hugh," Nina said, her confidence buoyed from taking a stand.

"Suit yourself." Hugh was curt, but Nina didn't get the sense he was going to give up that easy.

"Can't you just tell me why you thought we should talk?"

Nina hit the exit ramp going ten miles over the speed limit, forcing her to pump the brakes to keep in control. She would be home in a few minutes. Time was running out, and every part of her wanted to know what, if anything, Hugh had to say. Again, she regretted giving him her phone number. Why had she been so cavalier about it? Now he could call her anytime, day or night. He could even threaten to tell

Simon she'd contacted him behind his back. She felt foolish and angry with herself, but there was nothing she could do about it now.

"I'll tell you this much," Hugh said. "You're not safe."

Nina's body seized as though she were moments away from a car crash, bracing for a collision.

"Why on earth would you say that?" Her question leaked out in a breathy whisper.

"Are you going to help me out here or not?" Hugh's patience was gone.

"What do you want?"

Nina didn't have to elaborate.

"Let's say an even grand."

An audible gasp rose from her throat. *Over a week's salary.*

"No," she said firmly.

"Okay. Okay. How about five hundred then," Hugh countered. "I have Venmo. You can send it to me right now."

Nina had no idea what Venmo was.

"What are you going to do with the money?" she asked.

"What do you care?"

Nina seldom gave money to panhandlers, because once she did, the choice of how they spent it was no longer in her control. Instead, she'd buy gift cards to a coffee shop or a fast-food place for those in need, and she donated to homeless shelters every year, even when money was tight. Five hundred dollars to Hugh Dolan could end up in his arm, killing him. She didn't want that on her conscience—couldn't handle that guilt.

"I'm sorry, Hugh. I can't do that."

"Suit yourself," Hugh said, and with that, the call went dead.

CHAPTER 35

Nina arrived home shaken and anxious, trying not to let it show. She had to focus on Maggie and the latest crisis. Daisy greeted her in the foyer, so excited that she reared up and put her front paws on Nina's waist, just like the day she'd come home from the lake in a police cruiser with blood matted in her fur.

Connor ambled in from the kitchen, drinking a ginger ale out of a tall, ice-filled glass, even though sodas were for weekends. The look he sent his mother was one of pure desperation.

"When do I go to college?"

He thumbed in the direction of the living room, where Nina found Maggie sulking on the couch, TV turned off.

"Hi, sweetheart," Nina said, sitting down beside her daughter. She placed her hand on Maggie's back, hoping to comfort her. Simon came into the room still dressed in his khakis and polo shirt from the school day, glasses in place, magnifying the worried look in his eyes. Maggie propped up on her elbows to glare at him.

"Why is *he* here?" she asked.

Nina tensed. "Young lady, you do not speak to Simon—or anyone for that matter—like that. Is that understood?"

"She's upset," Simon said. "And here I am, everyone's favorite scapegoat."

For once he sounded wounded. There may have even been tears in his eyes, and for good reason. The war between Simon and Maggie must have been taking an emotional, perhaps even a physical, toll on him. Nina comforted Simon with a quick hug. She felt an irrational fear bubble up that he could smell Hugh on her, as if they'd had an affair instead of a phone call.

"Where do you think it could be?" Nina asked, referencing the missing lab report. "Did you retrace your steps?"

Maggie made daggers with her eyes. "I put it in my backpack, and then when I went to hand it in to my teacher, it wasn't there. Where would it be?"

"Um, your room," Connor said. "Have you been in there? It's like a hurricane went through it."

"Yeah, because I've been looking for my stupid lab report."

"Well, how about printing off another copy."

"It's late so we already got a zero."

"Then why do you even need to find it?"

"Because I want to make sure I didn't misplace it, which I didn't, dummy."

"Maggie, that's enough!" Nina snapped.

Maggie shook off the rebuke like a boxer who had taken a jab to the chin.

"Whatever," she said, sliding off the couch. "It doesn't even matter now." Off she went, storming upstairs to her room, slamming the door.

Nina followed, and nearly had a heart attack when she entered Maggie's bedroom. "Hurricane" wasn't quite the right description—it was more like a hurricane had detonated a bomb. Drawers were open, papers were everywhere, and clothes from the closet now carpeted the floor.

"Oh, Maggie," Nina said, bending down to start the cleanup. Usually she'd have made it her daughter's responsibility, but not tonight, poor thing. She was obviously a wreck.

Maggie rested on her bed, facedown, head under a pillow, while Nina gathered up loose papers from the floor. If she hadn't had her head turned to the wall, Nina might not have seen the flash of white showing at the bottom of Maggie's desk. Pulling the desk away from the wall, Nina watched as a stack of stapled papers fell to the floor. She examined the cover page with widening eyes:

The Effects of Stress on Body Temperature
Lab Report by Maggie Garrity and Benjamin Odell
D-Block, Ms. Stone

"Is this what you've been looking for?" Nina asked, holding up the report for Maggie to see. Bolting from her bed like she'd been electrocuted, Maggie snatched the report from Nina's hands.

"Where did you find this?" she demanded.

"It was behind your desk," said Nina.

"No. No, it was not. I looked."

"Behind your desk? Really? You checked there?"

Maggie seemed suddenly unsure.

"Well, that's where it was," Nina said.

"I don't believe it!" Maggie spat out the words. "*He* must have put it there."

"Maggie!" Nina didn't mean to raise her voice, and felt even worse when her daughter flinched. Simon appeared in the doorway, drawn to Maggie's room by the commotion.

"What's going on?" he asked, the hurt still lingering in his eyes.

"This is what's going on." Maggie, red-faced, her jaw tight and teeth clenched, snatched the paper from Nina's hand and held it up for Simon to read the front page. Nina had not seen her daughter on the verge of a complete meltdown since her toddler years, but felt certain one was coming.

Simon read the cover page, nonplussed. "What's this?" he asked. "Is it the missing lab report?"

"It was behind her desk," Nina explained. "It must have fallen there."

"It didn't *fall* there, Mother," Maggie said with a growl in her voice. "*He* put it there."

"Enough!" Nina's booming voice bounced off the bedroom walls. Now she, not Maggie, was the one about to have a meltdown. It was everything—Glen, Wendy Cooper, Teresa, Simon, Maggie, Hugh, all of it, bubbling up into one volcanic eruption. "That is enough! Enough with these accusations! Maggie, what in heaven has gotten into you?"

"I put the report in my backpack," Maggie said, tears in her eyes, her voice cracking with emotion. "I remember doing it."

"Well, you must have thought you did. Again, I'm asking: Did you specifically look behind your desk while you were tearing your room apart?"

The place Maggie looked was at her feet.

"I think so . . . I don't remember."

"I'll take that as a no," Nina said. "Maggie, I understand that you miss your dad. I get it. I really do. But I'm running out of patience with you. I don't know how to help you get over the fact that Simon is a part of our lives now. Do you need a new therapist? Go see mine if you want. I'll call in the morning. I'm at a loss here, but we have to do something."

Nina felt utterly defeated. Just as her life was finally coming together after so much heartbreak, Maggie seemed determined to tear it apart. When she'd agreed to these new living arrangements, Nina never considered her relationship with her daughter would hit such a nadir.

"Whatever. You're never going to believe me anyway," Maggie said, stomping out of the room like she was putting out little fires beneath her feet.

When her daughter was gone, Nina slumped onto the edge of the bed and sighed deeply, feeling on the verge of tears. Simon sat next to her and placed his arm lovingly around her shoulders.

"Well, at least you found the lab report," he said encouragingly. "I'll talk to her teacher. We'll get the grade fixed."

"Thank you," Nina said appreciatively.

"But Nina—"

Simon seemed hesitant. Panic flooded her. *Did Hugh call?*

"I didn't know you were seeing a therapist," he said.

Nina's blood froze. She realized she had let it slip in the heat of the moment.

"Oh yeah . . . I know. I've been meaning to talk to you about that."

That's when Nina explained how she got Dr. Wilcox's name from Ginny.

"I had a bit of a breakdown after we moved in."

She reassured Simon she was perfectly ready for this new phase in her life, but still needed to sort through her feelings about Glen. She also confessed to wanting something for herself, a little part of her life that she didn't have to share with anybody.

Nina didn't mention Hugh, of course, or how she and Dr. Wilcox had talked about Simon and his insecurities, but now at least that topic could be broached without it being too awkward. She worried Simon would be wounded or upset, but his face was brimming with sympathy.

"We can't keep secrets from each other, Nina," Simon said in a sweet, understanding tone of voice. "It's not healthy for a marriage."

CHAPTER 36

Hours after everyone had gone to sleep, Nina was wide awake. She gazed up at the blackness of the bedroom ceiling, wondering if she had reason to doubt the man lying next to her. The cadence and rhythm of Simon's breathing while he slept wasn't as strange to her as it once had been, but she wasn't fully accustomed to it either. Years of marriage to Glen had carved a familiarity that was impossible to duplicate.

The contrasts between Simon and Glen were both subtle and profound. Simon slept on his right side; Glen his left. Simon's calf muscles were more developed than Glen's, but his arms were less so. Simon folded his tees and polo shirts with the precision of a clothing retailer, rinsed with mouthwash *before* using toothpaste, and so on. In so many ways he wasn't Glen, and yet there were similarities, too: the way he smelled no matter what cologne she bought, the things he said, the truck he drove, gifts he purchased—all reminded Nina of the last man to share her bed.

Was it because she missed Glen, couldn't get him out of her mind? Or was she looking for patterns instead of seeing simple coincidences? More important, were there darker connections between her two great loves, reasons to doubt, signs she was missing just as she had missed them before?

When Nina closed her eyes, it was Hugh's face she saw, the one from the mug shot—a disheveled, broken man, who could have been minutes from his last fix when his picture was taken. How on earth could she trust that person—a drug addict extorting her for money—over the man sleeping beside her?

You're not safe.

Hugh's words, like Maggie's warnings, hissed at her from the dark. So what to do?

Nina listened to Simon's breathing, felt his arm, which was warm to the touch. Warm because *he* was warm. He was warm, kind, and good to them. They *were* safe, she thought. Safe in a new home, in their new life together, safe from the betrayals and heartaches she'd suffered, and safe financially, too. It wasn't like he was a stranger. They'd been together for almost two years, not a few weeks. This wasn't some random hookup, Nina reminded herself. They were in a committed relationship. They *owned* a place together. If something were direly wrong with him, surely the questionable behavior would have surfaced by now.

But there were *changes,* she realized. Not with Simon, but with her. Her appearance had changed, with a new hairstyle. Her relationship with her daughter had changed. The frequency with which she saw her friends had changed.

You're not safe.

In the quiet dark, Nina's subconscious began to guide her, urging her out of bed and downstairs to do a little more digging on her own. She still had not fixed up the first-floor office in the way she had envisioned on move-in day. Pictures she had planned to hang on the walls remained on the floor, sitting next to the unopened cans of the Manchester Tan paint she had yet to apply to the walls. The room held a desk, a chair, and not much else. But at least it was a private space where she could conduct her inquiry away from prying eyes—not that any of those eyes were open at the moment.

Nina powered up her laptop. *It's natural curiosity,* she told herself while navigating to the Google homepage. She typed the name "Hugh Dolan" into the search field, thinking perhaps there'd be a link to some exculpatory evidence that would make it possible to trust him, but no such luck. It was the same information as before: links to his arrest records and mug shots that the police routinely put online as a public service.

She thought again about Simon's parents—what were their names? Strange how she didn't know off the top of her head, but then again, they weren't coming over every Thanksgiving to carve the turkey. Still, it was something she thought she should know.

Nina heard a creak and froze. She listened for the sound of footsteps but heard none. Probably it was the house settling, whatever that meant. It was something Glen would tell Maggie whenever she heard noises in the night. The tender memory put a little crimp in Nina's heart. Why did Glen have to blow up all their lives? What awful thing had he done to make it necessary for him to kill himself or run away?

Nina compartmentalized those thoughts to focus on the names of Simon's parents. Eventually, she remembered: David and Elizabeth Fitch. She searched for the father's name first. After David's military career he went to work for a defense contractor, but his background wasn't distinguished enough to earn him permanent archiving on the Web. Thinking about Simon's parents made Nina think of hers as well. Maybe she should book a trip to Nebraska, go visit Nonni and Papa for a while, head there for Thanksgiving. Her mother couldn't travel because of a hip problem that was going to be fixed with a full replacement, but Nina could go to them.

Maggie would love it, and Connor had a break between

football and basketball seasons. It was disconcerting to realize the plan she'd formed in her head did not immediately include Simon. Because it would be hard on Maggie, Nina told herself, and because her father, who had adored Glen, hadn't yet warmed to the new man in her life.

Because you're not safe, Hugh's voice told Nina. *Your dad knows it. Parents have an instinct for this sort of thing.*

Pictures, if I only had pictures of Emma, thought Nina.

Whatever photographs there'd been of Allison had been turned to ash. Perhaps photos of Emma and Simon together would reveal something hidden about him.

But there were no photographs, nothing from Simon's past to ground her, nothing to give shape to his history. All Nina had to go on was the life they had made together. Nina reflected briefly on her time with Simon—his courtship that had begun with his finding Daisy, which had led to dinner out, and then to a moonlight beach walk, a kiss at the lake, and eventually his touching proposal, which she had declined, but with a promise that it wouldn't be long—a promise she fully intended to keep. That's how life worked, Nina believed. That's how things happened. It was random. She recognized that most moments were out of her control. She didn't know that she'd fall for the teacher when he brought Daisy home, just as she didn't know the father of her children would turn out to be a complete stranger.

And in the world of random happenings, how likely was it that lightning had struck her twice? What was the possibility that she'd realized her greatest fear and made another terrible choice in a man? It was inconceivable, that's what it was. Statistically, it would have to have about the same probability as winning Powerball.

But people win Powerball, Nina.

The little voice in her head was speaking up again.

Nobody is guaranteed a happily ever after. Nobody.

"Shut up," Nina said to the voice, and returned to her search.

Nina typed Emma Dolan's name into the Google search field. She'd done this before, but for some reason she hoped there'd be a picture of her in one of the online obituaries. Again, no such luck.

Nina opened a new browser window and popped over to LinkedIn, which had nothing to offer her, before checking Hugh Dolan's Facebook page again. She thought maybe he'd been friends with Emma and her profile existed in memoriam, but Emma was a ghost in this world and online. Nina's gaze traveled upward, where she noticed her Facebook Messenger icon indicated a new message.

She was about to click it when she heard a sound, a soft creak on the stairs. Her hand hovered over the icon. It could be Maggie or Connor, coming down for some reason, but it could also be Simon.

Why are you afraid? Nina asked herself.

But she knew the answer: she was looking into Simon's life without his knowledge.

Simon's words came back to her: "We can't keep secrets from each other, Nina. It's not healthy for a marriage."

Still, her curiosity won out, and she clicked the icon, not caring that those footsteps were growing louder. She held her breath, her hands shaking, pulse quickening, as she read the message from Hugh.

Are you ready to talk yet? The offer stands at $500.
You're not safe.

The footsteps were getting closer.

"Nina?"

It was Simon's voice. He appeared in the doorway, holding the phone he was using as a flashlight.

"What are you doing sitting down here in the dark?"

But it wasn't dark. Her laptop was on, her face alight with a bluish glow. Nina felt his eyes on her, taking in what he saw, assessing her, or so it seemed.

"I couldn't sleep," Nina said groggily, hoping she wasn't overacting. She was more alert than if she'd downed an espresso with a Red Bull chaser. She closed the browser window containing her Facebook page as Hugh's message flashed in her mind: *The offer stands at $500 . . .*

"Honey, what's wrong?"

As Simon walked over and put his arms around Nina, she realized there was a second browser window still open with Emma Dolan's name all over the search results. She closed that window quickly and turned to look up at Simon, hoping to distract him.

"It's late," Simon said. "What are you looking at?" His voice was cold and measured.

"Just . . . stuff . . . nothing . . ."

"That's strange, you've never done that before," he said.

"Like I said, I couldn't sleep, with Maggie and all." The words tumbled from Nina's lips as a believable explanation came to her. She had to crane her neck to look up at him as Simon loomed over her. As she turned her head some more, she could see he was gripping the back of her chair with force. His face shifted, hardening, realigning into the shape she'd seen that day with the tree branches, an unsettling dark anger—maybe the same face he had shown Maggie.

Stop it, Nina! she scolded herself. *It's all in your head. It's Hugh getting to you. This is Simon. This is the man you love and who loves you. Stop freaking yourself out.*

Nina closed her eyes briefly, and when she opened them, it was the old Simon she saw. The look was gone. He knelt down beside her, giving her shoulder a gentle squeeze.

"Let it all go," he said sweetly.

Nina felt foolish, and angry with herself. If there was any-one to be suspicious about, it was Hugh. She had to make a decision. One way or another, she had to let all this nonsense go. There was simply no reason to suspect that this beautiful man who had come into her life when she needed him most was anything but wonderful.

Tension left her body as she powered down the computer.

"Come back to bed, babe," Simon said as he led Nina upstairs.

His warm voice made her relax. He'd drawn down the covers, and Nina climbed underneath. Gently he rubbed her back until her eyelids grew heavy.

"You have nothing to worry about," he whispered in her ear, then kissed the back of her head. "We have everything we need." As he continued to rub her back, it was as if he were erasing her doubts. Soon her limbs felt heavy, and be-fore she knew it, Nina was fast asleep.

She awoke with a start to find it was still dark outside. The clock on the cable box read 5:30, thirty minutes before her alarm would sound. She leaned over to see Simon sleeping peacefully beside her. But why had she awoken so suddenly, pained by a gnawing anxiousness? Then it came to her: Simon was asleep, but had he been the whole night? Was there any chance he might have snuck downstairs, opened the laptop, and launched a browser window? If he did, he might have been in for quite the surprise. In her distracted state, Nina had forgotten the one thing she had meant to do before returning to bed.

She'd forgotten to clear the browser history.

CHAPTER 37

Don't eat, don't drink, don't cooperate, and watch your children die.

That was the message drilled into Glen's head time and time again. But it wasn't only threats that had made Glen obedient. There were the beatings. Though they had lessened over time, the irregularity of them had Glen always on edge.

They came and went with Simon's mood, like he was the weather, stormy or calm, hard to predict. He used Glen like a punching bag to take out his frustrations. They were near constant in the initial months. Simon had wanted to be with Nina and the children the same day he took Glen, but at some level he understood feelings would have to develop somewhat naturally.

There was punishment for fighting back. One effective counterstrike would quickly get Simon to break off his attack and move to the safe zone outside the box. Once there, he'd hit Glen with a police-grade Taser capable of shooting upwards of thirty feet away. Glen had received enough jolts to zap the fight out of him, literally. His conditioned strategy to any acts of violence was to shield himself as best he could from the blows while waiting for Simon's storm to pass.

As Simon grew more complacent in his new life with Nina, the beatings became less frequent, until they stopped altogether. But when the door to the box flew open, Glen knew something terrible was coming his way.

He had been enjoying a dreamless sleep, so much easier than the other kind. The basement lights were on, so he could see Simon's face as he neared. Fear bubbled in Glen's gut. He recognized the familiar look in Simon's eyes.

The blackness was back. The darkness. The rage.

Cocking his fist, Simon threw a punch that connected hard with Glen's face, just below the right orbital socket. It was a solid strike, though Glen was sure Simon pulled back a bit. For obvious reasons, he couldn't bring Glen to a hospital.

Simon threw another punch to the head, but this blow Glen deflected. Instead of fighting back, Glen's Pavlovian response kicked in. Box. Taser. Defend only. Wait it out. For the next volley, instead of going high, Simon went low. Glen had no idea what was coming. He went to the ground, moving his hands up to cover his face a split second before Simon's kick sank into the fleshiest part of his abdomen. Glen gasped as air sprang from his lungs. He rolled to avoid Simon's next attack, but couldn't roll far enough and was kicked twice in the back. The sudden movement pulled on his ankle restraint, gouging out a chunk of his flesh.

Blood seeped from an open wound to Glen's lower leg, setting a dark stain against his gray sweatpants. To avoid the next volley, Glen rolled onto his stomach, but Simon straddled him and threw more punches to the back of Glen's head, grunting like a rabid animal as he landed blow after blow. Glen bucked and squirmed beneath Simon, trying desperately to worm his way out.

"Simon! Simon!" Glen said, pleading. "Stop! Please! Stop! What's wrong? Talk to me. I can help."

Simon panted, and his fist went back yet again, but this time, he didn't throw the punch.

"You can't help," Simon said, softly and dejectedly. The fight was out of him. The storm had passed, or so Glen thought.

Simon stomped out of the box and over to the television. He hoisted up the TV, unmindful of the cord plugged into the wall, and with a grunt, lifted it over his head, his face clenched in anger. Glen cowered, shielding himself with his arms, afraid the appliance would become a projectile.

Simon had highlighted how this particular TV was glass-fronted, as if it were a selling point. Glen pictured shards of broken glass gouging out an eye as it crashed down on his head, but instead Simon brought his arms forward slowly, and set the television down gently. There was an audible exhale as Glen let go of his breath.

"You can't help," Simon said, crumpling to the floor, hiding his face in his hands.

Glen tried to clear away the blood pouring from his nose, managing only to smear it all over his face like war paint.

"Get me some bandages," Glen said, lying facedown, panting hard. He used his stained mattress to soak up some blood. "Get me some bandages, and let's talk. Let me help you figure it out, whatever it is."

Simon went upstairs and returned with a first-aid kit, along with a paper cup of water. He spent several minutes cleaning Glen's many wounds and applying bandages to all the injuries, including the gash to the ankle and a cut to his chin. The beard made it difficult to get the bandages in place, but Simon managed to stop most of the blood flow. He gave

Glen the cup of water. Sitting cross-legged on his blood-soaked mattress, sipping the water, Glen watched as Simon surveyed his handiwork.

"I'm sorry I went off on you like that. It was uncalled-for," said Simon, slumping on the floor nearby.

Glen gingerly rubbed the back of his head, feeling the tender lumps that had formed. "Why did you attack me?"

"I was angry. Needed a release."

The weather . . .

"What happened?"

"I'm not going to say."

"Is it Nina?" Glen sounded panicky. "Is she all right? Maggie? Connor? Are they okay?"

"Yeah. They're fine, Glen. Don't worry. I'm not going to hurt them."

Glen considered Simon almost impassively. "You know I don't believe that's true," he said. "You can't control yourself. Look at what you did to me." He pointed to his numerous injuries. "You're a sick man. You need help."

For a moment there, Simon looked like he was about to agree. "Nina's seeing a therapist," he said in a low voice.

Glen was taken aback. He had expected so much worse. "What's wrong with that? She's been through a lot."

"No, you don't get it. She's talking about me. I know it. She's talking about me and she's going to leave me."

Glen understood that would be the worst decision for everyone. It was strange for him to want Simon with his wife, sleeping in his bed, to be a part of his children's lives, because the alternative was too horrible to consider.

"You don't know that for a fact."

"I do. She's looking into my life, searching Emma's name. She'll figure it out. It's that damn therapist. She's making her doubt me."

Glen closed his eyes, thinking. When he opened them, he

fixed Simon with a pointed stare, his expression serious and reserved. Now was the moment to make his request, and Glen thought: *NICE GUY, a secret message, hope.*

"Let me talk to Maggie. By phone this time," Glen said. "Listen to me, Simon, this therapist business is about Maggie. Your plan to use her to make Nina quit her job is *causing* the problem. I know Nina better than you. Trust me. If we can get Maggie on your side, Nina won't have any reason to see her therapist anymore. We'll come up with another way to get Nina to quit working if we have to."

Simon mulled this over.

"Why would you want to do that?" Simon sounded skeptical. "Why help me?"

"You know the answer." Glen understood it was a risk to suggest he could coerce Nina through a proxy, but he had to make his case; he had to convince Simon to trust him, to follow his lead. "I'll do anything to protect my family, and you told me you wouldn't hesitate, not one second, to harm them if Nina rejects you, or loses interest. Tell me it's not true."

Simon couldn't deny it.

"Look, I'm trying to save their lives." Desperation leaked into Glen's voice. "You can do away with me. I don't care anymore. Kill me if that's what has to happen. But I can't let anything happen to my family."

A thoughtful look came to Simon's face, but the darkness in his eyes lingered.

"So admirable," he said. "Such conviction. Nina's told me time and time again how you were unavailable to the kids, how you were so work-obsessed. I don't get it. How do you stay so strong for them?"

"They're my children." Glen's voice was shaky.

"You have regrets, right?" Simon's expression brightened. He loved feeling superior to Glen.

"Who doesn't?"

This seemed to interest Simon, and Glen sensed his opportunity.

"Tell me about them," Simon insisted. "I can't make the same mistakes."

All this time together they had talked about what Glen did right and wrong in his marriage to Nina, but the conversation never went much deeper, and seldom focused on the children. The truth was Glen wanted to share. He was hungrier for conversation, for human contact, companionship—even from his captor and abuser—than he was for food. That's the mind for you. Adapt, or die. But Glen knew also that sharing might give him what he was after, so he spoke the truth.

"I have a lot of regrets," he said.

Simon looked intrigued. "Go on."

"Nina and I, we had this dance we did," Glen said, sounding a wistful note. "The more she focused on the kids, the more I retreated into my work, because I didn't feel needed at home. I became a provider instead of a father."

"Meaning?"

"Meaning, I took my children's childhood for granted." A lump sprang to Glen's throat. "I could have been more hands-on, more involved. Instead, I was the guy who never played with them enough. But I didn't know *how* to play cars or dolls, and I was never comfortable with babies. And it wasn't like Nina was asking me to do more. No, she was perfectly happy to take on all the responsibility. She made it seem like she was doing me a favor, but in reality, I think it might have been the other way around."

Glen took a moment to put pressure on the cut to his lip and apply another layer of gauze on the cut to his ankle.

This was good. Simon was being attentive, listening and interested.

"Anyway, the kids grew, cats in the cradle, got older, more independent, all that, but my habits didn't change. I was in the stands watching them play sports, sometimes helping with homework, but I was always distracted—on my phone, checking emails, putting out fires at the bank that I could have let burn. I focused on my work because that was the role I had carved out for myself. By that point, I didn't know my kids all that well. It was Nina who knew what stuffed animals to bring on vacation, what food they'd like, what activities they'd want to do. Me? I existed in the background."

Simon closed his eyes, as if picturing Glen's life in vivid detail, zooming by with the speed of a bullet train, regrets piling up with the miles.

"Your honesty is really touching," said Simon.

"When Maggie turned ten," Glen continued, "I made a promise to myself to get more involved in her life, but I didn't even know how to begin. I started reading to her at night, and that became our big father-daughter time. Just a book. The last one we were reading was *A Wrinkle in Time*."

That one hurt. Glen needed a moment to regain his composure.

"I tried to get Connor into fishing because that's what I liked to do, but he didn't take to it at all, and I didn't try to find something else for us to do together. I just threw up my hands as if it wasn't meant to be. Instead of working harder to fix it or talking it out with Nina, I slipped back into my familiar role."

"The worker bee." Simon's smile was almost a sneer.

"Work was my identity. It always had been."

Until it was gone, Glen thought. And he could never get it back.

"So you of all people understand why Nina has to quit her job," Simon said.

Work. What was it with Simon and Nina's job? What was it triggering for him?

Glen decided now was the time to ask again.

"What you're doing to Nina and Maggie," he said, "playing mind games, making Maggie insecure and suspicious, that's the wrong way to go. I know Nina. She'll think it's the relationship that's causing all the problems, and she'll leave you before she leaves her job. Maggie and Connor, that's *her* identity."

"She loves me too much," Simon said dismissively.

"I'm telling you, you're wrong," Glen said. "You've believed what I told you all the other times. Why not now? Let me talk to Maggie by phone. I'll fix it, even if it means Nina staying with a monster like you. I can't let you hurt my family, Simon. I can't let it happen."

Glen knew he was pushing his luck calling Simon a monster, but the physical restraint he'd endured over the years had yielded to an imperative to strike back, even if only verbally. He expected some retaliation for the invective, but instead, the darkness in Simon's eyes left in a rush as a dim light slowly rolled in.

"A monster . . ." he said, talking softly to himself, as if an idea were coming to him. "That's it. That's perfect. It's exactly what I'll do. Good, good thinking, Glen. Maggie might not be enough to get Nina to quit. What we may need is a real *monster* to push her over the edge. Okay, we'll make that call together. Not yet—but soon."

Panic gripped Glen. He had miscalculated. Simon didn't care if Maggie embraced him or not. He didn't believe Nina would ever leave him, not when he had his insurance policy chained inside a box to help smooth things over. But somehow, in the course of this conversation, Glen had given Simon a new idea to coerce Nina into doing his bidding. He was going to create a monster—though what that entailed exactly, Glen couldn't say.

At least he had agreed to a phone call.

It was something.

It was hope.

Simon extended his hand. Glen took it and sealed the deal.

CHAPTER 38

That week and into the next was an especially busy time at The Davis Family Center. Oddly enough, given all the human drama Nina dealt with, it was something of a respite from her battles on the home front. Simon explained he had bruised his knuckles in a fall at school, but secretly Nina wondered if he had punched a wall in frustration. Maggie had decided to give Simon the silent treatment; a consequence, she explained to her mother, of her continued belief that *he* was to blame for the missing lab report—refusing to take any responsibility of her own. It was no surprise when, once again, Simon used Maggie's behavior as proof this was not the best time for Nina to devote herself to work outside the home.

Something else about Maggie had been troubling Nina of late, and her motherly instinct told her it had nothing to do with Simon. It was normal, expected, for her daughter to pull away at this age, but for some reason, the distance felt different. When pressed, Maggie said it was nothing, but she couldn't deliver the rebuttal with eye contact, and Nina could hear the strain in her daughter's voice. There was something Maggie was holding back, Nina felt sure of it.

Either way, she was ready to move on with Simon while

continuing to help her daughter adjust. She was equally ready to forget all about Hugh Dolan, who had stopped messaging when it became clear that she would not pay him a dime.

Now more than ever, Nina was sure the whole thing had been nothing but a scare tactic on his part, a way of drumming up money for his habit. He had seen an opportunity and taken advantage of it, nothing more. As for Nina's investigation into Simon's past, that was over and done with as well, erased like the browser history she had taken care of before Simon had woken up that day. She had felt foolish for thinking he might have snuck downstairs while she slept to check up on her activities, but regardless, she had to get rid of the evidence.

All this nonsense and noise was in her head. Nina credited the work she'd been doing with Dr. Wilcox for her renewed determination to jettison the baggage she'd been lugging around, to give in completely to Simon and trust his love.

At her therapy appointment Nina wasn't sure where to begin. Should she talk about seeing Teresa again after all this time, and what she had revealed, as well as her lingering doubts about the extent of the affair? She hadn't told Simon about Teresa, in part because it would have required a lengthy explanation as to why she went looking, not to mention the possibility of revealing her deception on the night she visited Carson.

What about Hugh? Or maybe the focus should be on Maggie's latest accusations that Simon had stolen her homework (reason unknown). Perhaps it was best to discuss the pressures of her new job. But of all the people and things she could have discussed, it was Connor's face that flashed in Nina's mind, specifically his broad grin as he'd showed off the Bowflex machine he had helped put together. So that's where she began.

"How did the gift make you feel?" Dr. Wilcox asked after Nina explained Simon's big surprise.

"Well, part of me, of course, thought it was quite sweet of him."

Dr. Wilcox keyed in on Nina's hesitation. "And the other part?"

"I hate to use the word."

"It's fine to say, I promise."

"I guess . . ." Nina cleared her throat. "I guess the word that came to mind was 'controlling.'"

Dr. Wilcox's brow furrowed. "In what way?"

Nina explained how Simon had been deeply disappointed that she chose to go out with her girlfriends rather than work on the lawn as he had wished.

"In fact, my friends want us to work out together this coming Saturday, but it doesn't feel right or fair to leave Simon alone with Maggie on the weekend, especially now that I have a home gym to get my sweat on. So I backed out, disappointed them, again."

"Why do you think he bought you that equipment?"

"I'm not sure," Nina said.

Dr. Wilcox ruminated a moment. "Sounds to me a bit like the insecurity he displays around your job," she observed.

Nina nodded, because indeed there were parallels.

With patience and professionalism, Dr. Wilcox had helped Nina shine a light into the dark places, revealing in clear detail the damage Glen had inflicted on her psyche. Affair or fling, the hurt along with the ripples of his betrayal, had grown into a rip current that threatened to drag her and Simon under. Perhaps a joint session with Dr. Wilcox was the life preserver they both required.

It was decided. Nina would ask Simon to join her at therapy. She felt it would be the start of a new beginning for them.

She even established a new mantra: *Get your head on straight, get your life on track, and get your family healthy again.* To show her commitment, Nina picked up the phone to call Ginny and honor the promise she had made to Simon. It should be easy, she told herself. She had plenty of practice canceling plans with her friends.

"Come on," Ginny said in a plaintive voice after Nina broke the news. "It won't be the same without you."

"Sorry, I'm *really* sorry, but I'm swamped here. I can't do it, Gin," Nina said, looking at the mini mountain of papers and folders on her office desk, thinking it wasn't exactly a lie.

Ginny's lengthy silence said even more than her words. She didn't come right out and blame Simon, or rehash old concerns, only because she didn't have to.

"Work can wait," Ginny eventually pleaded. "This is us, the gang, the gals, once a year."

"I wish I could go, I really do, but my clients need me," Nina said, exchanging one kind of guilt for another. She loved her friends dearly, and it broke her heart into pieces to disappoint them. But Simon was a factor, and his concerns were valid and had to be taken into account. Barring some serious ailment or act of God, Nina made a silent vow that this would be the one and only girls' weekend she'd ever miss.

"Work, work, work," Ginny said, sounding annoyed now. "How did they get on without you before, huh?"

Nina returned a nervous laugh. "That's how much they needed me," she said.

"Well, no wonder Simon thinks you're having an affair."

Nina's breath clogged. "What?"

"Yeah, I saw him at Dunkin' Donuts, and he told me about how busy you've been, how he thinks you might be shacking up with somebody at work. My words, not his."

Hot anger raced through Nina's veins. "What were his words *exactly*?" she demanded.

"I don't know . . . I mean, I think he was just kidding, right? He said something about you hooking up with some-body at the office. I didn't find it very funny, actually it was kinda weird, so I didn't press him on it. I sort of ignored it, until now, because, well, I can kind of see why he might have made that remark."

"I'm not having an *affair*," Nina said, feeling the muscles in her neck tense, her pulse rising. "That's really hurtful." How could Ginny, of all people, be so unaware of how that comment came across? Nina had told Ginny and Susanna about meeting Teresa, what she'd learned of Chris the stalker, and of Glen's drunken indiscretion that, considering the source, could have been more than a one-night fling, so she had to know it was still a deeply sensitive subject.

"Oh. My. Gosh. I am the biggest ass," Ginny said, finally making the connection. "I wasn't thinking, honey. I was up-set about the weekend, is all. You know how much I love you."

Nina let her anger settle so that she could redirect it to where it belonged—at Simon.

She ended the call with a promise to talk later and got Simon on the phone.

"Hey, babe," he said, sounding delighted to hear from her. "What's up?"

"Why would you say that to Ginny?" Nina's voice quaked from a second jolt of adrenaline.

"Say what?"

"Tell Ginny you thought I was having an affair." She spoke through gritted teeth.

"What? She said that?" Simon sounded utterly perplexed.

"You two were in line together at Dunkin' Donuts, and

you told her you thought I was so busy at work because I really was having an affair. That's incredibly hurtful, Simon, especially given what I've been through. You know how sensitive I am about that. Why would you say that to my friend?"

"Because I didn't," Simon said indignantly. "I remember that conversation quite clearly. What I believe I said is that they wouldn't let you come up for *air*, and if she misheard that somehow, well, that's Ginny's problem, not mine."

Nina's outrage left in one great breath, followed soon after by a string of apologies.

Once again, she'd doubted Simon, and once again, he had a perfectly reasonable explanation.

"It's okay, babe," Simon said, himself sounding a bit out of breath, like his pulse had spiked as well.

But it wasn't okay. Like the incident with the TV remote, or when her start date had cost them all a surprise vacation, or her sneaking around about Hugh, the hours she'd been working, Maggie's struggles with him—all of it ended up making *her* feel guilty, as if she'd done something wrong.

Simon did his best to reassure Nina it was no big deal. He was already over it. He was far more concerned about what he was going to wear out to dinner with the superintendent of schools and his wife tomorrow night. Nina uttered a small gasp.

"What dinner?" She had no memory of any dinner plans.

"I told you about it last week," he said. "I even reminded you about it this morning before work. Dinner, tomorrow, with my boss and his wife; we're going to Surf and you said you wanted the crab bisque."

I did? thought Nina.

"Simon, honey, that's . . . that's not possible."

Simon laughed almost playfully, but with a hint of annoyance, too. "Well, it *is* possible, and it is also happening, and we did talk about it."

"What time tomorrow?" she asked.

"Five," he said.

"I can't go," Nina said. "I have a client appointment, and I can't cancel. I'm so sorry. I swear we didn't discuss this."

The voice in her head again, the guilty one, spoke up: *But you probably did talk about it—just as you probably told him to make damn sure the TV got turned off at six, because you are distracted, because you are working too much, too hard. And it's bad for Maggie, for your struggling family . . .*

Simon sighed.

"Dang," he said, accustomed to finding alternative words for cursing because of his students. "We made the plan last week. When did you book the client?"

"Monday. Rona has been piling on the work."

"It's my bad. I should have written it down for you, sent some text reminders, something. Seriously, no worries. You've got a lot on your mind with this job of yours. I'll be better at communicating our plans so we won't have a mix-up like this again."

They said their good-byes. Nina did her work, met with her clients, helped straighten bent lives, and in the quiet moments, had a fleeting chance to reflect. Her thoughts went to Simon, the accusations she made about him, the suspicions she harbored, and the dinner plans she screwed up, all of which left her wondering if she had it in her to be a good wife to anybody.

CHAPTER 39

The phone rang at five o'clock exactly. Of course, my phone was in my hand. I must have checked the ringer a dozen times to make sure it was on. I was terrified of missing his call.

When I first heard his voice I thought my ears were playing tricks on me. I thought, *No way, this isn't possible, it's a dream; it can't be him.* But then he called me "Bunny" and I lost it. It was the hard, couldn't take a breath, felt like I was going to pass out, full-on sobbing kind of cry. I was alone in my bedroom but had to muffle the sound with a pillow because Mom was somewhere, downstairs probably. I didn't know where Simon and Connor were, if they were even home, and I didn't much care. All that mattered to me was that for the first time in nearly two years, I was talking to my father. His voice was warm, exactly as I remembered, soothing like hot chocolate on a cold day.

"Hi, Bunny," he said again. "Hi, my sweetheart."

"Daddy? Is that you?"

I don't know which was shakier, my speech or my body.

"Yeah, it's me. It's Dad."

He spoke softly, doing his version of the loud library whisper, or maybe he was exhausted, I don't know what. I tried to answer him, but felt like my throat was full of sand, almost like I was having an allergic reaction.

"Hey, Bun, I know this is hard, but talk to me. Let me hear your beautiful voice again."

Earlier that day, I'd received a Talkie message from Tracy Nuts letting me know that my father would call at five o'clock sharp, so I should have my phone handy and be somewhere we could talk privately.

Daddy!

All day, I had barely been able to contain my excitement. It was the only thing I could think about, and sitting through my classes had been the worst kind of torture. And now that it was happening, I couldn't find any words to say. I heard his voice, his actual voice, and my tongue was tied in one big knot.

"Maggie, are you there? Did I lose you?" He sounded panicked.

"Dad—"

Turned out talking to my missing father was a lot harder than I thought it would be. I moved into the closet, closing the door behind me, thinking an enclosed, dark space would be comforting, wishing I'd brought Daisy for emotional support. I needed her now more than ever.

The start of our conversation was a lot of back and forth. *I miss you, Bunny. I miss you, Dad. I can't believe I'm hearing your voice. I can't believe I'm hearing yours.* That went on for a bit, him and me, both of us full-on blubbering. But the tears stopped when he said, "I can't talk for long."

I snapped right back into myself. I got that every word mattered. Every second counted. I couldn't, wouldn't let him go again. He had to come back. I had to convince him to come back.

"Where are you?"

Finally, I managed a sentence where I wasn't choking on tears.

"I'm safe. That's all you need to know."

"Where?"

"I can't tell you, honey."

"Are you close?"

"It doesn't matter."

"To me it does. I need to see you."

"That's . . . that's not possible."

"Why not?"

"Because I've done something. Something terrible. And I can't come home. You have to understand that."

Those hot tears returned to flood my eyes.

"Why?" I croaked out what had to be the saddest one-word question ever.

Dad gave a big sigh. "Some things I can't explain."

"What about us? You can't just disappear. You can't leave us again—with him!"

"Maybe it won't be forever," Dad said, using the *be patient* tone I recognized. "But it has to be for now."

Then he started crying harder. It was anguished; beyond upsetting. I shriveled up inside. I didn't know what to do, because I was the kid, and kids aren't supposed to comfort their parents. So I listened to my father cry, and occasionally I'd chime in with a nervous "Daddy, are you okay?" but for the most part I let him cry. And then all of a sudden he went silent, like he had had a heart attack and died.

"Dad?" I whispered his name, so afraid he was gone, that I'd lost him, that the call had been dropped, or worse. "Are you there?"

Then I heard a noise, a little creak I recognized right away as the sound of footsteps coming up the stairs. I sucked in a breath, held it, waited. Another creak, as my father's words, his text messages to me, flashed in my head: *IF SHE FINDS OUT, IT COULD BE VERY BAD FOR ME.*

What would happen to him? I wondered. "Very bad" covered a lot of ground. The footsteps. They were getting closer. Was it Connor? Simon? Mom? I focused on the sound.

"Dad," I whispered again. "Someone's coming."

I opened the closet door a crack and slipped out, crawling on my hands and knees. I managed to keep the cell phone where I could see it, making sure I didn't lose the call as I slithered over to my bed. I heard a knock.

"Maggie?"

It was Mom.

For the first time, I noticed the number. The area code was 802. Wherever that was, I knew that's where he was calling me from. I climbed into bed and pulled the covers over me. I put the phone under my pillow and kept it by my head, feeling the hum, the buzz of electricity, a little reminder that my father was right there, keeping me safe, keeping our secret safe.

"Honey?" It was Mom again, from behind the closed door. "May I come in?"

I took in a deep breath, but my heart was racing anyway.

"I'm fine," I answered, realizing too late that wasn't her question.

"Maggie?" Mom was confused, and the door was opening. I turned my head to see my phone peeking out from beneath the pillow. That's how close we were—me, Mom, and Dad—to being together again. All I had to do was move my pillow and she'd see I was talking to someone from the 802 area code.

Very bad for me.

Can you keep a secret? I trust you. Only you.

I shoved the phone farther under the pillow.

Mom entered my room, looking around, surprised to find me in bed. Then she saw my face and her expression turned to worry.

"Honey, what's wrong?" She came in and sat down beside me. "Are you not feeling well?"

"Nothing," I said, sniffling.

She touched my shoulder.

It hurt, real physical pain, not to talk to my father. It took everything I had to keep myself from pushing the pillow away, to make sure he was still on the phone, to scream out, "MOM! MOM! It's Dad! He's alive! He's okay!"

But I couldn't break his trust. I couldn't bring myself to give up his secret—our secret.

"You're crying," Mom said, stroking my hair, her hand only a few inches from the phone.

"I was just . . . just thinking about Dad," I said, giving her a half-truth.

"Oh, Mags," Mom said, in that mom voice. "I know this is so difficult for you."

I swallowed hard, forcing my eyes to meet hers. She leaned on the bed, her fingers brushing against the pillow where I'd hidden the phone. My stomach clenched and released. She shifted position, her hand moving closer to the phone. I took in a breath and held it.

"Do you need to talk? I know I haven't been as available to you as I should be."

I need you to go, I was thinking.

"I'm fine," I managed. "I just want to be alone."

Mom felt my forehead, looking a bit puzzled. She knew I wasn't acting like myself.

"Okay," she said, concern in her voice. "But if you want to talk, I'm here. I love you."

"Love you, too," I said, watching her go, unable to wait for her to get out of sight before I started to reach under the pillow.

When the door clicked closed, I put the phone to my ear. "Dad, are you still there?"

CHAPTER 40

Glen couldn't speak even though he heard Maggie repeatedly ask for him.

It had been painful and wonderful to talk to his daughter, to hear her beautiful voice, but hearing Nina's, not having prepared for the possibility, made it impossible to utter a single word. His throat closed. The emotions came hard—guilt, regret, self-hatred, all of it pouring down on him in an avalanche of grief.

"That's her voice," he finally managed.

"You're still there!" Maggie exclaimed.

"Your mom. I heard her voice."

"She's not in the room anymore. She's gone. It's safe to talk."

"God, I love you all. I miss you all so much." Tears stung Glen's eyes.

"Please let me tell Mom," Maggie said, whimpering her plea. "I can't keep this a secret."

Glen checked in with Simon, who was standing next to him, holding the Taser to his neck.

Simon hit Mute on the phone. "Won't have to. Not long," he said in a low voice. He hit the Mute button again.

"You won't have to keep it secret for long," Glen said. "We'll tell them soon."

He knew he'd have to embellish a bit to make the conversation sound natural, but he couldn't deviate from the main message. If he did, Simon would jolt him—fast. He had threatened repeatedly to drive to the house and end it for everyone if Glen tried to warn Maggie in any way. He'd do it then and there, he vowed. Glen took him at his word.

Simon hit Mute again.

"You gotta get somewhere safe," he instructed.

Mute off.

"But I have to get somewhere first. I have to get somewhere . . . somewhere safer."

Simon pantomimed putting a phone to his ear and mouthed the words "Nina" and "Connor."

"And when I do, you can tell Mom and Connor that I'm all right. Tell them I'm alive and well. Maybe I can even call, like I'm doing now."

He looked over to Simon, hoping for approval. He had guessed right. Simon's expression remained placid.

"Where are you calling from?"

Simon shook his head and Glen understood. They'd rehearsed this answer.

"I can't tell you that," he said. "You've got to trust me, okay?"

Simon gave a nod. Maggie said okay.

"Can you come home?"

Simon shook his head. Hit Mute.

"Ask about Nina," he said in Glen's ear.

Unmute.

"No, honey, I wish more than anything that I could, but I can't. What about Mom? Is she hanging in there?"

Glen's mind was churning, thinking how to work in something, that one little reference to tell Maggie about the danger, perhaps reveal something of his location. But he had pondered it, turning his ideas this way and that, coming up with nothing. Anagrams for Simon, like "minos," were nonsensical.

He had tried to think up a sentence where the first letter of each word would spell out a secret message, like he did with "NICE GUY," but ran into the same problem. Nothing sounded natural, so Simon would know. For days Glen had barely slept, thinking, thinking, but his mind wasn't sharp anymore.

"Mom's with Simon now," Maggie said, as if that said it all.

Mute again.

"Is she happy?"

Glen knew that was for Simon's benefit, and wondered: *Does he think Nina confided in Maggie?*

"Is she happy? Does she love him?"

Maggie fell silent for a moment. "No. She's not happy. She loves you."

Darkness seeped into Simon's eyes.

Glen made a noise, a little clearing of the throat. He was delaying. Time was running out . . . he had to get the message to her, now. But Simon was watching him closely. One wrong word . . . one slip. Fear chilled his blood and held him back.

He wanted to scream, "CALL THE POLICE, I'M A PRISONER AT SIMON'S," but couldn't risk it. He had timed it, all sorts of variations, and thought it would take two, maybe three seconds to get the words out. A Taser fired faster than that. Maybe Maggie would catch enough to make some meaning of it, maybe not. All Glen heard in his head was his daughter screaming, begging for her life as Simon moved the knife from one side of her throat to the other.

He felt his opportunity slipping away.

Simon pointed to the cue cards on the floor, which he had

written out prior to the call. He had returned the LED light so Glen could see the words.

"I know adults, Maggie, and I understand kids, too," Glen said, reading from card number one. "You miss me, you miss the way things were, but it can't be like that again. Not ever. Now listen to me, and listen carefully, even if you don't understand what I have to say."

Simon pointed to the second cue card. Glen read from it.

"I'm hiding for a reason. I've done bad things. I've hurt people."

"Who? Who have you hurt?" Maggie sounded wounded and in utter disbelief.

"That's none of your concern."

Glen went slightly off script there, but Simon seemed good with it.

"Your mom has done some bad things, too. Things that have contributed greatly to my situation. Trust me, she's no angel."

Back on script.

"What things?" Maggie asked, still alarmed.

"Things I can't tell you. Things I have to handle myself, okay? I'm still angry at your mom for what she did to me and I have to do something about it. It can't go unpunished. I'm not saying I'd hurt her. I'd never do that, and I'd never hurt you or Connor, but something has to be done. Understood?"

"No, I don't . . . I don't understand at all. What do you mean you have to do something about it? Do what?"

Simon tapped his foot on cue card number three.

"That's not your concern. Now, if this Simon person is treating you well, helping out financially, it makes things easier for me. I can't provide for you all like I once did, and he can." This part of the script was Glen's idea. He had to embellish a bit to address Maggie's specific comments, but knew to keep to the main points. "I don't expect you to understand, but having Simon there with you gives me less to worry about. It's up to you to find a way to make the peace. It's important and it's what I need you to do."

It sickened Glen to ask his daughter to enter into a truce with Simon, but he had no choice. If he was right, and Nina left Simon instead of her job, doing so for Maggie's sake, it could prove deadly for them all.

It took some convincing, but Glen eventually got Simon to agree it would be better if things were less fraught with tension at home. The question was how to get there. He knew Maggie wouldn't respond well to a demand, but suspected she'd be more malleable to guilt. He eventually settled on financial concerns to coax his daughter into making nice with Simon, but equally important to him, if not more so, was the coded message he still hoped to deliver, and for that, he knew time was running out.

"I've given this a lot of thought," Glen read on. "Simon can take some of my pain and worry away. All I care about is that you children are protected and looked after."

"If you want me to be happy, then please come home," Maggie said, her voice breaking again, basically sobbing out the words.

Simon hit Mute.

"Tell her to stop asking for you. I'm sick of it."

Unmute.

"You've got to stop, Maggie," Glen said, sensing if Maggie pushed too hard, Simon might push back harder. Now . . . he had to say something now. But what? *First Simon's demands,* he thought. *Make sure she understands. Protect her. Save your daughter.* "You can't keep asking me to come home. Do you understand? Make it better at home. If that means making peace with Simon, then you do it. If you do, then we can talk again. That's a promise. I love you so much, Bunny. I—"

Simon hit the button that ended the call. And that was it. It was over. He had failed to alert Maggie to the family's peril. He had let them all down. A crushing sorrow overcame Glen as he slumped to the floor of the box. Simon fished out a tissue from his pants pocket and handed it to Glen, who was crying now. From the same pocket he produced a scalpel, tweezers, and a test tube that might have come from the school science lab.

"Okay, good job," he said, giving Glen's shoulder a gentle squeeze. "This should work nicely. I expect to see a new and better Maggie and a happy, more content Nina. But there's still more to do, much more, starting with turning you into a monster."

CHAPTER 41

Simon went alone to dinner with the superintendent and his wife and arrived back home at close to nine o'clock in the evening, carrying a newly purchased plumber's snake he had bought while running errands after school let out. The pesky clog in the bathroom sink had not cleared after earlier attempts with boiling water, baking soda, and salt. He slipped on a pair of gray sweats and went to work on the clog while Nina folded clothes on the bed.

Again it hit her, how strange it was: a scene as normal as could be, but with a new cast member in place, as if Simon were Glen's understudy.

"How's the drain coming?" Nina asked as she laid one of his polo shirts flat on the bed, folded the sleeves back, smoothed the fabric with her hands, carefully folded the sides, and then folded it in half, trying to match the way Simon did it, remembering the instructions on the YouTube video she had watched. Admittedly, she felt a bit insecure, oddly territorial about domains that had once been entirely her own. She had never felt this way with Glen—a need to keep a spotless kitchen and an organized, tidy home, now that the chaos of moving was long gone. But for reasons unclear to her, Nina felt a silent judgment from Simon at times. There was nothing ever spoken, no quip to make her prickle, but a glance, a look that implied unmet expectations.

Any little thing out of place—a picture hanging crooked, a shoe not on the shoe rack, a salad not made, a bed left rumpled—he would tend to it with a resigned air, as if to say this little fragment of disarray had everything to do with her job, their main source of contention.

And so, Nina found herself researching the best ways to fold a polo shirt, if for nothing else than to chip away at the doubts building up about her domestic abilities. This business of messing up Simon's dinner with the superintendent had rattled her. It wasn't like her to forget a plan. She didn't even remember hearing about it until it was too late to alter her schedule, all because she'd been preoccupied with work—or at least that's what she told herself, echoing Simon's words.

If Simon held any lingering resentment about the dinner, he masked it well. Upon his return home, he'd talked glowingly about the school, support for his curriculum, additional money for the robotics team, and the improving test scores across the district. He also shared his worry about the growing epidemic of vaping among young people, another topic that had come up at dinner.

"Have you talked about vaping with Connor and Maggie?" Simon asked from the bathroom.

"No," Nina said, feeling guilty because she had become well-versed on the issue thanks to her clients.

"It's really a massive problem," he said. "The THC in the oils these kids are using is way more concentrated than the stuff we had, and a single JUULpod has about the same nicotine level as a pack of cigarettes. Can you believe that?"

Nina could, because she had read up on it.

"You really should talk to the kids about the dangers," Simon said.

Nina heard: *You're not being a good mother.*

"Or I can," he added. "If you'd prefer . . . at least to Connor. You wouldn't believe all the ways that kids hide this stuff. You have to keep an eye out for behavior changes—moodiness, slipping grades, asking for money." Simon laughed to himself from the bathroom. "Look who I'm telling, an expert."

An expert who hasn't talked about it with her own kids, thought Nina.

"Speaking of behavior changes, have you noticed anything strange about Maggie?" Nina asked.

Half of Simon's body appeared in the bathroom's open doorway. He rubbed a hand dry on his sweats.

"Besides acting like I'm the worst person in the world? No."

"She's been . . . different lately," Nina said. "There's something up with her."

"Talk to her about it," Simon suggested, as if Nina hadn't considered that possibility.

"Yeah, I know, and I will, I'm just asking if you've noticed any changes."

"She still hates me, Nina, and I don't think that is going to change anytime soon."

Nina heard the hurt in Simon's words and her heart ached for him. He was trying so hard to make it work for everyone, Maggie included. Once again that voice rose up inside her, blaming her for not having paved a better path. She wondered how she could have made it easier for everyone. Could she have better prepared Maggie for the transition? Why hadn't she waited longer to take a job?

Simon returned to the sink and Nina to her laundry when she heard him cry out, "Ah, got you, you bugger!"

A moment later, Nina was in the bathroom, observing water from the running faucet flowing unencumbered down the drain. The plumber's snake stood almost triumphantly on the vanity; its tip browned with gunk fished out from the offending pipe.

"Well done," Nina said, giving Simon a gentle kiss. "What should we do with this?"

Nina held up the snake, having adopted Simon's penchant for keeping a flawlessly clean bathroom.

"Put it under the sink," he said. "I'm not completely confident the drain won't clog again."

Nina opened the cabinet below, while Simon intently studied the water running from the faucet to see if his work really was done.

Inside the vanity, Nina spotted something she'd never seen before: a small, brown glass bottle that looked like it belonged in the medicine cabinet. She took the bottle out and examined the label. It read R&H IPECAC SYRUP, which she had a vague recollection was used to induce vomiting.

The safety seal had been removed, and it was obvious some of the contents had been dispensed. Her mother had kept a bottle around the house, and Nina recalled doing the same when Connor was little in case of accidental poisoning. But with poison control hotlines, ipecac was rarely recommended now, and people were encouraged to discard it. Nina had learned this from one of her online courses and remembered having tossed out the medicine ages ago.

"Is this yours?" Nina asked, holding up the bottle for Simon to see.

A grim look crossed his face as if Nina had unearthed something more than a bottle.

"Yes," he said quietly.

"What on earth do you have it for?" she asked.

Simon shut off the faucet and took the bottle from Nina's hands. He looked shaken, his eyes glazed over.

"I bought it for Emma," he said, a bit darkly. "More

accurately, to use on Emma. It was a just-in-case measure because she was a pill-popper. I haven't really talked about it with you, but in addition to her depression, she was addicted to pain medication. It happened before the opioid crisis was in full bloom, so she stockpiled quite a bit from different doctors, something I found out after the fact."

Nina thought: *That's how she got the pills to kill herself.*

"They kept on prescribing even though she had overdosed twice. After the first time, I bought the ipecac, and I gave it to her before we went to the ER. Then her doctors told me it was dangerous to induce vomiting. I don't know why I kept the bottle. Funny, the things you can't seem to part with. Honestly, I didn't even realize I'd brought it here."

Nina didn't know which of Simon's belongings were part of his history with Emma. Was the blue ceramic mug he favored a present from her? Had they been antiquing together when they stumbled on the leather love seat or that area rug in front of it? There was never a good opportunity to inquire that didn't feel slightly ghoulish. Emma rarely came up in conversation, for reasons Nina understood all too well. It had taken many, many months of silent rumination, not to mention a push from her friends, to open up about the most unpleasant moments of her own life. Again, Nina thought of Dr. Wilcox's advice that Simon should seek professional help, but soon that was replaced by another thought, a darker one.

You're not safe.

Hugh's words again. Hadn't she put him out of her mind, settled on a picture of him as a drug addict—like his sister, as she now knew? Is that how Hugh had gotten hooked? Had he been siphoning pills off Emma? Nina took a moment to think about stepping a toe or two over the line. What knowledge she couldn't acquire in her online searches, perhaps she could find out from a primary source.

"What was she like?" Nina asked. She caught a glimpse of herself in the bathroom mirror, and for a second it was a stranger looking back at her. She wondered when this new hairstyle would feel normal to her.

"Who? Emma? Why are you asking?"

An edge invaded Simon's voice, a whisper of how he sounded when he found her on the computer, secretly venturing into his past. He eyed her warily, but his expression remained affable.

"I don't know; I'm just curious about the people in your life, your marriage, is all. We don't ever talk about it."

But her thoughts spoke more truthfully: *Because I want to know more about Hugh . . . I want to know if I should trust him, and really, if I should pay him.*

Simon stood behind Nina and wrapped his arms around her. He studied their reflection in the bathroom mirror, rocking her back and forth as if swaying to music only he could hear.

"I don't talk about it because I'm with you. We don't talk about Glen all the time, do we?"

He kissed the top of Nina's head, the reflection of his eyes staying locked on hers.

"No, I suppose we don't," said Nina. "But maybe we should."

Simon pulled away, looking suddenly confrontational. "Why? What good would that do?"

"I'm just curious, is all," Nina repeated, her heartbeat picking up as she edged toward the truth. "I want to know all about you, including your past. Did you and Emma ever talk about having children? What did you two fight about? Why do you think she took her own life? There's a big part of your life I don't know anything about, Simon. Maybe you're holding on to something, and, well, talking about it would make things better."

Trying to read Simon's emotions was like looking at a blank canvas.

"Better in what way?"

Nina felt her resolve begin to retreat. "You know, better with me, your issues with my job."

"What issues?"

Nina waited anxiously for a crackling smile that didn't come. "Are you serious?"

"My only concern is that you working is bad for Maggie," Simon said, venturing into the bedroom, with Nina following. "You yourself said she's acting strangely. I wonder why?"

"That's not fair," Nina said, responding directly to his sarcasm.

"I told you what would happen," answered Simon.

"Why are you being like this?"

"Like what?" Simon snapped.

"Mean," said Nina.

Simon picked up the clothes that Nina had folded and brought them to the closet, where he carefully shelved them.

"I'm not being mean," he said, talking in an almost saccharine tone, a few ticks from being condescending. "I'm simply stating the facts as I see them. Maggie is struggling, and, well, I'm not surprised."

Guilt and anger exploded like fireworks going off inside her. Color flushed her cheeks.

"I don't get why you keep harping on my job. It's an issue of yours and I don't think my working has anything to do with Maggie's behavior. I'm merely trying to get a better sense of your life before us, learn a bit more about Emma, and Hugh, and what they were like. That's all."

Simon emerged from the closet with a bemused look on his face. His arms were folded tightly across his chest, head cocked slightly to one side, his eyes appraising Nina curiously.

"I don't remember ever mentioning my brother-in-law to you," he said tonelessly.

Nina's thoughts flickered. She searched for the right words, some satisfactory explanation, but her throat convulsed, a hitch entering her breathing.

"I'm . . . I'm sure you did, at some point," Nina said nervously. "He must have come up in conversation and you forgot. Where else would I get the name?"

Simon's eyes raked over her with an assessing glance.

"Hmmm, I think I would have remembered."

"Well, I'm positive you mentioned him," Nina said assuredly. She hoped the bravado camouflaged her mounting discomfort. Simon did not seem dissuaded.

"He's a drug addict, and I told Emma to be careful with her medication because of it, but she never listened. We were robbed more than once, and I'm sure it was Hugh's doing. I think Emma was sure, too, because she kept forgetting to set the alarm—sister helping brother. Do you remember *that* conversation, Nina?"

A jagged energy came from Simon. His eyes dimmed. Deep channels creased his forehead. He stepped forward, an almost threatening gesture, and Nina felt a sudden urge to retreat. The next instant something shifted again, so quickly that if Nina hadn't been on alert, she'd have missed it entirely. In a span of a few beats, his expression went from withering to wary to affable. It was as if a director had yelled "Action!" and Simon immediately slipped into character.

"I must have talked about him," he said. "Guess I forgot."

"You frightened me," Nina admitted.

"Well, Hugh frightens me," said Simon. "Brings up bad memories."

Simon sat on the bed, and Nina sat down beside him.

"It's hard for me to talk about Emma."

Nina's inner voice spoke loudly: *Now . . . now is your moment.*

"Maybe . . . maybe we should talk to someone together," she suggested.

Simon's eyebrows arched. "Who?"

"My therapist, Dr. Wilcox."

Nina tossed out the suggestion, nervous how Simon would respond.

For a moment, he again was that blank canvas, but soon enough a thoughtful look crossed his face, followed by a light of recognition.

"Sure," he said, giving her hand a squeeze. "I think I'd like that."

* * *

In the morning, Nina called Dr. Wilcox's office with hope in her heart, eager to make that appointment, but her call was put through to the answering service. She spent the rest of her morning conducting a home visit with Michael Cooper, which took her mind off Simon and everything for an hour. The Cooper children had the day off from school, and Michael was working from home, so the timing was good for everyone. What did she learn? Marriage is hard. Michael was lovely. He and Wendy, as she found out, broke up because of the same behaviors she and Glen had been dealing with—too much other stuff and not enough them. The kids were fine at Michael's. It was a perfectly safe environment, and her recommendation would be for joint custody, end of story.

Not long after leaving the Cooper home, Nina's phone rang. She thought it might be Michael calling, letting her know she'd left something behind, but instead it was someone from Dr. Wilcox's office.

"I got your message just now. I'm sorry, we're trying to get to all of Dr. Wilcox's patients. There's . . . there's been a terrible . . ." Nina heard the sharp intake of breath over the phone. "There's been a terrible tragedy," the woman finally got out.

"Oh, my God," Nina said. "Is Dr. Wilcox all right?"

"No, she's not," said the woman. "There was a home invasion."

Nina had heard something about that on the New Hampshire news channel but did not recall that a victim had been identified.

"The doctors aren't sure she's going to make it."

CHAPTER 42

I met Ben in the library during lunch period to catch him up on the conversation with my father. We found a quiet corner near the biography section for us to talk. Reliving the conversation I had with my dad brought all those messy emotions right back to the surface. When the tears came, as I knew they would, Ben was at the ready with a tissue. It was sweet how much he cared, but I felt terrible about monopolizing our friendship with my problems.

"I'll tell you when you become annoying," Ben said with a smirk that almost put a smile on my face.

"Thank you," I said, dabbing my eyes, feeling exhausted and more than a bit embarrassed. Ben must have thought I went through the day crying.

"Do you remember the area code where he called you from?" he asked.

"It was an eight-oh-two," I said. With my emotions so supercharged, I had forgotten to look up the location. Ben took my phone, and two seconds later he had the answer.

"Vermont," he said.

"Vermont?" My voice inflection implied it was the last place in the world I thought he might be. "What's he doing there?"

Of course Ben couldn't answer, so instead he gave a shrug. "Could be he's there. Could be the call was spoofed."

"Spoofed?"

"Caller ID spoofing," said Ben, as if those extra words would jog some memory. "It's a hacker thing," he explained. "You can make calls that look like they're coming from anywhere in the country, the world even. It's super easy to do, and I think it's even legal."

"You don't own a cell phone," I said, eyeing him suspiciously. "How do you know all that?"

"There are other ways to get on the internet, Maggie," he said, kind enough to not punctuate his observation with a "duh."

I took my phone from him so I could see what was on the screen, and there it was, clear as could be: an area code search showing 802 as belonging to the entire state of Vermont. We'd gone to Vermont a few times on family trips, including during the February vacation before Dad had disappeared. We went skiing at Jay Peak, a mountain near the Canadian border, and it was so cold that I spent most of the time in the indoor waterpark.

They had this ride called La Chute, which is French for "you'll scream your face off." Riders enter a tube something like sixty feet in the air, and then drop almost vertically, going fifty miles an hour before you hit the loop, a 360-degree put-your-stomach-in-your-nose total freak-out. Connor wouldn't do it, but Dad would. We probably scrambled our brains riding that thing over and over again. Maybe that's why he snapped and had to go into hiding.

"So you *don't* think he's in Vermont?" I asked.

Our librarian shushed me from behind her desk. I guess I'd shouted at the thought of yet another of my father's deceptions.

"I'm hypothesizing. It's a possibility," said Ben, talking like a science teacher.

"And I know he loves to fish. He'd go every Saturday," I said, feeling a powerful need to defend my father, trying to dispel the possibility of yet another of his lies. "So why not go there? Doesn't Vermont have great fishing?"

"Why go anywhere at all?" asked Ben.

"Back to that," I said. "The big mystery is why he left in the first place."

"Tell me again what he said."

So I told him, as best as I could remember. I wished now that I had recorded the call, if only so I could've heard Dad's voice again. It had been a disturbing, strange, emotional, and confusing conversation. I kept hearing him crying; something I'll never forget.

"Sounds to me like it's really important to your dad that Mr. Fitch looks after you all, like with money and stuff," Ben said, reflexively using Simon's last name, because we were in school. I nodded, having had the same impression.

"I get it," I told him. "I just don't get why he can't come home, and why I can't tell Mom or Connor that Dad's alive and well. And why would he say he's done bad things and hurt people? And what did Mom do? He's blaming her for something and told me it can't go unpunished. What's that all about?"

Ben gave another shrug. "I don't understand my parents. How the heck can I understand yours? But he told you to make nice with Simon, right?"

Again, I nodded. "Yeah, make the peace because Simon's helping out financially and my dad can't." I made it sound as if sucking up to Simon would be harder than taking one of Ben's math tests. "I suppose I could get Mom to quit her job. That would make Simon happiest of all."

Ben looked confused. "Why does he care if she's working?"

I laughed because I lived it and Ben didn't, but still, he'd picked up on something that had never made sense to me.

"He says it's because of me—I need my mom around more, I'm really fragile right now, and I need her full attention."

"You seem to be doing fine," Ben said. "More than fine. Like, you dealt with Laura Abel and all that stuff while your father was missing. That doesn't make sense. Maybe Mr. Fitch thinks *he* should be the one to make all the money."

"Maybe," I said.

"But Seabury's not cheap," Ben added. "You'd think he'd be psyched your mom was making extra money."

That was a head-scratcher for me, too. We all knew teaching wasn't a path to riches.

"Could be he has family money," suggested Ben.

"Possible. My dad said he was going to check into Simon. Maybe he did. Maybe he found out Simon's rich and that's why he wants me to make the peace." I paused because something wasn't sitting right with me. "But Simon has to rent out his house to afford ours," I added.

A surprised look came to Ben's face. "Really? That doesn't sound rich to me. We have a ski condo that we rent, and it's like a super-big hassle. My dad is always complaining about renters, cleaning, maintenance, all that stuff. If he had the money, he wouldn't rent it to anybody."

"Well, Simon rents his," I said, not really seeing Ben's point. "It's got access to the lake and is close to skiing, so he says it's filled up pretty much all the time."

"How much is the rent?" he asked.

"I don't know," I said, annoyed now, because what did rent have to do with my father? "We don't really talk about it."

"You've been there?"

I nodded. "We went swimming there once or twice, back when he was getting ready to move in with us." I pursed my lips together like I had sucked on a lemon.

"So you know what it looks like?" he said.

"Yeah. Sure."

Ben went to work on my phone. "What are you doing?" I asked.

"Trying to figure out how much rent he gets," Ben said.

"Why?"

"We're trying to get a sense of how much money he's got, right? So this rent, plus his job, minus what your house costs, should tell us something."

I didn't get a strong feeling that Ben knew exactly what he was talking about, because as kids we didn't deal with money. Even so, it was an interesting exercise, so I went along with it. Ben had pulled up all the rental properties in Seabury listed on Airbnb, which was one of the websites his parents used to rent their ski condo.

I looked through the pictures from the search results, but none of them were of Simon's place. He had a small ranch home with an attached garage and a nice green lawn. The listings here were cottages mostly, or places that looked like ski lodges, or extremely small houses that were right on the lake. Simon's place had a short walk down a narrow path to a small rocky beach where you could swim or launch a kayak or a canoe, neither of which Simon owned.

"So, none of these?" Ben said, as he scrolled through the list again.

"No, none."

Next, Ben checked out VRBO, another rental website he knew about. The properties here were similar, some were the same, but none were Simon's robin's-egg-blue ranch home. We checked Craigslist and a few other sites Ben found using Google, but again not one of them listed Simon's home.

"Maybe he *is* rich," I said. "I mean rich enough that he doesn't have to rent out his place."

"Yeah, sure," said Ben, a bit absently, because he was thinking of something. "But why bother lying about renting it?"

I fell silent until a thought struck me.

"I don't know why," I said. "But I may know someone who might help us figure it out."

CHAPTER 43

Unable to sit still, Nina paced the tiled floor in the main lobby of Lakes Region General Hospital, waiting for Ginny and Susanna to arrive. Ginny cried upon learning the horrible news from Nina. She was Dr. Wilcox's patient as well, and Susanna had asked to join the quick noontime visit as a supportive friend.

She called Simon to share the terrible news. He stammered before he spoke—shocked, she thought, like everyone.

"So, she's . . . she's definitely going to make it?"

Nina found his phrasing odd. He did not sound hopeful, but more like he couldn't believe it was possible.

"The doctors aren't sure," Nina said. "I'm at the hospital now. Ginny and Susanna are on their way."

There was a long pause.

"Okay," he said, lengthening the word as if in thought. "That's just awful. I'm really sorry. Keep me posted, will you?"

Nina told him she would and said her good-byes.

As she waited, a recurring question spun a web through her mind, trapping her thoughts: *Who would have done this? Was it a patient? Someone with a grudge? Or was it simply a random attack?* Nina pushed aside those questions to focus on her friends. She realized it was the first time in ages that Las Tres Amigas had been together, but the grim circumstances made it a joyless reunion. They hugged, Ginny dabbing at her eyes, causing Nina's eyes to fill as well.

"What have you heard?" Susanna asked.

"Let's go," said Nina. "I'll tell you on the way."

They signed in as visitors and followed the signs to the third floor, where Dr. Wilcox had been moved after leaving the ICU. To everyone's collective disappointment, she was asleep when they arrived. A sweet-faced nurse agreed to let them leave the bright bouquet Ginny had purchased, along with a card Nina had selected.

The cubicle was small and crammed with machines. Nina didn't know a thing about all of the tubes, IVs, and equipment hooked up to Dr. Wilcox, but she had no difficulty understanding the extent of damage someone had inflicted on her.

Gauze bandages covered much of her head, and hideous black-and-blue bruises made Dr. Wilcox's face somewhat unrecognizable. *Did she fight off her attacker?* Nina wondered. *Are those defensive injuries to her hands? Did her assailant use a knife?* Nina swallowed hard. Her gaze traveled back to the battered and bandaged face, taking in the horrific stain of violence.

"I'm so sorry," she whispered. "Can I touch her hand?"

The nurse to whom Nina directed her question returned a quick nod. "She's heavily medicated, but I'm sure she knows you're here and I'm sure she's grateful."

They stayed only a few minutes, as instructed, before taking themselves to the coffee shop across the street from the hospital. Nina got their drinks without needing to ask for anybody's order: a chai latte for Susanna, an espresso for herself, and a green tea for Ginny. It was a reminder of how close she was to these women, how well she knew their tastes, personality quirks, everything, and how little she'd seen them lately. Again, Nina found herself crediting Simon's prescience. She was no longer readily available to anybody—not just her daughter.

Nina carried the drinks over to the table where Ginny and Susanna sat talking.

"I can't get over how awful she looked," Ginny said, giving her tea a cautious sip.

The women talked for a time about Dr. Wilcox, the horror of her injuries, and how they might support her during the recovery process.

"Who do you think did this to her?" Susanna asked, her voice a whisper, as if the assailant could be nearby.

Nobody had a good answer. Nina contemplated sharing how she and Simon had planned to start couples therapy with Dr. Wilcox, but something silenced her. She knew the impetus was the tense exchange they'd had about Hugh. It would be hard, if not impossible, to talk about Hugh Dolan without telling her friends how she'd contacted him, his attempt at extortion, to say nothing of the reason he thought they should meet.

You're not safe . . .

She had no desire to dredge up Ginny's and Susanna's growing concern about Simon. Soon the conversation segued from Dr. Wilcox and possible suspects to more familiar topics—kids, town gossip, and committee nonsense. Everyone laughed when Ginny told a story about finding a mouse in her car, which really put an end to the pall that had made even mundane chitchat feel weighty.

"It's good to talk," Susanna said.

Ginny's eyes turned serious. "We need to make it a priority to see each other more often," she said with authority. "What happened to Dr. Wilcox is a wake-up call to us all. Any day could be our last."

"You just never know," Susanna concurred. "But Nina, you've got to own this more than anybody. We don't see you anymore."

Nina tensed at the jab, which had hit on an uncomfortable truth.

"That's not true," she said, feeling an immediate need to go on the defensive. "We've seen each other."

Ginny and Susanna exchanged a knowing glance.

"Girls' weekend," Ginny said. "Workouts you can't do with us because you have a home gym."

She said "home gym" with her nose in the air like it was highfalutin'.

"Movie dates you canceled," Susanna said, getting her phone out. "And we're not leaving here without making a firm plan for dinner. Let's go to Cucina Toscana again. I'm dying for the calamari. It was amazing. Nina, you would know that if you hadn't blown us off the last time."

For a moment, Nina had no idea what Susanna was talking about, but then she recalled the evening Simon had gotten suddenly and violently ill, forcing her to cancel dinner plans at that same restaurant. Something else coalesced in Nina's mind, another memory, this one more recent—the bottle of ipecac syrup she'd found under the bathroom vanity.

She had assumed Simon brought it in the confusion of packing. People often kept outdated meds around. Of course, it was plausible he'd packed it by accident. But something else was possible, too, Nina realized. *Simon could have used the syrup on himself.*

Nina searched for a motive, some reason Simon would want to purposely make himself violently ill. Her thoughts flashed to Teresa, and to Chris, her obsessive boyfriend who'd faked having cancer to keep Teresa by his side. A fierce chill crept up her spine. *He wanted to keep me home. He wanted to keep me with him. Did Simon use Maggie that night as a ploy to keep me from leaving the house?* Nina put herself back in that moment, remembering how they had both been reluctant to leave Maggie alone, especially when Simon was so ill. Had it all been an act? *Could he be using Maggie now, manufacturing emotional problems for her to try and force me to leave work?*

Nina came to the stunning possibility that Simon could be waging an elaborate bit of psychological warfare, instilling doubt and worry in her for his own gain. The word "controlling" tumbled through her mind once again.

"You okay, hon?" Susanna asked with a concerned look in her eyes. "You've gone a bit pale."

"I'm fine," Nina answered quickly. She knew her friends would have her back, that they'd be the first to pile on Simon, warn her away, but Nina wasn't ready to hear the accusations. This could well be in her imagination, and unless she had proof, she would continue to protect the life she and Simon were building together.

"Just thinking of Dr. Wilcox, is all."

Ginny and Susanna acknowledged the shared sentiment with weighty expressions of their own.

Nina sipped at her espresso, contemplating her next move.

There was a bank nearby. She could make a quick five-hundred-dollar withdrawal and could probably sit down face-to-face with Hugh in an hour or two. She'd pick somewhere safe, crowded. She'd make sure there was good parking for a quick escape. He wouldn't try anything, not in daylight hours. A little bit of money to discover if there was any truth to his dire warnings suddenly seemed like a very wise investment.

CHAPTER 44

Was it stupid and foolish to meet with a potentially danger-ous man?

That was the question on Nina's mind as she sat down across from Hugh Dolan. She didn't know anything about him, not even how he got here, or where he came from. Did his drug addiction make him impulsive, desperate? Did he plan to take her by gunpoint to the ATM for another with-drawal? She'd found him where he said he'd be, in a booth in the back of the Bar and Feather, a speakeasy-themed res-taurant in downtown Seabury. Nina had picked this meet-ing spot because it always drew a sizable crowd even in the early afternoon. Simon was coaching robotics after school, so running into him wasn't a concern.

The first thing Nina noticed was the look of surprise on Hugh's face when he set eyes on her, as if something about Nina's appearance startled him.

Even though the restaurant was dimly lit, the curtains drawn to keep out sunlight, Nina didn't need to see well to know that Hugh Dolan lived a hard life. He looked like his mug shot, but in person his narrow face was more weather-beaten. His skin had no color save for pockets of acne that stuck out like constellations of red stars. Gray streaks ran through greasy hair that fell to his shoulders, and the odor of cigarettes was noticeable from across the table. His arms barely filled out the faded jean shirt he wore. Despite his appearance, to Nina's professional eyes he didn't give off vibes that he posed any physical danger. Then again, she knew the lengths some addicts would go to for their fix, so she refused to dismiss the possibility outright.

Hugh ordered a whiskey shot with a beer chaser from the black-clad waitress. Nina asked only for a glass of water.

He studied Nina through sunken, hooded eyes, saying nothing for a time until she got the unspoken message. From the wallet she kept in her monogrammed Coach bag, Nina produced five crisp one-hundred-dollar bills. She slid them across the table to Hugh, who counted the money twice, folded the bills carefully in half, then stuffed them in his shirt pocket. After the waitress came by with their drinks, Hugh took his shot, ordered another, and downed half the beer.

"You got this, right?" he said.

Nina heard the steely edge to his voice, casting fresh doubts on her earlier supposition that he wasn't prone to acts of violence.

"Yes, I'll cover the tab," Nina said, correctly guessing his intent. "But you're not driving, are you?"

She hated how nervous she sounded, wary he might exploit any weakness on her part. Hugh smirked knowingly.

"I can handle myself," he said. "You look like her, you know that? Your hair mostly."

Reflexively, her hand went to her head, forgetting for a moment she'd dramatically altered her appearance.

"I look like who?" she asked apprehensively.

"Like Emma."

Nina's heart sailed to her throat. Now she understood the look of surprise when he first set eyes on her. She hadn't thought that Hugh might bring a picture of the elusive Emma Dolan, but now she prayed he had.

"Do you have a photo of her?" Her voice was barely above a whisper. Perspiration prickled her forehead.

Hugh took out his phone and tapped the screen before presenting Nina with an image of a smiling woman, sitting on a rock at the ocean.

"Happier times," said Hugh a bit wistfully.

She saw a vague similarity in their faces, Emma's being thinner and longer than Nina's, her nose less pronounced, but the hair was unmistakably the same—a bob with straight bangs and swept sides. A pit opened in Nina's stomach. It was unsettling to gaze into the face of her near-doppelganger, a dead one at that, but what did it mean?

"I see the similarities, but lots of men have a type," Nina said, feeling a sudden urge to be protective of the man she still loved.

"True," Hugh said. "But Simon Fitch isn't like lots of men."

Nina stiffened in her seat. This was the true purpose of her visit: to find out if there was any truth to Hugh's alarming claims. She probed his eyes, studied his body language, searching for any of the telltale signs of deceit she was trained to recognize. Seeing none, she again studied the picture of Emma Dolan, a woman in her forties with a haircut from a different era.

"What do you mean by that?" she asked.

Hugh downed the second whiskey the waitress brought over before enjoying a few sips of beer. He cleaned the foam from his thin lips with the back of his hand.

Nina lost patience with him. "If I'm not safe," she said, talking hurriedly now, "why wouldn't you simply explain it to me over the phone? Why the insistence on the money?"

Hugh looked at her like she was dim. "Are you asking where's the goodness in my heart?"

Hugh rolled up his sleeves to reveal for Nina a thin, near-bloodless arm, dotted with scars recognizable as needle injection marks.

"I gave my heart to something else. But I'll make good on my promise. I'll tell you the truth. That was our deal. So tell me, has he isolated you from your friends and family yet? Does he make you question things? Does he try to control your life? Trust me, Nina, you're not safe."

Nina's throat went dry as a jumble of thoughts came to her, starting with Susanna and Ginny, who not long ago chided her for being so unavailable. But there were always valid reasons causing her to cancel plans with her friends, and Simon wasn't keeping her from seeing her parents, as Hugh had implied. She hadn't seen them because she didn't want to bring the stress of Simon and Maggie's difficulties to Nebraska, simple as that. *Or is the strife something he's cultivating partly for that purpose?* The question she asked herself took her by surprise. She contemplated Hugh's other allegations.

Does he make you question things? Does he try to control your life?

Nina went silent as her thoughts flickered back to their first big blowup in the new house, the one over the TV remote and the instructions she'd had no memory of giving. And there were other small, rather inconsequential happenings that didn't seem to amount to much when taken as separate incidents, but as a whole began to form a disturbing pattern. There was Maggie's perspective: the trip to Niagara Falls that she clearly thought had been fabricated to make Nina feel guilty about her new job; Simon's thoughtless remarks at the school assembly; the missing homework; and of course, the dark look Maggie had described that Nina, too, had seen on that odd morning when Simon was preparing to cut the neighbor's tree branches.

And don't forget the day he bought you a home gym so

you wouldn't have a reason to work out with your friends, she told herself.

She thought about the dinner with the superintendent that Simon swore he had told her about, and the inappropriate remark about an affair—the one he later denied making to Ginny. *Controlling?* Perhaps.

Nina caught a glimpse of her distorted reflection in Hugh's near-empty beer glass, seeing again the haircut she had gotten at Simon's—what was it? Suggestion? Or was it more than that? No, she'd done it on her own, Nina told herself. She had willfully, enthusiastically, gone to that hair appointment, and made the dramatic change to look like the model in the magazine. A hair appointment Simon had made, she reminded herself, with hopes she'd style her hair to look like Emma Dolan. Other thoughts came to her, a swirl of doubt stirred up as if Hugh were a whirlwind churning up the uncertainty lurking within her. She recalled the mixed message Simon had sent about the job after gifting her the Coach bag, and found herself wondering if he *was* intentionally making her question things.

Nina had been deceived before, but the way Simon looked at her, loved her, the things he said, the note he wrote and put in that bag, his touch, the way he connected to her, all made her believe to her core that she wasn't being lied to this time around. And every doubt Hugh's accusations had conjured could easily be countered with some logical explanation.

Safe or not? Who to believe?

"Why do you keep saying I'm not safe?"

Hugh raised his head. His red-rimmed eyes bored into Nina's. His fierce gaze made her cower inwardly, but she didn't let it show on her face.

"Emma didn't kill herself," Hugh said. "*He* killed her."

The accusation did not come as a shock. Simon had told

her very clearly that the police had questioned him. Standard procedure—interview the spouse.

"Why would you say such a thing?" she asked.

"Because I know," Hugh answered flatly.

"The police didn't think so," said Nina. "They'd have arrested him."

"That's because they're idiots," Hugh said.

And you have a lot of reasons to dislike the police, thought Nina, seeing Hugh's mug shots in her mind.

"I think my money bought a better answer than that, don't you?"

"I know my sister," answered Hugh after a moment's pause, "and she wasn't suicidal." He picked up his phone, again showing Nina the picture of a smiling woman at the seashore. "Does she look depressed to you?"

Nina felt a burst of sympathy for Hugh. "Depression wears many masks," she said. "I know it's hard to accept, but what we see on the outside doesn't always reflect what's going on inside." Nina thought it highly doubtful he'd read excerpts from Emma's diary, as she had.

"You sound just like the police," Hugh said bitterly. "They jumped right to suicide because Emma was seeing a therapist. But she wasn't in therapy because she was depressed. Simon was making her crazy. She never saw her friends. She stopped seeing me, our parents, all of us. There was always some issue, and Simon was at the center of it all."

Nina had a theory: Hugh needed someone to blame for Emma's death and found the perfect scapegoat in his former brother-in-law. It gave him a motive for his accusations. What she still didn't have was evidence to refute his claims.

"He controlled her," Hugh continued. "What she did. Where she went. Everything. He took her over, completely, even what she looked like."

"That doesn't prove anything, Hugh."

"Yeah, and neither did her suicide note. It was short and sure as shit didn't explain why she did it. All it said was: *I'm sorry. I can't take this anymore.* What the hell is that? It could have been a note she'd written after a fight. For all I know he had copied her handwriting."

"Seems like a bit of a stretch to me," said Nina.

"Maybe, maybe not. What I do know is that Emma had never talked about taking her life. It happened out of the blue. One day she's fine, and the next she ODs intentionally on her pain meds and Ambien."

But Nina knew all this. Just as she knew that the police had questioned Simon after his wife's death. They'd done a deep dive into his computer, looking for affairs, incriminating Google searches, illegal drug purchases on the Dark Web, contacts with nefarious individuals, recently purchased life insurance policies, finding nothing to make them remotely suspicious. They had talked to friends who said Simon was a wonderful, attentive husband. There were no signs of abuse, no reports of domestic violence.

"Had your sister overdosed at any other time?"

Hugh returned a grim nod. "Yeah, it happened a few times. Her chronic pain was getting tough to manage."

"Why was she on pain meds?"

Hugh shrugged. "I don't know what started it. Emma had a good career as an accountant before she quit her job. That was about a year after she and Simon got married. Simon blamed the job for her downfall; said it was too much pressure on her. You ask me, I don't think he ever wanted Emma to work. Didn't like her having her own money. You know that's one way abusers try to control you. Like pushers, man, they make you dependent."

That revelation would have alarmed Nina, but Simon was extremely generous with his money, even putting her on his checking account, and he'd been excited when she got the job, only voicing major concerns after Maggie started having troubles.

"He was always going on about how he could provide," Hugh continued. "Then one day, seemingly out of nowhere, Emma starts suffering chronic pain. Work pressures, she said, but I think Simon somehow put the idea in her head so he could get her hooked on pain pills. Next thing you know, she's popping opioids like they're Pez candy. Don't get me wrong, I appreciated her habit." Nina caught the glint in Hugh's eyes. "Back then, man, it was like any unexplained twinge got an oxy prescription and refills to go with it. Eventually, she ended up leaving her job. She couldn't function anymore."

Nina knew one cause of chronic pain was depression, which aligned with Simon's story. As a whole, though, despite decades of research, the condition was still poorly understood and notoriously hard to control.

Work pressures. Depression. Chronic pain. Drug abuse. Interesting, thought Nina. Was Simon afraid that Nina, too, would become overwhelmed with her job and stop functioning, as Emma had done? Maybe Nina's career was a reminder of all he had lost. A part of Nina relaxed because she believed that yes, indeed, that was exactly the case.

"What can you tell me about her other . . . overdoses?" Nina gulped on the word.

Hugh's face turned harder, more serious. "Why are you asking? What did Simon tell you?"

"He said he tried to help her, that he tried to induce vomiting."

Hugh thought a beat before his expression changed as a memory came to him.

"Oh, yeah. Weird you bring that up. We were in the ER waiting room—Simon, my parents, and me. I remember the docs told him to never do that again if she overdosed."

There was no delay between her question and the answer, suggesting to Nina that Hugh didn't have to think before he spoke.

Relief washed over Nina. *Simon didn't lie!*

"Look, I get that I don't exactly have my life together. But that's no reason for you not to believe me. He killed her," Hugh said glumly, then shrugged. "But my conscience is clean."

It was clear Hugh *believed* Simon was responsible for his sister's death, but he hadn't convinced Nina of the fact. On top of that, Nina had a possible new understanding of Simon's concerns around her job, his irrational fear that she might end up as dysfunctional as Emma.

Nina set her business card on the table and stood to go.

"Hugh, I'm sick to my stomach that I may have fed your habit, but I had to know what you wanted to tell me. Now that I know, I sincerely regret paying you. If you give me the money back, right now, I'll use it to fund your drug treatment. I'll pay more if needed. Please, Hugh, please. You need help."

Hugh laughed and shook his head in mild disgust.

"No, lady," he said firmly. "You do."

CHAPTER 45

Last week Connor threw a touchdown pass, his first ever, but it wasn't enough to give his team a win in the playoffs. Bad for him, good for me, because now he had a free afternoon to help us figure out the mystery of Simon's rental property. When I told him what Ben had found out, Connor was intrigued—not because he thought Simon was up to anything, but because he saw it as a way to help ease some tension at home. Like me, Connor loved our mom, and unlike me, he liked Simon. He wanted things to be lovely and peaceful, so if proving there was nothing going on would get me off the Simon warpath, he was all for helping.

It was Connor's idea to borrow a time-lapse camera that belonged to the father of his best friend, Luke. Apparently, and I'd only just found this out, hunters use time-lapse cameras to help track their prey. Didn't seem fair to me, but I got it—you have to know where the animals are to shoot them. In a way, we were like hunters, staked out in the woods across from Simon's home by the lake. We rode our bikes there, Ben, too, and kept them out of sight behind some trees. There were neighbors on each side of Simon's house, but the trees would keep us well hidden.

Connor went to work attaching the camera's straps to a

tree in front of Simon's place. He checked the line of sight to make sure he could get a good shot. The camera was boxy and camouflaged like hunting gear. It was easy to miss, even close up. From our hiding spot, we couldn't see the lake behind the house, but we could feel the cold breeze blowing off the water. The clouds were thick and heavy, and I hoped the rain would hold off until evening, as predicted.

I had on a sweater and wool hat but forgot my gloves, leaving my fingers frozen as icicles. Ben's glasses kept fogging up, and he had to clean them frequently on his jacket sleeve. We were down on the ground, where it was even colder, pulling dead leaves around our bodies like animals making a nest. Connor, who was more into skiing than I was, didn't seem bothered by the chilly temps. He pushed and pulled at the camera, making sure it was secured tightly in case the wind picked up.

When he finished, Connor came over to where Ben and I were half buried, looking down at us like we were a couple of crazies.

"What are you two doing on the ground?" he asked.

"We're hiding in case someone shows up," I whispered.

"Stop whispering," Connor said in a loud voice, sounding annoyed. "Nobody is around here. You're being a little freak."

I got up, leaves raining down from my body as I stood. Ben did the same.

"Is the camera all set?" I asked.

"All set," he said. He took out his phone and showed us the app that controlled the camera's settings. "I set the time-lapse frequency to fifteen minutes, and the duration is set to all day. The photos automatically get deleted every few hours."

"What happens at night?" asked Ben.

"Shuts down to save battery," Connor said. "It'll power on by itself at sunrise."

"Isn't Luke's dad going to wonder what happened to it?"

Connor had said something about the camera costing over two hundred dollars, so I figured he'd notice it was gone.

"Nah, he bought a new one. This has been in a box for like, a year. No problem there." Connor's smile faded as a serious look came to his face. "But you and you," he said, pointing at me and Ben, "need to stop with this nonsense about Simon once I get proof that nothing is going on here."

I nodded because that was the deal I'd struck with him. I was okay with it, too. Even if this didn't work out, I still had my other secret hope about how we'd get rid of Simon—the one about our dad.

I wondered if Dad was camped out in the woods of Vermont like we were camped out now. I had messaged him on Talkie every day with no reply, and tried the number he had called me from countless times, but never got an answer. As much as I wanted to know where he was, why he left, I had to know what Mom did to him and what he planned to do about it.

Then I thought about our last call suddenly going dead. I tried not to think the unimaginable—that *he* was dead in a ditch somewhere, that the people chasing after him had found him, those kinds of thoughts. But I had this knowing, a deep-in-my-bones kind of knowing, that he was fine, that he was going to come back and everything would be like it had been. He'd get over his anger at Mom, whatever that was all about; Mom would realize she loved Dad, not Simon; and we'd be a family again. I believed this even if our spying expedition turned out to be a big waste of time.

With no warning, and seemingly for no reason at all, Connor gasped and his eyes grew wide with fright, as if something terrible was about to happen. He looked every which way, his body crouched, tense, head darting, searching for the safest route to run.

"It's a drug dealer," he whispered in a mocking way. "No, no, it's a prostitute."

Connor straightened and curled his lip at me in disgust. "Really, you two clowns have been streaming too much crap on the internet."

I shouldn't have told Connor what we thought we might find, but he'd demanded some kind of explanation for the stakeout, and Ben's theory about prostitution or drug dealing was the best one we had.

Connor was done. He was going for his bike. It was a long ride back home, a lot of it uphill. Mom was at work, thinking I was at Ben's house, and Simon was out of the house, we didn't know where, when we left, but we all had to get home soon or questions might get asked.

"Listen," Connor said, taking a serious tone. "You've got to get over this Simon business. I mean it, Maggie. After we prove this was a waste of time, no more. You've got to accept the fact that Dad is dead and Simon is in our life now."

My heart shattered because Connor should know—no, he *had* to know; he deserved the truth as much as I did. It wasn't fair of me to keep the secret from him. No matter what our father thought, I *could* trust Connor. I'd explain that Dad would be in danger if the police found out he was alive. All I had to do was show him the Talkie messages we'd been exchanging to feel a million pounds lighter. The harsh wind felt like a slap across my face, like it was my father's hand punishing me for breaking my vow.

"Connor," I said, reaching for my phone. "There's something . . . something I need to tell you."

But before I could get the words out, I heard the sound of

car wheels coming down the road. All three of us froze like deer sensing a predator.

"Get down," Connor said in a harsh whisper, no joking this time.

We all went down quickly as the car came into view. But it wasn't a car, it was Simon's truck, which I recognized even before he turned into the driveway, flashing us his signature bumper sticker: I'M A TEACHER, WHAT'S YOUR SUPERPOWER?

"What's he doing here?" whispered Ben, who looked extremely nervous, like this was the first time he'd done something wrong and was about to get caught in the act.

"I bet he's meeting a prostitute," Connor said with a grin. "It is his house, dummies."

Ben shook his head in disgust as if to say Connor was too immature for his liking.

"Quiet," I hushed them as Simon got out of his truck. He did not look suspicious, worried, hurried, or anything like that. He looked exactly like, well, Simon—khaki pants and a heavy jacket over what I presumed was some kind of polo shirt. He closed the door of the truck with a bang. Connor shifted position and a large branch snapped under his weight. The crack drew Simon's attention, and his head pivoted in the direction of the noise.

I let out a gasp, loud enough for Ben to shush me. We lay frozen on the ground as if encased in ice. Simon's probing eyes searched the trees for the source of the noise. I turned my head to look at Connor, who didn't look so cocky anymore. He must have been thinking what I was thinking: *We can't explain being here.* Talk about things getting awkward at home.

Ben was breathing loudly beside me. I watched Simon advance down the driveway, his gaze locked on the woods.

"Oh shit, I think he sees us."

Connor's warning got Ben ready to bolt, but I held him down. Even that little bit of movement rustled the leaves underneath him, drawing Simon forward right up to the top of his driveway, then beyond.

When he crossed the road, Simon walked to the edge of the woods, put his hands on his hips, and stood perfectly still. Ben's breathing became increasingly shallow. I risked a glance. His face was white as a sheet. Dots of sweat popped up on his forehead even in this chill.

Simon took a single step into the woods. I heard leaves crunch under his foot. For a second, I thought Ben was going to get up and make a run for it. I moved my hand, slowly as could be, over to Ben, whose cold fingers interlocked with mine. We made eye contact. I tried not to breathe too hard, too fast, but I was quaking inside. Turning my head, I watched Simon take another step into the woods, peering through the trees, now no more than fifteen yards from our hiding spot. Ben squeezed my hand harder. I was coiled so tight I thought I might spring up by accident. Out of the corner of my eye, I could see Connor looking as nervous as I felt.

Simon took another step. I held my breath. I'm sure both Ben and Connor were doing the same. He fixed his gaze right on the spot where I was hiding, and I swore he saw me, but instead of advancing, he turned and started walking back to his driveway. Moments later, he was inside his house. We waited. Nobody moved a muscle for what felt like an hour, but it was probably only a few minutes.

"Okay," Connor whispered. "Take the bikes through the woods. Don't get on them until we reach Black Oak."

I nodded as I stood. My legs were stiff and cold. We formed a line, Connor in front, me in the middle, Ben taking up the rear. We kept low as we pushed our bikes as quiet as could be over the dead leaves carpeting the forest floor.

I took the whole terrifying encounter as a sign from Dad to keep his secret at least for one more day.

I turned my head to look back at the house and felt my stomach drop when I saw that the curtains in the front room were parted. From my position, I could see Simon looking out the window in our direction. Then, I watched as he pulled those curtains closed.

CHAPTER 46

Regret is an awful thing. It filled Glen with shame and sadness. There were things he missed, of course. Football games. Lacrosse games. Cookouts. Fishing. Those hazy memories that would flitter in and out of his mind at random intervals all the days he sat chained in the box. But regret was its own special kind of torture. It was more potent than depression, boredom, longing, even memories. Because at the root of regret lay helplessness—an inability to change a desired outcome.

If only . . .

Those, he'd come to believe, were the two most destructive words for the mind.

If. Only.

If only he'd told Maggie to run.

If only he'd passed a message to her.

If only he'd kept his mouth shut at his job.

If only he hadn't gone to the Muddy Moose.

If only he appreciated his family more.

If only . . .

Glen kept hearing Maggie's voice over and over in his head, sweet and unsure, and the sound crimped his heart anew. He had failed his family in a whole new way. He had one chance, one swing of the bat, and he had missed. Simon would never let him talk to Maggie again. He had made that abundantly clear.

Glen's stomach rumbled with hunger. He'd been left with no food. He embraced the pain; he deserved it for his failure.

Swing and a miss . . .

But hours went by, and maybe even days; hard to track time down here.

All he knew was that Simon hadn't visited the box, maybe for the longest stretch yet.

Is this how I'm going to die? Glen asked himself over and over. Left alone. Completely forgotten. If so, at least he wouldn't have to bear witness to his family's suffering any longer. At least he'd be gone.

His bathroom had a foul reek. The water he'd been rationing was running low. The batteries of his LED light were nearly out of juice, but it didn't much matter. He couldn't read even if he had wanted. His mind was elsewhere. Soon he'd be in the dark. Then he'd waste away. Maybe it wasn't so awful. He considered it almost romantically. One day he'd close his eyes . . . and then all those regrets would be gone. Someday someone would crash through the wall of the box to find his bones shackled to a chain. Then, those who mattered to him most, assuming his family was still alive, would at last have some closure.

Glen was entertaining these thoughts when the door to the box flew open, and light flooded in. Simon was there, looming in the doorway.

"Did you say something to Maggie? Did you get a message to her somehow?"

"No," Glen said, cowering, slinking away. His first inclination was always to move to safety, but there was no safe corner in the box. Simon stayed rooted and Glen quickly got the sense he didn't come to hurt him; he came for answers.

"I think she was here, with her friend. Now, why would that be?"

Glen got anxious, too. *Why would that be?*

"She's probably curious about you. She's inquisitive. It's her nature."

"Hmmm . . ."

Simon appeared lost in thought. "Maybe so," he said, rubbing his chin. "But if I find out you're lying, Glen . . ."

He didn't bother finishing.

"Nina's been in contact with my ex-brother-in-law, Hugh," said Simon. "Why?"

"Who is Hugh?"

"Emma's brother. He's a junkie. A loser. I decided to start checking Nina's Facebook app on her phone. Careless girl never logs out. Sure enough, she and Hugh have been exchanging messages about me. He wants to meet her. Maybe they've already met. Now, why would Nina reach out to him? What's she thinking?"

Glen was Simon's best source for information. Knowing Nina the way he did, he could venture a guess.

"Obviously, she's looking into you. Something's made her nervous and she wants to know things about you. Things you might not be sharing."

"The therapist?" Simon wanted the source.

"For sure, that."

"I thought the same. But I also went to the Muddy Moose—see if Teresa Mitchell returned. That would be a problem. Remember her?"

Glen said nothing.

"Well, she is back. I bet you *anything* Nina went to see her. If she did, she'd have found out your love story was just a little one-night stand. Why, why, why does this all have to get so complicated?"

It sickened Glen to imagine what Nina must have thought

of him all this time—a liar, a thief, an adulterer. His spirit lifted somewhat at the possibility she'd learned part of the truth.

Glen knew that Simon had carefully planned the setup with Teresa. He loved talking about his cleverness. At first he wasn't going to use Teresa's name in that text message he sent Nina. When Simon learned Teresa had taken off, leaving no forwarding address, and nobody counted on her coming back, he decided to add more detail, thinking it made the story more believable.

The pictures he'd sent, coupled with the lie, had served their purpose well. As long as Nina believed Glen had enjoyed a torrid affair, it made it easier for her to move on with another man—specifically Simon.

Simon made a tsk-tsk sound. "I didn't think she'd go looking for that waitress after all this time. Damn therapy."

And that's when Glen knew Simon intended to kill Teresa, if for nothing else than out of sheer vindictiveness.

"You must be hungry." A kinder look came to his face. "I'll make you some eggs. Then I got to get home for dinner. Pasta primavera tonight. Yum. Maybe I'll come back later and let you watch TV. I'm thinking you're going to be really interested in the evening news."

"The news?" Glen was confused.

"Yes, sir—the monster is on the loose."

Glen went cold inside. "Simon, what have you done?"

"You'll see soon enough. Thought I did a better job of it, but no worries. I wore a mask. It's not like she's going to identify me or anything, and besides I left plenty of reasons for the police to look elsewhere."

Glen's mind wandered, as it tended to do, from this thought to that, and he wasn't concerned about monsters, or the news.

He was thinking about Maggie.

Why was she here?

Maybe he *had* gotten a message to her, unwittingly even? Was it possible? And just like that, hope returned—hope tempered with a great deal of worry.

The house was alarmed; not with one system, but two. The second system was a solar-charged backup in case of a power failure. That backup alarm sent an alert directly to Simon's cell phone anytime someone entered the house.

Glen prayed nobody got the foolish idea to come looking here alone.

Simon was about to shut the door, but turned back to Glen.

"I think Nina's going to quit this time. I really do." Simon looked quite pleased with himself. "If not, I've got one more thing to try. Anyway, here's to hoping."

The door clicked shut. Alone again.

Glen's LED light flickered . . . flickered . . . and returned him to darkness.

CHAPTER 47

There was something odd in the air at dinner, something strained. Meals had been quieter in general with Simon at the table, but usually Nina couldn't hear the clink of a fork on a plate or a gulp of water going down. Tonight it was different, but when pressed, nobody owned up to anything being amiss. Connor took his usual mini-mountain helpings of pasta; Maggie ate her food solemnly with Daisy splayed out under the table at her feet; Simon served Nina the asparagus drizzled with olive oil, all with little more said than "Pass the bread, please."

Nina wondered if the tension had to do with the disagreement she and Simon recently had about Thanksgiving. Simon did not want to go to Nebraska, saying that his continued difficulties with Maggie would make the trip too uncomfortable and would ruin the holiday for everyone. To assuage Nina's guilt at leaving him behind, Simon assured her that there were plenty of teachers with whom he could celebrate the day.

Hugh Dolan's words flashed like a neon sign illuminating lingering doubts: *Has he isolated you from your friends and family?* Nina dismissed the notion. Simon was happy she was going home for the holidays; he said so himself. *He* was the one staying behind, for *his* reasons. Even so, none of this felt right to Nina. Family meant everything to her. The thought of this divide between her daughter and Simon and its impact on other parts of her life was incredibly upsetting.

"Maggie, honey, you look tired, are you feeling all right?"

Nina was concerned about the dark circles ringing her daughter's eyes, her wan complexion, and worried she might be coming down with something. *God, please don't be the flu.*

"You do look a bit . . . stressed, Maggie," Simon said, delivering an odd pause. "That must have been a difficult homework assignment you and Ben were working on."

To Nina's ears, Simon's tone sounded a bit off, almost mocking, as if he were suggesting Maggie and Ben had been engaged in some other kind of activity, maybe the sort a boy and girl with raging hormones might test out. But Nina knew better. Ben was Maggie's friend, nothing more.

She knew that Maggie had gone to Ben's that afternoon to study for something, but hadn't pressed for details, because once again, her mind had been on her caseload. Guilt about the holiday, worry about Maggie, it all ate away at her appetite, but Nina took a bite of pasta to be supportive of Simon's efforts in the kitchen.

She was about to ask Maggie if the lab report grade had been adjusted as Simon had promised, when the doorbell rang. Daisy barked wildly. Nina looked puzzled—popover visits from Susanna had ended when she'd moved in with Simon.

"I'll get it," Connor said, up from the table in a flash, with Daisy close on his heels. Nina heard him open the door, heard Daisy's excited barking, and then heard a familiar voice from her past. The man assured Daisy he wasn't a threat, and soon enough the barking stopped. The last time she'd seen him, he'd been bringing Daisy home to her. A moment later, Connor came back into the kitchen with Detective Eric Wheeler following.

Wheeler still wore a military-short haircut, but looked like he'd put on some weight. He was here alone, and Nina didn't know if his previous partner, Detective Murphy, had been reassigned or had moved on.

"Sorry to interrupt dinner," Wheeler said to Nina, "but I was wondering if I could get a moment of your time. In private."

Nina was up from her seat the instant she laid eyes on him. She knew he had come with news about Glen. There could be no other reason for the unannounced visit.

"Of course," Nina said, her gaze shifting over to Simon, who looked as tense as she felt. "Simon should join us. We can go to my office. Kids, stay here a moment."

Nina's voice quavered slightly. Maggie and Connor exchanged worried looks, while Nina, Simon, and Detective Wheeler departed the kitchen for the office, where the framed pictures were still on the floor.

"What's going on?" Nina asked nervously.

"No easy way to say this, so I'm just going to come out and say it," Wheeler began.

Nina took hold of Simon's hand. *His bones,* she thought. *They finally found his bones.*

"The DNA analysis of hair fibers from the assault of Dr. Sydney Wilcox came back from forensics this afternoon."

Why is he telling this to me? Nina wondered. *Why is any of this my business? I'm just a client. Why not tell Dr. Wilcox's family?*

Wheeler said, "The samples came back a hundred percent match for Glen Garrity."

CHAPTER 48

They gathered in the living room like it was another family meeting. There'd been too much going on to make those meetings a weekly occurrence as Nina had intended, but now there was more, much more, to add to the agenda. Simon and Nina sat on the love seat. Maggie and Connor were on the sofa. Detective Wheeler sat on a chair Connor had brought in from the kitchen.

Connor was red-eyed from crying. Only fifteen minutes earlier, he had learned the bone-jarring news about his dad, but nobody could believe it was true. But it was true, Nina told herself. Hair and fiber samples taken from the crime scene matched Glen's DNA with 100 percent certainty. Even bits of his skin had been scraped from underneath the victim's fingernails, left there as she'd fought for her life. It was a fact: Glen had broken into Dr. Wilcox's home and assaulted her viciously, mercilessly.

But why? What could possibly be his motive for the attack?

In their private meeting, Detective Wheeler had learned of the connection between Nina and Dr. Wilcox, but he was no closer to an answer regarding motive than she was. Nina turned her attention to her daughter, whom she thought looked oddly placid. She assumed Maggie was in shock, and maybe that's why she did not look as bewildered as the rest of the family.

"I know my dad," Maggie said flatly. "He wouldn't have hurt that woman."

Nina didn't share a fraction of her daughter's conviction. Glen—his life, his choices—made it impossible to discount the improbable.

"What makes you say that, Maggie?" Detective Wheeler asked.

Nina caught something in her daughter's expression—the eyes mostly. A weight was there. She could see it clearly, *had* seen it clearly for days now, even at dinner tonight before the big bomb dropped. Maggie was holding something back. Glen was alive. Glen was around, nearby. Maggie was acting oddly. Nina put it all together and came to an extremely unsettling conclusion.

"Sweetheart," Nina said to Maggie, her voice low, thinking she might have figured something out. "Have you been in touch with your father?"

Guilt radiated off Maggie like a miniature sun. Her eyes filled and then the tears streaked down her face like a pipe had burst. Her body shook as she gulped for air between anguished sobs. Nina crossed the room with hurried steps, taking her daughter in her arms. Connor looked utterly shaken, as if he'd absorbed a brutal hit on the football field and couldn't catch his breath. Only Detective Wheeler didn't look completely stunned, or even slightly surprised. No doubt he was accustomed to people keeping all sorts of secrets.

For the next fifteen minutes, Maggie confessed to everything: the Talkie friend request from Tracy Nuts; her promise in subsequent messages to keep the secret; their phone conversation from a number she had traced to Vermont.

"What did you do to make him run away?" Maggie asked

her mother with tears in her eyes. "Dad told me you did something and that's one of the reasons he had to disappear. What did you do?"

"Nothing," Nina said. "I did nothing."

"What exactly did he say? You can tell us; it's safe to tell us now."

Wheeler's relaxed approach seemed to have the intended effect of getting Maggie to open up.

"He told me to get along with Simon better because he wouldn't have to worry about money and stuff, and then he said . . . he said he was hiding for a reason, that he had hurt people, but he said Mom did bad things, too, and that she was partly responsible for his situation and he couldn't let it go unpunished." Maggie's speech was rushed as the words came tumbling out. "I didn't understand any of it."

Nina stifled a gasp. What had Glen become? She had barely known him to get angry. What could have filled him with such rage? What role could she have possibly played in that transformation? And why viciously attack a perfectly innocent soul to punish her? Was that the punishment he'd told Maggie about? How would he even know she was seeing Dr. Wilcox? None of it made any sense. For whatever reason, Glen had laid the blame squarely on her shoulders. How dare he accuse her of anything? She had been nothing but a loyal and loving wife to him. How could Glen possibly point at her when *he* had been fired at work, *he* was lying, *he* was stealing from his family, *he* had hooked up with the waitress and perhaps others?

Nina didn't have many answers, but after piecing together events from the past few days, she understood at least one thing.

"You were talking to your father on the phone when I came to your room the other night, weren't you?"

Nina sounded incredulous, but not upset. Thinking of her

own father, she believed she would have done the same had roles been reversed. She hugged Maggie even tighter, letting her cry, knowing every tear her daughter shed was a little less weight to carry.

"It's okay, sweetie," Nina said, rocking Maggie in her arms the way she had when she was younger.

"He told me I couldn't tell anybody. That I had to keep it a secret, that it would be very bad for him if I told you or Connor, like he might be killed or something if anybody found out."

"It's very good of you to be honest with us, Maggie," Detective Wheeler said. "For the time being, I suggest everyone stay extremely vigilant. Maggie, we'll need your computer, your phone, to run forensics, see if that can help us pinpoint a location."

Nina wanted to see those secret messages Glen had exchanged with Maggie, but she'd speak with Detective Wheeler about it in private. She didn't want her daughter having anything else to worry about.

"Is Glen a threat?" Simon asked the detective. "Could he show up here?"

"Anything is possible now," he said.

Simon cupped his face in his hands. Nina pulled Maggie into her body, keeping an arm draped around her shoulders, her protective motherly instincts taking hold.

"You need to talk to the bank where Glen worked," Nina told the detective. "He was fired from his job years before he disappeared, and I think something there set this whole train in motion."

Wheeler made a note.

"Speaking of jobs—Nina, your job," Simon said, looking first to Nina and then to Wheeler. "Is it safe for my wife to keep working?"

Nina eyed Simon strangely, and even Maggie had the

wherewithal to key in on his miscue. Nina was still Glen's wife, not Simon's. Wheeler, none the wiser, answered with authority.

"Well, that's going to be for you to decide. Obviously, I think whatever steps you can take to minimize your risks, it's advisable to take them until we get this situation under control."

Nina knew Simon would interpret Wheeler's assessment to mean that, at a minimum, she should take a leave of absence. Maybe she would, but not until the Cooper case was officially resolved. Besides, they weren't going to barricade themselves inside their home. Yes, Glen was out there, somewhere, but she had a life to live. Her bravado, while admirable, was also cold comfort. Glen must have been following her. How long had he been spying from the shadows? The question chilled her to the core.

Another thought came to Nina, this one more frightening. Perhaps Glen would come for the children, take them from her. Who knew what he was capable of? But there were steps she could take until his capture. She'd drive the kids to school and drive them home, or Simon could. She'd cut back on her hours, no problem there, but she wouldn't quit. Better to be at work, Nina reasoned, than home alone where she'd be more vulnerable to attack. She and Simon could work out the logistics later. Right now, the more pressing task was getting her family situated into this new normal.

"How will you catch him?" Nina asked.

"We're working on it," Wheeler answered. "Look, it's obvious that Glen's in the area, and it's obvious that he's violent, and he's probably been following you, Nina, for a while now. Maybe the attack on Dr. Wilcox was his way of punishing you for whatever it is he blames you for. We just don't know his motives, but we do know that you're going to need protection, and we'll do all we can to provide that.

"We're going to have a police detail parked outside your house. They're on their way now. They'll be here all night, maybe for the next couple days. Hopefully we'll arrest him soon."

Nina thanked the detective for his efforts, but she didn't feel any safer. Compounding her anxiety, what Wheeler had said struck her hard. Was he right about Glen's motives? Was there some twisted symbolism in his target? Perhaps. What better way to exact revenge on someone he blamed, errone-ously or not, than harming the person committed to helping her? Nina believed—hoped—that Glen wouldn't attack her, or Simon for that matter. They were providing for the chil-dren, and according to Maggie he wanted no harm to come to her or to Connor. But he could go after one source of comfort in Nina's life. Would he threaten others—possibly Susanna or Ginny?

Grateful as she was for police protection, these past two years had taught Nina that anything was possible.

CHAPTER 49

Lunch again, eating with Ben like usual, only this time everything was different. It had been four excruciatingly long days since I found out my father was out there, somewhere, and the police considered him armed and dangerous. He wasn't a missing person anymore or presumed dead. He was a *wanted* man. He had attacked a woman, nearly *killed* her. And now everyone—and I do mean everyone—knew my father was suspect number one in the crime. Once again, Maggie Garrity was the center of attention. Shoot me now.

Ben had been right about one thing: Dad was never in Vermont. He was nearby all this time. I still couldn't wrap my head around it. My father was sick and needed help; at least that's what Mom said.

I took a bite of my sandwich and then a bite of Mom's homemade brownie, all while watching Justin, Laura, and my former friends chatting it up three tables away.

"So what now?" Ben asked.

I gave him a brownie, that's what, and gobbled down another. "My dad's not answering any of my messages."

"You're still trying to reach him? Isn't he, like, dangerous?"

"He's still my dad. And he's not dangerous to me, so yeah, I'm still trying. I'm using Connor's phone now because the police have mine."

"Crazy."

"For sure. You know what else is crazy? Simon, that's what."

"Yeah, I guess this didn't change any of that," said Ben. "What about the camera?"

The camera was still operational, and Luke's dad wasn't missing it, so we didn't have to return it anytime soon. The battery life was impressive—weeks, if not months, running on a bunch of AA batteries. We could look at the pictures transmitted via Wi-Fi to an app on Connor's phone, but it wasn't producing much useful information except that Simon was the only person who ever went to his house. We knew it wasn't being rented—at least currently—but that's all we knew.

"He's really pissed that my mom won't quit her job," I said. "Like *really* pissed. He keeps telling her it's not safe to keep working until the police get my dad."

Ben cringed, which I interpreted to mean he partly agreed.

"She won't listen," I said, in a way that made it clear I was proud of my mom's bravery. "She's at work right now, in fact."

"Well, your dad . . . he seems to have some . . . some issues to deal with," said Ben, approaching the subject cautiously.

I was about to defend my father, say that I didn't believe the evidence, when I felt the first sign of trouble. The tightness started in my throat, like the feeling of a hand around my neck, making it hard to get down a breath. My skin prickled and tingled as panic turned my body rigid.

I heard Ben call my name in a worried voice. "Maggie, you all right? Maggie?"

I saw people get up from their seats in a flash, some breaking into a sprint, gathering around me, circling, closing in on me, closing . . .

"What's wrong?" That voice belonged to Justin D'Abbraccio, crying out as he ran toward me. But I knew what was happening. Panic clamped around my heart. I could feel my lips, my eyes swelling as I fought for air.

"I think she's having an allergic reaction!" Ben screamed.

"What did she eat?" someone asked.

"Nothing. Just her lunch. She had brownies, maybe those?" Ben sounded on the verge of tears.

"My pen," I wheezed.

Ben was already fumbling with my backpack. This wasn't my first allergy crisis, so I knew I had to stay calm or I would make the situation worse.

My vision was blurring, but I could see Ben unzip the backpack. He felt around the big compartment for the special carrying case containing two EpiPens. I had two pens with me at all times in the unlikely event a pen malfunctioned or more than one injection was required. His search became increasingly frantic as he looked through various pouches and compartments for the case. He came up empty.

Sharp pains made me clutch my stomach, groaning. Scarlet bands started to streak across my hands and I felt them burn into my face. My breathing became increasingly shallow as the panic inside me deepened.

"The pens! It's not here . . . it's not here, Maggie." I heard Ben's terror, and watched as he dumped the contents of my backpack on the ground, searching with increasing desperation. He rifled through various pockets and pouches, again coming up empty.

"Where is it? Where is the case?" he cried with fright.

I stumbled off my chair, wheezing as my eyes lost focus.

"The nurse! Someone get the nurse!" It was Justin's voice I heard.

If I could have talked, I would have told them any EpiPen would do. Somebody in the lunchroom had to have one. The scarlet bands on my hands spread to my arms. The rise and fall of my chest quickened as I fought to get air down my swollen throat.

Is this what dying feels like?

I looked at Ben through gauzy vision.

My pens are in my backpack, I wanted to say, but I couldn't get out the words. Light slowly faded from my eyes. I knew the pens were in there, but I hadn't bothered to check because I *never* take them out.

I started to make an alarming sucking noise as I heard someone say my lips were turning blue.

"Where's the nurse?" Ben shouted. "Hang on, Maggie."

His voice was the only thing keeping me from succumbing to total panic.

Someone knelt down behind me. Though my eyesight was hazy, I could see it was Laura Abel. She gently stroked my hair, and then took hold of my trembling hand, grimacing at my cold and clammy skin.

"Maggie," Laura said, touching my rash-covered face. "You stay strong, okay? Help is coming." Laura's voice broke as tears spilled down her cheeks.

Each of my labored breaths sounded to me like a final gasp. The rapid pace of my skittering heart thundered in my chest.

"Laura—Laura." I squeaked out her name through my swollen lips.

"We're here. We're all here," Laura said, and I could tell she was struggling to stay calm. "It's going to be all right."

Time slowed to an excruciating crawl. I shut my eyes

tightly and saw my father's face flash before me, but I knew he wasn't going to get here in time to save me.

As people gathered around, closing the circle tighter, I could feel my throat continue to swell.

"The rash is all over her neck, face, and arms," Laura said, now cradling my head in her lap. Ben looked on, helpless as could be, my backpack splayed open on the floor beside him.

"I'm scared," I said, barely managing to get out the words.

Ben took hold of my hand and I squeezed back weakly. I'd never felt so helpless in all my life.

"Maggie!"

For a second I thought it was Connor calling my name, but when I looked, I saw Simon running toward me, holding something in his hand. The school nurse was right behind him.

"Pens! I have pens!"

Simon, suit blazer flapping behind him like a cape, charged through the cafeteria at a full sprint. Working quickly, he pulled a pen from the carrying case, then removed the blue safety cap as if he'd practiced it before. Swinging the pen in an arc, he jabbed the orange needle cover into my thigh at a ninety-degree angle. I heard the click. Simon held the pen in place for a full ten seconds. Even with my vision blurred, I could see the indicator change color. The medicine had been dispensed correctly. I massaged the injection spot, feeling the epinephrine swim through my veins.

My eyes closed and the world around me grew darker, then darker still. In that moment, I left my body, feeling nothing but an unbelievable kind of lightness, like I could float away, far, far away, free from gravity. As I drifted off and the blackness became more pronounced, a single thought flickered through my mind before all thoughts ended.

Did Simon get the injection into me in time?

CHAPTER 50

A young female ER doctor took forever to complete a battery of tests that confirmed what Nina could tell merely by observation: Maggie was healthy enough to go home. It was a relief for everyone, especially Maggie, who was dreading the thought of spending the night in the hospital—the same hospital where Dr. Wilcox was still a patient.

There'd be no visiting her therapist this time. Nina's focus was on her daughter—and besides, she felt too guilty to pay a visit. After all, it was her husband who had administered the savage beating. Glen was out there somewhere—profoundly, violently angry with her, and anytime, day or night, he could show up.

Nina had been at work when she got Simon's panicked phone call about Maggie and had driven to the hospital at a reckless speed. She kept Simon on the phone with her as he followed the ambulance with Maggie inside. He knew Nina was coming from The Davis Center. As a concession to ease his worry for her safety, Nina had agreed not to leave the office for client visits and was now getting home before sunset.

The police continued to conduct random patrols during the day and kept a single unmarked car parked outside their home at night, but that hardly seemed a long-term solution. The only answer was to find Glen, to catch him, but how? They were no closer to knowing his whereabouts even with the information extracted from Maggie's phone. According to Detective Wheeler, Glen had expertly hidden himself using technology that turned him into a digital phantom. Nina didn't know Glen to be particularly tech-savvy, but he certainly was smart enough to have picked up the skills. He could be anywhere, Nina was told, which she had interpreted to mean he could have followed her to the hospital right now.

"You really need to make sure you have your EpiPens on you at all times," Maggie's doctor had instructed, taking a sterner tone than Nina thought necessary.

"The pen case was actually in the backpack, in a zippered pouch Ben didn't check," Simon said. "There was a lot of confusion, so it's completely understandable he missed it. Lucky for us, the nurse keeps a supply on hand."

Nina could picture the scene in her mind, the utter pandemonium in the cafeteria as Maggie's breathing slowed while her scarlet rashes deepened.

"Ben feels terrible about it," Nina told her daughter. "He's really upset and blames himself."

"I called the Odells to let them know you were going to be fine," Simon added.

"Do you know what caused the reaction?" Nina asked the doctor, who returned a somewhat indifferent shrug. Her job was to stave off death, and so as far as she was concerned, this was mission accomplished.

"It's hard to say. Could have been cross-contamination from a food-processing plant," the doctor offered. "It's rare, but I've seen it before."

Nobody was going to analyze what Maggie had for lunch that day. In the rush to get to the hospital, it had been left behind and then discarded by custodial staff. Even so, Nina would carefully revisit every scrap of food she'd prepared and contact any company she suspected of cross-contamination in case a recall was in order.

She phoned Ginny and Susanna to update them on all that had happened. Both friends offered to come to the hospital for moral support, but Nina assured them she was fine on her own.

There was another matter weighing on her, one Nina could not discuss with Simon, or her friends: Hugh Dolan had reached out to her again. In his message, which had come to her via text earlier in the day, he had offered more information on Simon, including files containing his personal research into Emma's death, along with a promise that there'd be no fee attached. Hugh claimed to like Nina, said that he'd appreciated her kindness, and wanted to clear his conscience that he'd done everything in his power to keep her safe.

Hugh's sudden altruism was not entirely convincing. Of course, Nina wanted to see those files of his, scour them for something the police might have missed, but she doubted he had anything for her apart from plans for another shakedown. Besides, Simon had once again shown himself to be a loving, supportive, and concerned partner, everything she could have hoped for in a moment of crisis.

The next call Nina made was to her parents, who were understandably distraught to hear the news. Nina assured them as best she could that Maggie was going to be okay, and described Simon's heroics in detail.

"It's good to know there are still good men out there." Her father's jab was obviously directed at Glen, and it was the first indication he was warming to Simon. Nina took it as a good sign, but doubted it would be enough to convince Simon to put aside his issues with Maggie and come to Nebraska with them for Thanksgiving. Perhaps Maggie would be grateful to Simon, though, and would come around all on her own.

Since they'd arrived at the hospital separately, Nina and Simon had to get home separately. Simon drove his truck while Nina followed in her car. Maggie, her voice a bit weaker, complexion paler than normal, talked about Laura Abel, specifically the kindness she'd shown.

"Nothing like a near-death experience to make you realize that stupid things are stupid, I guess," her daughter said.

Maggie's observation brought Hugh to mind again. Maybe she should reach out to him, check out those files he'd offered. Maybe it wasn't another attempt at extortion. Maybe there was good in him, too, because there really was some good in most everyone, including Laura Abel.

Nina thought grimly of Hugh's words of warning, concluding that really nothing was safe. Marriages, new relationships, life itself, it was all incredibly fragile, it could all come undone with a single bite of food, one picture of a waitress, one warning from an ex-brother-in-law. The best Nina could do was to listen to her heart, trust her instincts, and those told her that Simon *was* good. More than good— throughout today's horrifying ordeal, he had been a godsend. He had helped save her daughter's precious life, and for that, she would be forever grateful.

Simon unloaded the car while Nina got the kids settled. Connor had stayed at home with Daisy, but the stress of the day worked as a sleeping potion. Both children were out as soon as their heads touched the pillow.

Nina returned to the kitchen, where she scoured the ingredients she had used for Maggie's lunch, including the ones in those brownies.

"I've used that brownie mix before," she said, sounding perplexed, looking through the trash for the box the mix had come in. "I don't get it."

"It's probably some cross-contamination, like the doctor said," Simon suggested. "Let me check the recycling bin."

Simon went to the garage, and moments later he returned with a flattened box of brownie mix that made Nina do a double take.

"That's not the brand I buy," she said, taking the box from Simon. She went to the pantry where she kept other boxed mixes. "Here," she said, showing Simon the mix she always bought. The packaging looked similar, but the box in Simon's hand was a brand Nina had never purchased before. Using her phone, Nina checked an allergy website she turned to whenever a food item gave her any questions. Their motto—*If You Can't Read It, Don't Eat It!*—were words Nina lived by.

"This product isn't safe," Nina said, as she scanned the clear warning on the website indicating that this particular brownie mix was manufactured on equipment that also processed tree nuts and peanuts. "I wouldn't have bought this." Nina's voice shook with anger and disbelief. "I'd *never* get this."

Simon took the box from her and eyed it curiously.

"You went shopping a couple days ago, right? You must have been distracted," he said. "You've got a lot on your plate. With Glen, your job—look, it's too much for anyone. The mistake is completely understandable, but I've been warning you something bad might happen if you didn't quit."

How could I do that? Nina asked herself. It was so out of character. If anything, she was the *most* thoughtful and conscientious about ingredients in their food. It simply didn't register.

A thought struck her. She could check. Nina went to the mudroom where she kept her purse. From inside she fished out her wallet. She always stuffed a stack of receipts in there, and soon enough found the one from her last shopping trip.

She scanned the items.

Fruits. Vegetables. Milk. Eggs. And toward the bottom

were the packaged goods—pastas, canned soup, and there, near the very end, was a $3.99 purchase for her brand of brownie mix, the one she'd bought for years, the same mix she was sure she'd used to bake those brownies. The box Simon had shown was similar in appearance to her brand—both had large red logos—but the receipt was proof she hadn't made a mistake.

Simon's words struck her like a punch.

I've been warning you something bad might happen.

One warning too many. This one was like a flash of light exploding in her mind, blinding her momentarily. And then she could see it clearly, so it had to be possible.

She went from the mudroom to the bathroom directly off the kitchen, hoping she'd gone there unnoticed.

Closing the door gently, Nina locked it behind her, not wanting to say anything until her racing heart slowed enough for her thoughts to come together. Right now, those thoughts were flashes, quick answers to Hugh's questions. *Has he isolated you from your friends and family yet? Does he make you question things? Does he try to control your life?*

She wanted so desperately to believe in Simon that she had bought into every rational explanation for every behavior. But now, seeing things in a new light, the answers to every one of Hugh's questions was a resounding yes. She replayed the incidents one more time to make sure, categorizing them in her mind as she did. When she studied her reflection in the bathroom mirror, her hairstyle, so dramatically new and different, made Nina think a stranger was staring back at her.

If Simon had shown her the brownie mix she normally purchased, maybe she'd have believed cross-contamination. Instead, he went for something to make her doubt herself, to convince her that her work was making her careless and distracted, nearly causing the death of her daughter. Job or no job, Nina was too experienced, too damn vigilant, to make a mistake like that.

She thought of the wedge he'd begun to put between her and her parents. She thought of all the ways Simon had kept her from seeing Ginny and Susanna—all of it and more designed to make her doubt herself.

Why all this business with Maggie then? Nina tried to puzzle it out. Maggie wasn't the source of Simon's distress. It was the job, the damn job. She thought of Emma again, of Hugh's warnings, and the answer was simple and in front of her all this time: control. If Maggie were in crisis, Nina would be forced to reexamine her priorities. Eventually, when it got bad enough, she'd *have* to quit. And now look what her job had done—or so Simon was saying. Just as he had said to Emma.

And how likely was it that Maggie's EpiPens weren't easy to find? Ben Odell was the most competent boy she'd ever met. He wouldn't have missed seeing the case. It was always in Maggie's backpack, unless . . . unless the pens really weren't there.

Could Simon have removed them? In all that chaos, how easy would it have been for him to slip the pen case back into her backpack with nobody noticing? As easy as putting a drop of peanut oil in the brownies. And why do it? Well, there's nothing like the near-death experience of a child to make one reconsider her priorities, that's why.

Nina returned to the kitchen to find Simon pacing the room. He read the ingredients on the box in his hand, looking baffled, head down, like he was studying for an exam. She gripped the kitchen counter to steady her shaking hands. Simon looked up at her.

"I'll call the company first thing in the morning," he said. "Tell them the packaging similarities nearly caused a deadly mistake."

"Get out," Nina whispered.

Simon's eyes widened as if disbelieving what he heard. "Nina, what?"

"Get out," she repeated, hissing the words in a low voice. She swallowed her anger and fear.

Simon's surprise deepened. "What . . . what are you talking about? Nina, you're stressed . . . you're not thinking clearly."

"I'm *finally* thinking clearly," Nina said, stepping forward. "Get out of my house. Get out now." She growled the order through gritted teeth.

"It's *our* house, Nina," Simon said. "Or did you forget?"

Simon didn't sound or look furious or even surprised anymore.

"In ten seconds, if you don't start packing a bag, I will go outside to the police car currently parked in front of *our* house and tell them that you tried to kill my daughter."

As it turned out, Glen had finally, albeit unwittingly, done something to help her. The police were already here.

"Are you crazy?" Simon's voice carried an edge of anger, as the darkness in his eyes deepened. "You have no proof of that."

"No, I don't." Nina summoned strength and conviction she hadn't known she possessed. "But it'll ruin your teaching career, and that's just the start."

In a flash, Nina played out in her mind what would happen if she marched down the walkway, banged on the window of the police car parked curbside, and cried for help. She knew the laws, because more often than not, the police called in social workers when they lacked legal authority. They would investigate her claims for sure, but this was not a domestic violence incident. There were no signs of struggle or violence of any kind. She was well, the children were fine, nobody was drunk or high, and Simon would of course be on his best behavior. She had no marks on her person, so she couldn't lie about being hit or choked. If she did, Simon would claim the charges against him were fabricated and she'd be the one in trouble.

No doubt, if she did raise a ruckus the police would probably call for backup. The children would awaken. The authorities would interview Simon in the house, not down at the station, because they'd have no cause to arrest him. They'd simply want to know why Nina was making these allegations. And he'd have an answer.

"I'm sorry for all this craziness, officers," she imagined Simon would say. "Nina's been under tremendous stress because of Glen and now this terrible incident with Maggie. I just need to get her to bed. She'll be better in the morning."

Nina could make a scene. Beg for help. But again, what crime had been committed here? She could try to explain the long string of events that had led her to the conclusion that Simon was dangerously manipulative, but not without sounding like a lunatic. Her best bet was to bluff and hope that Simon wasn't as intimately familiar with police procedure as she was.

Simon took a threatening step forward. Nina held her ground, forcing herself to gaze into the blackness of his eyes, seeing in them something deeply disturbing.

"Go upstairs, pack a bag, and get out of here. Get out before I make things much worse for you."

Nina could see from Simon's pained expression that her words had packed the intended punch.

"I love you, Nina," Simon said, sounding as sweet and sincere as she'd ever heard him. "You need help, serious help. But I'm not going to put you under any more stress. I can tell you're at your breaking point. So I'll go. Okay? I'll leave, right now, but remember, this is *my* property, too."

My property . . .

His comment evoked a memory of those tree branches. Everything in Simon's world, Nina thought, from his clothes to the people in it, needed to be ordered, neat, to fit inside defined compartments in his mind.

"I expect you to get over whatever is going on with you right now and to invite me back into my house very soon." Simon's tone was severe, borderline threatening. "Otherwise, I'll be forced to take action on my own."

"Action?" Nina's brow knitted as her voice rose in pitch.

"You're a social worker," Simon said. "You of all people know it's not acceptable to leave children in a dangerous situation. Your thoughtlessness could have killed Maggie today."

Was he threatening to accuse her of being an incompetent parent? Yes, that's exactly what he was doing, she decided. Threatening to take the children away from her.

"And don't forget Glen is out there somewhere," Simon continued. "What if he wants his kids back? Who is going to stop him? You? The police? You need me, Nina, you need my help."

"Help with what?"

"Protection, for one, from Glen. But most important, I need to teach you how to be a good mother." Simon glared at Nina, piercing her with an icy chill. "I'm a teacher. It's what I do. I educate. And you have a lot to learn before you can be the wife and mother I expect you to be. There is a right way and a wrong way to be, for everything and everyone. That includes you."

Simon left the kitchen. Finally, Nina felt like she could breathe again. Still, she followed him upstairs, praying he wouldn't try to do anything to the children. She carried her phone in one hand, 911 pre-entered and ready to send, and in the other was a kitchen knife hidden behind her back. Her heart hammered in her throat while she watched Simon pack a single bag. Minutes later he was downstairs.

He opened the front door and stepped outside onto the porch landing. He stood there a long while, a suitcase of clothes in one hand, the leather bag she'd bought him for a birthday gift in the other. He kept his back to Nina.

Without any sort of good-bye, Simon closed the door softly behind him, and then he was gone.

CHAPTER 51

The evening after I nearly died was Sports Award Night at the high school. Unfortunately, I had to go. Connor was getting some big award so he had to be there, and Mom didn't want to miss it, because she's a mom. Our world might have been turned upside down, but that didn't mean we couldn't do normal things, too.

Mom was worried about me, of course, but not worried enough to let me stay home alone. With Dad back in the picture, she was concerned he might show up at the house. Maybe he'd try to take me, she said. Or worse. I wasn't worried. Dad would never hurt me or try to kidnap me, but Mom didn't see it the same way, and I wasn't going to argue.

Either way, I felt pretty good. I had rested at home all day, with no side effects from the allergy attack. I probably could have gone to school, but I didn't want all the attention. Everyone checked in with me anyway—including Laura Abel. We talked by phone (real voices, not just texts) and it was a bit awkward, but it was also kind of okay. I'm not talking rainbows and unicorns or anything like that. I wasn't going back to my old crew—no way. But I realized it was easier not to carry all that anger and resentment around. In a way, just by being nice, Laura had made it possible for me to leave her and Justin and the rest of the meanies behind for good. I call that progress.

I figured Simon would be joining us at the big event, but no, he didn't. In fact, I hadn't seen him all day. When I asked Mom, she told me we'd talk about it after the awards night. That gave me a big lift.

"Talk about it" sounded like code for "we got into a huge fight and he's gone," maybe for good. I looked around the crowded auditorium for signs of Simon but didn't see him anywhere. It wasn't his school, but still, I figured he might have shown up, invited or not, to watch Connor get his award.

Connor was around somewhere with his team. The football team was always the grand finale. Groan. This evening was going to take forever, and we'd have to stay until the end.

At least Ben was with me. He'd gotten his parents to drop him off even though he didn't have any siblings who were getting awards. But he wanted to see *me,* make sure I was okay. Mom hugged Ben tightly and wouldn't let go for the longest time. I could tell it embarrassed Ben, but I also knew how much he appreciated it. It was Mom's way of letting him know she didn't blame him for what happened.

"Don't ever do that to me again," Ben said, taking the seat next to mine.

"Like I'm planning on it," I shot back.

We shook on it, but Ben didn't seem relieved.

"It *wasn't* there," Ben whispered to me as the auditorium lights dimmed. "I looked in every pouch, every single one. It wasn't there, Maggie. I swear to you."

Ben told this to me on the phone earlier, but now he could look me in the eye so I'd know he had no doubt about it.

"But Simon *found* it," I said to him, still trying to puzzle it out.

Then something clicked for me, and judging by the *OMG!* expression on Ben's face, it did for him as well.

"Do you think—?" Ben didn't finish the thought because he didn't have to. We were on the same wavelength now.

I remembered something from that day, a vision of Simon running toward me. Something had been different about him, but what? I asked Ben about it, but he didn't know either. So we sat in silence, hardly paying attention as the fall sports teams and individuals got recognized—team spirit award, most valuable player, most improved, yadayadayada. I clapped when I heard applause, but my brain was elsewhere, trying to recall what had been different about Simon that day. My memories were scattered. I could see faces in my mind, and remembered the terrible fear and the horrible feeling of not being able to breathe. I'd never experienced a feeling of panic like that and prayed I never would again.

Ben was positive that my EpiPens were not in my backpack. One hundred percent sure! There was only one possible explanation—Simon had removed them the night before, like he did my lab report.

So, how would he have slipped the pen case into my backpack later when I was having my reaction? He must have had them with him. But where? In his hand? No, I remembered him running toward me holding one pen case, the one from the nurse's office, not mine. Could he have hidden my case in his pants pocket? Maybe, but it's pretty bulky. So where else?

Then it struck me—the one place Simon could have easily concealed the pens. I knew something had been different about him. Yes, he had on his usual polo shirt and khaki pants combo. But he was also wearing a suit jacket that day, something he *never* did. I remembered it clearly now, waving behind him like a flapping cape as he ran. And that's when I knew Ben was right about the pen case and Simon was a monster.

* * *

For the rest of the evening program I tried to come up with a way to tell Mom that Simon was a nutcase—bad pun intended. If he took my pens, which I believed he had, it also meant he poisoned my food. I could only imagine what Mom would say: "Here we go again, Maggie." I'd never felt so connected to the boy who cried wolf in all my life. This accusation, more than all the others, would seem so outrageous, Mom would never, ever believe me. I was completely stuck. Unless . . . unless her promise to talk later meant she already knew.

Connor was in the front seat as we drove home, carrying a plaque to commemorate his coach's award. Mom didn't seem to be her usual beaming, proud mom self. We were silent for a bit until Mom spoke up.

"Kids, I didn't want to say anything earlier because this was Connor's day and I didn't want to spoil it. There have been some . . . developments at home with me and Simon."

I was on the edge of my seat. Connor looked at Mom all concerned, like he was bracing himself for the worst. I was doing the same, but his bad news would be good news for me.

"We've had some difficulties getting along and I've asked Simon to leave for a while."

Connor's eyes shot open wide. "What? Why? What did he do?"

"It was nothing he did. We're just not getting along."

"No, he did do something." The words came spilling out of my mouth before I knew what I was saying. "He poisoned me. He took my EpiPens, put something in the brownies, and then he slipped the pen case into my backpack."

"Maggie, enough with you and Simon!" Connor sounded really ticked off.

"What makes you say that, Maggie?" To my utter surprise, Mom didn't sound angry at all. I told her my theory about the sport coat. Connor shook his head in disbelief, but Mom stayed perfectly still.

"Okay, sweetie," she replied.

She said it absently, like she was lost in thought.

"I'll make some hot chocolate when we get home and we'll all talk about what's going on, okay?"

Connor nodded his agreement. I leaned my body forward to put a hand on Mom's shoulder.

"I love you, Mom," I said.

She glanced at me in the rearview mirror, and the look in her eyes told me everything I needed to know.

She believed me.

* * *

We entered the house through the garage door, and the first thing I expected, I didn't get: Daisy didn't start barking. She always barked whenever we came home, because she knew it was her job to protect us. I thought maybe she was sleeping, so I went to the living room to look for her. But she wasn't there.

"Daisy!" My voice bounced off the walls as I listened for the sound of padded footsteps that never came. I ran to the kitchen to look for Mom and Connor.

"Daisy's not here," I said, tears welling in my eyes.

"Of course she is," said Connor confidently. "She's probably sleeping."

We checked all over the house, every room, under the beds even, but she wasn't there.

I kept calling her name over and over again: "Daisy! Daisy! Where are you? Come out. Please . . . please!"

My voice kept breaking into sobs. Even Connor now looked sick with worry. It wasn't until I was coming downstairs after checking all the bedrooms that I noticed what was wrong. The front door was open slightly, like we'd forgotten to shut it completely on our way out. I checked the screen door for paw marks, thinking maybe she'd gotten out the way she had before—that horrible day Simon came into our lives. But I saw no scratches and the screen was intact. Still, who had left the door open?

We called the police. There should have been a patrol car parked out in front of our house.

"They were called away because of a reported burglary in the neighborhood," Mom told me. "So they didn't see anyone take her."

Then Connor spoke up, and surprised us all.

"What if Simon reported the burglary to get the police to leave so he could come here and take Daisy?"

"Where would he take her?" Mom asked. "Are there hotels around here that allow pets?" She didn't make it sound like Connor's theory was far-fetched.

"He's not staying at any hotel," I said. Connor and I took turns telling Mom about the rental house, our theory about the place not being rented, and how we sort of proved it.

Mom looked upset, but more about us taking risks than us spying on Simon.

Then Connor's face lit up.

"What is it, honey?" Mom asked.

"The camera," he said. "It's still operational. It's not running at night to save battery, but if he has Daisy, we might be able to get a picture of her."

"Who cares about pictures? Let's go there now and get our dog back," I said.

"No!"

I jumped at the sound of Mom's hand slamming against the kitchen table.

"Nobody goes back to that house. Nobody. Is that understood? I'll call the police. You let me handle this," Mom said.

I wasn't about to disagree.

CHAPTER 52

They spent the weekend without Daisy—a whole heart-wrenching, gut-churning, sleepless, brutal weekend.

Nina arrived at the Seabury Police Department for her scheduled meeting with Detective Eric Wheeler, hoping for some kind of development. This was her second trip here.

On her first visit, the detective had assured her he was conducting a thorough investigation, and while he had yet to update Nina on his latest findings, she wasn't entirely in the dark. She knew something of Simon.

According to her spies, Ginny and Susanna, he was at school, teaching his Monday classes like all was normal. Maggie was staying home under protest. In her mind, it was unconscionable to give Simon any control over her life. Nina did not want her daughter to be in the same building as that man, but Maggie did have a point that school was the safest place for her. Glen was still out there, somewhere, and the police were no longer keeping watch over the house.

Nina had hoped she'd have proof by now that Simon had taken Daisy, or poisoned Maggie, and then he'd be put on leave or fired outright with criminal charges pending, so her daughter could return without worry. Such wasn't the case.

Her other option for getting Simon out of the picture wasn't panning out either. She had called Hugh Dolan, texted him numerous times, sent him Facebook messages, but gotten no answer. She had imagined marching into Wheeler's office holding irrefutable evidence that Simon was a killer. Unfortunately, Hugh had vanished, proving himself unreliable, which really wasn't surprising.

Nina had fretted the last few days away—everyone had, with Daisy gone. Twice she had nightmares about Glen showing up at the house with a knife to annihilate his family, his anger boiling over into a murderous rampage.

She had awakened bathed in sweat. Nina was left on her own to protect her children, and Ginny's suggestion to buy a gun no longer sounded ridiculous to her.

Meanwhile, other stresses began pinging away, including paying the mortgage. She was formulating plans to move out. Let Simon have the damn house; she'd go live with Ginny or Susanna if she had to.

In an ironic twist, Simon had at last gotten what he desired: Nina decided to take a leave of absence from her job. She had stopped by The Davis Center first thing in the morning to deliver the news to her boss, Rona, in person. She gave vague excuses of a difficult family situation and no timetable for her return. Nina filled out some paperwork and that was that. Maybe they'd fire her, but she couldn't trouble herself with those concerns, at least not until she got her dog back and Simon was out of the picture.

There was no perfect time to step away, but this moment was as good as any. She'd finished her report on the Cooper case, recommending joint custody for the children. There'd be fallout from Wendy for sure, but Nina wouldn't be in the office to hear it. Instead, she was at the police station, seated in an interview room, getting Wheeler's take on his part of the investigation. He did not look like a man about to deliver good news.

"Let me go over what we've done and where we're at," he began. "We interviewed most of your neighbors, and nobody saw Simon leave your house with Daisy."

"Okay," said Nina, nodding. She had expected this answer, because she had checked with her neighbors as well. She had also contacted Granite State Dog Rescue, put up posts on the Seabury community Facebook page, and once again pinned missing dog posters around town, but so far none of those efforts had yielded any results.

"What about the burglary?" Nina asked.

"We investigated and found nothing. The person who reported the incident said he was a tourist from out of town and heading home when he saw something suspicious."

"Have you spoken to him?"

"Called. No answer."

"That's because it was Simon."

"Not according to the name he gave us."

Nina knew when a conversation was going nowhere.

"What about Simon, have you spoken with him?"

"Of course," Wheeler said. "And you can guess what he told us."

"He doesn't have Daisy. And before you ask, his neighbors haven't seen a dog out in the yard, or seen Simon walking a dog, or heard barking, for that matter.

"Simon did tell us that you two got into a fight and he's living at his other home until you work something out. That's not a crime, Nina. People break up all the time."

"Sure, but they don't always steal a dog when they go. Detective, Daisy is part of our family, and we need her back." Nina's voice shook with a mix of frustration and sadness.

"Look, Nina, we want to help, but we've got our hands full with you. Glen, Simon, your dog—you're like a full-time project here. Have you tried talking to Simon?"

"No." Nina kept her head down, afraid if she looked the

detective in the eyes she'd crack and tell him what she suspected he'd done to Maggie. She had no proof other than a
store receipt that he'd laced her brownie with peanut oil and
no idea how Simon might retaliate if the police questioned
him about it. Until she got her dog back, Nina did not want
to take any unnecessary chances. Maggie was fine. They
were all fine . . . all but Daisy.

"Can't you just get a search warrant?" Nina pleaded. "Go
in there and look for yourself?"

Wheeler's deepening frown told her the answer was no.

"That's a big ask. We need probable cause, a court order,
all of that," he said. "And right now, we don't have it."

"I kicked him out of the house, and the next night my dog
goes missing. That should be proof enough."

Wheeler's mouth tightened, telling her it was not. He
glanced at his files. "According to the report, the front door
was partially ajar. You really need an alarm system."

"We called an alarm company—well, Simon did, after you
told us Glen attacked Dr. Wilcox. But the company couldn't
get the install scheduled until next week."

Wheeler glanced at his case file. "From what I'm reading
here, it's not the first time your dog has gotten out through
an open door." Nina took the comment as victim-blaming.

"Yes, I know that, but—"

She halted mid-sentence, feeling suddenly immobilized.
With all that was going on, she hadn't seen the parallels
clearly until Detective Wheeler inadvertently brought them
to her attention: the first time Daisy had gotten out she'd
faulted herself for leaving the front door partially open.
What if she hadn't left it open either time? What if someone had been inside her house and taken Daisy, leaving the
door ajar to make it look like that was how she had got out?
And what if that same person miraculously found her dog
in the woods and brought her back, adding burrs to her fur

to heighten the ruse? She became upset enough for Wheeler to take notice.

"Are you okay?" he asked.

"No, I'm not," said Nina, as the magnitude of what she was now realizing struck her with great force. Simon could have ingratiated himself into Nina's life and the lives of her children predicated on a terrible, cruel, and calculated lie. It was entirely possible he had taken Daisy that day and brought her back so he could play the hero.

And she had no doubt he'd taken her again.

From her pocketbook, Nina removed her last-gasp effort—the printout of an image Connor had shown her that morning. They'd been monitoring pictures from the camera across from Simon's house on an app Connor downloaded to his phone. She hoped for a clearer shot. This one was a bit like the Loch Ness Monster—grainy, blurry, and extremely difficult to make out.

Nina was reluctant to admit she was spying on Simon. She certainly had concerns about the legality of a camera pointed at a private residence. But there were other ways to explain the image she was presenting.

"Look at this," she said, sliding the printout across the table. Wheeler unfolded the printout and studied it closely.

With her index finger, Nina circled a dark, oblong shape that could have been anything, including a bit of curtain or a shadow. But in this context, she knew, as did the children, that the indistinct shape was without a doubt their Daisy.

"What's this?" Wheeler asked.

"It's my dog, in the window of Simon's house. You can see her?" Nina made it sound like the answer should have been a resounding yes.

Wheeler took another look. "Where did you get this?"

"I took a picture of Simon's house when I went looking for Daisy. Is that illegal?"

Wheeler said it wasn't, but his expression also said he didn't necessarily believe her story. Thankfully, he didn't press her for a better explanation.

"Yeah, I can't get a search warrant off this, if that's what you're asking," he said, handing Nina back her printout.

"But that's Daisy!" Nina sounded exasperated.

"It could be anything, which is exactly what a judge would say. I want to help you, I really do, but our hands are tied, legally tied. I can't get a search warrant, so I suggest if you think Simon has your dog, go talk to him and try to get her back."

Nina took that as her cue to leave. She thanked Detective Wheeler for his time, thinking to herself that she might have to do more than just talk.

With a hopeful heart, Nina tried Hugh Dolan's number again, figuring it was her last shot at getting Detective Wheeler on her side. If the police weren't going to believe photographic evidence, perhaps Hugh had some key fact in his possession, something that would turn a suicide into murder and a murder investigation into a search warrant.

Nina listened to the rings—one, two, three—expecting her call to go right to Hugh's gruff voice mail greeting. Someone answered this time, but to Nina's surprise, the speaker was female. She had a thick New England accent and a smoker's voice, coarse as sandpaper.

"Who's this?" said the caller.

Nina introduced herself as a friend of Hugh's and asked if she could speak with him.

"Hugh's dead," the woman said curtly. "I'm Catherine, his girlfriend. Well, his sometimes girlfriend."

Nina went cold inside.

"Dead?" She drew out the word, her voice quavering slightly. "What happened?"

"Overdose." Catherine was matter-of-fact about it, as if

this sad outcome was long expected. "I found him a few days ago. We were supposed to hang out, but he didn't show, so I called the cops. And they found him, in his apartment, needle still in his arm."

"I'm . . . I'm so sorry for your loss."

Nina wasn't sure what to say, or how to say it. As her thoughts swirled, a sinister possibility came to her, leaving her breathless and unsteady on her feet.

"Say, who are you again?" Catherine asked, now sounding suspicious, like Nina might be a rival for her dead lover's affections.

"I'm a friend . . . again, I'm so sorry . . . you have my deepest condolences."

Nina ended the call abruptly as her thoughts raced ahead. It was entirely believable that an overdose was how Hugh would meet his end, and guiltily she considered having contributed to his demise, but another, more disturbing possibility tugged at her: Simon. Had he done something to Hugh, given him drugs that would kill him? It was possible, just as he had done to Maggie. Nina no longer required any files to believe Emma Dolan had met her fate at Simon's hands, but she had nothing to offer the police except for more speculation.

CHAPTER 53

Simon brought Daisy to Glen for a visit. Might as well, or so he said, since everyone was now staying under the same roof. During the course of his captivity, Glen had seen glimmers of kindness from Simon. Not every moment was spent torturing and tormenting. To do so simply required too much effort. He must have understood at some level they were all living beings with needs, wants, and desires. Some part of him must have held fragments of compassion. Some part of Simon was human.

Daisy went completely berserk when she first saw Glen, spinning in circles inside the box, licking his face, his arms, his hands. The second visit was more of the same. The third no different from the first. Dogs were the best that way.

Simon watched this reunion joylessly.

"Time is running out," he said. "Why hasn't Nina asked me to come back? She has to know I have her dog. At least she should have called by now."

Daisy had calmed enough to rest her head on Glen's lap, and it felt like a touch of heaven.

"It's not going to work," Glen said as he gave Daisy some

gentle pats. She didn't notice his chain, had no idea they were both on leashes. "Give Daisy back. We'll come up with another way."

Glen knew Nina's rejection of him would cause Simon to snap.

Then the blood, the knife, live video feed of his family's murder.

Simon shook his head defiantly. "No. No, it doesn't work like that. She needs to come to me. I was so close, too."

"Close to what?" Glen's voice rose in exasperation. Despite the circumstances, all of the suffering, he had to know. What was it all about? What drove this man to such lengths? Why Nina?

"It doesn't concern you," Simon said. "Nina needs to come around, that's all. Things are going to get bad, Glen, if she doesn't. They'll get so much worse."

There was only one way for it to get worse.

Glen stilled. He swallowed hard, trying not to think the thoughts racing through his mind.

"What are you going to do?"

"I took you," Simon answered flatly. "If I have to, I'll take her, too."

The darkness in his eyes deepened.

"The children?" Glen tried to keep his voice level.

The look on Simon's face said enough. Empty. Void. Expressionless. Soulless.

Glen understood well enough. The box would become Nina's new home. Perhaps the police would search the basement, but it was doubtful they'd find the hideout. It was too well concealed. Glen and the children would be disposed of somewhere and Simon would go on.

After a time, Simon yanked Daisy out of the box and

closed the door behind him. Darkness again. No new batteries for his lone light. Dark as a coffin. Dark as death.

Glen screamed, and screamed again, but nobody on the outside, not even Daisy, could hear him.

CHAPTER 54

It wasn't often I won an argument with my mother, but by Wednesday she had agreed to let me go to school. I knew she wasn't comfortable with it, but I wasn't comfortable letting Simon control my life. I missed Ben and I was falling behind in my work. She agreed I'd be safe there as long as I kept to the plan and stayed indoors. I was given strict instructions to avoid Simon at all costs. If he spoke to me, I had to ignore him. I also had to keep my backpack with me at all times, and there were no brownies from a mix in my lunch that day.

After first period, I had to get to science, which unfortunately required me to walk by Simon's classroom. I would have done anything to avoid it, but there were only so many ways to get there.

Ben was with me because we had class together.

"Are the police doing anything?"

He was worried about Daisy, too.

The hallway was noisy, crowded with kids, as it always was between classes.

"Not a thing," I said with disgust. "If anyone thought Simon took me, they'd break down his damn door. But since it's a dog, well, 'Go and talk to him.'" I said this in a deep voice, like I was imitating the police. "That's their response

for you," I said, back to my normal voice. "Like he's not totally suspect! Daisy's there. I know it. I *feel* it."

Ben seemed to agree.

We were nearing "Mr. Fitch's" classroom and my stomach did a flip. I think I slowed down, and Ben knew why.

"Want me to go ahead, see if he's in there?"

"No," I said. "We'll go together."

We walked side by side, every step a bit more tentative
than the last as we neared the creeper's classroom. At the
open door, I tried to keep my eyes forward, but I couldn't
resist looking. I turned my head just a bit, just so, and there
he was, standing at the front of his classroom wearing his
dumb polo shirt and dumb khaki pants. Same old Simon.
The leather bag my mom bought him was on the floor next
to his desk. It was so wrong that he still used it. I mean, this
guy poisoned me and stole our dog! How could they let him
teach children? What a whack job!

I tried to turn my head before he saw me, but Simon caught
my eye and there it was—the look I had tried so hard to record. Even from a distance I could feel its heat. He wanted
to kill me, no antique gun this time. He would shoot me dead
if he could, that's what his eyes were saying.

Simon made a thin-lipped smile, but the darkness didn't
leave him. He put his hand up, fingers waving at me, and the
smile on his face grew wider until his teeth were showing.
To me he looked ghoulish, like the worst Halloween mask
ever. I wanted to scream and run away, but instead I froze in
place. I couldn't move a muscle. Simon continued to stare at
me, until Ben finally dragged me away, and that broke the
spell.

"What a freak," he said as we walked away, but this time
at a faster pace.

"A freak with my dog," I snarled. "If I could get at his
briefcase, I'd take his keys and go get her myself."

Ben stopped suddenly and grabbed hold of my arm. "What did you say?"

"I said I'd go get the keys to his house, which he always keeps in that bag, and go get my dog myself."

It was all talk, of course. *Maggie's big show!* But I was feeling extra combative at that moment.

Ben locked eyes with mine, no blinking, deadly serious. "You mean it?"

I gave him a funny, sideways glance, because I wasn't sure I'd heard him right. I kind of laughed it off.

"It's not like I can go in there and just take his keys," I said, rolling my eyes at him.

Ben looked around like he was scanning the hallway for something. Then, he locked on his target.

"You got one chance," he said to me, showing me a single finger. "One. Take it."

"What?"

I didn't know what he was talking about, but off he went, like a sprinter, backtracking toward Simon's classroom. I reached out to stop him, but he was moving too fast. I told myself he wasn't doing what I thought he was doing. But sure enough, he had Justin D'Abbraccio, my former pal, the boy who started all the whatnot with Laura Abel, in his sights, and he was heading for him with a determined look on his face.

"Hey, Justin!"

Justin whirled to see Ben storming at him, hands balled into fists at his sides. When he got to within spitting distance, Ben reached out a long, skinny arm and took hold of the front of Justin's T-shirt.

"What the—?"

Justin looked like someone had dumped cold water on his head—it was that kind of shock and surprise.

"You really should learn to be nicer to people, you know that?"

Even when he was being aggressive, Ben sounded polite. He shoved Justin with some force, and that wasn't polite at all. Laura Abel was nearby and she and a bunch of her cronies moved in close to watch.

"Hey, back off, Odell," Justin said, sounding a little unsure. "What's your problem?"

"You." Ben gave Justin another hard shove and this time Justin shoved back.

"What the hell, Ben?"

Justin couldn't understand what was happening to him, and honestly, neither could I.

"Maggie is a nice person and you've been nothing but mean to her and I've had enough of it."

Justin didn't look like he wanted to fight, but the kids who gravitated to the action were salivating for one. Ben gripped Justin's shirt harder. Justin grabbed Ben's. And that was all it took. It was a full-on kid fight. No punches thrown, just a lot of going around in a circle, holding on to each other's clothes, trying to drag the other person to the floor. One second we're on our way to class, and the next it's WWE, Seabury style. It took me a bit to figure out what the heck Ben was up to, but when I saw Simon bolt out of his classroom, along with a few other teachers, well, then I got it.

Ben wasn't defending my honor. I mean, cute if he was, but he wasn't.

He was creating a distraction.

I knew I wouldn't have long. I slipped into Simon's classroom unnoticed (I hoped), which was now empty because the action was out in the hall, and went right for the leather bag on the floor. The noise level was like a fire drill on steroids. Nobody would hear me rustling about.

It took two seconds to feel around inside the bag before my fingers brushed up against his keys. I grabbed them, put them in my pants pocket, closed up the latches, and went back out into the hall. When I got there, Simon and another teacher were pulling the combatants apart. Ben caught my eye and I gave him a thumbs-up sign. He smiled sweet as could be. Then I took off to find a quiet place where I could call my mom.

CHAPTER 55

Nina didn't waste one second getting to the school. Maggie was waiting for her in the nurse's office, feigning a stomach-ache. She talked to her daughter in private, and made the exchange. Of course Maggie wanted to go with her to Simon's place, but Nina's denial was firm. So she agreed to stay put with the nurse, where she'd be safe and looked after, recuperating from nothing, while Nina went on her mission.

She was furious with her daughter for taking the risk, but at the same time incredibly proud of Maggie's bravery and ingenuity. Ben's, too. It was actually a stroke of genius, though Nina doubted the kids had thought it through, especially since Maggie said it was a spur-of-the-moment decision.

Either way, according to Ben's research—and plenty of photographic evidence gathered by her children—Simon's home would be without renters and vacant while he was at school. She hoped he hadn't changed the alarm code, but if he had, she'd lie to the police and tell them Simon had given her permission to check the house for her dog. Why have his keys? It would be a case of he said, she said. If Daisy were there, Simon's denials wouldn't carry much weight. Getting the keys back to Simon would be easy. She'd leave them in the school parking lot—or perhaps she'd just toss them down a storm drain.

* * *

It was a few minutes after eleven thirty in the morning when Nina pulled to a stop in front of Simon's home. The air carried a bit of a chill, portending winter, and as if in answer to that thought, she heard the geese that nested on the lake. A moment later, Nina saw them taking off in chevron flight, en route to a warmer climate.

The house had an attached garage and a well-kept lawn, one of the few in the neighborhood not blanketed with fallen leaves. Somehow, he was keeping up with the maintenance here.

Maker Lane, where Simon lived, was a quiet street in a part of town Nina seldom frequented. She didn't know any of Simon's neighbors. Not that it mattered, not that she would have called on them. She'd come here for one purpose only: get in and get out as quickly as possible, hopefully with Daisy. She stuffed her cell phone and a leash into the pocket of her dove-gray jacket, leaving her purse in the backseat of her car. She wanted to enter the home as unencumbered as possible.

She didn't see Simon's pickup truck anywhere, and after checking the home's exterior and seeing no lights on inside, felt confident that he wasn't around.

She found the right key. There was a faint click as the lock disengaged. She opened the door, hearing the beep-beep-beep of the alarm. All went silent when she entered the code, and Nina breathed a sigh of relief.

She had watched Simon turn the alarm on and off many times and automatically committed the sequence to memory. Nina thanked her social work training for sharpening her observation skills, as well as Simon's complacence with keeping the same alarm code.

If she had second thoughts, Nina couldn't act on them now. She was here. She had no choice but to push forward. A split second after setting foot inside, however, she knew something was wrong—terribly wrong.

As a childless bachelor, Simon didn't own much furniture. What he had acquired, he had moved into the new home. He had told her he bought new furniture for the renters, so she expected to see couches, chairs, tables. But the home was stripped bare of everything—there were no rugs, no plants, no nothing. Even the walls were smooth, no markings where pictures might have hung.

It looked to her like nobody lived here, but when she checked the floor with her fingers, not a speck of dust collected on the tips. Someone was keeping the home spic and span, just the way Simon liked it.

Nina peered down the front hallway before taking one tentative step followed by another. With nothing to absorb the sound, her footsteps echoed loudly, and her heart stayed lodged firmly in her throat. She listened. Did she hear something? A scratch? A bark? No, the home was as still as a morgue.

"Daisy? Are you here?" Nina's voice bounced off the walls as she ventured farther into the quiet, empty house.

Emboldened, she wandered about, noting the lack of furnishings in each room, the dearth of comforts of any kind. She passed through a spotless kitchen, where there were some signs of actual life—dishes drying on a wooden drying rack, pots on the stove. She checked inside the refrigerator. There was milk, along with cheese, eggs, and vegetables for a salad. Someone was eating, but she didn't see any dog food, and that was upsetting. Maybe Simon was telling the truth. But every fiber in her body told her Daisy was here, somewhere, so she kept searching.

Eventually, Nina made her way to the master bedroom, which was at the end of a short hallway. It was the room where she and Simon had first made love, but what had once been a cozy space was now nearly barren. There was a mattress on the floor and bedside it a lamp, no end table. The bed was made, neat and tight like a soldier's bunk.

Nina's gaze went to three framed photographs hanging on the walls, the only pictures she'd seen in the entire house. Her blood froze. She approached and studied the images carefully. One picture was clearly of Emma Dolan, but lacking the genial smile she'd worn in the image Hugh had shown her. This portrait was far more subdued, taken in black-and-white at what looked like a photography studio, with her hair styled as Nina's was now. The second picture was of Nina, a photograph of her that she remembered Simon taking in a park after she'd gotten her new hairdo. It, too, was printed in black-and-white, mounted in a simple black frame with a white mat.

It was the third photograph that left Nina shaking.

This was another picture of her, only it *wasn't* her. The woman in the photograph was leaning up against a tree in a verdant park, and unquestionably in her twenties. And strangely enough, she looked just as Nina had at that age. Judging by the woman's outfit—plaid, pleated miniskirt, a high-neck sweater, platform shoes—it was a style Nina might have worn in the '90s. The haircut, however, was the same as Emma's, the same as Nina's—a bob with straight bangs and angled sides. While Nina and the person in the third photograph shared uncannily similar facial features, the younger woman had the saddest eyes she'd ever seen.

"Who are you?" Nina whispered, touching the glass as she

traced her fingertips along the contours of the young woman's face, so similar to her own.

She surveyed the rest of the room, not that there was much to see. She noticed now what she hadn't before: a small book on the bed. It was the only book in the room and possibly in the entire house, which was odd for someone who studied history and enjoyed building robots as a hobby.

Nina picked up the book and studied it. She ran her hand over the textured cover of brown leather. She dragged her fingers along the edges of the yellowing paper. It smelled old, like a vintage volume an antique dealer might own. Only when she opened the top cover and flipped through the crinkly pages did she realize it was somebody's handwritten diary.

At first, she figured the diary was Simon's, but while the neat and looping handwriting was as legible as a teacher's might be, it was remarkably different from his. The lettering looked familiar, and she remembered where she'd seen it. Simon had shown her a few pages of Emma Dolan's diary when they were talking about her depression. The handwriting was unquestionably the same. But when Nina turned to the inside cover, searching for an inscription, she found the name of Allison Fitch.

A sinking, sick feeling washed over Nina. Not only had Simon lied about the diary belonging to Emma, he'd also lied when he told her he had no pictures of his first wife. There was at least one photograph of Allison Fitch, and it was hanging on the wall directly opposite her.

CHAPTER 56

Nina held her hand over her mouth to stifle the gasp rising from her throat. She sat on the edge of the neatly made bed, the diary splayed open on one leg, and began to turn the pages.

From the very first entries, it was evident that Allison Fitch, Simon's first wife, was an abused woman. Nina read page after page of her pain, angst, fear, hope, and self-doubt, feeling the burn of guilt for violating the confessions of a woman in crisis, yet unable to resist the imperative to push ahead.

She realized Simon must have carefully selected passages from the diary to mislead the police into thinking Emma had been depressed to the point of suicide. In reality, they had been the words of another woman. The entries made no note of the date or year. It would have been easy for him to photocopy passages that weren't particularly incriminating and glue them into a blank book to support his assertion that Emma was depressed, countering Hugh's claims of abuse.

She read on.

Well, I screwed up another plan. Got the date wrong. My mistake, but I'm always messing up something,

*aren't I? Simon's right. I'm a total screw up. Anyway,
I cleaned the kitchen to try and make it up to him,
but didn't do it to his standards, so once again I'm a
failure. Guess I'll try harder.*

Hugh's words came back to Nina: *Does he make you question things?* Nina recalled the countless times Simon had accused her of failing to remember something and thought: *Not things, people; he makes the women in his life doubt themselves.*

These were Allison's private thoughts, and for a moment Nina struggled to wrap her mind around the fact that Simon read them to himself in bed like it was *Jane Eyre.*

Her breath caught, all color draining from her vision, after reading one particularly illuminating passage.

*I get what I have to do. I have to leave him. Yes, yes,
yes, I've said it before. Heard it a thousand times,
too. But it's not easy. I don't have any money. He's
taken it all. I don't even have access to the bank
account. I didn't understand what I was signing. He
made it seem like it was important, but when I asked
ONE simple question, he snapped at me and asked if
I trusted him. So I signed it and when I went to take
out money that's when I found out I wasn't on the account anymore. I don't have any credit cards, and all
the tips I make I give to Simon to pay the bills. God,
I wish he NEVER came to the restaurant that night. I
wish I never left with him. More than anything, I wish
that I never met Simon Fitch!*

Nina realized Simon had told her another lie. He and Allison weren't college sweethearts. She'd been a waitress or something, maybe down on her luck when he met her. She was probably young and without the means to support herself. It would have made it easier for him to take control of her life. Nina wondered how long they'd dated before the abuse started.

Some of what Allison shared in her diary revealed a more volatile side to Simon than Nina had seen. Intuition told her his methods hadn't changed with the years, but he had refined his technique considerably.

> *I got home from the bar and Simon was already in a nasty mood. He looked at his watch and said I should have been home 13 minutes ago. 13 minutes! Like he had timed it. I told him the buses were running late. He told me I should have called and I said, yeah I should have, but I said it really sarcastically. I didn't think it was a big deal, but he got up off the chair and came at me fast. He grabbed my hair and yanked my head back so hard I cried out in pain, and told me to watch how I spoke to him. But he didn't hit me, so it's no big deal. It was just words. Words don't leave marks or bruises.*

It wasn't all a living nightmare. Earlier passages attested to Simon's sweetness, his charm, how much he truly loved her. It was clear for the first time in her life that Allison felt adored and treasured. It must have been intoxicating to a young woman with little life experience. It had been for an older woman; Nina knew. Allison wrote about a moonlight stroll on the lakeshore, dancing to music of wind and waves, and Nina felt sick remembering how Simon had courted her.

> *I think what he loves most about me is my sense of style, how I'm not like all the other girls. I've got*

such a thing for the 60s and 70s, the fashion, the way
women wore their hair. Simon loves my new haircut.
He said I looked like a movie star. He thought I was
so creative. I showed him the magazine where I got
the idea from and he said I was more beautiful than
the model.

The magazine.

Was it possible the magazine Allison referenced was the
same issue of *Vogue* Simon had shown her—the one Nina
had used to model her hairstyle? She had never checked the
date on the cover, so it could have come from another decade;
it could have belonged to Allison.

Nina spent too much time on the bed, flipping pages, reading passage after passage, forgetting for a moment she had
broken into Simon's home. She began to skim the pages, taking in what she could as quickly as possible, aware it was not
in her best interests to linger, but unable to pull herself away.
Certain entries stuck out like a lighthouse beacon sending its
danger warning.

I told Simon I didn't feel like he was paying enough
attention to me and he snapped and said I was being
too sensitive. He says I'm always nagging him about
this or that. All of a sudden I'm defending myself
when I was trying to talk about my feelings. I guess I
just have to do better. It's my fault. I know he hates it
when I criticize him. His father criticized him con-
stantly so it's hard for him to hear. I'll be more care-
ful next time. And he's right. I am too sensitive.

All I am is a failure. I can't do anything right. Can't
fold his shirts right. Can't cook a good meal. I'm not
adventurous enough in bed. I feel like I'm constantly

*saying sorry. And when I tell him how he hurt my
feelings, he just says I misunderstood him. I don't
know what to think. But I think he's probably right.
Okay, that was a first. He hit me. And it hurt. Really,
really hurt. But in fairness I did call him a son of a
bitch. That's because I wanted to go out with Heather
and Marie and he wouldn't give me any money, and
I wasn't about to ask them for cash. He said we were
running low and couldn't afford a night out, but I
worked for that money. It's mine! Right? Anyway, he
punched me. Closed fist and all. And afterwards he
was so so apologetic. He actually threw up, he was
that upset! He was crying, crying, crying, telling me
how sorry he was, begging me not to leave him, that
he didn't mean for it to happen. He gave me two hundred dollars and told me to go out and have the best
time ever. Said don't worry about him and that he'd
be fine. But I couldn't go out, not with him so upset.
He's never lost his temper like that before. Something
must really be bothering him. Anyway, I didn't think I
had enough makeup to cover up the mark, so I stayed
home. We ended up having a good night watching a
movie, but he wouldn't go to bed until I promised I
forgave him. So I did.*

*We are working so hard on the relationship. I think
it's making a real difference. We're not in therapy,
not yet anyway. Simon says we can't afford it. But
we're talking a lot and he really wants to change. I
know it. We're going to get through this. Together.
I love him and he loves me. And that's what matters.
He's had such a hard life. I mean both his parents
died not that long ago. It's traumatic. Even though
his father was really abusive to him and his mother,*

it's still really hard. He's going through a lot. I'm really hopeful for our future and I know I can help him change. I just know it!

I don't see my friends anymore. Simon hates them. All of them. He says he doesn't trust them. Calls them a bunch of phonies. I told him he's wrong, but he's so sure of it that he said it's either them or him. Like what I am supposed to do with that? Leave? Move out? And go live where? I have no money. None. And we're working so hard on us, too. I'll give it some time. I know we can figure this out. And then I'll ask Marie if she called me a bitch behind my back like Simon said she did.

Simon's been horrible lately. I think he yells at me just to see me cry. It's like I do nothing around here. I cook. I clean. I work. I contribute! I am important, but he makes me feel so insignificant sometimes. I feel like I'm constantly walking on eggshells. He says I'm always upset about something and that's why my friends don't like me anymore. Maybe he's right. Before Simon came along I was nothing, and without him I'll be nothing again.

I've stopped cooking because Simon's being so mean to me, which is really pissing him off. But he's always upset with me about something, isn't he? I'm perpetually subpar in his eyes. Any chance he gets, he'll point out how other wives treat their husbands, but not me. I'm not a good wife at all. It's hard to take these constant comparisons, but I guess the verbal slaps are preferable to the other kind.

Simon hit me again and I told him that was it. I was
going to leave him. He said if I did that he'd kill me.
He said it quickly, too, like he had planned it out
already. I don't know what to do. Honestly, I'm really
scared. He's been in this black mood for the longest
time. I feel too ashamed and embarrassed to go back
home. I mean, I ran away. My parents haven't heard
from me in years. I'll never live it down! No, I have
to figure this out on my own. It's my fault. I'm doing
it. I'm triggering his behavior. So if I'm responsible,
I can fix it.

Nina passed through episodes of more heartache and
abuse. Allison fell short of Simon's expectations time and
time again. The beatings did not end.

I'm a week out of the hospital. I can walk fine. The leg
will heal. Everyone believed Simon, like I knew they
would. I'm clumsy enough to have fallen down the
stairs. If only they knew. But I can't tell my friends.
I can't tell anyone because I'm afraid. He'll kill me
if I try to leave him. I know he will. I should kill
him first. I should stab him in his sleep, a knife right
through his cold, beating heart. But you can't do it,
can you, Allison? Because you are weak and pathetic,
just like he says you are.

Allison even repeated something in her diary that made
Nina shiver with grim reminders of the last words Simon had
spoken to her:

Like Simon says, there is a right way and wrong way
to be, for everything and everyone.

As Nina neared the final entries, things seemed to take a turn for the better. That's when Allison got pregnant.

I can't believe it. I'm going to be a mother. Maybe this will change everything. Maybe a baby is all that we've been missing. God, I pray that's so. Please. Please make it so. I'm so excited but nervous, too. I can't wait to tell Simon. He'll be overjoyed.

And from what Nina read, he was overjoyed, at least for a time. But Simon could not control his nature. He'd yell and scream when the house was in disorder. He'd badger and berate, but at least the beatings seemed to stop. There were no entries detailing any physical abuse during her pregnancy. But there were plenty of allusions to emotional isolation and loneliness.

Now he's telling me I have to quit my job. He says the stress is bad for the baby. I don't know what to believe anymore, but I still gave them my notice.

A group of people from the bar got together for a good-bye party and gave me some money so I could buy things for the baby because I wasn't having a baby shower. Simon said those were bad luck. I wouldn't give the money to Simon to put in the account, so he hit me in the stomach. He hit the baby! That decided it. I'm going to get a job, a secret job that pays me very well. But it has to be something I can do without him finding out, so I can't go back to the bar. All I need is just enough money to get away, and then I'll start my new life with a new name.

I'm so done being afraid. I'm going to get money and then I'm going to leave him for good.

The baby changes everything.

That was the final entry. Those were Allison's last words.

CHAPTER 57

Nina's heart sank. She looked at Allison's picture again, hoping, praying she got away. But perhaps not. Maybe Simon had found out she was going to leave him. Had he killed her? What happened to the baby? The diary answered none of those questions.

Closing the small book, Nina rose from the bed as a gnawing fear took root. She knew better than most how difficult it could be to leave an abusive relationship. But even with all her training, she had fallen into a similar trap. Now she'd done it again, staying inside Simon's orbit, in his home, far longer than prudent.

School was still in session, she had that going for her, and the alarm had been disabled so Simon would have no reason to suspect anything amiss. Then again, he might have noticed his keys missing, and that could trigger him to check the house.

Her mounting anxiety went full bloom as she processed the dire reality of the situation. Nina understood it now: she was the carbon copy replacement of Allison, who'd left Simon heartbroken, or was dead and buried by his hand. Simon had used Nina to try to overcome the deep-rooted sense of rejection he had harbored ever since Allison had taken with her Simon's child and vanished, never to be seen or heard from again.

How long had he lusted for me? Nina wondered. Probably from that first day when they had met at the D.A.R.E. meeting almost seven years ago. The timeline gave her new insight into a terrifying possibility: When had Emma died? Soon after that meeting? Nina calculated the dates in her head. Yes, it was around that time, she decided. It was possible—even probable, given what she'd learned—that when Simon met Nina he decided to substitute one version of Allison—Emma—with a near-perfect replica. There was no doubt in Nina's mind that a side-by-side comparison of a recent picture of herself and one of Allison Fitch as a forty-something-year-old woman, would look as close to identical as different DNA would allow. Nina now saw herself as Simon saw her: his chance to fix the past, to bring Allison back to him.

Maybe Simon had killed Emma because two near look-alikes would have been confusing for him. Or perhaps he had wanted Emma's money and a fresh start. Nina couldn't say.

Hard as it was, she tried to put herself in Simon's twisted brain. With Emma out of the picture, what had he done next? He'd bided his time, hadn't he? Like a patient hunter lying in wait, planning his attack, for years, perhaps. Thinking, always thinking, how he could ingratiate himself with Nina, waiting for that perfect opportunity to strike. And then the opportunity presented itself when Glen disappeared, leaving her and the children vulnerable, giving Simon the chance he needed to make his move.

My God, she thought. *Heaven help me.*

The onslaught of revelations left Nina dazed, so instead of making a hasty exit as she'd intended, she wandered down the hall in something of a trance, leaving the diary on top of the comforter where she had found it, making sure to smooth out the indentation of her body. She briefly contemplated taking the book, to use it as irrefutable evidence of what Simon really was, but didn't want him coming after her to get it back. Simon Fitch was more dangerous than she'd ever imagined, and now she not only feared for her life, but for the lives of her children as well.

At the end of the hall was the door that led to the basement. Nina had never wandered through the house when she was there with Simon, but once he had shown her his cellar. Remarkably clean and ordered, it had stayed in her memory. She noted now how the door was tightly sealed at the top, bottom, and sides. A thought prickled at her. Daisy could be down there.

You'd have heard her barking, Nina told herself.

Maybe. Or maybe not. Maybe the door is sealed so sound can't escape. Or maybe she's down there dead. Maybe he killed my dog.

Every fiber in her body told her to leave, to get out of that house right away, but she couldn't go, not without checking first. She didn't want to stay in this house a second longer, but she had to know.

Setting her hand on the brass doorknob, Nina gave it a twist. It turned in her grasp. She pulled hard to open the door. It was stiff at first, but the seal eventually gave way. She looked down the hall toward the front door, scared that Simon might appear. But the house was as empty and still as when she'd arrived.

The open cellar door revealed a steep stairwell. The room below was impenetrably dark. Not a trace of light anywhere.

She peered into the blackness, heart hammering in her chest. She was feeling around the top of the stairs for a light switch when she heard a bark.

CHAPTER 58

"Daisy?"

Her call was answered with more barking.

Nina found the light switch. A naked bulb dangling from a cord illuminated a steep, slat staircase made of unfinished wood. Dizzy with fear, Nina descended the stairs slowly, one creaky step at a time, holding on to the wood railing for balance. Her heart knocked hard enough to mask the sound of her footsteps. The farther she descended, the louder the barking became.

Get my dog and get out . . . get my dog and get out, she repeated to herself.

"Daisy?" Nina called her dog's name again as if she could answer; sure, so sure it was Daisy's bark, the way a mother knows her child's cry. Her breath came in shaky sputters, a whistle of fear pushing past her trembling lips as she continued her descent.

Nina stepped into a dark enclosure, the light from the lone bulb unable to penetrate the space below. She peered into the blackness. Daisy's barking was loud and to her left, somewhere in that pitch dark.

She thought she heard a noise to her right, or was that in her head? Nina froze, petrified. Closing her eyes tight, she drew in a sharp inhale. Simon was down here. He had *been* down here, waiting for her in the dark. He was always one step ahead. Simon—Simon the patient hunter—had hidden himself in the basement. Knowing Nina as he did, like a subject he had studied in school, a topic he'd mastered, he knew she would come, and she did just as he'd predicted, marching right into his trap. What would he do to her if he caught her here? Kill her? Dump her body in the same grave where he may have buried Allison?

She waited for another sound but only heard the desperate barking of a dog—her dog. Nina pushed aside all grim thoughts to focus on finding light.

Her fingers brushed up against a support pole, where she found a second switch that powered on bright overhead fluorescents. She turned, half expecting to see Simon, a twisted smile on his face, but instead, encountered a wide-open, nearly empty basement, as neat and devoid of possessions as the rest of the house. Taking in the room, Nina noticed a television propped up against a wall on the other side of the stairs, its snaking black cord plugged into the nearby outlet. *How strange to see a television in this empty space,* she thought.

She turned her head in the opposite direction, toward the barking, and there she was—Daisy, her beloved dog, crated, looking healthy as could be. The crate was large enough to allow Daisy to move about freely, and so she did, her body clanging loudly against the metal barricade in wild, uncontained excitement. Daisy could see and smell Nina. She knew what home was, and home had come to her.

Nina's heart leaped for joy. There did not appear to be a lock on the crate; escape should be easy.

Get my dog and get out.

Nina went to the crate. She crouched down to undo the latch, and managed to get the leash out of her coat pocket without dropping her phone. Daisy broke into a frenzy of barking.

Opening the crate a crack, Nina struggled to secure the leash to Daisy's collar. Her dog was nonstop motion, barking, yipping excitedly, and kissing any part of Nina within reach of her tongue. The moment Nina stepped away from the door, Daisy shot bullet-like out of the crate. With a burst of startling strength and speed, she dragged Nina to a wall behind the stairs. Nina resisted by tugging hard on Daisy's leash to pull her in the opposite direction.

"Come on! Come on!" she urged.

She didn't want to go back through that house, but there was no other way out. Again, she jerked the leash hard, but Daisy continued to resist.

Eventually, Nina got to the stairs, and up she went, surprised she had to pull Daisy, and with some force, to get her to leave.

Out! Out! Get out! The voice in her head was screaming now.

At the top of the stairs, Daisy dug in and wouldn't budge, so Nina gave the leash another hard tug. The house was quiet and still. To her left, she could see the front door. Escape was only feet away. Her heart lifted. It was mission accomplished. She'd go straight to the police and they'd arrest Simon for dognapping. She wondered if perhaps she should get the diary, thinking the authorities would search for Allison and reopen the investigation into Emma's death, but now wasn't the time. She had to leave. Every part of her was urging her to go.

Good-bye, house. Good-bye, Simon.

As Nina reached for the front doorknob, her cell phone rang.

CHAPTER 59

Instinct made Nina retrieve her phone from her coat pocket. It could have been Maggie calling from school. Simon was there and she was thinking crisis.

She saw the call was actually from Connor. Nina was about to answer when Daisy gave a hard yank, pulling the leash free from her loosened grasp as she went for her phone. Spinning quickly to catch her, Nina lunged for the leash, but Daisy was too fast. In a blur of motion, Daisy bolted for the door to the basement, which Nina had left open in her haste.

Down she went again, putting her phone back in her coat pocket, not answering Connor's call.

Get my dog and get out.

Nina returned to the basement to find Daisy barking wildly at the wall behind the stairs, pawing at the brick.

"What are you doing?" Nina shouted as she reached down to gather Daisy's leash. She pulled hard, but Daisy held firm. Nina gave the leash another tug, gritting her teeth in frustration.

"Come on," she urged, her temper rising as if she were dealing with an obstinate child.

Instead, Daisy went down on her stomach, paws outstretched, before rolling onto her back, refusing to make eye contact.

"No! Come!" Nina scolded.

What is Daisy trying to say? A trainer had once told her that hierarchy was important in the canine world. Could Daisy be attempting—in a respectful manner—to inform Nina that she wished to disobey her command? Perhaps. Or maybe it meant she was afraid. If so, it would be an emotion both currently shared.

Nina thought of Allison, gone somewhere, taken, killed, thought of Simon finding her here, and pulled on the leash again, this time with more force, knowing every second counted.

"Come on," she growled.

Daisy allowed Nina to drag her a couple feet on her back before righting herself.

There, thought Nina. *Let's go.*

But Daisy dug in and began moving in reverse, as if she were playing a game of tug with an invisible rope toy, pulling Nina toward that same wall she'd visited before.

No more games. Nina went for the collar. She'd carry her out of here if she had to. But now, standing so close to the wall, Nina could see something she hadn't noticed before. There appeared to be the very faint outline of a door. Daisy kept her nose to the wall, barking excitedly. Using her fingers, Nina traced the edge of the outline, searching for some kind of a latch, but there didn't appear to be any way to open it.

She would have left, but Daisy was so insistent that she simply had to know why. But how did it open? She had no tools, nothing she could use to pry it ajar. What was behind there?

It's Allison . . . it's her body . . . it's her bones.

Feeling desperate, Nina pressed against the wall in random places, looking for some kind of pivot point, but the door, if there was a door, wouldn't budge. She reached higher for added leverage, and her hand pushed against a brick above her head. She heard a click and a popping like an airlock giving way. The crack in the door widened. A jagged energy coursed through her body. Nina set her fingers against the edge of the crack and gave a hard pull. The door swung open easily, the hinges not making a sound. A pungent aroma, truly an animal-like scent, filled her nostrils.

Nina's mouth opened in a scream, but no words came out.

He looked back at her blankly, his eyes wide with disbelief. Daisy darted into the room behind the stairs with unbounded joy, her barking ricocheting off the concrete walls.

"Am I dreaming?" he asked in a whispered voice.

Nina knelt before the man with the ankle restraint around his leg and touched his bearded face with great care and tenderness.

"No," she said, caressing him, tears stinging her eyes. "You're not dreaming. I'm here, Glen. I'm really here."

CHAPTER 60

This was not the man portrayed on the missing-person posters that Nina had distributed all over New Hampshire. That photo had captured Glen's rugged good looks: the hard-to-tame wavy hair with the side part he favored, eyes a bit brooding, neatly trimmed beard glinting red, and a proud smile because, after all, he had just hiked up a mountain.

Then there was this man: hollow, bloodless skin pock-marked with ugly bruises, deep red scratches, and lesions on his arms and face that had to have come from a recent beating. He was shockingly pale, eyes darkly ringed, and cheeks sunken like those of a castaway. A thick and tangled beard, descending well past his chin, trapped dried food like a spider's web. His hair, unruly as his beard, draped long past his shoulders. His body was decaying while alive.

He was chained like a prisoner, and dressed like one, too, in a gray sweatsuit that hung loosely over what once had been a fit, well-muscled body. He began blinking rapidly, his eyes adjusting to the blazing light. Nina stood shakily, taking one step back, scanning the room, as if the answer to what to do next would be found nearby.

When the overheads were off, Nina had noted that

the darkness was impenetrable. Now she knew why. The basement had casement windows that were covered with blackout shades. Certainly those windows had been sealed tight. There was no way out for Glen, not with a chain locked around his ankle.

"Oh, dear Lord," she said.

The ground seemed to suddenly drop out from under her, her balance gone. Nina sank to her knees again, landing with a painful crack of bone on cement. The room went spinning—the walls, the floor, Glen, Daisy, all of it now a blur.

Blood thrummed in Nina's ears as her vision went black. Fear added weight to her body, pulling her down, down into nothingness. Again that smell, musty and rancid, wafted from Glen's prison, powerful enough to make her eyes water and sharpen her focus. She came to, snapping into herself.

She fixed her gaze on Glen. The despair in his eyes filled her with profound sorrow. Glen inched forward, the rattle of his chain making Nina cringe.

Get out! Get out! Get out!

The voice in her head was back, screaming to her this time.

Nina emerged from her fog and began to crawl toward Glen, her body trembling. She entered the room partway, reaching for the chain, pulling uselessly on his restraints.

Glen pursed his lips, still blinking, working hard to speak the words that were starting to form.

"He has the key," he managed, his eyes traveling to the heavy-duty lock securing the ankle restraint to his body. "The chain is welded to the base. You can't break it."

Nina saw such pain in Glen's eyes. Was that for all he had done or for what Simon would do to them? Daisy was elated, her tail wagging like wipers in a rainstorm. The room may have been soundproof, but it couldn't block out Daisy's incredible sense of smell.

"I'm so sorry," Glen said, his voice breaking. "I'm so sorry for everything."

Nina was checking the key ring for one that might unlock Glen's restraint, but put them away to take his hand in hers. His skin was raw and brittle. Their eyes met, and when he didn't look away, when his eyes never left her face, she took in his grief and his sorrow and knew with certainty he'd been down here since his disappearance. He'd been living in the room behind the stairs for nearly two years.

"Oh, Glen, no, no, I'm the one who's sorry." Nina's voice broke as tears filled her eyes. "I'm so sorry for what happened to you."

"How long have you been in the house?" Glen sounded like he'd just come out of a dream. "The room is soundproof. I can't hear a thing in here."

"Not long," Nina said, forgetting for a moment the time she had spent in the bedroom.

"You shouldn't be here," Glen said. "He'll know."

"No, I turned off the alarm, and Simon's at school. We're safe."

The hairs rising on her arms didn't agree.

"There's . . . there's a backup system." Glen croaked out the words, his voice hoarse, weak as an old man's. "It's hooked up to his phone. If anyone comes inside the house when he's not here, he'll know it. Get out. Get out now and call for help."

Panic rose in her. Prisoner or not, Glen was the one thinking more clearly, and if he had known how long she'd spent reading the diary, he'd have yelled at her to run. A plan formed in her mind: she'd flee, get outside, and drive a safe distance away before calling the police.

"I'll go for help," Nina said, walking backward, unable to avert her eyes from Glen.

The numb shock was beginning to abate, her brain firing now. The place had two alarms, not one. Simon was at school, a fifteen-minute drive away. But she'd been in his house twice as long. He had to know she was here—who else would it be?—so why wasn't *he* here? What was he doing? Was Maggie in danger? Had he taken her? Did he plan on striking some kind of deal—her love . . . for her daughter's life? Is that why Connor had called?

Nina was reaching for her phone when she heard something skid across the floor like a hockey puck.

Peering down, she settled her eyes on what had caught her peripheral vision. It took a moment to realize the object by her feet was a leather diary.

Oh, God, no.

And the lights went out.

CHAPTER 61

She was plunged into total darkness, a black void surrounding her. A noise now near her. Movement, a quick shuffling, barring the only way out, shoes scraping against the floor. Nina went completely still, her fight-or-flight response battling for a decision. What to do? There was nowhere to run. She couldn't see, but she heard his voice coming from the nothingness surrounding her—two words, pure ice.

"Hello, Nina."

"Leave her alone," Glen cried out, his desperate plea coming from Nina's right, while Simon's fast footsteps approached from her left. He knew this space, how to maneuver in it, even without light.

Nina went for her phone to call for help; it was the only clear thought she had. But it took a moment to get it out of her jacket pocket, then more time to get her fingers in the right places to make the call.

Simon was on her. The light from the phone's display had helped him track his quarry. He grabbed Nina by the shirt and drove her into his body. At the same instant, he raked the phone from her grasp, causing her to drop it to the floor with a loud clatter. Still holding her by the buttons of her blouse, his foot went up, then down onto the phone with his heavy shoe, over, and over, until it was pulverized glass and plastic.

Darkness again.

With a grunt, Simon dragged Nina away from Glen, out of the hidden room, and over to a nearby wall. His hand soon found a switch and with a flick returned them to the light.

Nina needed a moment for her vision to adjust. When it did, she saw he was dressed for work. Everything about him looked normal, even the placid expression on his face. But those eyes, those black eyes were as empty as this house.

"We need to talk," he said.

Daisy came bounding over to them, her leash dragging behind her. She knew Simon, his scent. He was a friend, and she must have thought this was some sort of a game. She went up on her hind legs, to put her front paws on Simon's waist, but Simon pushed her, and down she went.

With a grunt, Simon threw Nina up against the wall, clamped his hand around her throat, and started to squeeze. As her vision dimmed, Nina could feel her eyes bulging in their sockets. Daisy seemed to sense something shift in this game of theirs. She moved away, growled, head dropping low, approaching slowly, cautiously.

Simon was breathing heavily, like he'd just finished a jog.

"I had to borrow a car. Home emergency, I said, and my truck battery was dead. Your damn kid—so difficult, no discipline, no respect. You should have raised her better." Simon drifted off as if in thought. "She came here to spy on me. Did she say that nobody was staying here? No renters? Is that why you thought to come here to look for Daisy?"

Simon's grip around her throat constricted the air to Nina's voice.

"I took her to punish you," Simon explained. "I'd have brought her back, eventually, like I did the last time, once you realized you needed me in your life. But it's no matter now. I guess in a way this had to happen. No more secrets. Now we can be together as we really are."

Simon reached behind his back with his free hand to remove a gun he had tucked into the waistband of his khakis.

He put his finger on the trigger, pressed the barrel up against Nina's forehead hard enough to leave an imprint.

She could sense what he was thinking. *Pull it. Pull it.*

She heard Glen's muffled pleas through the partially open door to his prison.

She saw Simon's finger tense around the trigger. Fear bubbled in her throat. Her breathing became constricted as his grip tightened.

The determined look set on Simon's face left no doubt in Nina's mind that he was gathering his resolve to strangle her, or to shoot her dead.

She waited, the anticipation unbearable. *How much will it hurt? Please be quick,* she prayed. A desperate longing to see her children once more surged through her, a need more powerful than her desire to breathe freely again. *Who will take care of them? My parents? Would Simon even let them live?*

"Please, Simon . . . you don't have to . . . do this."

Nina's words burned with raw emotion. Simon said nothing and in his silence a steely bolt of terror struck her hard. She waited . . . and waited for an end that didn't come. Something shifted in Simon. Nina sensed his hesitation. He couldn't bring himself to pull the trigger. He didn't want her to die, *couldn't* let it happen. Instead, he began to caress the side of her face, running his fingers back and forth across her trembling lips. His black eyes flickered with bits of light, like the gasping final flames of a candle at wick's end, his internal conflict bubbling to the surface—to kill her or let her live; to end his twisted dream or try again.

Daisy wasn't comforted. She barked at Simon. He had fed

her, petted her, loved her, and played with her, so why would he be hurting her person?

"It's okay, Daisy. Relax," Simon said.

Keeping the gun pressed to Nina's head, Simon let go of his hold on her throat. Stretching his arm, eyes never leaving Nina's face, Simon felt the floor until his fingers brushed against Daisy's leash. He straightened, having managed to keep the barrel of the gun aimed at Nina the entire time. He maneuvered the three of them over to the crate. He put Daisy inside, closing the door behind her. Daisy barked in protest.

"I wouldn't hurt her," Simon said, using his free hand to caress the side of Nina's face. "She brought us together once before, and she's brought us together again." He pushed her hard against the wall.

"Nina," he whispered in her ear, moving his hand again to her throat, applying light pressure, his way of letting her know that by gun or hand, he was in charge. "I'll get rid of him," he said. "Glen didn't love you. Look what he did to you. With Teresa, look what he did."

Simon pushed harder into her body. "I love you, Nina," he said in her ear, stroking her face with his hand holding the gun. "I love you so much. And you want to be with me, too, don't you?" he said, still speaking softly.

Nina knew not to antagonize him. Better to keep him off-balance, keep him talking.

"Yes, of course, of course I do," she said, breathing hard.

"I have a box in my closet with two hundred thousand dollars in it. Two hundred thousand. It was Emma's money, and thanks to her will, now it's ours, her gift to us. I kept it here in case of an emergency. We'll go somewhere. We can live off that money. Believe me, you'll be so happy. I'll make you so happy."

She forced her body to relax even while his other hand

continued to grip her neck. She was responding to him, letting him know how much she liked his plan, while Daisy, still locked in the crate, let her presence be known as well.

"Please, Simon, please let her go," Glen called out from his room. "It won't work. It can't ever work now."

But Nina wasn't focused on Glen. All her attention was given to Simon. *Control your breathing. Control your fear. Make him believe.* She forced herself to relax. It *could* be as he wanted, or that's what she was trying to tell him with her body, leaning in, pressing against him. Even with his hand still clutching at her throat, Simon *was* getting the message. She saw joy blossom on Simon's face. He relaxed his fingers, letting air, precious air, rush into Nina's lungs. He pushed against her harder, kissing her ear, her neck. She responded to his touch, her fingers now tugging at his hair, a soft noise escaping her lips.

Nina drew in a breath. She placed her lips against his ear. "Simon," she whispered, breathing heavily, pushing into him. "Simon," she said again.

"Yes, yes," Simon said breathlessly.

"Simon."

A piercing cry exploded from Simon's mouth after Nina brought her knee up fast and hard, ramming into his crotch with all her might. Simon's hand flew up in reflex, and the gun went off—two loud pops that put holes directly in the ceiling, sending bits of plaster raining down on them.

He slumped to the floor, gasping for air. His body lay motionless, blocking the bottom stair—the only way out. Nina had no idea if Simon had managed to hold on to the gun or not as she tried to hurdle him to make her escape. But he seized hold of her ankle as she went up and over and would not let go. Nina hopped awkwardly on one foot to stay upright as Simon managed to slowly get to his knees, still holding her ankle in his viselike grip. With another push and groan,

Simon was soon standing. He kicked Nina's other foot out from under her and she went down, hard, using her hands to break her fall.

Nina spun onto her back. She looked up in horror as Simon loomed over her. Fury pulsated in his face. He began to drag her toward Glen's room by the ankle, limping to compensate for the pain in his groin. With no balance, no leverage, Nina tried to twist free, but could not. Simon pulled her toward him like a fisherman reeling in his catch. He let go of her leg to take hold of her from behind, wrapping one arm tightly around her chest, lifting her into him as if she weighed nothing. Nina kicked and thrashed to slip free, but it was impossible to break his hold.

Now she got her answer as to what had happened to that gun. With his free hand, he put the weapon back to her head.

"Calm down, Nina," he said, huffing and hobbling, compensating for his injury. "Just take it easy. Okay? You don't want this going off accidentally. You don't want to leave Connor and Maggie without a mother."

That got Nina to still. Daisy went wild, her barking escalating. Driven by instinct more than anything—fight or flight—Nina snapped her head forward and bit Simon hard on the arm he'd used to wrap around her chest. Simon yowled in pain as he tossed Nina onto the floor. The left side of her skull connected hard with the television. She lay there dazed, her vision blurred. Inching toward her, Simon aimed the gun—a gun she'd never known he owned—at her heart.

"Don't!" Glen cried out, as loud as his weakened voice could carry. "Leave her alone. Leave her, Simon. Please."

Coming as far forward as his chain would allow, Glen pawed frantically to get to Simon, but the chain wouldn't let him go far enough. Simon moved in front of Nina, still pointing the gun at her. As she struggled to stand, Glen made another useless lunge. His chain pulled tight, sending him

momentarily airborne. He crash-landed hard to the ground.
But he had distracted Simon, enough for Nina to get back to
her feet, pick up the television, all sixty-something pounds
of it, and fling it at Simon with the adrenaline-fueled angry
cry of a shot-putter. Simon easily sidestepped the projectile.
Shards of broken glass from the screen exploded on impact,
shooting out in all directions. He surveyed the wreckage and
made a tsk-tsk sound, like a disappointed parent.

"Well, that's a waste," he said, as if it puzzled him that
Nina would destroy a perfectly good television. "But I'm
thinking in a few minutes nobody will be needing it."

His threat went unacknowledged, but Nina understood
if things didn't go his way, they would die—perhaps they
would *all* die. She was panting from exertion and terror,
standing behind the stairs between Simon, who blocked her
only way out, and Glen, trapped in his room.

"Your answer to my question will decide what happens to
the children," Simon told her. "I want you to know that. So,
Nina, now it's the moment of truth for us. I love you. Do you
love me, too?"

Simon lowered his weapon. His arms hung at his sides.
There was nothing crazed about him. He was calm as could
be. He looked to Nina like a teacher standing at the front of
his classroom, hoping someone would give the right answer.
That someone was her. Nina understood that any other words
would bring her a bullet.

"Yes, I—I love you, Simon." Knowing what he wanted
to hear, of course that's how she'd answer, but why on earth
would he believe her?

Her only hope was that desire and obsession would oc-
clude his thinking. Simon closed his eyes and lifted his head
to the ceiling as if basking in some hidden glow. "Say it
again," he said, his eyes still closed.

A flash of movement drew Nina's attention to the space

behind him. To her shock and relief, she saw Detective Eric Wheeler quietly descending the slatted basement stairs. She could see him clearly in the open space between each step.

"I love you, Simon," Nina said, more loudly this time and with feeling, while Wheeler crept panther-like down into the basement. He had his gun drawn as he moved cautiously from stair to stair, motioning with his hand for Nina to keep talking, keep Simon distracted.

"I love you," Nina said again, her heart racing in terror. "We'll make it work. Don't worry about anything, Simon. It'll be the two of us. I'll be your second chance with Allison. Just the way you want."

With that, Simon opened his eyes. He looked hopeful, relieved, somehow at peace. Nina's body quaked as a faint smile came to his lips.

"Thank you," he said. "You don't know how happy you've made me."

Wheeler came into full view, a stair creaking under his weight as Simon sprang out from behind the staircase. Whirling around to face him, Simon fired three shots—*pop, pop, pop*—before Wheeler fired one. His bullet sank harmlessly into a concrete wall; all three of Simon's sank into flesh. Wheeler tumbled down the stairs, spilling onto the concrete floor, spreading blood everywhere.

Simon went to him. Wheeler, on his back at the bottom of the stairs, gazed blankly at the ceiling. Pulling the gun from Wheeler's weakened grasp, Simon tucked it into the waistband of his khakis. He looked down at the detective as though he were assessing something too bizarre to comprehend.

"Detective," he said sorrowfully, "why on earth are you here?"

Nina watched the erratic rise and fall of Wheeler's chest. "Connor. . . . worried . . . called," he managed to wheeze.

Simon sounded surprised. "Why would he be worried?"

Nina swallowed a gasp. She'd forgotten about the camera in the woods. It was still taking pictures in the daylight. Connor must have been checking for signs of Daisy and maybe saw a picture of Nina entering the house. He would have at least noticed her car parked in the driveway. There must have been another picture of Simon's arrival, and Connor would have known she was still inside. That's why he had called her. And when she didn't answer, he called the police.

Good boy. Good boy, she thought.

Nina moved out from behind the stairs to take a tentative step toward them. Trying to sneak up on Simon while he had his back to her was like playing the children's game, red light, green light.

Simon stood to the side of the staircase closer to the dog crate, Wheeler splayed out at the bottom step, Nina creeping up from behind. Out of the corner of his eye, Wheeler watched Nina approaching. Then he looked away, focusing as best he could on Simon—to keep him from noticing her, she thought hopefully. Nina continued her silent advance, bending at the knees to pick up something off the floor.

Wheeler spit a gob of blood from his mouth. "Officer down. Backup—call for backup . . . call, backup."

He was disoriented. A pool of blood darkened his shirt. Every word he spoke was a struggle. Nina now knew the detective hadn't asked for backup when he came to investigate. No additional police were coming. Help *wasn't* on the way.

Simon covered his mouth with his hands like he couldn't believe what he'd just done. His shoulders slumped as though he was supremely disappointed in himself.

"I'm so sorry for doing that to you," Simon said, indeed sounding genuinely remorseful. "You've been . . . helpful to my efforts. You did a really exemplary job. End of watch, that's what the police call it, right?"

Simon raised his gun, aiming it at Wheeler's head, but lowered it as he surveyed the rest of him. There was no need to fire another bullet.

"Why?" Wheeler had to know what he was dying for.

"For love. For a second chance," Simon said.

Wheeler's fading gaze looked past Simon at Nina, who had snuck up close enough to be within striking distance, wielding a huge glass shard from the smashed television like a dagger.

She thought of Maggie, at lunch, gasping for air as her swollen throat closed up. She thought of the EpiPen she had driven hard into her daughter's thigh on more than one occasion. *It's just another pen,* Nina told herself, thinking of the glass. *Do it again. Do it again.*

Nina locked her eyes on her target. Swinging her arm in a similarly wide arc, she drove the glass shard into the side of Simon's neck with powerful force. When the glass had penetrated the skin and dug in far enough to do damage, Nina yanked hard, slicing open her palm in the process as Simon's neck split wide. The severed veins made a ripping sound as jets of dark blood sprayed geyser-like in a horizontal direction.

Simon sank to the floor, dropping his weapon to clutch at his bleeding throat, choking to death on his own blood. His legs spasmed as his body jerked about wildly.

Reaching for the gun Simon dropped, Nina picked it up, and retrieved Wheeler's weapon as well. She thought about shooting Simon, but preferred to watch him writhing, gasping, dying as blood poured from his body in rivers. She looked over at Wheeler. His wide eyes were open, seeing nothing. His chest no longer rose or fell.

Nina had taken CPR as part of her numerous certifications.

She pumped hard and fast on the middle of Wheeler's chest while Simon gagged on his blood. With her hands soaked in Wheeler's blood and her own, Nina delivered rescue breaths she knew were pointless as she watched Simon die. She could deliver all the rescue breaths in the world; Wheeler wasn't taking them. His eyes were milky with death. There was no point in doing anything more, and Simon was still alive.

Nina had something important left to do. She approached Simon without caution, knelt down next to him, not caring that his blood was getting all over her shoes, her pants.

"Where is Allison? Did you do something to her? Where is she? Where is the baby?"

Simon gazed up at Nina with a look of pure bewilderment.

"Give her peace, Simon," she said, pleading now with urgency in her voice. "Did you hurt her? Do you know where she is?"

Simon's breathing grew labored. He gurgled on his blood. Time was running out. He was going to take this secret, if there even was one, with him to his grave. But she had something else to say. The last words she wanted him to hear. The last words he'd ever hear.

"I want you to die knowing I don't love you. I. Don't. Love. You."

Confusion sparked in Simon's eyes before a profound pain set in. In that moment, Nina felt certain Simon had heard and understood her. She saw recognition linger in his eyes for a moment before the light went out of them for good.

CHAPTER 62

Lakes Region General Hospital, the same hospital where Maggie and Dr. Wilcox were treated, had a new patient. Glen was malnourished, and despite his efforts with bodyweight exercises, had lost tremendous muscle mass, but overall he was in surprisingly good health. The nurses trimmed his beard, tended to his cuts, and pumped him with antibiotics to fight off possible infection. He was feeling woozy from the medication, but alert enough to give multiple statements to the police, who were reeling over the death of their fallen brother. It would be a long time before Seabury recovered from Simon Fitch.

The media was on the story. Already the headlines were juicy, and online, PSYCHO TEACHER OBSESSES OVER FIRST WIFE LOOK-ALIKE was getting plenty of shares.

But Nina wasn't focused on what people were saying. This was a time for her family to heal. And the best treatment for Glen was seeing his children again. Maggie had hugged her father so hard Glen pleaded with her to let go. She brought *A Wrinkle in Time* with her, thinking her dad might want her to read to him at his bedside.

"You're so much bigger," Glen said. "I missed so much. I missed you all so much."

The tears fell freely. Maggie, biting her lip, trembling with emotion, couldn't find the words.

"I tricked you, Bunny."

"Bear," Maggie reminded him, struggling to speak while a sad smile crested her lips. "You're supposed to call me Bear. Remember?"

Glen's laugh was tinged with sorrow. "I forgot. I keep forgetting that."

Nina rested her hand on Glen's bony shoulder. So much of him was gone, both physically, and emotionally. They'd all recover, even Dr. Wilcox—all except for Hugh, and Detective Wheeler, and Emma. Maybe Allison. Or maybe she did get away.

"It was the worst thing, lying to you like that. I wanted to tell you . . . but I . . . I couldn't." Glen made his confession with his eyes shut tight, those never-ending tears rolling down his cheeks. "I didn't mean to let any of you down."

Maggie broke into a sob, eventually clearing her eyes with the back of her hand.

"You . . . didn't let me down, Daddy," she managed. She took a big gulp before she could say more. "If you didn't tell me to make nice with . . . with him . . . Ben and I wouldn't have thought to look at the house . . . and . . . and . . ."

Maggie couldn't finish; instead she went back to hugging her father again. They all enjoyed a group hug.

What would have happened? Nina wondered. Without Maggie and Ben, she might never have thought to look for Daisy at Simon's house. Glen could have been left for dead. Eventually, Simon would have shown his true colors. Most likely, at some point he would have killed them all, Nina was sure of it. Glen hadn't failed them. He had saved them.

"Daisy's the real hero," said Glen, brightening as a tender laugh escaped him. "Thank God for her sense of smell."

"And her loyalty," added Nina. "She wouldn't leave without you."

"You could have left the house with her and nobody would have known I was still in the basement."

Glen laughed again, this time with notes of astonishment and awe. His survival had been so tenuous. One event linked to another, starting with Dr. Wilcox, who led Nina to Teresa, then to Hugh . . . Hugh, who knew who Simon really was . . . Maggie, who unwittingly clued in to something being amiss with the rental property . . . Daisy, who had found Glen . . . Connor, who had stayed vigilant.

It took everyone Glen loved most to save his life and the lives of his family.

Connor wiped away tears. The nurses and doctors were giving the family space to reunite.

"Dog of the year," Connor said, barely holding it together. "I love you, Dad."

And then Connor fell to pieces, and so did Nina, and Maggie cried even harder, as the nurses, keeping their distance, got teary-eyed as well.

Eventually, everything and everyone settled. The kids, still numb, took off to get something to eat, leaving Glen and Nina alone for the first time.

"How are you feeling?" Nina asked. It was a loaded question, but what else could she say?

Glen closed his eyes, shaking his head in disbelief.

"I . . . I just feel so guilty and ashamed. It's my fault."

"Stop . . . this won't do us any good."

"But I'm responsible."

"No you're not, Simon is," she said, with a lack of conviction.

Glen wasn't entirely wrong, Nina thought. He had done things—terrible things—that had made them vulnerable to

Simon. He had stripped his family of security and lied for years about his job. She had accepted Teresa's version of their affair, but still . . .

"I want to talk. I want to tell you what happened. How it happened."

"Not now. You need to rest. There'll be time for that later."

"I'm so sick of time," Glen said with a sneer of disgust. "It's all I've had."

Nina tried to wrap her mind around it. Two years. He'd been kept in that horrible space for almost two years. No doubt, Glen was struggling to grasp it as well.

"He drugged me. That's why I did . . . with Teresa . . . why it happened. I wasn't in my right mind." Glen ran his tongue across his chapped, dry lips. "We didn't have an affair. I swear to you. I know you thought that we did, and it tore me up inside. But it was only once, and Simon orchestrated it all."

Nina nodded. "I had pictures, you know—including one of you giving Teresa a big kiss. It was quite believable."

"Simon sent them to you. Put a name to the face to make it more credible when he found out Teresa had left the area, probably for good. He wanted you to think I was with her so you could move on from me."

"Well, it worked. We'll talk about it, too, all our regrets— later though, after you rest and get your strength back."

"Regrets," Glen muttered under his breath, his gaze drifting to another time and place. When he looked up at Nina, he was present again. "I thought a lot about those in the box. But I want you to know why I was in Carson. Why I lost my job at the bank. It's important you know."

Nina glanced at the bandage covering the cut to her palm from the glass shard she had turned into a weapon. She could still hear the skin rip as she pulled the makeshift dagger across Simon's throat. It was as if she could feel his warm blood on her skin.

"Let's get you healthy. Focus only on that for now. Then you can tell me your story. And I'll tell you mine."

CHAPTER 63

A week later, Nina showed up at the hospital with a bottle of whiskey. Truth serum. Glen had finished his daily physical therapy session, but instead of going back to his bed, he and Nina found an empty conference room where they could talk and drink.

It was time.

They sat next to each other on a hard-cushioned couch. Glen looked much better with each day. His color had returned; his cuts and abrasions were well on the way to being completely healed. His doctors were impressed with his progress, and the nurses and PT therapists managing the lion's share of his care and rehabilitation were equally encouraged.

Nina and the kids had come to see Glen every day, but he had requested this private session with his wife. He was tired, beaten, battered, but he had to cleanse himself. He had to purify.

They both did.

"I like your hair," Glen said.

Nina had cut it short, modern and stylish.

"Thank you," she said. "I couldn't stand it the way it was one second longer. Bad memories."

They shared a quiet laugh. Nina poured two fingers of whiskey for each of them.

"Am I even allowed to drink?" Glen said slyly, sneaking glances like he was getting away with something.

"Not long ago this would have been the only medicine you'd have been given. So drink up."

"Don't tell the nurses," Glen said. "They're very protective of me."

That was a bit of an understatement. Those nurses were hawkish at holding the media at bay. The story of a man imprisoned in a soundproof box wasn't dying down anytime soon.

"Cheers," Nina said, lifting her glass.

They both kicked back the first drink, and Nina poured them another. Truth serum. She'd tell Glen everything, but first, Carson.

It all started with the bank. If Nina hadn't been left in dire financial straits, Simon's efforts might not have worked so effectively. Instead, he had taken advantage of a perfect storm, a confluence of events that had nearly served his purpose. So now it was a moment of reckoning. Why had Glen lied to her for all those years?

"I lost my job."

Nina appeared nonplussed. "So you got fired. Why? And why not just come to me?"

"No—no," Glen said, sounding impassioned, a man with pride still in him. "I didn't get fired for something I did wrong. I got fired because I was suspicious that my bank was acting unethically. I tried to report it, but the CEO wasn't interested in hearing what I had to say. I guess he preferred the profits."

Nina became more intrigued. "Unethical, how?"

"Branch managers at my bank were opening hundreds of

unauthorized accounts, issuing unauthorized credit cards to our customers so they could charge all sorts of fees. The scheme was netting big dollars."

"Just like Wells Fargo," said Nina.

"Screwing customers out of their hard-earned money isn't the exclusive privilege of the big banks."

"So they fired you for trying to blow the whistle?"

"I wasn't just fired," Glen said, sucking down the whiskey like water. His lips were moving more freely with each sip.

"Go on," Nina said.

"Before they got rid of me, senior management—and I'm pretty sure it was at the CEO's direction—trashed me in my Form U5."

Nina looked perplexed. "Form U5?"

"It's like a report card for people who work in financial services—or at least, anyone who works as an investment advisor. I had one, even though I didn't really need it for my job. If you have one, a hiring manager looks at your U5 more than your résumé. Those comments in my U5 immediately turned me into poisoned goods. The system works well if a worker takes advantage of a customer, but if an employer unfairly defames an employee, it's impossible to get it corrected, and it means the end of your career. There is no recourse. No organization you can turn to for help. One black mark on the U5 and you'll never get a job in finance again."

Nina nodded. She got it now. Glen didn't just lose his job. He'd been blackballed. He was persona non grata in a career and an industry he loved.

"I thought I was finally earning enough to stop worrying about every little expense—and then overnight, I couldn't get a job as a teller in Podunk, Anywhere. My U5 followed me like a curse."

"That's outrageous," Nina said, sounding genuinely upset.

"Why didn't you tell me? I'd have understood that story a heck of a lot more than you secretly draining our bank accounts."

"Why didn't I tell you?" Glen repeated the question with a pitiful little laugh. "God knows, I should have. I didn't start out intending to do what I did. I thought I could handle it on my own, that eventually I'd land another bank management job, one that didn't need a U5. I only went to Carson to fish, away from everyone who knew me, so I could think, come up with a game plan, a plan B.

"Instead, I found out that when you're approaching fifty and you've had only one career path, forging another isn't a quick and easy thing to do. In my case, it was impossible. I kept thinking my luck was going to change. My résumé would land on the right desk, or something like that, but no. After a year of failure and constant rejection, I had to accept my fate. We were destined for bankruptcy no matter what I did."

Nina puckered her lips, looking unconvinced. "I still don't see why you didn't tell me. You were the noble knight in this tale, trying to do a good deed, and you got a raw deal for it. I would have been on your side. What? You didn't want to worry me, is that it?"

"You don't get it," Glen said, hiding his face in his hands. His breathing turned shaky. "The job was all I had. It was who I was."

"That's not true. You also had a family. You were a dad."

"Was I?" Judging by Glen's expression, either the whiskey or some memory had suddenly turned bitter. Nina poured them each another splash. "I was a father, sure, but I wasn't a dad."

"Not sure I'm clear on the distinction."

"You're not a father. You couldn't understand."

"Try me."

Nina thought Glen was going to clam up. This was the hard part. She took a sip of her drink, and Glen did from his as well. The alcohol was loosening them both. Maybe they could be honest with each other for a change. It wasn't about money and work. This was about their relationship. A rift in the marriage, the same kind of gulf the Coopers couldn't cross, had made it impossible for them to see and hear each other. That is, until Simon.

It was obvious to Nina now—so many signs, signs she'd missed. Simon had wanted the best possible source of information to make Nina fall in love with him. Glen was Simon's Cyrano de Bergerac—the man who could teach him what to say, how to act, how to be around her.

She fit perfectly into Simon's picture, and Glen was his guarantee that he wouldn't fail with her, and to her continued astonishment his plan had nearly worked. The gifts Simon bought her, that opal necklace, the eggplant dish he'd made, movies and TV shows they both enjoyed, his orangey-woodsy smell, things he'd say to her, even the truck he owned—all so comforting to a woman in distress, so familiar. And that special attention he'd paid to Connor, his eagerness for time together as a family, it had all come from the same source, little tips Simon extracted to ensure he got his prize.

It sickened Nina to think of the time she had spent in Simon's bed, making love to him, while her husband had been chained up below, perhaps aware she was there, calling out to her in a voice she couldn't hear. Her children, too, had come to Simon's, toured the house, gone to the lake, unaware their missing dad was so close by. Simon was so twisted that he probably got off on the danger.

"You and the kids. That's what I thought about the most down there. I thought how I'm going . . . to . . . miss you all so much."

When Glen's voice broke and he began to weep, Nina reached over to take hold of his hands, consoling him.

"It wasn't all your fault, Glen," Nina said. "It took me a lot of therapy to come to terms with the role I played. Maybe if I had helped you forge a stronger bond with the kids, you would have taken a different path. But I was selfish. I think I wanted them all to myself. I liked making all the decisions, liked having them come to me. I needed them, maybe even more than they needed me. But I'm not that person anymore."

Nina took her hands away. It was her turn and she wanted no comfort as she fumbled her way through her admission.

"I know you're carrying a lot of guilt for what happened, but I've got my fair share of it, too," she began. "I'm the one who let Simon into our lives so quickly. I ignored my better judgment, my own doubts, Maggie's warnings, misgivings from my parents and my closest friends. I was needy and vulnerable, and I put us all in danger and I have to live with that now.

"You've paid your price and I've paid mine. We can't erase the decisions we made, we can't undo what happened to us, but hopefully, we can try to rebuild."

"With what? I have no job. We have no money."

A slim smile crested Nina's lips.

"I thought about that," she said, "so I got us a cushion."

And that's when Nina shared what she really did when she'd gone upstairs to call the police from Simon's place using Simon's cell phone. Obviously, she could have made the call from his basement.

She had gone to the bedroom at the end of the hall, and again saw the picture of Allison Fitch, who bore such an uncanny resemblance to her. But she had other things on her mind.

She opened the closet door.

He said it was here, didn't he?

There was hardly anything in the closet, making it easy to locate the box she was after. It was big enough to hold a pair of hiking boots, but there was no footwear inside.

"Two hundred thousand dollars, cash, tax free," Nina told Glen. "I put the box in my car before I called the police. I didn't tell the kids. They don't need to know."

"You clever girl." Glen was smiling.

"We deserve that money for what we went through. But I'm putting some of it into a nonprofit in Hugh Dolan's name to support addiction recovery."

Glen nodded in approval.

"You know, he killed Hugh," he said. "He broke into his apartment, subdued him, shoved a fentanyl-laced injection into his arm—revenge for his interference, that's what he told me."

Nina wasn't surprised. She already knew Simon had spied on her Facebook messages, so in a way, she had played a role in Hugh's death. The money wouldn't cleanse her conscience, but it would help take away some of the guilt.

"Remember how we met?" Nina said.

"Match dot com," Glen said with a laugh.

"I always wanted a better story to tell," she said. "My broken jar of pasta sauce. We might not have the greatest how-we-met story, but we do have a good story to tell."

From a pocket, Nina produced a business card belonging to a major book publisher. A large figure was written on the back.

"I suspect it's too soon for you to tell our story right now," Nina said. "It's too soon for me. But when we're ready."

Nina had plans for that money. In addition to funding drug treatment in Hugh's name, she intended to provide for Detective Wheeler's widow, and fund an effort to track down Allison Fitch, and if necessary, try to locate her remains. There was no way to make this up to Dr. Wilcox, but fortunately she was back on her feet and eventually she'd be able to resume her practice.

Glen's eyes misted over as he leaned in, put his mouth close to Nina's ear, and whispered, "I'm just so grateful we're alive to tell it together."

They hugged.

At last, finally, after all this time, she harbored no doubts. This was her husband. The man she loved. True, he had made a terrible choice by not confiding in her, but she had made terrible choices of her own. They were flawed together— like all marriages, perfectly imperfect. With time and counseling, Nina had total confidence she could get over Glen's deception and his lone indiscretion. The mind was funny like that. It could adapt, shift, change directions like sand in the wind.

In another week, he would be officially discharged and they'd move back in together as a family. Nina had rented a new house in Seabury. She had the money. Ginny and Susanna were helping with the move—once again, the comfort of friendship.

As Nina pulled away from Glen's embrace, she caught sight of something, or someone, over his shoulder. Simon was in the room with them, a gaping wound in his neck, blood splatter in his hair, on his face, his clothes. She didn't flinch, didn't scream. It wasn't the first time she'd seen him.

Nina closed her eyes, opened them, and when she did, he was gone.

EPILOGUE

MAGGIE GARRITY, ESSAY FOR THE DARTMOUTH COLLEGE ADMISSIONS APPLICATION.

QUESTION: *The lessons we take from obstacles we encounter can be fundamental to later success. Recount a time when you faced a challenge, setback, or failure. How did it affect you, and what did you learn from the experience?*

It is easy to judge other people. It takes no effort at all. Sit back, look at their choices, and decide what you would have done. It's as simple as that. But when you're safe inside your home, on your couch, petting your dog, it's easy to overinflate your capabilities. Why not imagine you'd be a superhero. Of course, you (amazing person) would punch and kick your way to safety—whatever the danger. But here's what I've learned after my ordeal, the greatest obstacle I've ever overcome: until you live it, you don't know what you would actually do. What you think you'd do is nothing but a fantasy.

If you google my name, you'll see story after story about what happened to my family and me. It wasn't pleasant. It was the worst time in my life. I nearly died. We all did.

Some people judged my father harshly for what had happened. They called him a coward for not finding a way to get a message to me, or even trying to make an escape. They thought the man who had taken him prisoner had brainwashed him into developing a psychological alliance with his captor, which is known as Stockholm syndrome.

But these people who judged him weren't shackled inside a 512-cubic-foot room for nearly two years. My father did what he had to do to survive.

We all did.

So don't judge.

I wasn't always good at this myself. There was a time before that I judged kids who are different—kids who are super studious, kids who don't look or act "cool," kids who don't do sports, or any of the "right stuff." That's a lesson I learned the hard way.

Toward the end of seventh grade and the beginning of eighth, I was the target of a bully and was cast out of my social circle. I found myself alone all the time, walking to classes alone, studying alone, eating lunch alone day after day. And you better believe I was judged. Some thought I deserved taunting and teasing. Some just wondered if there was something wrong with me. But there was one who offered his hand. One day, while sitting in the cafeteria, a boy I once judged and dismissed, a boy who was an outsider himself, asked if he could join me for lunch. I was reluctant at first, but then we started to talk and I found that this boy, a boy I never would have considered before, was smart and funny, generous and kind.

That was Benjamin Odell. He turned out to be my best friend and he's one of the reasons my family is still alive.

We live in a fairly small community and I know that after my father's disappearance, some people had plenty to say about my mother. They said she took up with a man too quickly. They said she put us in harm's way by bringing a dangerous and deranged person into our lives. They judged her without understanding my mother or our situation.

Those who know my mother well know her to be a smart woman who was very protective of her family. This time she just failed to see the danger in front of her, in front of us all. And she wasn't the only one who failed to see. My brother was also fooled. And all those who judged her . . . would they have been fooled, as well? Quite likely. This person tricked a lot of people.

For reasons I don't understand, I saw what my mother and my brother could not. From that terrible time, I learned to trust my own instincts and to fight for what I know to be right. And in time, maybe *just* in time, my mother and brother came to the same understanding, and together we did what we had to do to save our lives.

I learned something else from my awful experience. I learned about the woman at the heart of it all, and, no, it's not my mother, even though that's what the stories say. Victim Zero is a woman named Allison Greene. That's her real last name. I won't use her married name because I know she would not want it.

Allison was a battered woman. She was trapped in a horribly abusive relationship. I've read her diary many times. I know her story well. I've also been looking for Allison for years—a lot of us have. I use the internet to try and find her and I guess you would call me an amateur sleuth. I haven't uncovered any leads, but I'm still searching.

Allison was married for about four years and finally, she ran away from her abuser. Nobody has seen her since. At least we hope she ran away. She was pregnant when she disappeared and nobody knows if she escaped or if she had her baby, because her abuser took those secrets to his grave. And who was this abuser? He was the same man who was in our lives, the man whose surface ease and charm hid a murderous soul. Of course, we knew nothing of Allison, or of a baby, or of abuse, when our story started.

This isn't an essay about what happened to Allison Greene. It's about how easy it is to judge people like Allison—women who stay in abusive relationships or return to them. It can be hard to support someone who keeps returning to a danger-ous situation. You might think: What are you doing? You know better!

But you're not that person. You're not living it. You're not afraid for your life. You're not without financial means. You're not hopeful it can be different.

Judging others is easy. It makes us feel superior. But it doesn't help women like Allison, or my father, or my mother, or me, or anyone who is "different."

It hurts.

So what to do?

It's simple. Don't rush to judgment.

Have humility. Show empathy.

Ask: What can I do to help?

That's the question my mother asked my father on his road to recovery.

How can I help?

Three years ago, my parents renewed their vows. It was a beautiful ceremony, but we took a moment to acknowledge Allison, and all the women and men like her, people trapped in abusive relationships, and we said a prayer for them. My mother made a speech and everyone cried.

I believe we all want the same things out of life. We want to be loved, accepted, to belong to something, or someone, to feel wanted and valued. Sometimes we make poor choices on this journey. Instead of sitting in judgment of those choices, let's help each other get back on the right path.

That's what I've learned from the greatest challenge I've ever faced. That's how it changed me.

ACKNOWLEDGMENTS

The basic premise for this story came to me in that magical way that stories come to writers—via the ether. I wrote a first draft in 2015, and a funny thing happened on the way to publication: the book didn't quite work. So I did what writers sometimes have to do, I moved on, and worked on other books, came up with new ideas, but this story never left me.

In 2018, I returned to the novel, and as I often do, sought input from people whose judgment and opinions I trust. As I considered their different views, I was able to find the story hidden in pages of earlier drafts, and from my imagination, created the fictional world of the Garrity family, Simon Fitch, and Seabury, New Hampshire. The folks in my arena provided guidance and signposts for me to follow along the way and, with their advice, I took what I believed was a good idea and shaped it into something far better. These people deserve my profound gratitude and if you enjoyed the novel, then they deserve yours as well.

So without further ado, I need to thank my mother, Judy Palmer, for her many reads, suggestions, thoughtful edits, and encouragement along the way. My wife, Jessica, listened to every word and was helpful, as always, in clarifying the characters' motives and feelings. Special thanks go to Meg

Ruley and Rebecca Scherer, for helping me regain my footing anytime I stumbled with the ideas, the words, or just the walk along this path. To Jennifer Enderlin, editor and publisher extraordinaire, goes my deepest appreciation for her wisdom, grace, and undeniably great instincts for a good story. Jen, I'm forever grateful to be partnered with you.

Along the way, I got a lot of expert advice on police work from my friend and local law enforcer Sergeant Jonathan Tate, and loads of encouragement from Jane Berkey, who has been instrumental in the Palmer family writing legacy since she became my father's first and only literary agent. Speaking of my father, I'll always thank my dad for encouraging my pursuit of this crazy dream to use my time creatively to tell stories. We all miss you, Pop.

Behind the scenes are the people who make the book happen out in the retail world: Danielle Prielipp, Rachel Diebel, Paul Hochman, the St. Martin's sales team, the marketing and public relations people, Robert Van Kolken, Emily Dyer and the whole crew at Macmillan audio, the team at Jane Rotrosen Agency, all the freelancers, designers, back office folks, and I can go on. Additional thanks goes to my spotters, readers who follow my Facebook page and agreed to read the novel to look for any typos. Thank you, Dara, Joy, Becky, Lynne, Corky, and Kathy. You were of great service.

Writing is a solo endeavor that takes a village to bring to market. But readers are what make the hard work worth all the effort. So thanks for taking this journey with me. I hope you enjoyed the ride.

—D. J. Palmer
New Hampshire, 2019

Read on for an excerpt from

My Wife
Is Missing

the latest electrifying thriller from D. J. Palmer . . .
available soon in hardcover from St. Martin's Press!

CHAPTER 1

MICHAEL

As Michael Hart rounded the corner to his hotel room, he saw a small, lifeless shape lying on the floor of the hallway.

It was Teddy.

Teddy's arms were splayed open wide like the T-shape of a cross, legs straight as boards, feet pointed up at the ceiling. Still as stone, his two dark glassy eyes, black like onyx, gazed unblinking upwards, seeing nothing. Wrapped around Teddy's neck was his familiar blue kerchief, frayed at the edges from time and touch.

"What on earth are you doing here?" Michael muttered to himself, bending at the knees to retrieve the beloved stuffed bear. He uncoiled his fingers from the pizza boxes he'd been carrying to latch onto Teddy's plush arm. Careful not to tip tonight's dinner, Michael rose to standing. In the back of his mind tumbled a thought: *Where is Bryce?* Wherever Bryce went, Teddy went with him.

Michael endured a spurt of frustration—the kids dropping things everywhere, Natalie not thinking straight enough to keep track. Who was there to pick up the slack? He was, that's who. Chances were the old Natalie would have noticed Teddy had become separated from his owner. This new Natalie—his wife who managed only a couple hours of sleep on a good night, who suffered tremors, visions, and memory problems as a result, who these days had a fuse shorter than a matchstick—could have quite conceivably left one of the children behind (let alone a teddy bear) without realizing her oversight.

Michael exhaled his annoyance and concern in a single breath. No harm done. Teddy was safe. The cleaning crew hadn't swept him away. He figured Natalie and the kids had gone off exploring. Addison and Bryce had both been wide-eyed with wonder on their first trip up in the hotel's famed glass elevators so chances were they'd gone riding them again, and Teddy got left behind in all the excitement.

With the bear still dangling in his grasp, Michael gave the hotel room door a gentle kick, hoping the kids had returned from their adventures so he wouldn't have to fumble for a key. He waited. Down went the food (and Teddy) as Michael fished out a plastic rectangle from his wallet.

The room was dark when he entered. A heavy smell of vanilla and cedar clung to the air. It was a trick of the hotel trade, he knew; a little scent to help set the mood, like a new car smell. Normally the pleasing aroma didn't last long once the occupants arrived, but the vanilla odor was still quite strong. Something about it made Michael feel strangely alone.

Curtains thick as X-ray blankets blocked out the view of Times Square. He pulled them open to let in the last bits of daylight. They'd arrived close to sunset, and Michael couldn't wait to show Addie and Bryce the explosion of neon when darkness came. There was so much he wanted his kids to see and do here.

The city held a special place in Michael's heart. When he and Natalie were newly married, they'd make frequent trips from Boston to New York to take in shows and dine at fancy restaurants, but this was their first time coming to New

York as a family. Today was all about getting settled and acclimated to the neighborhood—their plan was to check out Times Square from above and then on the ground. Of course, Addison had already scoped out her primary stops, and no doubt the M&M and Disney stores would soon be getting some of Michael's hard-earned cash.

After setting the salads and pizzas on a dresser, Michael tossed Teddy onto the bed Addison had claimed. The cot Bryce would occupy for the five nights remained folded up in a corner of the room. The cot wasn't exactly unnecessary, considering his son could sleep perfectly well in a sleeping bag on the floor. Michael knew the kids would be comfortable here, but he worried how Natalie would fare. She couldn't sleep at home, and it had been a shock to him when she suggested they take a family trip to New York during the kids' April vacation.

"Are you sure?" he said in response. "What are you going to do if you can't fall asleep? Wander the hotel halls like Marley's ghost?"

"I'll be fine. It'll be good for us," Natalie assured him.

He saw the outline of sadness in her tight smile and in her eyes, which were the color of the dark ocean. She was already anticipating the difficulty, but clearly she wanted to do it, so he made the reservation.

Good for us, Natalie had said. Goodness knows they could have used some quality time together. It was something the marriage counselor had suggested. The truth was that he'd been planning to approach Nat about a getaway, just the two of them, leaving the kids with her parents for a stretch. More than family time, they needed to reconnect, or at least hit the reset button on their marriage. The past few months had been, in a word, eventful. But Natalie had insisted on getting away with the kids as well, so family time it would be.

It took some fiddling, but Michael finally managed to

get the room lights on—no small feat, given how modern hotels eschewed the old-fashioned switch for touch technology. Honestly, he was surprised everyone wasn't in the room eagerly awaiting his return, ready to pounce on the food. He checked his phone for a text from Natalie letting him know where they'd gone.

Nothing.

He checked the watch he wore obsessively—a throwback, Natalie called it. The Citizen timepiece with its thick leather band, darkened at the edges, couldn't send and receive messages, but it did tell him the hour was getting late.

They'd arrived in New York utterly famished after a four-and-a-half-hour car ride from their home in Lexington, Massachusetts. Michael had suggested going out to eat, but Natalie was too tired (no surprise there) and wanted takeout from a nearby pizza place she'd found on Yelp that had fantastic reviews. But given the dinner rush hour, delivery would take too long, so Michael was dispatched for pickup.

"Where is everyone?" he said to the empty room, plopping himself down onto the bed he'd soon be sharing with his wife. He sent her a text.

Food is here. Come and get it.

Wherever they were, he imagined the kids had to really be enjoying themselves to delay dinner for even a minute. A savory whiff of sauce and cheese tickled Michael's nose. He contemplated downing a slice, but managed restraint. He was a big believer in eating together as a family, and always made it a point to get home from his job at Fidelity in time for dinner. They'd only recently begun a new dinnertime tradition called Three Things, a conversation starter game that Natalie got off the internet. They'd take turns going around the table, each sharing one thing that had gone well that day, one thing they were grateful for, and one thing they'd have done differently.

Three things.

It wasn't easy getting the conversation going, and typically the kids launched half-hearted protests, but in the end Michael always felt the game brought him closer to the people who were closest to him.

He recalled Natalie's three things from the night before. They'd struck him as somewhat odd, just as this whole experience of returning to an empty hotel room felt odd.

Natalie had said:

"Today I got us all packed and ready to go."

"I'm grateful for the truth."

"I wish I'd done this sooner."

He had meant to ask his wife for clarification—what was it she wished she'd done sooner? Pack? And what truth was she grateful for? But then Bryce spilled his glass of milk, and those questions got lost in the aftermath.

Now, thoughts of that game—specifically Natalie's reference to her packing prowess—brought Michael's attention to just how clean the room was. He took in that vanilla and cedar smell again. It was as if they'd not yet arrived. Normally there'd be clothes strewn about, the TV blaring, and suitcases left open on the floor, but not this time. This time there was not an item in sight, as if Natalie had prepared them for a military-type room inspection.

In the bathroom, Michael splashed water on his weathered face and rubbed the dark stubble of a nascent beard. He looked aged well beyond his forty-three years, but stress can do that to a person. His marriage was on the rocks, but was there more to their troubles at home than he knew?

I'm grateful for the truth . . .

Noticing his reddish eyes, Michael went for his toiletry bag on the countertop, digging inside for the Visine. As he undid the zipper, a concern tugged at him, bringing with it an unsettled feeling not unlike the one he had experienced when he found Teddy all by his lonesome in the hallway.

All his senses were telling him something was wrong. He couldn't immediately identify the source of his unease, but as he scanned the bathroom, he realized what was amiss. He distinctly remembered Natalie getting her toiletries out of her suitcase because she had wanted to brush her teeth. Now there was only one toiletry bag on the counter, and it belonged to him. *Had she really put hers back in her suitcase?*

Michael's heartbeat picked up. Just a little.

He went to the closet directly across from the bathroom. There he paused, not quite ready to open the door. His thoughts gummed up as he took another look around the perfectly ordered room.

Two rambunctious children aren't this neat.

The smell of vanilla taunted him.

He gripped the knob of the closet door, his stomach in knots, and gave it a yank. It was dark inside, but he had no trouble seeing the outline of his black suitcase pushed up against the back wall.

One suitcase.

Just one.

His.